Praise for Rita Mae Brown's delightful novels featuring the unforgettable Hunsenmeir sisters . . .

LOOSE LIPS

"[Brown] does an admirable job of portraying the effects World War II has on a small American town. . . . [The] characterizations of Louise and Juts are acutely realistic."　　*—Arizona Republic*

"Brimming with Brown's comic sense of social posturing and missteps, her rich novel lets readers laugh with her at the personal foibles that seem to loom so large in small-town settings."　　*—Booklist*

"Time has honed Brown's literary skills but not lessened her love for these characters."　　*—Library Journal*

"Surprises . . . come from Rita Mae Brown's comic timing and her affection for eccentrics."　　*—Seattle Times*

SIX OF ONE

"Joyous, passionate, and funny. What a pleasure!"
　　—Washington Post Book World

"No matter how quirky or devilish, Brown's people cavort in an atmosphere of tenderness. . . . It is refreshing to encounter this celebration of human energy."　　*—Chicago Sun-Times*

"Brown has some of the same effervescent yet secure trust in her local characters that Eudora Welty feels for hers. . . . When history nicks them, they slap right back."　　*—Kirkus Reviews*

"A lively and very lovely book."　　*—Publishers Weekly*

BINGO

"This is vintage Brown."   —*Publishers Weekly*

"Delightful . . . Rita Mae Brown is still a hoot."
                                                  —*Philadelphia Inquirer*

"*Bingo* beams with Brown's fondness for her characters and her delight in the oddness of the world of Runnymede."
                                                  —*Boston Herald*

"Joyously comic."   —*People*

"Longtime fans will welcome back Nickel Smith, this time coping with a surprising passion. . . . New ones will flock to *Bingo*'s vividly drawn characters (like the lustful Hunsenmeir sisters) and tart, loving humor."   —*Self*

"Hilarious, superbly written fiction."   —*Booklist*

"Genuinely funny."   —*Los Angeles Times*

LOOSE LIPS

RITA MAE BROWN

BANTAM BOOKS

New York   Toronto   London   Sydney   Auckland

LOOSE LIPS
A Bantam Book

PUBLISHING HISTORY
Bantam hardcover edition published 1999
Bantam trade paperback edition / May 2000
Bantam trade paperback reissue / February 2008

Published by
Bantam Dell
A Division of Random House, Inc.
New York, New York

Book design by Ellen Cipriano

Library of Congress Catalog Card Number: 98-56079

Bantam Books and the rooster colophon are registered
trademarks of Random House, Inc.

ISBN 978-0-553-38067-5

Printed in the United States of America
Published simultaneously in Canada

www.bantamdell.com

BVG   15   14   13   12   11   10   9   8   7

In memoriam
Johnny Holland
June 14, 1983–January 2, 1999

PART ONE

1

Life will turn you inside out. No matter where you start you'll end up someplace else even if you stay home. The one thing you can count on is that you'll be surprised.

For the Hunsenmeir sisters, life didn't just turn them inside out, it tossed them upside down, then right side up. Perhaps it wasn't life whirling them around like the Whip ride at the fair. They upended each other.

April 7, 1941, shimmered, a light wind sending Louise's tulips swaying. Spring had triumphantly arrived in Runnymede, which straddled the Mason-Dixon line. The residents of this small, beautiful town, built around a square before the Revolutionary War, waxed ecstatic since springtime warmth had arrived early this fateful year. Probably every year is fateful to someone or other, but some years everyone remembers. On April 7, though, Fate seemed far away, shaking up countries across the Atlantic Ocean.

Julia Ellen, "Juts," slammed the door to her sister Louise's house. She pursed her lipstick-coated lips and blew a low note then a higher note, like a towhee bird. Snotty bird-watchers like Orrie Tadia Mojo, Louise's best friend from her schoolgirl days, called it a Rufous-sided towhee. Juts always pronounced it two-ey, since it uttered the note twice.

Hearing no response, Juts whistled again. Finally she yelled, "Wheezer, where the hell are you?" Still no answer.

Juts had celebrated her thirty-sixth birthday on March 6. She'd always possessed megawatts of energy, but as she zoomed through her thirties she accumulated even more energy, the way some people accumulated wrinkles. The only person who could keep up with her was Louise, four years older; since Louise lied shamelessly about her birthday everyone "forgot" her exact age except Juts, who held it in reserve should she need to whack her sister into line. Cora, their mother, remembered also but she was far too sweet to remind her elder daughter, who was having a fit and falling in it over turning forty. This momentous occasion had just occurred on March 25. Even Juts, out of pity, pretended Louise was thirty-nine at the birthday party.

Both sisters roared through life, although they roared in different keys. Juts was definitely a C major while Louise, an E minor, could never resist a melancholy swoon.

Juts stubbed out her Chesterfield in the glass ashtray with the thin silver band around the edge.

"Louise!" she shouted as she opened the back door and stepped out.

"I'm up here," Louise called from the roof.

Julia craned her neck; the sun was in her eyes. "What are you doing up there? Oh, wait, why should I ask? You're singing 'Nearer My God to Thee.'"

"I'll thank you to shut your sacrilegious mouth."

"Yeah, yeah, you walk on water. I came over here to take you to lunch at Cadwalder's but you're such a pill I think I'll go by myself."

"Don't leave me."

"Why not?"

Louise hesitated. She loathed asking her younger sister to help her because she knew she'd have to pay her back somewhere, sometime, and it would be when she least wanted to return a favor.

"Oh." Julia tried to conceal her delight as she spied the white heavy ladder behind the forsythia bushes, a rash of blinding yellow. "Gee, Sis, how awful." She started walking away.

"Julia, Julia, don't you leave me up here!"

"Why not? I can't even crack a joke around you but what it gets turned into a spiritual moment by Runnymede's only living saint. Oh, let me amend that, by the great state of Maryland's only living saint."

"What about Pennsylvania?"

"We don't live in Pennsylvania."

"Half of Runnymede is over the line."

"You mean over the top, don't you?" Julia crossed her arms over her chest.

"You know what I mean." Irritation crept into Louise's well-modulated soprano.

"Pennsylvania is so much bigger than Maryland, kind of like a tarantula compared to a ladybug. I'm sure there are lots of living saints in Pennsylvania, probably in Philadelphia and Pittsburgh, but then again—"

Louise cut her off. She knew when Juts was heating up for one of her rambles. "Will you please put the ladder up?"

"No. Mary and Maizie will be home from school in two hours. They can put it up."

Louise's younger daughter, named after Julia Ellen, had been given the nickname Maizie to distinguish her from her aunt.

"Now listen, Juts, this isn't funny. I'm stuck and those noisy kids might not hear me when they get home. Put the ladder up."

"What do I get out of it?"

"Maybe you should ask what you don't get out of it." As Louise edged toward the roofline, little bits of asphalt sparkles skidded out under her heels.

"Bet it's getting hot up there."

"A tad."

"What are you offering me?"

"No more lectures on your smoking or drinking."

"I hardly drink at all," Julia snapped. "I am so sick of you claiming that I drink too much."

"I have yet to see a Saturday night that you don't fill with whiskey sours."

"One night out of seven—it's Saturday night, Louise, and I like to go out with my husband."

"You'd go out whether he was here or not."

"What's that supposed to mean?"

"It means you can't live without male attention and if I were your husband I wouldn't let you out of my sight."

"Well, you're not my husband." Julia dragged out the heavy ladder but didn't prop it against the gutter of the roof. "How come your nose is out of joint, anyway?"

"Isn't."

"Is."

"Isn't."

"Liar."

"You expect me to be Mary Sunshine when I've been stuck on this roof for hours."

"What are you doing up there, anyway?"

"There's a bird's nest in the chimney. I removed it."

"Any birds in it?"

"No, although I'd let them stay until they were big enough to fly. Honestly, Julia."

The exasperation in "Honestly, Julia" told Juts it was time to strike. "I'll put this ladder up if you give me that hat you bought last week."

"The one from Bear's department store in York?"

"One and the same."

"Julia, I love that hat."

"So do I, and you have more money than I do. Come on, Louise, I've got to have something to wear to church on Easter."

"I'm not made of money, Juts. Pearlie and I manage better than you and Chessy do."

"Boy, you really don't want to get off that roof, do you?"

"I do. I'm sorry. You know I speak my mind."

"That's what you call it. I call it sitting in judgment." Julia ran her fingers through her honey-brown curls and turned again to leave.

"All right!"

She stopped. "The hat, Louise—the minute you get off that ladder."

"Yes."

Juts heaved the ladder to its feet; it wobbled for a moment, then she pushed it toward the roof, where it stopped with a wooden *thud*. "I'll hold it."

Louise turned over, her hands spread out on the roof. She slid a little but stopped her descent by turning her feet on their sides. She reached over with her foot, found the first rung of the ladder. Carefully, she backed down. Once down she entered the house without a word to her sister. She slammed the back kitchen door so hard that all the ceramic figurines with the nipples painted in red nail polish shuddered in the living room. It was Pearlie—her husband, Paul—who did the painting. Louise said he was artistic. Julia declared with a straight face that most men have a deep craving to paint the nipples on statuary and she left it at that. To Chessy she referred to her sister's home as the Titty Palace or T.P.

Juts opened the door, closing it behind her as her sister tromped back into the room. She thrust a big navy-blue hatbox, with *Bear's* in graceful script across the top, into Juts's hands. "Here, you damned chiseler."

Wisely deciding not to argue about being called a chiseler, Juts carried the hatbox by the crossed heavy ribbon on top. "Come on, let's get a chocolate frappé. On me."

Louise thought about it a minute, realized she was very thirsty, and murmured, "All right."

As they walked toward Runnymede Square, Juts again asked, "What's the matter?"

"Nothing's the matter. I was perched on that roof too long. I even thought about jumping off."

"It's a good thing you didn't. You would have ruined your forsythias." Not that Juts believed her. She knew something was nibbling away at her sister.

"Ruined my shoes, too."

"Could have broken your ankle."

"Or my neck—why, I could have been killed."

"Nah." Juts smiled. "Only the good die young."

"You're awful."

"No, I'm Julia."

"You're my awful Julia." Louise giggled as she pushed open the door of Cadwalder's drugstore.

"You girls just missed your mother," Vaughn, the eighteen-year-old son of the owner, called from behind the fountain. "She left with Miss Chalfonte not fifteen minutes ago."

"On foot or in the Packard?" Louise inquired.

"The Packard." A folded towel was draped over one arm. He leaned over the marble countertop at the fountain. "What'll it be?"

"Lime sherbet and a new life."

"Mrs. Smith, you're a caution." He laughed, using an old expression from the 1880s.

"That's not what I call her." Louise cast a baleful eye at the hatbox secure under the counter stool.

"Okay, no lime sherbet until summer, I know. I want a giant chocolate frappé and a hot tea on the side."

"And I want a strawberry frappé with coffee on the side."

"Okeydokey." Vaughn lifted the square black covers and

began flipping ice cream into heavy ribbed glasses. "Isn't this spring something?"

"The best," both women agreed.

"Hard to believe there's a war on."

"It won't last long," Louise airily predicted.

"And what makes you think that?" Juts's stomach growled.

"Because England never loses a war unless it's to us."

"I hope you're right—" Vaughn's voice trailed off as he calmly poured coffee. "We never really finished the Great War, you know?"

Louise blinked. She didn't know, and at that moment she wanted her strawberry frappé, not a reflection on recent history from a kid.

"Vaughn, remind me how old you are," Louise asked.

"Eighteen."

"You're not thinking of running away to Canada and enlisting, are you?" she pressed.

He blushed, making his freckles disappear. "Uh, gee, Mrs. Trumbull."

"I thought so." Louise reached for her coffee before he put it on the counter. "Wait and see. Maybe we can stay out of this one."

"Yes, ma'am."

"What amazes me about war is a bunch of old men start them. Right?" Juts's small audience nodded so she continued. "Then young men fight, get wounded or worse, and the old farts sit back and reap the reward. Makes me sick. Thanks." Vaughn slid her the tea over the counter.

"If you were a man, would you enlist?" Louise asked Juts.

"Sure, to get away from you."

That made Vaughn blush again because he wanted to laugh but didn't want to offend Louise. Everyone in Runnymede knew of her temper; Juts's, too, for that matter.

"Ha, ha," Louise dryly said and eagerly dug into her creamy frappé.

"I've been meaning to tell you, Louise—you haven't been yourself lately." Juts smiled. "And it's a big improvement."

Vaughn burst out laughing. Louise jammed her spoon into her frappé, brought out a luscious bit of ice cream with strawberry syrup, and flipped it onto her sister's surprised face.

Julia answered in kind. Vaughn involuntarily took a step back and pleaded, "Ladies."

"There's only one lady here," Louise said grandly.

"Yeah, and she's forty years old."

2

Light shone through the Limoges china. It was so thin that it was translucent. At the rim of each piece a thin red line surrounded by a thin gold band circled the cup, saucer, or plate to intertwine in a *C* for *Chalfonte*.

Celeste Chalfonte, beautiful, willful, and in her middle sixties, unfolded the linen napkin on her lap. Across from her, Ramelle Chalfonte—her lover of thirty-nine years and the wife of Celeste's brother, Curtis—did the same.

The aroma of eggs, sunny-side up, sizzling bacon, and fresh biscuits filled the breakfast room on the east side of the house.

"Do you have the *Clarion*?" Celeste asked for the South Runnymede paper.

"No," Ramelle answered.

"What about the *Trumpet*?" She asked for the Yankee Runnymede paper.

Ramelle shook her head. "No."

Celeste rang a small silver bell. Cora Hunsenmeir, in her late fifties, appeared.

"Your Highness."

"One of those days, is it?" Celeste noted. "Where's the paper?"

Cora left without a word and reappeared to place the folded *Clarion* by Celeste's left hand.

Snapping open the front page, Celeste's gaze was drawn to a photograph of two familiar faces. Harper Wheeler, the sheriff of South Runnymede, stood between Cora's two daughters.

"Oh, dear." Celeste inhaled, then showed the evidence to Ramelle. She turned her light eyes up to Cora. "Why didn't you tell me?"

Cora shrugged. "Well—you'd find out soon enough."

"Are they in jail?" Ramelle sweetly inquired as she took the paper from Celeste.

"Harper Wheeler wouldn't keep them there. He said no jail is big enough for those two." Cora sighed. "Harmon Nordness wouldn't let him put one in the North Runnymede jail, either."

Celeste, standing now to read over Ramelle's shoulder, chuckled. "Sorry." She caught herself.

"Go right ahead," Cora said.

Soon both Celeste and Ramelle were laughing.

Ramelle read Popeye Huffstetler's byline out loud: ". . . 'The source of disagreement, according to Vaughn Cadwalder, was over why Mrs. Chester Smith would enlist in the Army. Mrs. Paul Trumbull took offense when Mrs. Smith, her sister, declared she would enlist just to get away from her. Both ladies are free on bail posted by their respective husbands. Sheriff Harper Wheeler lectured Mr. Smith and Mr. Trumbull on controlling their wives.

Mr. Smith was quoted as saying, "Not even Adolf Hitler could control Juts." Mr. Flavius Cadwalder, owner of Cadwalder's drugstore, has refused to press charges since both Mr. Smith and Mr. Trumbull have promised to pay in full for damages, which are estimated at three hundred and ninety-eight dollars.' " Ramelle drew in her breath. "Three hundred and ninety-eight dollars! My God, Cora, what did they do?"

"That depends on who is telling the story." The heavyset woman shrugged her shoulders.

"What do you think?" Celeste asked her friend and servant of many decades as she sat back down. She was too hungry to continue reading over Ramelle's shoulder.

"Louise was stuck on her roof—"

"What?" Ramelle interrupted.

"She was cleaning out a bird's nest from the chimney. The ladder fell and Juts came along hours later. Except she wouldn't put the ladder up until Louise gave her that beautiful Easter hat she bought at Bear's."

"You know, I always thought Julia had the makings of a great politician." Celeste bit into a biscuit, light as a feather.

"One says 'apples,' the other says 'bananas.' " Cora poured Ramelle fresh coffee. "Some of this fuss is because Mary and Maizie are like to drive their mother wild. What little patience Louise has is—" Cora waved her hand to indicate that patience flew away.

"It's hard to imagine Louise as a mother," Celeste said. "It's even hard to imagine Louise as a wife. I keep seeing this little girl with long curls playing the piano in my parlor." She tapped the back of the paper, which Ramelle eagerly read. "Of course, it's hard to imagine you as a mother with a twenty-year-old daughter."

"Yes." Ramelle laughed. "But mine is a grown woman in California. Juts and Louise are overgrown children right here under our noses."

"Well, Cora, how are the husbands going to raise three hundred and ninety-eight dollars?"

"I haven't asked."

"If I were you I wouldn't inquire too closely." Celeste felt the delicious bacon crunch between her teeth.

3

Chessy Smith ran his fingers over the deep grain of cherry wood. Walter Falkenroth was paneling his extensive library with cherry. The *Clarion* had to be hauling in money hand over fist, because Walter's new house was as big as an airplane hangar. Chessy took the leftover wood home to build two nightstands for Juts. Chester Smith owned the hardware store in town. To bring in extra money he would build cabinets, chairs, and tables in a workshop at the back of the store. This way he never wasted time. If it was a slow day in the store he'd still be productive.

Juts breezed into his workshop. Even though they would be fourteen years married in June, she always gave the twoey whistle, then knocked on the door. Partly this was out of respect but partly it was for safety's sake. If her big, blond husband was bent over a band saw or a jigsaw she didn't want to startle him. As it was, he was just checking the dimensions of his nightstand drawings.

"Come on in."

She pushed open the door. "Honey, it's dropped to forty-eight outside. You'd better fire up the stove."

"Not going to be in here long. I'll be home in a minute."

She sat on a heavy oak bench. "Are you still mad at me?"

Julia Ellen's merciless vitality could wear down an iron man. Her flagrant disregard for propriety had made her exciting when they first met. It still made her exciting, but there were moments when Chessy would have settled for a docile wife, one not given to smashing glassware at the drugstore fountain because she was furious at her sister. They had also smashed the huge mirror behind the marble-topped counter. He and Paul would be in hock for the rest of the decade.

"I don't know where I'm going to get two hundred dollars."

"One hundred and ninety-nine dollars," she quickly corrected him.

He pressed his lips together. "Right."

"She started it. I swear, ever since she's turned forty she's twitchy. That and the fact that Mary is getting carried a little fast by Extra Billy." Julia referred to Mary's boyfriend, a good-looking kid who believed rules were meant to be broken.

"I'm going over to Rife Munitions to get a part-time job. Pearlie's going too."

"You can't do that!" She slammed her fist on the bench, hurting her hand. "Ouch, goddammit."

"We have to do it, Juts. There's no other place we can pick up work quickly. It's the munitions plant or the canning factory, and Rife owns both of them."

"Well, you could go up to Hanover and work for the Shepards. There's always work in the shoe factory up there or on the horse farm."

"Can't afford the gas."

"What are you talking about? We aren't that poor."

He leveled his lustrous gray eyes into his wife's gray eyes; they both had the same unusual eye color. "Don't you read the newspapers? Julia Ellen, we're going to war. It's only a matter of time . . . and when we do, gas will be one of the first things rationed."

"Fiddlesticks. Isn't that why FDR pushed through the Lend-Lease—so we wouldn't have to go?"

"No, that's how he's trying to keep England afloat."

"Europe can settle its own scores. We went over there once. The American people won't stand for it again."

"I'm telling you—we're going in."

"How do you know all this?"

"Been talking."

"Women gossip. Men talk." She smiled. "You are all bigger gossips than we are."

"Makes no matter. I've got to raise that two hundred dollars somewhere."

"One hundred and ninety-nine dollars!" she shouted.

"That one dollar counts for a lot, doesn't it?"

"Yes. You can't work for a Rife. You know what they did to our family."

"That was a long time ago. Brutus paid for blood with his own blood. Pole and Julius are a little better than their father." He referred to Napoleon and Julius Caesar Rife.

She ground her teeth. "You can't do this to me. You and Pearlie will break my mother's heart."

"Already talked to your mother."

"Behind my back?" She hit the bench again and wished she hadn't.

"Since when is talking to your mother going behind your back? She understands that the money has to come from some-place."

"I'll get a job. I'll go back to work at the silk mill."

"They're full up."

"How do you know?"

" 'Cause I went there first."

Outraged, Juts leapt up and kicked the bench over. She slammed the door and hurried down the street.

Chessy sighed. She'd be sure to make life miserable for as long as it pleased her. He figured he'd better drop by Cadwalder's for a sandwich. He wouldn't be getting any supper tonight.

4

The wind picked up. Juts strode with her head down. A car horn beeped twice. She glanced up. Louise motioned to her from behind the wheel of Paul's black Model A. She ran over and hopped in, glad to be out of the wind.

"Where's Pearlie?"

"Home."

"Does he know you have the car? He never lets you take the car."

"I ran right out of the house and took it."

"Oh, Louise."

"I'm sick of him telling me what I can do and when I can do it. I paid for this damned old rattletrap the same as he did. Maybe not in dollars and cents, but in hard work. So if I want to drive it he can sit on a tack. He's too damned cheap to buy a new car. He says we have to run this one until it dies. Well, Sister, let's just run it until it does."

That said, Wheezie pressed the accelerator, let out the clutch, and they lurched forward.

"You two have a fight?" Julia stated the obvious.

"Son of a bitch." Since Louise rarely swore, the eruption must have been a real Vesuvius.

"Us, too. Rife?"

Louise nodded. "You and I had an argument yesterday. A few drugstore items were broken. My husband acts as though we have marched on Atlanta and burned it to the ground." Louise sounded extremely rational, her voice oozing maturity.

"The *Clarion* didn't help."

"When I get my hands on Popeye Huffstetler his eyes will pop. Besides which he can't write."

"He does all the ground work for St. Rose's so everyone will back him up. People believe what they read." Julia referred to St. Rose of Lima's Catholic Church, where Louise was a devout member and Popeye performed sexton duties. Julia was a staunch Lutheran, partly out of faith and partly to drive her older sister crackers.

Louise took a corner on two wheels. " 'Wrecked' havoc, he said—we 'wrecked' havoc at Cadwalder's. And old Flavius Cadwalder is charging us retail for the damages. The least he could do would be to charge us wholesale, after all the business we've given him. Besides, it's *wreaked,* not *wrecked*. I told you he couldn't write."

"Everyone gives him business. He's got a monopoly." She sucked in her breath. "Louise, slow down."

"Scaredy-cat."

"I might go to heaven or hell, but will I go home?"

"Clever." Louise grimaced but she did slow down.

"Sisters and brothers fight. I don't see why everyone picks on us. We always make up."

"Righto." Louise had recently heard this on her favorite radio show, which glorified brave Britain. "Yes, we did, but that nauseous—"

Juts interrupted. "Noxious."

"You know what I mean, don't correct me, that fat Harper Wheeler made sure his picture was in the paper between the two of us. The only reason he gets reelected is that no one else wants the job. He's up again next year."

"We could run for sheriff."

That idea flickered, then died. "We'd have to pick up drunks and they'd puke in the backseat of the car."

Julia ditched her own idea. "What about a flower shop?"

"The Biancas have that sewed up. Runnymede is too small for two flower shops."

Juts flopped back in her seat as Louise again let the clutch out unevenly. "Bet it's going to freeze again tonight. I'm cold," Juts complained.

"Put the blanket around your legs." Louise patted the plaid blanket neatly folded on the seat between them but her steering wobbled.

Juts grabbed the wheel, which made Louise yank it harder in the other direction. "Watch where you're going."

"Keep your hands to yourself!" Louise corrected the big swerve. However, she scared an oncoming driver half to death.

"Frances Finster looked peaked." Julia commented on the driver's appearance.

They drove in silence along the bumpy country roads west of town. Louise swung back east as the long red rays of the setting sun lent a melancholy tincture to the rolling hills of Maryland.

Julia piped up. "We've got to do something, Louise. Otherwise our husbands will go to work for Rife Munitions."

"I told Pearlie I'd leave him if he did that."

Julia whistled. "Even I didn't get that radical."

"March 17, 1917, doesn't seem that far away. Memory's like that." Before she realized it Louise had driven to Dead Man's Curve, a nasty twist of road, bloodred now in the sunset. She stopped the Ford. Both sisters got out and peered over the steep incline where their mother's lover, Aimes Rankin, had been killed, his head bashed in and his body tossed over the curve those many years ago. No one believed it was a motorcycle accident. Aimes had tried to found a union in the Rife Munitions factory, which was doing a booming business thanks to the Great War. It had originally come into prominence during the War Between the States, when the original founder, Cassius Rife, safely on the north side of the Mason-Dixon line, secured huge contracts from Washington. He was accused of shipping arms into the South. Since nothing could be proved against him no charges were ever brought. He wasn't the only war profiteer engorged on the dead of that hideous conflict, but he was the one everyone believed had worked both sides of the fence.

Julia swayed over the drop, cold air stinging her face. "I miss Aimes."

"He was more of a father to us than our own father."

"Think we'll ever see our father again?" Julia wistfully asked.

"I don't know and I don't care," Louise answered. She was old enough to remember her mother's grief when Hansford John Hunsenmeir walked out on them.

"Momma says Cassius killed her father up here, too, for asking Congress to investigate Rife's business dealings. Must have been his favorite place. PopPop couldn't stand Cassius's double-dealing—" Julia paused a moment. "Sometimes I think hate is like a ball. It can't roll if everyone doesn't give it a push."

"I'm not talking about hate," Louise said. "I'm talking about honor. Our husbands can't work for a Rife, no matter which Rife it is. They're Brutus's sons and they're Cassius's grandsons and they've killed our people two generations running."

"I know." Julia's voice weakened. "But where are we going to get all that money?"

Louise shivered. "Let's get back in the car."

They clambered in and pulled the plaid blanket over their legs. Louise hugged herself to keep warm.

"I've been coming up with all the ideas," Julia said. "It's about time you had one."

"Dress shop."

"That's pretty good. We've got wonderful taste."

Louise again defected. " 'Cept we don't have any money for clothes to start up."

"There is that." A screech owl startled Julia. "Let's get out of here."

They motored around in the gathering black velvet of night.

"I think better on a full stomach," Julia grumbled.

"Where do you want to go?"

"Dolley Madison's is too far away." Juts loved the little restaurant set over a creek on the Pennsylvania side. "Blue Hen is good but kind of pricey."

"Let's go to Cadwalder's."

"Umm, we'd better wait awhile before going back in there."

"I'm driving by." Louise, determined, rambled down the Emmitsburg pike, which fed into Runnymede Square. Once in the square she zoomed around the north side just for effect, then jolted to a stop in front of the drugstore.

"Chessy." Julia noticed her husband's car parked out front.

"And I'll bet you dollars to doughnuts he's got Paul with him."

"Damn. I'm really hungry but I don't feel like seeing them."

Louise pulled out in case Pearlie looked outside the big window. She drove over to the bakery. "Doughnuts are better than nothing."

"Yeah," Julia agreed.

Millard Yost's face fell when the Hunsenmeir sisters pushed through the door. "Hi, girls," he managed to say.

"Hi, Millard," they replied.

"Sure hope you two are getting along today." He nervously laughed as his fingers drummed on the expensive glass display cases.

"We're thick as thieves." Louise laughed.

"And hungry. How about one dozen glazed doughnuts, six cake doughnuts, and six chocolate-covered doughnuts."

"All right." He immediately began filling the order.

"And two coffees."

"Sweetie—" he called.

His wife, Lillian, entered from the rear. The Yosts lived behind the store. "What?"

"Could you get the girls two coffees while I do this?"

"Hey, Millard, are you trying to get rid of us?" Julia joked.

"No, no," he lied.

"Really, what happened at Cadwalder's was, uh . . ."—Juts glanced at Louise and decided not to get into it—"unfortunate."

"There you go." He handed over the doughnuts in a bright white paper bag as Lillian gave them coffee in heavy mugs.

"We can't take your mugs."

"No, no, you all just keep them." Millard made change.

"Can't we eat here?" Louise inquired.

Lillian pointed at the clock. "Closing time."

"Now, you girls just go on and keep those mugs." Millard ushered them out the front door, locking it the minute Julia's back foot hit the pavement.

They climbed back into the car. "Jeez, Sis, think everyone's going to be like this?"

Louise grabbed a chocolate doughnut. "They'll forget."

"Maybe we'd better not go into shops together."

"I still don't think it was that bad. If it weren't for that horrible Popeye Huffstetler."

"Well, even if he hadn't put the picture in the paper I guess it would have gotten round." Juts sighed.

"The *Trumpet* only carried a small column on it. We'll shop in Pennsylvania."

"They don't like to admit that the *Clarion* got the scoop." The glazed doughnut seemed to melt on her tongue. "You know, Wheezer, we can't keep these mugs."

Louise studied the hefty white mugs with a thin dark green line painted around the top.

"Is your doughnut spoiled?" She knew Juts felt bad.

"No. Best doughnuts in Maryland. It's just, I wish Chessy wasn't working so hard and now he's going to work nights too. Just because—you know."

"Yeah. You shouldn't make fun of my age and you stole my new hat."

Juts sang out, "If you want it back, go climb up on the roof and I'll knock the ladder away. See how long you perch up there."

Louise started to get mad all over again, then caught herself. She also caught sight of her husband in the rearview mirror. Scowling, he was heading straight for her, Chessy in tow. "Uh-oh." She handed her sister her half-full cup as she started the motor, but Pearlie, a wiry, fast fellow, grabbed the door handle before she could pull out.

"I ought to fan your hide," he said as the Yosts pretended to count money inside the store.

"You're so cute when you're mad."

He opened the door, reached in, and cut the ignition. "If you've burned out my clutch on top of everything else, Louise, I will lock you inside the house until you learn how to behave."

Juts said nothing. Chessy stood outside her door, his arms folded across his forty-two-inch chest. She smiled sheepishly, opened the door, and handed him a doughnut. Even though he'd eaten a hamburger with all the trimmings he could always eat more.

"Cake. Your favorite."

"What have you two been up to?"

"Nothing." Juts innocently ate another glazed doughnut.

"Louise, get out from behind that wheel," Pearlie said.

"I have to drive my sister home."

"No, you don't. Chessy's car is right over there."

Louise slid next to her sister, drawing comfort from her nearness. Juts didn't get out of the car, even though Pearlie thumped down behind the steering wheel.

"Come on, Juts," Chessy politely suggested.

"Wait a minute. We feel terrible." Juts hung her head. She did feel terrible but not that terrible. Louise jabbed her lightly with her elbow. Juts snapped her head up. "We don't want you two working at night. It's not just Rife Munitions. You both work so hard, we hardly see you now."

Chessy leaned against the open passenger door of the car. "Well, honey, you girls get together and you can't behave. Somebody's got to pay the bills."

"We were silly. It was over a stupid hat." Louise sounded convincingly contrite.

"We're going to share it," Juts volunteered, then wished she'd kept her big mouth shut, for Louise beamed.

"That isn't going to pay off Cadwalder." Pearlie was resigned to his fate: working at night and living with an irrational woman—but then he'd heard they were all irrational.

"I'll sell the hat back to Bear's department store," Louise said with no conviction.

"We've decided," Julia announced in a surprisingly commanding tone of voice. "We are the culprits and we're the ones who must pay back the debt. We're going into business."

"What?" Pearlie appeared stricken.

"Yes, we are." Louise had no idea what Julia was talking about, but at this moment she was better off aligned with her sister than with her husband.

"We're going to open a beauty salon." Juts held up her hand as the men sputtered. "The start-up costs are low—we already have the curlers—and our only competition, Junior McGrail, is blind in one eye—"

"—and can't see out of the other." Louise liltingly finished the sentence for her, describing the daughter of Idabelle McGrail the First, who had gone to her reward in heaven last year, unlamented by the Hunsenmeir sisters.

Pearlie dropped his forehead on the steering wheel. "God help me."

5

I heard it from the horse's mouth." Juts put her palms on the dash as Louise popped the clutch, hurtling her forward. "Why don't you let me drive?"

"You—you? You were the one who smashed into Mother's front porch and sent my piano rolling down and—"

"That was a long time ago."

"Nineteen twenty-six."

"Nineteen twenty-five."

"Summer of twenty-six, Julia."

"I wasn't married until June of twenty-seven and I know when I had that small mishap—"

"Small, ha!" Louise's voice rose.

"Chessy didn't complain."

"He was courting you. I can tell you that new radiator cost plenty."

"My point."

"What's your point?" Louise grew impatient.

"We weren't married for two more years so it had to be the summer of 1925."

"Have it your way."

"It's not my way. It's a fact, pure and simple. Dammit, now you made me forget what I was going to say."

"You were talking about Lillian Yost."

"Oh yeah, I went in to return my mug. Did you return yours?"

"Yes," Louise said smugly.

"Oh, when did you do that?"

"The very next day, Julia, as you should have done."

"I would have." Juts wriggled in her seat. "But I had to—" She sat bolt upright. "Slow down, Wheezie!"

"I see the dog. I'm not blind."

"Where was I?"

"Lillian Yost."

"Oh yeah, Lillian said that Barnhart's on Frederick Street is up for rent."

"That's been up for rent for a couple of months."

"No sign's been in the window."

"You have to know who to talk to," Louise purred.

"I do! That's why I talked to Lillian Yost." Julia's face reddened. "She's a Barnhart."

"I know that."

"I could crown you. Will you please let me finish my story."

"All right. All right." Louise raised her gloved right hand off the wheel as if waving her off.

"I returned my mug. I asked Lillian what was going to happen to the shoe-repair shop now that her dad's retired. She said they were anxious to rent it to the right people. We're the right people."

"Did you tell her that?"

"Of course."

"And—"

"She smiled."

"Did she tell you the rent?"

"Yes. Forty-five dollars a month and we have to pay for electricity and heat. She says we'll use a lot of electricity. She said this would be a big undertaking and we would have to cooperate. Then she wanted to know if our husbands approved."

"What did you say?"

"I said they were ready for us to make some money."

"Well—" Louise's brow furrowed. "That's not an outright lie. Paul swears he isn't lifting a finger. I said, 'Fine with me. I've saved my pin money.' Little does he know how much."

"How much?" Juts's eyes had an eagle glare.

"I'm not telling you."

"Why not?"

"Because you'd think we had a safety net and we don't. It's my money, not yours."

"Did I say it was mine?"

"No, but I know how you think and money burns a hole in your pocket. It always has, Julia."

"Look who's talking . . . the big spender at Bear's department store."

"That reminds me. I want that hat for Easter," Louise stated.

"I get it for Easter. I said we'd share but I'm running the schedule or you're going back on the roof."

The clouds out of the west darkened and the temperature dropped.

"Feels like snow."

Juts opened the window and sniffed. "Smells like it. Won't be much. Gives me the blues, though."

"Yeah. How much work do you think we'd have to do to Barnhart's?"

"A lot. There's a nice little place on the alleyway behind the bank, if Barnhart's doesn't work out."

"We have to face the street and Barnhart's is right behind the movie house on the square. I wish we could get a place on the square—even if it's on the Mason side of the line . . ."

"Then we'd have Pennsylvania laws to contend with and Maryland's are bad enough. I hate politicians. Bunch of windbags."

"I'd like them better if they smoked better cigars."

This made Juts giggle because Louise was unintentionally funny. "Say, how did you get the car again?"

"I asked for it. Went right in the front door and said, 'Paul, I need the car.' "

"I don't believe you."

"I added that Celeste needed me to use it."

"Why not use Celeste's car?"

"It's too big. I couldn't drive it."

"You can't drive this one, either. I wish you'd let me drive."

"You're too impulsive."

"I didn't flick frappé on you. You started it and you can come on over and get the strawberry stain out of my dress, too."

"Chocolate is worse."

"Self-defense." Juts twirled her wedding ring around her finger. "Why is Celeste sending you to talk to her niece, anyway? I always thought Diddy Van Dusen's elevator didn't go to the top. She came by it honestly, though. Her mother was crazy as a bedbug."

Louise clamped down, making her lips a thin red line. "I worshiped Carlotta Van Dusen. She brought me to the true faith."

"Oh, that." Juts airily dismissed what would have turned into a rapturous report of conversion. "You might as well tell me because I'll ask Mom. If she doesn't tell me I'll ask Celeste."

"Isn't that something about Francis Chalfonte getting a big job in Washington with FDR and hiring Rillma Ryan?" Louise referred to Celeste's handsome nephew, in his forties. Rillma had graduated from South Runnymede High the previous year. Celeste was overrun with nieces and nephews.

"Big beans. Tell me."

"My lips are sealed."

"Not if I punch you in the mouth, they aren't."

"Don't be childish. Some things are best left unsaid. Besides, you'd blab it all over town and then what?"

"You really want your ass kicked, don't you?"

"Don't be vulgar, Julia, it's unbecoming." She sniffed, then said, "Give me the hat back."

"I will not."

"Then stop pestering me."

"I volunteered to share the hat. That's more than you ever did."

"You only volunteered so you'd look good in front of your husband. You never would have done it otherwise. You can be very selfish sometimes." She held up her gloved hand again. "But when the chips are down you're the best."

"A Hunsenmeir trait." Juts was determined to weasel Louise's mission out of her. "I don't remember McSherrystown being this far. I'm going to sleep."

"We're almost there."

"A five-minute nap is better than nothing."

"Are you giving me back my hat?"

"You don't want me to take a nap?"

"I want my hat back. After all, my arrangement with Celeste could affect *you*."

"You can tell me if you're successful with Diddy. If you aren't then I won't know what I've missed." Julia cleverly shut her eyes.

A slight twinge of worry rose in Louise's breast. She had thought she had Julia where she wanted her. "It's really a good deal."

"Uh-huh."

"Celeste wants us to succeed."

"Good. She can be our first customer."

"Ramelle dresses her hair."

"And everything else." Juts opened her eyes. "Think people make love when they get old? Those two are pretty old."

"Women don't really make love that way. They're companions who kiss now and then."

"And a bear doesn't shit in the woods."

"Will you stop being so *vulgar*. I've got to get in the right frame of mind to visit Diddy."

Juts warbled "Abide with Me" and then broke into "Holy, Holy, Holy."

"You're a big help."

"I'm so glad." Juts smiled like the Cheshire cat. "I hope Diddy isn't even there—physically, I mean. She's never been there mentally."

"Elizabeth's scattered, I grant you that, but she's smart where it counts. She's taken over the academy now that Carlotta has gone to her reward. You can't be but so dumb to do that, you know."

"I'd like my reward right here on earth."

"A camel will slip through the eye of a needle before a rich man will get into heaven."

"Written by some poor sod, I guarantee it."

"That is in the Bible!"

"You aren't the only person in the family who has read the Bible. I just don't *believe* all of it, that's the difference, and furthermore, I don't want to get stuck with Diddy Van Dusen. She bores the living shit out of me."

"You'll do as you are told."

"Oh, and who is telling me?"

"Celeste."

"Wait a minute, Sister, this is your mission, not mine."

"I need you."

"I'm not doing one single thing. I'm here to keep you company. You and Celeste can cook up whatever you want. Leave me out of it."

"But you'll benefit."

"I'm not listening to that horseface blabber on about the building program and the exercise program and the music program. Uh-uh." She shook her head.

"If I can convince Diddy to keep her stock shares in the Chalfonte business, Celeste promised to pay our store rent for one solid year. Now you have to help."

"What's Diddy's shares got to do with us?"

Louise checked her lipstick in the rearview mirror, not a good idea as she ran off the road. "Whoops." Confession of a confidence affirmed her importance. She was loath to indulge too much, however.

"Whoops, shit—you ought to let me drive."

"You can't drive Pearlie's car."

"You can't either." Juts smirked.

"You know, you think I don't know what you're doing—but I do. You think I'll let down my guard and tell you everything that Celeste told me, but I won't. Furthermore, I'm tired of your constant harping on my driving. You repeat yourself. I'm sick of it."

"Well, Wheezer, I'm not as dumb as you think, so there." Juts ignored her sister's driving comments. "The Chalfontes are planning some kind of merger or fishing for a big government contract and Diddy will throw a spanner in the works because it will be for war stuff. Diddy is a pure pacifist. Chalfontes manufacture ball bearings, so . . ."

"You keep your mouth shut."

"I am." Juts sighed heavily. "Doesn't it make you wonder how Major Chalfonte did it? Our grandpa came home after the war and didn't do squat."

"Mmm." Louise slowed to take a nasty curve up ahead. "Major Chalfonte used to say, 'The war taught me that machines are the future.' So he started making ball bearings."

"He died before you were born."

"I know that."

"Then don't talk as though you knew him."

"Celeste told me that . . . I did know him, sort of."

"Tell me why Celeste will pay our rent for a year but not the damages?"

"Because if we work we'll have to learn something."

"I have learned something."

"Oh?"

"Never to sit next to you when you eat a strawberry frappé."

Louise exhaled loudly. "You wear me out. I have to be sharp for this."

" 'Beautiful savior, king of creation'—" Julia sang.

"Stop it."

"I have a good voice."

"Did I say you didn't?" Louise checked her wristwatch. "Another couple of minutes."

"Are you sure we're on the right road?"

"Julia, how many times have I run up the road to McSherrystown?"

Juts kicked off her shoes and flexed her toes. "I'm kind of sorry Barnhart's closed."

"Go over to Cashton's."

"If there's enough business for two shoe-repair stores there's enough business for two beauty salons. I wonder how Junior McGrail will react?"

"Smile to our faces and tear us down behind our backs."

Julia paused. "How's Pearlie with this?"

"Says it will never work—but he hasn't taken a job at Rife Munitions."

"Is he still mad at you?"

"Maybe a little. He's too worried about Mary to fuss with me. She's working on my mood, too. If we had the money we'd send her to Immaculata Academy."

"Won't do any good."

"A Catholic education is the best there is and Immaculata is one of the best schools around."

"I don't mean that. I mean she'd sneak out with Extra Billy no matter where you sent her. She's in love and she thinks she's the only person who's ever felt this way. You were like that once. Your ass runs away with your head."

"I most certainly was not. I had sense. Mary, however, does not."

"Louise," Juts chided her. "You *swooned* over Pearlie. You wrote his name in your schoolbooks and Miss Dwyer sprouted blotches when she saw you had defaced state property. You were awful."

"I was not. I didn't lie to Mother."

"No."

"And I didn't sass her. As for you, you were a pest."

"With good reason. Pearlie would give me a dime to leave you two alone. I made a real haul." She smiled. "I think you were more in love with Pearlie than I was with Chester. But you were younger when you met him. I love Chessy but I don't think I was quite so wrapped up in him."

"No, but then you've always been independent."

"He's still mad at me."

"Oh."

"He comes home late from work and he reads the newspaper. He hardly talks to me."

"Chessy?" This surprised Louise. Her brother-in-law was an even-tempered man.

"Yesterday he took Buster for a forty-five-minute walk."

Buster was their Irish terrier, a joyful, expressive fellow, devoted to Juts and Chessy as well as to the cat, Yoyo.

"So? Chester loves to walk Buster."

"I know, but usually I go with him."

"He's worried sick about the money."

"Well, so am I!" Juts put her shoes back on. "I think my feet are growing. Anyway, I'm doing something about the mess we made. I'm willing to work but Chessy says it takes money to make money. I sure hope you get somewhere with Diddy because then we won't have to use up so much money getting started."

"Yeah." Louise was worried, too. The reason she had gone to Celeste in the first place was to ask for a loan. Before she could open her mouth Celeste had asked her to intervene with Diddy. Since Diddy and Louise had gone to school together and remained friends, Celeste's request made some sense. Louise readily agreed. It spared her the humiliation of being in debt to her mother's boss. Once she caught her breath she asked for one year's rent. Celeste laughed and called her shrewd. Scared was more like it.

"You know what Chessy said to me last night?" Juts went on. "He said the most dangerous food in the world is wedding cake."

6

Diddy Van Dusen lived the asceticism of the extremely rich. Self-denial in such lavish proportions gagged Juts. She would gladly have taken the castoffs that Diddy dispensed to the poor. Not that Juts was terribly poor, but she realized that in the class scheme of America she was hanging on to the lower middle class by a thread. Good bloodlines shored her up although not as much as Louise, who shouted D.A.R. the minute she felt threatened. Illustrious ancestors had never put a penny in Julia Ellen's pocket, so she abstained from the great Southern vice of ancestor worship.

Now, walking through the grounds of Immaculata with Diddy, she tried to be cheerful.

"We've built another dormitory since last you were here."

"Wonderful," Louise cooed.

"We try to keep some rigor in their lives—after all, life is filled with tests." Diddy's strong features balanced her fair coloring. She resembled a Van Dusen more than a Chalfonte.

"Do you ever get tired of it here?" Juts blurted out.

Diddy stopped by the sundial in the middle of the central quad. "No, I'll carry on Mother's great work."

"Your mother was a saint."

Juts fought back a smirk as Louise drenched Diddy in praise about her departed mother, herself, and Immaculata. By the time Juts got back in the car her facial muscles ached from the strain of false smiles.

Louise crowed over her victory.

"—at the mere mention of godless people, Carlotta quivered. But it's true, you know."

"What's true?"

"Julia Ellen, you haven't heard a word I've said."

"Yes, I have. You talked about the British and the Germans fighting in North Africa. It was North Africa, wasn't it?"

"Don't you read the newspaper?"

"I read the sports page from cover to cover. The Orioles are going to be great this year."

"Juts, no one cares about a minor-league team but you. The Orioles are small beans and the International League is tee-ninetsy."

"Baseball is baseball!"

"Well, as I was saying, I brought up the sale of her stock and told her flat out that Celeste sent me over, knowing how I care about these important moral concerns."

"Ha."

"I do so care—anyway, I told her that bad as the world is right now, it will be far worse if the Communists sit back and let Germany defeat everyone, then come in and beat a weary Germany on their way to mopping up all of Europe. They don't believe in God. They believe everything is about money."

"Isn't it?"

"Julia!"

"All right, all right. Good job. Celeste will be grateful."

"A year's rent!"

Juts brightened. "How about a striped awning outside. Red and white."

"Green and white."

"That'll look like a grocery store. We have to be more colorful and we can't give Junior anything to carp about. She'll have to make it up—know what I mean?"

"Well—"

"Red and white."

"Red and white," Louise agreed.

Juts watched clouds, a deeper gray, rolling in from the west. "Louise, I'm real proud of you. I couldn't have talked to Diddy. I can't even talk to my husband."

"Oh, that will pass. What you need is a baby."

"It's not like I haven't been trying. He won't go to the doctor. I even told him that I've gone and I'm okay."

The first raindrop splattering on the windshield forced Louise to slow down. "I hate to drive in the rain."

"That makes two of us when you're behind the wheel. Why don't you let me drive?"

"I told you, Pearlie would die or kill me. The only reason I got the car today was that he wants to stay on the good side of Her Highness."

"He's no fool. Hey, Wheezer, pull in at that Esso station, will you? I need a Co-Cola."

As Juts pulled two cold bottles out of the big red cooler, Louise watched as the raindrops splashed, mixed in with light sleet.

"Now I'll have to wash and wax the car."

"Men love their cars more than they love us."

"Pearlie says the car is more dependable and doesn't throw dinner plates at him."

Juts popped the cap off the bottle. The metal cap fell down in the slot with a click. She handed the bottle to her sister.

"I'm taking Celeste's money to Barnhart's tomorrow morning. How about if you meet me at the store at nine?"

"Good by me."

They clambered back into the car, the rain and sleet beating down in gray sheets.

Juts piped up. "Let's wait until this blows over. Anyway, I want some peanuts."

"You can't eat them in the car. One little shell and my husband will skin me alive."

"All right. All right." Juts slammed the door, dashing for the little office.

She brought roasted peanuts and two more Cokes to Louise, who got out of the car. Cold, they huddled under the overhang, eating and drinking.

"Damn, it's getting nasty," Juts complained. "Ever notice how spring gets your hopes up and then whammo, you're back down on the floor? Kinda like my Orioles. I'm going to buy a true baseball cap this year."

"You get fat by talking and thin by swinging a bat. That's what Aimes used to say."

Juts brushed off her hands, the salt falling down like tiny sparkles. "Can't wait for late summer when I get boiled peanuts. Is there anything better than that?"

"Momma's fried chicken."

"Hmm." Juts took a hop-step to the car. "Funny what you remember. Aimes did say that, didn't he? I remember him saying, 'What you don't have in your hand, you can't hold.' "

They rode back to Runnymede. Juts was unusually silent.

"Are you worried?"

"About what?"

Louise replied, "About going into business. There's a lot to do."

"No."

"It's not like you to be quiet. You're getting to be like a light-bulb, Julia, you switch on and off these days."

"My mind wanders." She shifted her weight. "I don't know. I have a funny feeling."

"Like someone's going to die?" Louise imagined disaster in large portions.

"No."

"Have you seen any blackbirds pecking at your window?"

"For a Catholic you sure do set store by signs."

"I do not, but everyone knows a blackbird pecking at your window means someone's going to die, and soon."

"No, I don't think anyone is going to die. No."

"Did you skip your monthly?" Louise's voice rose hopefully.

"Nah. And will you stop pushing me."

"I'm not pushing you." Louise inhaled and her voice lowered into the important-information register. "But I know that no woman is truly complete and happy until she has children."

"Mary and Maizie make you jump for joy."

Louise pooh-poohed that sarcastic comment. "Growing pains. They'll grow up. We did."

"I wonder. Sometimes I think no one grows up, we just grow old."

"Women grow up, we have to." She slowed as she neared Julia's small house with its neatly trimmed hedges. "Maybe you're tired. I feel edgy when I'm tired."

"No, I'm not tired. Not after two Co-Colas. I just have a

funny feeling. Like life is going to throw me a curveball." She paused a moment, then pulled herself back up with a big smile. "That's why I need that Orioles cap."

7

Rambunctious lived up to his name. By the time Celeste returned to the stables from what was to have been a relaxing hack, she was exhausted, out of sorts, and wondering if age was creeping up on her. If she heard the phrase "still beautiful" one more time, she thought she'd scream. A biting wind out of the north lashed her face. Her cheeks glowed rosy and moist.

"How was he, Miz Chalfonte?" asked O. B. Huffstetler, Popeye's brother.

"Naughty. You know how he can get when he wants to see if you're asleep at the wheel."

O.B. laughed. "Time for a come-to-Jesus meeting?"

"I'll give him a day to think about it. If he's bad tomorrow then I expect I'll have to remind him of his manners." She slumped in a chair in the tack room as O.B. untacked Rambunctious, now an angel. She called out, "When's your wife due?"

"Another six weeks or so. Starting to tell on her."

"I should wonder." She used the old phrase that was actually a form of agreement. "You'll be a good father."

"Thank you, ma'am."

"You know, your brother is in deep trouble with the Hunsenmeir sisters."

"I told him last night that he better write something good about them real soon or his goose will be cooked."

"Cooked, he'll be pâté."

"Ma'am?"

"He'll be cooked, then ground up into little pieces."

"Oo-whee." O.B. shook his head.

"I have an idea that might help him." O.B. stopped brushing Rambunctious and looked over the horse's withers as she continued.

"You know the girls are opening a beauty salon in Barnhart's old shoe-repair shop. Maybe on the day they open their doors for business, Popeye could write a story. Any new business is worthy of the *Clarion*'s attention, after all."

"Wish I was as smart as you, Miz Chalfonte."

"That's very kind of you, O.B., but you know more about horses than I could if I had three lifetimes to learn. There are many different kinds of smart."

"Thank you, ma'am."

"Doesn't it surprise you that you and Popeye are from the same family? You're so different."

He started brushing again. "Popeye always thought he was better than the rest of us. Going to the University of Maryland put the cherry on it."

"For Carlotta it was her summer in Rome in nineteen hundred and three. She saw one too many cardinals in a red dress. I think if you can get along with your family you can probably get along with anybody."

"You got a point there." He paused. "My brother better do something fast. He's twenty-five and can't find a girl to please him. I never saw such a picky man."

"Miss Chalfonte." A voice called from the end of the stable where the big doors were open.

"I'm in the tack room." Celeste recognized Rillma Ryan's voice.

Rillma greeted O.B. as she passed, then bounced into the oak-paneled room. "Thank you so much."

"For what?"

"For getting me the job in Washington."

Celeste noticed how soft Rillma's brown eyes were, how glossy her black hair, her lips perfectly shaped. She'd known Rillma was pretty, but somehow in the last few weeks she had matured into a beautiful woman, or maybe Celeste was just now noticing.

"I'm glad you can go. It's a wonderful opportunity. And you'll be a big help to Francis. He's like all Chalfontes, a strategist, not a tactician. I know you'll take care of the details in his office."

"If there's anything I can ever do for you, Miss Chalfonte, please tell me. I'll do anything, you know." Rillma exuded excitement.

"I'll bear that in mind."

"Well, I've got to race back and pack up."

"When do you leave?"

"Monday."

"Ah, then you do have a lot to do."

Impulsively, Rillma kissed Celeste on the cheek, then dashed out again as breathlessly as she had arrived.

As she watched the beautiful girl reach the open doors, her youthful figure surrounded by a burst of light, Celeste felt a catch at her heart and wondered if she'd made a dreadful mistake.

8

Chester Smith was foot-weary from the dance of politeness. Walter Falkenroth, Chessy's biggest customer while his new house was being built, was not an unkind man, but when he said "Jump" he expected Chessy to reply "How high?" If Chessy hoped to find some peace in his mother's kitchen, though, he was doomed to disappointment.

Chessy's mother and his wife cordially detested each other and had done so since he and Juts began dating. Their wedding day saw all their friends at the service but not Mother Smith, who feigned illness. Keeping both women happy, or at least away from each other's throats, took elegant sidestepping.

Mother Smith, built like a credenza, scrubbed her sink as she lambasted him.

"—by the nose."

"Now, Mother."

"She does, she leads you around by the nose. The rest of the family will be here and you should be here, too."

"We go through this every year." He sat on the floor, his legs straight out as he leaned back to fix a hinge on a low cabinet door to the right of the sink.

"Your place is with me. Not with those Hunsenmeirs. They're not our kind of people. She can go to her people, you can come home." When her son did not reply she continued. "You married beneath you, Chester." She sighed an artful sigh. "Those things happen, but you don't need to keep company with them. You belong here on Easter Sunday with your brothers. Oh, Uncle Will is coming up from Richmond and Uncle Lou is taking the train in from Harrisburg."

With a grunt, Chessy tightened a screw, the powerful muscles on his forearm also tightening with each turn. "Mother, Christmas dinner here, Easter dinner there. Let's not fuss."

"I'm not fussing. I'm trying to get you to see the light." She turned off the water after wringing out her dishrag. "In order to rise in this world, one must mix with the right people."

"I'm doing okay."

"You could do better."

"I like what I do."

"You're the eldest, Chester. You should set an example. Joseph received another promotion." She paused and before she could say "at Bulova Watch," where Joseph worked, her son quietly interrupted.

"I'm not as smart as Joseph and I'm not as ambitious as Sanford." Chester carefully did not use his brothers' nicknames in front of his mother, who thought them common. "I get along."

Rupert Smith, a big, broad-chested man like Chester, opened the back door. "Hello, Son."

"Hi, Dad."

"Chester, don't use slang in my presence."

Rupert placed the folded newspaper he carried under his arm on the table as though it were fine china. "I'm ready for a cold beer. Will you join me?"

"Sure."

"If you two are going to drink spirits, then you go out on the back porch. I don't want anyone coming in the house and—"

"Jo, we're going to drink our beer right here in the kitchen."

She slapped down a wooden spoon. "Then you can fetch it yourself."

Rupert crossed over to the tiny wooden icebox with the ice compartment on the top and pulled out a long-necked brown bottle of good Pennsylvania beer. He handed one to Chester, then opened his own beer and the paper. Rupert's idea of visiting was to read the headlines out loud.

"Says here a man was arrested in Hagerstown for posing as a financier from New York City."

"Rupert," Jo cut in, "tell your son to come to Easter dinner."

"I expect he knows that, dear."

Exasperated, she stormed out of the kitchen. "You men always stick together."

Rupert ignored her and read another headline. " 'Nevada lashed by storms.' " He read in silence. "Out there two inches of rainfall is a flood. I'd like to see the West."

"Me, too." Chester drained his bottle. He needed to head home. "Dad, I've got to get back."

"Oh." Rup glanced up from his paper. "Why don't you try and stop by after church on Easter. It will make life easier here."

Chester felt a wash of battery acid in his stomach. "Dad, it's not that simple."

Rupert said nothing, returning to his paper. Chester washed out his beer bottle, dropping it in the garbage can under the sink. He walked down the hall to say good-bye to his mother, who was polishing the big mahogany dinner table.

"Bye, Mother."

Focusing on her task, she growled, "You could make an exception just once. After all, this may be the last time we're together. You know Lou's not been well."

This was too familiar a ploy for Chester to rise to the bait. "I'm sorry to hear that."

"When you have children we *will* refashion our holiday schedule."

"It's been a long, dry spell." He smiled tightly. None of his brothers had children, either.

"You have all married barren women."

"Maybe it's us."

Sharply she said, "Oh, no, it isn't. Our people have never had that problem, not your father's people." She shook her head. "It's the wives."

"If I don't get by Sunday, you have a happy Easter, Mother."

He left by the back door. Without a word, she continued polishing. His father kept his nose in the paper.

Chessy opened his own back door a half hour after he said he'd be home.

Juts, wearing her apron with flowers on it, greeted him. "You're late, goddammit, and I burned the liver."

"I stopped by Mother's."

"That battle-ax kept you just to spite me."

Chester kissed Juts on the cheek, removed his coat, then washed his hands. "Be ready in a jiffy."

She called after, "Was she on the warpath about Easter dinner?"

"I don't know, honey, it goes in one ear and out the other. You know I don't pay any attention to her."

But he did. Chester paid attention to everybody, and sooner or later his silence would become an unbearable burden.

9

Surely He hath borne our griefs and carried our sorrows: He was wounded for our transgressions, He was bruised for our iniquities.' "

" 'All we like sheep have gone astray: and the Lord hath laid on Him the iniquity of us all.' "

As Pastor Neely read the introit for Good Friday, Juts, smartly turned out in subdued colors, veil over her face, automatically read the responses. The liturgy appealed to her; she knew it by heart for the entire ecclesiastical calendar.

She shared a hymnal with her mother but her mind wandered even as her lips carried the correct, dolorous response. " 'Hear my prayer, O Lord: and let my cry come to thee.' "

Juts was counting names in the congregation, mostly women. The men didn't or couldn't take off work today, but she knew that every lady sitting in sad repose would dutifully drag her husband to Easter service. A sick person would be carried in on a stretcher. No one missed Easter service.

She numbered three Elizabeths, two Katherines, and one Kitty. One Mildred, one Florence, her age. Then it struck her that names tag a generation. Not the classic names, but the Mildreds, the Myrtles, the Roses.

She wondered what she would name a daughter. Certainly

she didn't want to copy anyone around her. She discounted Dorothy because the Maupins had named their tiny baby Dorothy and that child strongly resembled a ferret. Dora sounded like a fat whale, Eleanor like a priss, and Bernice was the name of a girl who ought to grow up to work in a millinery shop. None of those would do. Bonnie was too bouncy, Lucille a touch old-fashioned for this new generation. Margaret wasn't too bad, but Juts didn't want to be classic, she wanted to be original.

Of course, if she ever bore a son, that would be easy: Chester junior.

Before she could further muse on this subject, great velvet curtains were drawn over the stained-glass windows—the altar and pulpit already being draped in black velvet—all lights were extinguished, and a chilling silence fell over the worshiping women. It was three o'clock, the hour at which Jesus surrendered His spirit to His father.

Julia Ellen, not overfond of the Old Testament, or even some parts of the New, wondered why the fathers were so cruel, starting with God. Abraham was willing to sacrifice his only son. Moses cared not a whit for his own. Nothing good really happened until the New Testament. At least those stories didn't scare her when she was a child, although Good Friday gave her the creeps. Sacrifice held no appeal for Juts, even one made nineteen hundred years ago.

When the organ gave a rumble, the curtains opened, and she breathed relief. She was even happier when the service ended. She and Cora filed down the aisle to shake Pastor Neely's hand as he stood at the door to the vestibule to greet them.

Once out on the sidewalk of the square, the temperature in the mid-fifties, she looked for Louise, emerging from St. Rose of Lima's.

"There she is."

And there she was, swathed in black with deep purple

highlights, her veil shimmering over her face, tiny little squares embroidered into the mesh.

"Mother." Louise walked across the square, glanced around, and said sarcastically, "Junior McGrail ignored me. In church. That's a good Christian."

"Pig fat and bone idle, that one," Juts said.

"Where are the girls?" Cora inquired.

Louise turned around just as Maizie skipped down the steps, forgetting the solemnity of the occasion.

"Walk like a lady, Maizie."

A furrow on Maizie's young brow gave a fleeting indication of what she might look like as an old lady.

"Hello, G-Mom. Hi, Aunt Juts."

"Don't call your grandmother that. Really, Maizie, it's Good Friday and you're standing in the square in front of God and everyone."

"Oh, Louise, don't be too hard on her," Cora said.

Louise ignored her mother. "Where's Mary?"

"Still in church."

"What's she doing in there?"

"I don't know." Maizie shrugged, which meant she did.

Louise, hands on hips, prodded. "Your sister flies out of church like an arrow. Now, stop trying to fool me. What's she doing in there? Is Extra Billy in there?"

"Mom, Billy's not a Catholic."

"One more reason not to like him." Louise pursed her lips.

"Oh, Wheezie, stop trying to be more Catholic than the pope."

"Julia, if you'd open your eyes—"

Juts snapped back, "And if you'd open yours you'd realize you're pushing Mary into that boy's arms. If you didn't knock him every five minutes, she'd tire of him."

"Don't tell me how to raise my daughter. You're not a mother. You don't know anything."

Cora placed her bulk between the two. "I don't want a rumpus. Louise, go on back in there and fetch her out. Juts, button your lip."

Louise stalked back up the steps and into the church.

Julia whined, "She started it."

"Have enough sense to shut up," Cora commanded. "It's Good Friday." She put her arm around Maizie. "How do they expect you to grow up when they haven't?"

Maizie giggled. "Uh-oh."

That exclamation was due to the sight of her mother propelling a scowling Mary down the steps, bumping her from behind with the purple purse, a little swat here, a little swat there.

Louise strode past the three, calling over her shoulder, "Meet you at the store. We're going to have a little talk." She prodded a recalcitrant Mary again.

Juts laughed, knowing Mary was going to get hell.

"Talk—they'll have a come-to-Jesus meeting."

Maizie whispered, "Billy snuck into St. Rose's last night and left a love letter for Mary in the hymnal. But he must have gotten the pew wrong because it wasn't in our row. Mary's flipped through every hymnal in there."

"Oh, for Pete's sake." Juts laughed. "Mom, don't you think Louise is making too much out of Extra Billy?"

"Come on, let's walk over to Frederick Street." Cora motioned for her daughter to start, then winked in the direction of Maizie, just ahead.

"Oh." Juts shut up, realizing Cora didn't want to talk in front of Maizie.

Maizie dashed for Cadwalder's. "G-Mom, can I get a soda?"

"Yes, tell Mr. C. I'm on your heels. I'll pay for it."

"I think I'll wait outside," Juts volunteered, prudent for once.

"I think you'll be out in the cold till you pay your bill, girlie."

"Where're Celeste and Ramelle? They're usually in church." Juts changed the subject.

"Having a Mr. and Mrs." This was Cora's euphemism for a knock-down-drag-out fight.

"Oh boy."

"Those two haven't had cross words for such a long time." Cora, loyal to Celeste, refused to elaborate. "I'll be right out."

Julia lingered on the square, waiting for her mother and niece. She smiled and waved at friends and foes. She passed and repassed and was quite stunned when Junior McGrail marched right by her, looking neither to the left nor the right, as she paraded into the drugstore.

Just then Cora and Maizie trooped out.

"Mom, Junior McGrail just gave me the cold shoulder."

"She nodded at us," Maizie chirped, thrilled to be able to contribute to an adult conversation.

"You might be taking bread out of her mouth," Cora said as they walked the two doors east to Frederick Street.

"I don't see it that way. There's enough hair in this town for two shops. Besides, hers is in North Runnymede and ours will be in South Runnymede."

As they walked into the former shoe store the three ignored Mary's tear-streaked face. Juts's Irish terrier barked a greeting to her.

"What are you doing here, Buster?" Juts addressed the dog.

"He was here when I unlocked the door." Louise spoke in an even tone of voice that meant she was struggling to control her temper. "Mom, what do you think?"

"You two have sure cleaned this place up."

"Now, I think the mirrors should line this wall, with cabinets underneath and big comfy chairs here so people can read while they're under the dryer."

"Louise, we also need chairs we can pump up and down."

"I know that. Right here will be the reception area with lots of music. I'm tired of feeling like I'm in a funeral parlor when I go into a beauty salon. And over here—"

"Girls, how are you going to get all this done?"

"What do you mean?"

"Cabinetwork is pricey and mirrors will put you in the poor-house, to say nothing of the plumbing for each sink."

"Chester can do the cabinetwork and Pearlie can paint. We'll scrounge up the rest," Louise replied forcefully.

"You two better get on the good side of your men."

"Paul will do whatever I tell him," Louise bragged.

"Mother, why would you want a husband that dull?" Mary flared up.

"Don't be a nit. If you don't get the upper hand with a man he will run with other women, drink, or gamble and then you'll both be in the shitcan." Louise shocked herself by saying "shit-can," but she'd had such a go-round with Mary that her guard was down.

"I don't want that kind of marriage," Mary stubbornly argued. "I want a man who loves me, who—"

"Love, oh Mary, don't make me laugh. What do you know about love?"

"I know it doesn't mean you give orders."

Louise advanced on Mary, who stood her ground.

Cora put a stop to the fuss. "Louise, there's plenty of time for her to learn about men."

"What I'm trying to get through her thick head is that if you lie down with dogs you get up with fleas."

"Mother!" Mary ran out, slamming the door behind her.

"Mary, Mary, you come back here this minute."

"Want me to go get her, Mom?"

"No, Maizie, you stay right here. She can't go find Billy because he's at work. She'll go home." Louise shivered. The heat wasn't on in the store. "Let's go."

"Louise, there's a time to wink as well as a time to see."

"Mother, stay out of this!" Louise grabbed Maizie by the elbow and pushed her out of the store, leaving the door ajar.

Julia watched her sister hurry Maizie down the street. "Louise thinks she knows everything," she said.

"She's not young enough to know everything." When Juts started to laugh, Cora smiled at her. "And neither are you."

"I never said I knew everything, but she's just pushing Mary at that boy, she's making him irresistible."

"I know that."

"Then why don't *you* say something?"

"Because everyone has to learn."

Juts reached down to pet Buster. "You mean everyone has to learn the hard way."

Cora shook her head. "Everyone's got to learn however they can."

"But you know Mary's going to get in trouble—maybe even big trouble. Extra Billy is wild as a rat."

"And handsome as a prince. Julia Ellen, escort me back to Celeste's," Cora said firmly.

"Okay." Juts waited for her mother to step outside into the sunlight, then locked the door behind her. "Mom," she whispered, "I'm afraid Mary will get pregnant."

"Might."

"That would kill Louise. The shame of it—not that I think it's the worst thing in the world but, well, it's not the best. Mary would be an outcast in these parts."

"If you take a person's lesson away from them they have to learn it later, and each time that lesson gets put off it gets worse and worse. I'm an ignorant woman, but I've learned that much in this life."

"You're not ignorant."

"Can't read or write."

"Lots of people can't read and write. Anyway, I have to think about what you said. I feel like I should do something. Maybe I should talk to Mary."

"Suit yourself."

10

The pilot light glowed like a blue moth's eye. Exhausted from the duel between passion and reason, Celeste stood over the stove. She believed she should be above showing emotion and she was angry at herself for arguing with Ramelle.

After all, she was the daughter of a war hero, T. Pritchard Chalfonte, a Confederate major who slogged through four years of deprivation and horror yet never complained. He was thirty-eight when his third child was born, and Celeste clearly remembered her father in his forties and fifties. The Chalfontes aged slowly, so the major seemed young for a long, long time.

Nor did her mother, Charlotte Spottiswood, vent whatever steam had built up inside her. Celeste reviewed her brothers and deceased sister; no matter how they differed, all practiced restraint. After the Great War, when two of her youngest brother's comrades returned, she learned that Spottiswood had died as befitted a Chalfonte, doing his duty and without comment. Although their father passed away in 1897, his legacy of quiet courage informed his children and their children.

Raising her voice at Ramelle seemed nearly as vile as if she had struck her. In all the years they had been together she couldn't recall a more vehement denunciation, not even when Ramelle became pregnant by Curtis and married him. Perhaps the loss of Spotts, still so raw, enabled her to overcome whatever jealousy she might have felt toward her other younger brother, Curtis. She tried to remember how she had felt. All that came to mind was her joy at little Spotts's birth. On reflection, 1920 had proved one of the happiest years of her life.

Ever since, Ramelle spent the winter and early spring in California with Curtis, the high spring, summer, and fall in Maryland. Spotts would turn twenty-one in a few weeks and she loved the girl as if she were her own daughter. Curiously, even though Ramelle was married to Curtis, the name on the birth certificate was Spottiswood Chalfonte Bowman—Ramelle's maiden name.

She did recall a subdued disagreement when Spotts decided to attend a Western college, Stanford, instead of Bryn Mawr, Celeste's first choice. However, she didn't shout. She merely pointed out to mother and daughter that the Eastern schools provided one with better connections throughout life. After all, there wasn't much power in the West that she could ascertain, so the leaders of the younger generation still graduated from Ivy League schools. Spotts graciously declined. She liked the West better.

Celeste even called Curtis, who said, "She's old enough to make her own decisions." She never remembered her parents saying anything like that to her or to her other siblings. Times had changed, and not for the better. She believed young people needed guidance. You couldn't allow them to do whatever they wanted to do. They were too self-indulgent for that.

However, she restrained herself, and Spotts hurried off to Stanford, which she loved.

This disagreement was different, though.

In the nearly twenty-one years since Spotts's birth, Ramelle had never altered the schedule. Now she declared she was returning to California because Curtis had enlisted. This was a big alteration.

Initially, Celeste had tried the reasonable approach. That didn't work. Then she tried bribery. That didn't work, either.

Finally, she lost her temper. Ramelle walked away from her, went to her room, and shut the door.

That didn't surprise Celeste. After all, had Ramelle shouted at her, she might have done the same thing or simply jumped in the Packard Twelve and roared off.

The teakettle whistled. She poured herself a cup and sat in the cozy glassed-in nook off the cavernous kitchen. Tea and tulips. She adored tulips, and masses of them swayed under the nook window. Spring took two steps forward and one step back. It had remained cool all week and Easter Sunday showed no promise of warming. However, the tulips didn't mind; they opened their flame-orange petals lined in black, their reds, whites, purples, and yellows in defiance of the crisp air. The cherry trees were more prudent. They were waiting for a toasty day in the mid-sixties.

Windblown light deepened to gold. In an hour the sun would set. Twilight had made Celeste ache ever since she was a child. The pain deepened with age. She couldn't understand how quickly the years flew by and it made no sense at all to her that she was in her sixties, although everyone told her she looked like she was in her early forties. Whatever her exterior, she had sixty-three years of memories. She loved her life. She wanted sixty more years. And she loved Ramelle.

The truth was, she was jealous. This jolt of self-knowledge made her put down her cup with a rattle. She'd never been jealous. Why now?

A light footfall in the kitchen made her turn around. Ramelle, in a red silk robe, the one Celeste had brought her from Paris, walked to the stove. She didn't see Celeste. So Celeste enjoyed the delicious experience of observing someone who doesn't know she is being observed.

She had learned many things over the course of her life, and one of them was that there is the self you know, that you show to others; there is the self you know, that you don't show to others;

there is the self others know about you, that you don't know; and
lastly, there is the self others don't know and you don't know, either. It takes a disaster, a catastrophe of some sort, to blast out the
self no one knows.

She watched Ramelle, such a graceful woman, blink when
the gas flames snapped around the burner. She wondered what
her lover knew about her that she didn't know. Perhaps it was better not to know, really.

"Come sit with me."

Ramelle jumped. "You startled me."

"I startled myself. I lost my temper and I apologize."

Ramelle waved her hand, dismissing the subject. "You don't
like change, my dear. As long as things go according to plan it's
fine. I juggled the plan."

"Am I that much of a tyrant?"

Ramelle joined her. "An enlightened one."

Celeste rested her head in the cup of her hand for a moment.
"Well—"

"Since you're so much brighter than the rest of us, we're all
rather happy that you organize life. I know I am."

"Oh, Ramelle, I'm not brighter than you are—just better
read." Celeste watched the light fall across Ramelle's delicate features.

"All the Chalfontes are highly intelligent—the Spottiswoods,
too." Ramelle mentioned Celeste's mother's family. "Breed the
best to the best and hope for the best. Isn't that what we do with
horses?"

"Yes." Celeste laughed, then added, "Mother favored
Carlotta."

"Oh, she did not. How could anyone favor Carlotta?"

"Carlotta married Herbert Van Dusen, an insipid soul, if ever
there was one. Mother thought he was eminently suitable because
he had a seat on the stock exchange, though that's about all he

had. His partners carried him along, but to hear Carlotta tell it you would have thought he had the rapacious wisdom of J.P. Morgan."

"She loved him, though. We all tend to overstate the virtues of those we love."

"Oh." Celeste took a sip. "Do you overstate mine?"

"No."

"What an elegant fibber you are, Ramelle. I don't understand why you want to go back to Curtis. He's too old for combat, but once this vulgar display of organized violence is fully orchestrated, he'll play his part. He is fifty-seven, you know."

"If he has his way he'll get into the fighting somehow. I think he has hated living in his brother's shadow all these years."

"Curtis survived the Great War. He acquitted himself with honor."

"Men don't think like that. Spotty died a hero's death."

"There are moments when I think men are the most peculiar animals God ever put on this earth."

"They say the same thing about us."

"Yes, I suppose they do." Celeste watched the gold turn to pink outside as the sun neared the waiting horizon. "Are you angry with me?"

"No. Well—maybe just a little. I don't like being yelled at. Honey, whatever happens with Curtis, I'd like to be with him until he goes."

"You could be together here."

"Curtis will run his business until he's given orders to go. You know how all your brothers are."

"You know, I never asked you—are you in love with Curtis?"

"Of course." Ramelle laughed. "He's so much like you, only—softer in ways."

Celeste wanted to say that Ramelle should love her more, but she paused, and instead replied, "He's fortunate."

"Oh, Celeste, Curtis is just Curtis. He's happy-go-lucky. He belongs in that California sunshine and in the film business. It suits him. He's one of those men who knows how to get things done—as I said, like you. Nothing stops Curtis, but then again, I suppose nothing stops Stirling, either; it's just that Stirling has always seemed old to me, even when he was young." Celeste's brother in Baltimore piloted the ball-bearing business.

"The price of being firstborn, I should think," Celeste said.

"I love you, you know. Always and ever."

"I love you, too."

"There. We've made up. Don't you feel better?"

"I'm not entirely sure. I feel somewhat relieved. I'm just cross with myself for losing my temper."

"You're only human."

"That's what disturbs me." Celeste laughed.

The front door opened and closed with a thud.

"It's me. Where are you two?" Fannie Jump Creighton, Celeste's friend since infancy, bellowed.

"Oh, Lord." Celeste sighed, for Fannie Jump could talk. "We're in the kitchen."

Fannie, carrying a heavy shopping bag, lumbered in, dropped the bag on the floor with a soft *clunk,* and said, "I was nearly run over. Kaput. Smashed into the afterlife with no hope of instant resurrection, I can tell you. Flattened, just positively flattened by that goddamned Extra Billy Bitters, who someone should put in jail—"

Celeste interrupted, "Someone will. In good time."

"Well, in good time might be now because he's got Mary in the car with Louise chasing and she's behind the wheel, may all the saints preserve us. You know that Louise couldn't drive her way out of a burning barn. And in hot pursuit of Louise is Chester Smith with Juts, Maizie, and Paul in the car and Paul is hanging out the window screaming, I tell you, just at the top of his lungs, for his crazy wife to slow down. I think we should call the sheriff. After all, it's a threat to the public welfare and the authorities ought to be alerted. But which side? I mean, you know how pompous Harmon Nordness can be, should Billy cross over into Pennsylvania. But the worst part is Mary's got a gun and she's shooting out the window, just firing away like cowboys and Indians!"

"What!" both listeners exclaimed at once.

11

Extra Billy flew down Frederick Street hanging left on two wheels as he made for the Emmitsburg pike, but he couldn't get the old deuce coupe under control. When he finally straightened the Ford out he fishtailed over the Mason-Dixon line. He careened around the northwest side of the square, swerving in front of the Bon-Ton department store. He ran up on the curb, then overcorrected, only to drive right into the beautiful square itself. Mary was waving the gun. When they bumped hard going over the curb, she shot into the roof of the deuce coupe, which scared both of them. Billy didn't watch where he was going and smashed right into the base of the Yankee general George Gordon Meade. The statue tilted just a bit but the deuce coupe sure got the worst of it.

Dazed, Billy spilled out of the car, sat down hard, then crawled up on all fours to pull a squealing Mary out.

Just then Louise, madder than a stepped-on hornet, also

jumped the curb and came to a lurching halt next to Billy's car. Chessy, far more prudent, stopped at the intersection by St. Rose of Lima's, cut the motor, and ran for the accident, as did Juts and Pearlie. On their heels were Celeste, Ramelle, and Fannie Jump, puffing hard since they had run from Celeste's house, which was close to the square.

Extra Billy, with presence of mind, grabbed the gun from Mary. "I didn't know she had it, honest, I didn't."

Louise yanked Mary to her feet, for she had slumped against the deuce coupe. "What's the matter with you?"

"Don't touch me! I hate you!" Mary wailed as she wrapped her arms around Extra Billy's slender waist.

"Touch you. I will whip you within an inch of your life!"

"No!" Mary screamed.

Pearlie, now at the scene, made a fist ready to hit the young man when Chessy, fast up behind him, grabbed his arm.

"Pearlie, that's not the way."

Extra Billy gratefully cast his eyes at Chester and then behind him to the trio of women tromping over the square. The two cars had mashed the flowers, which Celeste gingerly stepped over.

"I won't go home, I won't go home!" Mary shrieked.

"You'll do as I tell you." Louise reached for her but Mary twisted away, all the while clinging to Billy, gun still in his hand.

Celeste reached for the gun, neatly removing it from Billy's hand. "You won't be needing that."

"Uh—no, Miss Chalfonte."

"Is it your gun?"

"No, ma'am."

"It's Daddy's." Mary wept.

When Pearlie spoke, his voice was shaking. "You'd better come home right now. We'll straighten this out."

Maizie, eyes big as golf balls, observed the whole thing, her sister imploring her with looks, since Maizie was always her ally except when the two were fighting.

A siren in the background promised further unpleasantness.

"Shit," Extra Billy muttered.

"Don't swear in front of me!" Louise snapped.

"I'm sorry, Mrs. Trumbull, I'm sorry about all of this. It didn't start out like this. We were going to ride over to Baltimore and come right back, but—"

"Don't lie to me, Billy. You were abducting my daughter." Louise's voice was hard.

"Abducting! Hell, Wheezie, she about ran her legs off to get in the car. Car looks pretty bad," Juts said.

"Keep out of this, Julia! You're not a mother."

"Louise, will you calm down? Getting Billy arrested isn't going to solve anything."

"Don't you take her part!"

"I'm not, I'm—"

They all stopped to observe Harmon Nordness stop, lift himself out of the squad car, and size up the catastrophe, then, head down, stride across the debris.

"Hello, Sheriff." Chester tried to smooth things over. "We've got a bit of a situation here, but nothing we can't get sorted out."

"Thank you, Chester, I intend to do just that...." Sheriff Nordness licked his fleshy lips. "Who was driving the Ford?"

"I was," Billy declared.

"You usually run into statues, Billy? I've caught you at cockfights. I've hauled your poppa in drunk and disorderly with you in the backseat. But I believe this is the first time you and anyone else has ever wantonly defaced state property."

"It was an accident, Sheriff."

"Uh-huh." Harmon put his face right up to Mary's tearful one. "What have you got to say for yourself, girlie? I've got a report that you were shooting a revolver from this very car."

Mary wailed.

"Oh, Harmon, people do talk." Fannie Jump fudged it a little. "The gun in question happened to be in the backseat of the car and when Extra Billy encountered a little difficulty steering his car it bounced off the seat and discharged."

"Gee-od." Harmon spat a wad of tobacco juice on the ground.

"Crazy things happen." Juts smiled big.

"Yeah, 'cause crazy people make them happen." He turned on Juts, who took a step closer to Chessy. "Now folks, I'm going to have to run you all in. Extra Billy and Mary and whoever was driving the Model A."

"Me." Pearlie stepped forward.

"Pearlie, why'd you want to do a fool thing like that? That's not like you."

"He didn't do it, I did." Louise practically pushed her gallant husband out of the way.

"That's more like it."

"You can't take Wheezie without me." Paul put his arm around his wife's shoulders.

"Trumbull, I can do whatever the hell I want around here. I'm the law in this part of Pennsylvania."

"Indeed you are and I don't know how you do everything that you do. You're woefully understaffed, Harmon." Celeste's voice rang like silver. "But tomorrow is Easter. Why don't we all go home, go to church tomorrow, and ask for forgiveness. No crime has been committed other than repair work to George here, and I expect Extra Billy and Mary will have to make good on the statue."

"Yes, ma'am." Billy eagerly looked to Harmon. "Yes, sir."

Harmon, like most low-level officials, entertained a keen awareness of where local power resided. It definitely resided with Celeste Chalfonte even though she lived in Maryland. You just didn't rile the Chalfontes or Rifes or Frosts or other local worthies. Besides, the editors of the *Clarion* and the *Trumpet* could make him appear heartless for hauling kids into jail on reckless-driving charges before Easter, even if they did have it coming.

"Tell you what I'm going to do. I'm going to let you get these cars out of here. People who go to church in the morning don't want to be looking at this mess. Then I'm going to call down at Dingledine's Nursery and ask them to let you all in late to buy tulips and azaleas and then you all are going to plant these tulips and I don't much care if it takes all night. Then I will assess the damages and we'll figure it out from there." He glared at Juts and Louise. "Seems to me you girls already have racked up some expenses in this town."

Since the deuce wouldn't start, Chessy, Paul, and Extra Billy pushed it out of the park with Fannie Jump Creighton at the wheel. A still-outraged Louise, on a short leash held by her sister, stomped home to get gardening tools and lanterns.

Celeste and Ramelle, with Maizie, drove on old Route 140 to Dingledine's, where they had to talk Randy Dingledine into following them with a truckful of tulips, since the Packard could only hold so much.

"Now, Maizie, I don't want you to be upset by all this. Mary's in the grips of blind passion." Celeste searched around for the appropriate vocabulary for a fourteen-year-old girl.

Maizie sighed romantically. "I thought it was swell."

"Oh, God." Ramelle rolled her eyes heavenward.

12

Buster patiently waited on the southwest corner of the square, behind City Hall and in front of Christ Lutheran Church. Yoyo, his best friend, Juts's large long-haired tabby, sat next to him. Juts and Chessy, worn out from last night's plantings, had forgotten to tightly close the screen door on the back porch and the animals scooted out once they discovered the mistake.

The singing inside all the churches on the square swelled to a crescendo. The cat and dog exchanged glances, deciding this was extremely interesting, and trotted up the long steps to the heavy wooden double front doors of Christ Lutheran, opened to welcome the faithful.

Yoyo shot down the carpeted center aisle as Buster contemplated his next move. Yoyo's original intention was to find Juts and Chessy, but the intoxicating fragrance of massed flowers around the altar and communion rail proved too tempting. She picked up speed, hesitating only at the rail because beautiful needlepoint knee cushions were on the floor. This was heaven: something to tear and something to smell. A titter rolled through the congregation, a ripple from back to front. As Pastor Neely faced the altar he was unaware of the source of amusement. A pendulous lily proved more inviting to Yoyo than sharpening her claws on the needlepoint. She launched herself into the air and grabbed it with both paws, yanking it out of the arrangement.

The paprika-colored pollen sprinkled on the floor as well as over her long whiskers.

Juts, wearing the disputed Bear's department store hat, had her nose in the hymnal looking for the next hymn, and didn't know Yoyo was experiencing a religious moment. Chessy elbowed her. She glanced up and didn't see anything because Lillian Yost sat in front of her, her hat massive. The Hunsenmeir pew was in the fifth row and Cora was sitting in the middle; she didn't see Yoyo either.

Buster, curiosity peaking, followed the cat down the aisle but was waylaid by the heavy odor of chocolate. He ducked into the pew with the Falkenroths and the Cadwalders, where he found a chocolate-covered marshmallow bunny, which little Paula Falkenroth had hidden in her white purse. Paula giggled when Buster, docked tail wagging, slid up to her in the pew. She soon stopped when he reached right in the purse and snatched her candy.

"Daddy!"

"Hush," Walter whispered. He saw what Buster did but he also knew that Paula was forbidden to carry candy in her church bag. If her mother found out there would be a disagreeable discussion on the way home. Putting out a daily newspaper and building a new house used up Walter's reserves of patience. He wanted a calm Easter.

Buster scampered out the pew as parishioners turned their knees to the side.

"I want my chocolate bunny!"

"Paula!" Her mother reached over Walter's chest and pushed the child back on the pew.

Pastor Neely, still invoking many holy writs, faced the altar and couldn't turn around.

The acolyte proved useless. At fourteen he thought this escapade an improvement on the service.

Yoyo, thrilled with the easy conquest of the lily, attacked the entire enormous arrangement. Flowers scattered everywhere.

"Pssst," Juts hissed at her cat as she leaned around Lillian's shoulder.

Upon hearing her mother's voice, Yoyo paused from her frolic for a moment, then resumed her pleasures.

Cora started to laugh.

"Mother, you're no help," Juts whispered.

The more Julia scowled, the harder Cora laughed. Chester started laughing too, as did others around them.

Meanwhile, Buster tore down the center aisle, skidding to a stop at the Hunsenmeir pew, mouth drooling as he held his booty.

No wonder you come to church, the cat and dog seemed to say. *This is fun!*

Finished with his many invocations, Pastor Neely turned from the altar, face radiant with the message "He is risen," only to find two little furry faces peering right up at him, one smeared with pollen and the other fiercely holding a chocolate bunny.

Not content with her depredations, Yoyo leapt into the middle of the huge altar floral arrangement. Both tumbled onto the floor.

Juts rose, face beet-red, slid past her howling mother and husband, and stalked toward her pets.

Try as she might to maintain her dignity—after all, it was the highest holy day of the year—the sight of Yoyo, crazed with excitement, and Buster, jaws clamped on his prize, proved too much for Juts. She giggled.

Pastor Neely sternly glared down at her.

This made her laugh even more. Juts reached for Buster's collar. He didn't resist.

"Come on," she whispered.

He obediently followed.

"He's got my bunny!" Paula Falkenroth shouted.

"Good God." Walter covered his eyes.

Margot, his wife, whispered, "Paula, I told you not to bring candy to church."

"I forgot," Paula lied.

"Little girl, don't you forget that you're in a house of worship," her father warned.

"Well—" She twisted away as Buster walked past her, Juts's hand still firmly on the collar.

"I'll buy you another bunny, Paula," Juts promised.

The Cadwalders stared at Juts as if to say, "Why do these things always happen to you?"

She smiled weakly and continued on, then turned and called as low as she could, "Yoyo, come on, kittycat."

Not only did Yoyo ignore the kind entreaty of her mother, she experienced one of those fits of ecstasy known primarily to members of the feline family and certain Catholics. She raced through the plants on the floor. She soared over flower arrangements wherever she found them. Some she cleared, some she didn't. Galvanized into action by Pastor Neely's uncompromising stare, the acolyte chased Yoyo, which heightened her celebration of her own powers. She put the brakes on as the lanky boy lurched past her, then she wheeled and gracefully arched onto the altar, where two identical, magnificent arrangements reposed on either side of the large, chaste gold cross. Tempting as those arrangements were, her pursuer was gaining on her. She ducked behind the cross. As he reached for her, she saucily and defiantly reached right back to bat at him. Being a good sport, she kept her claws sheathed.

Then she dropped behind the altar and stealthily crawled to the side as the acolyte got down on his hands and knees, providing the congregation with the sight of his rump, not perhaps the typical object of worship.

Beads of perspiration appeared on Pastor Neely's forehead. Chester knew he should try and catch his cat, but he was convulsed with laughter and so weak from it he could barely move.

Celeste, Ramelle, and Fannie Jump sat in the third pew to the right of the aisle, pews being assigned according to when one's family participated in founding the church or joined it. Tears of laughter rolled from their eyes.

Yoyo, not one to shun the spotlight, realized she had the congregation in the palm of her paw. She zoomed out from the consecrated area, vaulted onto the back of a pew, ran along it as hands grabbed for her, then casually jumped off, only to catapult herself onto the exquisite maroon velvet curtains. She climbed the curtains into the balcony, where she discovered the organist, a family friend, Aunt Dimps.

Terrified that Yoyo would feel compelled to play the organ, Aunt Dimps stood, her back to the organ, her arms outstretched.

The sight of Dimps in this strange posture caused Yoyo to reflect upon her actions. She sat stock-still, cocked her head to one side, and then walked toward her.

"Good girl, good kitty, Yoyo." Aunt Dimps reached down to pick up the animal, who sauntered toward her.

Yoyo sidestepped those outstretched hands, leapt up, and landed *kerplat* on the keyboard. A dreadful screech boomed through the pipes, which so scared Yoyo she scooted off the organ, charged through the balcony aisle, and scurried down the back stairs, which emptied into the vestibule. She saw Buster and Juts out on the steps so she collected herself and walked out.

Juts, hearing the organ cacophony, had put two and two together. She crumpled on the steps, more from merriment than from shame, just as St. Rose of Lima's opened its doors, the worshipers spilling out like children let out of school.

O.B. Huffstetler, sharp-eyed, guiding his most pregnant wife down the steps, noticed Juts. He called back for Louise, who was coming out the door. "Louise, something's wrong with Juts."

Her eyes followed the direction of his finger, as did everyone else's.

As quickly as she could in her high heels, Louise ran down

the steps, her orchid corsage bobbing with each step. Pearlie and the girls, now alerted, followed, charging across the square.

Breathless, she knelt down by her sister. "Juts, Juts, are you all right?"

Juts laughed so hard she was sobbing. She couldn't respond.

"Aunt Juts." Mary also knelt down by the aunt she loved.

"What are Yoyo and Buster doing here?" Maizie asked.

That sent Juts into renewed sobs of laughter.

Pearlie bent over and gently put his hands under his sister-in-law's arms. "Uppie-do." He lifted her to her feet, where she sagged against him.

"I think we'd better get the doctor," Pearlie said.

"No." Julia shook her head, tried to say something, and then fell apart all over again.

By now the congregation of St. Rose's, as well as St. Paul's Episcopal, was gathering on the steps of Christ Lutheran.

"Is she all right?" asked Junior McGrail, who secretly hoped she wasn't.

Juts nodded.

"Well, what's wrong?" Popeye Huffstetler, ever the reporter, bluntly asked.

Juts kept laughing and pointing to the dog and the cat.

Junior, now upon them, remarked in a stage whisper to Caesura Frothingham, her best friend, "Imagine, Easter Sunday and she's got dirty fingernails. I wouldn't want someone to do my hair with dirty fingernails."

Try as she might, Juts couldn't scrub out the dirt from planting tulips and bushes all night.

Juts blinked back the tears. "Junior, you only have two hairs on your head."

Obviously, Juts was recovering.

Christ Lutheran's service ended and out rushed the rest of the congregation. Within seconds the details of Yoyo and Buster's adventure were being told. Most laughed. A few holier-than-thou types were scandalized.

Chessy, Cora, Celeste, Ramelle, and Fannie Jump howled with each detail of Yoyo's rampage being told.

Chester picked up a purring Yoyo. "Bet the devil made you do it."

This sent everyone into peals of laughter again.

Junior scanned the park. "I don't remember azalea bushes there." She pointed a pudgy finger.

"Oh." Ramelle shrugged.

"They're interspersed with tulips. As president of the Sisters of Gettysburg, I planted that with my girls, and it was solid tulips," Junior babbled.

"Hey—" Caesura, a former president of the S.O.G., exclaimed, "George Gordon Meade's statue is desecrated."

"He's listing to port," Popeye observed.

Fannie Jump Creighton, serving president of the Daughters of the Confederacy, carefully held her hands behind her back. "Always said Meade was tilted."

"You started the war!" Caesura snapped.

"I wasn't even born. Hell, you're so old, Caesura, not only do you remember *that* war, you probably led the Charge of the Light Brigade for the mother country."

"Well...well...I never! And on Easter Sunday." Caesura thumped her parasol on the steps. "You haven't heard the last of this, Fannie Jump Creighton. I know you're in on it somehow."

"Oh, balls." Fannie stonewalled her.

"How dare you." Caesura cracked Fannie over the head with her parasol.

"Idiot!" Fannie grabbed Ramelle's parasol and the two ladies dueled.

Buster barked and Yoyo's eyes got big as bowling balls.

Chester and Pearlie grabbed Fannie Jump, a substantial example of the female species, while Popeye and Pastor Neely, robes flapping, grabbed Caesura.

"This is dreadful. This is just dreadful," Junior wailed.

Caesura, shaken as a hen smoothing back its feathers, pointed her parasol at Fannie Jump. "I will have satisfaction."

"Now, Popeye, you've got to keep this out of the paper." Junior hung on Popeye's arm. He was already scribbling. Her weight slowed down his progress.

Getting nowhere with Popeye, Junior seized Walter. "You can't embarrass her this way. She was insulted publicly and you know how hard Caesura works for the community."

"Junior, I never tell my boys what to write."

"Then I am never advertising in the *Clarion* again!" That said, she thumped down the steps, Caesura in tow, just as Extra Billy Bitters, fresh from the Baptist service, bounded up the steps to Mary.

Louise smoldered.

"Honey chile," Cora whispered in her ear, "we've had confusion enough for one day."

Celeste smiled and sighed. "Mary and Extra Billy find each other more fascinating than we do."

"You forget how it feels to be young and in love." Ramelle beheld her broken parasol, as Fannie, now released, and panting, joined them.

"Blistering idiot. Caesura Frothingham is truly one of the stupidest women I have ever known. If she had a brain, she'd be dangerous. As it is, she's marginally amusing."

"Now, Fannie."

"Oh, Celeste, don't stick up for her."

"I'm not, but—"

Pastor Neely, not having shaken hands with them as was his custom at the end of each service, came over, his hand extended. "He is risen."

"Amen." Fannie solemnly shook his hand.

Pastor Neely then met with the Hunsenmeir group. "Louise Trumbull, what a happy surprise to have you on the steps of Christ Lutheran."

13

A t six-thirty on Holy Monday the phone rang at the Smith residence. Buster lifted his head off his paws, then put it back down. The phone always rang at six-thirty.

Juts, making her first pot of coffee while Chessy shaved, picked up the heavy black receiver. "Toodle-oo."

"We're not on the front page, thank God," Louise said, relieved as she scanned the details of the altercation on the steps of Christ Lutheran Church and the mysterious damage to George Gordon Meade. "Do you have your paper?"

"Yes, Buster got it. I'm opening it up right now. You're right." Then Juts flipped through. "We're not on the front page. We're on page two."

"Oh, no." Louise, in her excitement, had read through the front-page story, a war report that was continued on the rear page. She hadn't opened the newspaper. She quickly read: " 'Buster Smith and Yoyo Smith, an Irish terrier and a large long-haired alley cat, both owned by Mr. and Mrs. Chester Smith, joined the congregation of Christ Lutheran Church on Easter morning. Perhaps moved by Pastor Neely's sermon concerning the resurrection as a rebirth from our animal selves, the cat and dog contributed to the services. Yoyo Smith showed herself adept at flower rearranging and Buster Smith was in charge of refreshments.

" 'The highlight of the service came when Yoyo played the organ. Mrs. Smith declared her cat has always been musical, a fact confirmed by Sevilia Darymple, church organist. Mrs. Smith, the former Julia Ellen Hunsenmeir, with her sister, Mrs. Paul Trumbull, is opening a hair salon on Frederick Street behind the Strand Theater named the Curl 'n' Twirl. The grand opening will be May 15. According to Mrs. Smith, Buster and Yoyo will also be employed at the salon.' "

As Louise paused for breath, Julia said, "Pretty good free ad, isn't it?"

"I don't remember you giving Popeye an interview."

"I called him after we got home from Mom's Easter dinner. I guess we're even now," Juts said.

"No, we're not. That horrible article about you and me with that dreadful front-page picture. I mean, I looked like death eating a cracker and you looked, well, not yourself."

"Okay—but this is a good start, Louise. Popeye can do a little more penance."

"May 15." Her voice fell. "Do you think we can do it by then?"

"We have to. Anyway, now that Junior McGrail isn't advertising in the *Clarion,* let's make hay while the sun shines."

"She'll advertise in the *Trumpet.*"

"So, we'll get all the new people in South Runnymede."

"Julia, there are no new people in South Runnymede."

"Louise, you're such a pessimist, besides which I've got some really good ideas."

"That's what I'm afraid of."

14

The events of the last two days had drained Louise, but she didn't realize it until she met Juts at their store to pick out wallpaper. She sat on the floor with a thud. Her Boston bull, Doodlebug, squatted next to her, ignoring the entreaties of Buster to play.

"Julia, after what happened yesterday I should think you'd give Buster a rest."

"You're the one who needs a rest. You look like the dogs got at you under the porch."

Louise snarled, "Thank you so much."

"Jeez, Louise, if I can't tell you, who can?" Juts bent her head over the big wallpaper book. "These colors are good but the pattern is too busy. Chinese ladies under willow trees. Now, let's see—"

"Don't turn the pages so fast. You know, Juts, I still don't think this is such a good idea. The wallpaper will peel. We should paint and be done with it. A high-gloss."

Julia pointed to many cracks in the walls. "Do you know how long it will take to fix those?"

"Pearlie said he'd come on down in the evening and do every single one."

"He did?"

"He's being very cooperative. Any luck with Chessy?"

In a voice higher and thinner than usual, Juts replied, "He'll do it."

Louise sighed. "It's been a hectic week, hasn't it?"

"Hectic? It's been crazier than hell. Must be something in the air." She lifted the heavy sample book off her lap and gave in surprisingly easily. "If Pearlie will fix those cracks, then we ought to go with high-gloss."

"Something that won't show the dirt so easily." Louise was glad her little sister saw things her way for a change. "A good rich color."

"Basic black."

"Will you concentrate?"

"I am. I lugged this book over, didn't I? You know, we need a radio in here right now. We're going to be hours and hours on our feet, so let's get some music. Hey, don't forget the dance this weekend out at Dingledine's."

"I'm too tired to think about dancing."

Each year the nursery held a big dance at the old barn on the property. If it rained they went indoors, if not they danced outside on a specially constructed dance floor. The Dingledines knew partyers would pass through the nursery, see the spring shrubs and flowers, and maybe come back during the day to pick some up.

"Louise, why don't you go home and take a nap? I'll do this." Juts pulled measuring tape out of her pocket.

"I'm better off here. If I go home I'll find even more to do. Mary and Maizie aren't lifting a finger these days. All Mary does is moon, cry, or sing. Maizie gets distracted by Mary and then she's late doing her schoolwork. That comes first, so the chores—" She trailed off.

Juts, not especially riveted by tales of domestic arrangements, walked across the room. She held the tape with her thumb on the floor, then ran it up three feet. "Countertops this high."

"Wait a minute." Louise scrambled to her feet, walking gingerly for a few steps. Then she stood next to the tape, making imaginary grooming movements, reaching for scissors and combs. "Three inches higher."

Juts ran the tape up three inches. "Pretty good?"

"I think so. Let me hold it for you." Louise pinched the top of the tape, holding it steady.

Juts performed imaginary motions herself. "That's fine with me. Ought to work in case we take in other hairdressers, unless one is a midget." She reached for the tape. "Now, over here I think we should build a wall so we can have a little private space in the back."

"We've got a storage closet back there. Go sit in the storage closet if you need privacy. It's big enough."

"Louise, that will last ten minutes and we'll both hate it. All Chessy has to do is throw up some two-by-fours out to here, see?"

"And where do we get the money?"

"We don't. He can ask Walter Falkenroth for leftovers. There's always waste. It will cost us lathing and more paint, but we get privacy."

"What are you going to do with that privacy?"

"Smoke a cigarette, drink a beer, and play solitaire."

"You will not drink during working hours." Louise put her foot down.

"Don't be a pill."

"I won't have it. As for smoking, that cigarette is stapled to your lip. You don't need to go in the back room to puff."

"I happen to be smoking right now, but I don't smoke as much as you say. Anyway, it's awfully nice to sit down, have a drag and a hot cup of coffee away from the searching eye."

"Well..." Louise mulled it over. "Only if Chessy can get the wood free."

"Good." Julia clapped her hands, which made both dogs run over to her. "Sorry, guys." They sat back down. "We'll have to give Harmon's wife free haircuts, and let's see—who else?"

"Why?"

"Because he could have thrown Mary and Extra Billy in jail, that's why. Wheezer, are you sick or something? You're not firing on all pistons today."

"I'm pooped."

"I'd be pooped too, if my daughter ran off with a no-'count. Firing the gun wasn't her finest hour, either."

"She's high-strung."

"High-strung? She's certifiable!"

"Julia, there is nothing wrong with my daughter's mind."

"There is now."

"You usually stick up for her." A hint of anger crept into Louise's voice.

"No, what I do is tell you to lay off Extra Billy. The more she's around him, the more she'll see him for what he is, a very handsome piece of white trash."

"She's not your daughter."

"Let's not get into this. We're both tired. We've got one month left to get everything ready. I'm trying to find a salon that's going out of business. Maybe we can pick up equipment cheap. I called some shops in Baltimore and they promised to call back if they hear anything. Maybe you could call York and Hagerstown so all the long-distance charges won't be on my line. Chester's still mad about all this."

"He'll get over it. Say, did you see Rillma Ryan at the train station yesterday? I passed her coming back from Mom's. She looked so pretty all dressed up. Imagine having a job in Washington."

"Yeah, if I weren't a married woman I'd go on down myself. Men everywhere!"

Louise would die before she'd admit that she felt life was passing her by. She had never worried about that before, but lately the thought lazed through her mind like one of those biplanes with advertising streamers dragging along the beach at Atlantic City. You never knew when it was coming. You'd hear a drone and next thing you knew there it would be, the pilot waving as he came in just beyond the shoreline. Her streamer read, "You're getting old. How long have you got?"

"Julia—?"

"What?"

"Nothing."

"How about painting up to here a deep clear red and then putting up a chair rail and white above that?"

"That will look silly without wainscoting, and don't tell me you can get wainscoting for free, Julia, because I wasn't born yesterday."

"I didn't say a thing." Juts looked outside the window, saw Mary on the other side of the street, and checked her watch. "What's Mary doing out of school at one-thirty?"

"What?" Louise followed Juts's pointing finger. "I'll soon find out." She briskly walked to the front door, opened it, and called out, "Mary, what are you doing out of school?"

"They let us out early today, Mom." Mary crossed the street. "I went home but you weren't there so I came over here."

"Why did they let you go early?" Louise was suspicious.

"The boiler broke down so they let us out before it got too cold. It's only forty-five degrees. You can call Mrs. Grenville and find out for yourself," she said defiantly.

"Now that you're here, you might as well go to work." Louise let the challenge pass.

"That's why I'm here."

"Where's your sister?"

"She's on her way. I asked her to bring stuff."

About that time, Maizie waddled around the corner carrying two heavy buckets.

"You could have helped her."

Mary, without reply, hurried back outside, taking one of the buckets from her sister's sagging grasp.

Juts peered in the buckets when the girls came inside. "Tape, chalk, hammers, nails, oh, here's a folding measuring stick that's better than what I've got."

Louise turned up the thermostat on the wall. "It is getting pretty chilly, isn't it." The old radiators thumped. "We're going to have to bleed these radiators."

Juts grabbed tape and chalk and began marking the space on the floor where the cabinets would go.

"Mary, was this your idea—to help?"

"Yes, Mother." Mary smiled her biggest, sweetest smile.

15

Yoyo had been under house arrest ever since her Easter worship service. Eyes half closed, the cat sat in the window. Buster's barking as he rounded the corner sent her off the windowsill to the door. However, Juts knew a cat trick or two, so the minute she opened the door she bent over and scooped up the escape artist before one paw crossed the threshold.

"Gotcha."

Yoyo meowed in protest but dutifully allowed Juts to place her on her shoulder and pat her back as though she were a baby. She withheld the purrs until she smelled chicken in the sack Juts carried in her right hand.

Immediately following Julia was Mary, who quickly shut the door. She too carried a sack of groceries.

"Aunt Juts, where should I put this stuff?"

"Kitchen table."

They unpacked groceries, then Juts cut up the chicken, carefully scrubbing each piece of meat before placing it on a sheet of wax paper. Sprinkled over the wax paper were flour and spices she mixed for her fried chicken. Sitting on the counter were two brown eggs, which she was going to crack. She would roll the chicken in the egg, then dredge the chicken through the flour and spices. Fried chicken was her specialty.

Yoyo observed, whiskers occasionally twitching from the enticing aroma. The dog, riveted to the floor, followed Julia's every hand motion.

Since the girls had gotten out of school early, Juts had asked Mary to help her while Maizie stayed with Louise.

"Cut on the radio, will you, my hands are wet."

"Sure, Aunt Juts." Mary clicked on the left dial of the small wooden cathedral radio, which sat under the old clock. The huge radio reposed in the parlor.

The Smiths had little by way of possessions, but Julia loved her music. The kitchen table was wooden with a white porcelain top pinstriped in red. The floors were uneven plank oak. The cabinets were yellow with round red enamel knob handles. White curtains with red teapots hung over the windows. A pantry, big and airy, helped keep the kitchen organized, for Juts, like her sister and her mother, had to have everything pin-tidy. If Chester came home and hung his coat on the back of a kitchen chair instead of on a peg in the mudroom, he heard about it the minute Juts laid eyes on it. All the Hunsenmeirs were fiercely clean.

Julia hummed while she worked.

"Momma says you used to be wild as a March hare, Aunt Juts."

"Is that so?"

"She says I take after you."

"I see." Juts waited for the frying pan to reach the desired sizzling temperature. "What else does she blab about me?"

Mary, who looked like a younger, slightly larger version of her pretty mother, giggled. "She says if I'm not careful I'll wind up like you, struggling to make ends meet because I married the wrong guy."

"Your mother is full of—" She caught herself. "Funny ideas. Chessy is a good man."

"It's not that, Aunt Juts, it's that he doesn't make much money. She says you could have done a lot better—that Walter Falkenroth was in love with you and he's got tons of money, just oo-scoobs of it, and you turned him down."

Juts noticed Yoyo edging closer to the chicken, now rolled and dusted with flour. "Don't you even think about it." Yoyo returned Julia's stare. "What a disobedient child."

Mary laughed. "Guess she'll have to do the stations of the cross at church, huh?"

"Lutherans don't believe in the stations of the cross. Ours is checkbook religion. I bequeath to my dear sister all that mumbling, crossing, and getting up and down on the knees. She just eats it up. The more miserable it is, the more she likes it."

"Mom's going up to see Diddy again. Orrie's going with her." Louise's best friend, Orrie Tadia Mojo, was the confidante of her secret desires. In fact, every conversation with Orrie began, "Now, don't you tell a soul." Then Louise would forget she'd told Orrie, tell someone else, the story would get all over town, and Louise would round on Orrie, accusing her of spilling the beans.

"Means we're in for another spate of devotion." Juts placed a juicy chicken breast in the oil. The crackle startled her. "Hot, hot, hot." She fetched a heavy kitchen towel, spreading it out on the counter. When the chicken was finished she'd put it on the towel to soak up some of the oil.

"Aunt Julia—?"

"Hmm."

"Do you like Billy?"

"I think Billy is very handsome."

"He is." Mary blushed.

"I don't know if he'll settle down, honey. His people don't value stability."

Her clear eyes clouded over. "Oh, he will. He needs me. I can help him."

"Mary, every woman since Eve has believed that. I can hear her now, 'I'll give him this apple and maybe he'll get some sense in his head and go to work.' So what happened? Adam gets some knowledge and blames Eve for it. She didn't put a gun to his head. He didn't have to eat the damned apple, the weakass."

Julia's thoughts, quite unlike Louise's orthodoxy, made Mary laugh. "They didn't have guns then."

"She could have hit him over the head with a stick. No, he snatched that shiny red apple from her sweet hand. He takes a bite and discovers they're naked. Now I ask you, Mary, how stupid is that? The man must have been dumb as a sack of nails. Garden of Eden, my foot. It had to get cold at night, even in the Garden of Eden, so he needed clothes at night, right?"

"I never thought of it that way."

"That's my point. If you read the Bible and think about it you're left with more questions than answers. That's why no preacher ever really wants you to think. So Adam blames Eve and we're all in trouble. The big oaf couldn't face what he'd done. And to this day if a man gets in trouble what does he do—blames it on a woman."

"Extra Billy isn't blaming his troubles on me." Mary swelled with pride.

"Oh, Mary, give him time." Julia smiled, but understanding how fragile and wonderful first love can be, she quickly added, "I'm glad to hear he's shouldering the blame."

"Not only that, he's going to fix the statue. He asked Donny

Gregorivitch to help him 'cause you know Donny's dad has that big wrecker truck."

"What's he going to do with the wrecker truck?"

"Pull the statue upright and shore up the base. He's got it all figured out."

"Harmon know about this?"

"Yes, ma'am, the first person he told was the sheriff."

"Well—good. Now I have one little niggling question, a tiny worm in the apple—guess I've got apples on the brain." She paused and with her cooking fork speared the hot chicken, placing it on the towel, then dropped in more chicken, which crackled as it hit the oil. Yoyo tiptoed along the window ledge over the sink and chose to sit next to the cooked chicken, although she turned her back to it. "Yoyo, I'm on to you."

The cat flattened her ears, refusing to turn around.

"She's a real personality." Mary snapped the stems off Carolina okra, which they'd been lucky enough to buy fresh at the store.

"Everyone in this damned family is a real personality. Now, what I was going to ask you was, why were you and Extra Billy running away? I'll get to the fun later."

"We weren't running away, Aunt Julia." Mary's voice rose in self-defense. "Mom said I couldn't go out until I'd finished all my homework. Billy doesn't have a phone so I couldn't tell him that and when he came by the house I walked out to tell him. Anyway, Mom's standing there and she's yelling at me and carrying on and I just said, 'The hell with you,' which was awful, but I did and I got in the car and said, 'Let's go to Baltimore.' How was I to know she would go crazy and chase me in Daddy's car?"

"That part I know because your father called here and Chessy and I hurried over to get him." She took a breath. "Has your father ever spoken to you about Extra Billy?"

"Daddy says that he doesn't understand girls. He seems to understand Maizie well enough."

"Maizie's different from you. She's more like Paul."

"Aunt Julia, I love Billy. I want to marry him and spend the rest of my life with him."

"Oh, the rest of your life is a long, long time."

"I'll never love anyone else." She held the okra under the running water.

Juts wanted to say a number of things—practical, mature, or passing as mature; reasonable. She kept her mouth shut. Why burst the bubble? Life would take care of that sure enough.

"Has Billy asked you to marry him?"

"Not exactly."

"I see."

Mary hastily added, "He doesn't have enough money right now. Really."

Yoyo coyly glanced over her shoulder. Seeing Juts turn her back to grab a pot for the okra, she delicately hooked a small chicken wing and that fast was off the counter before Juts knew what happened.

Juts turned back to the stove. "Now, Mary, I think what has everyone worried is that you and Billy might be doing stuff out of the way."

Mary blushed cherry-red and shook her head. "No."

"That's good. I'm not as fussy about these things as your mother. I figure we're animals, after all, so I don't care if you do everything but—you understand?" When Mary nodded yes, blushing even more, Julia continued, "If you're going to bring children into this world it's important to be married and to be prepared for such a big responsibility—so be careful, honey."

"I am, I mean, I will, Aunt Juts." She reached for another dish towel in a drawer and patted the fried chicken on top. "I'll be sixteen in January and I can marry of my own free will then." She smiled. "I mark off the days in red every day on the calendar. And you know what really makes me mad, Aunt Julia, I just think it's so mean. Mother can be really, really mean. She says"—Mary

put her hand on her hip and imitated her mother's voice—
" 'Ignorance is bliss.' "

"If ignorance is bliss, why aren't more people happy?" Then
Juts noticed a little snail trail of grease across the kitchen floor.
Following it, she found a larger splotch of grease around the corner, which Buster was licking. Yoyo was curled up on the sofa as
though this had nothing whatsoever to do with her. Juts scowled,
then started laughing at herself. "God, it's terrible to be out-
smarted by your own cat."

16

If you don't hurry up, we'll be late," Juts nagged Chessy as she
tied his bow tie. "You're always late. You'll be late to your own
funeral."

"I'm almost ready," he said in a smooth voice.

Chester, prodded and pushed all his life by his mother and
now by his wife, habitually showed up a half hour late or more.

The phone rang twice, their signal since they were on a party
line, as was everyone in Runnymede except for Celeste and the
Rifes. Juts ran to the stairwell, picked it up, then growled, "It's
your mother."

Chester reached for the phone, his bow tie tied, his shirt crisp
and white, his pants pressed with a pleat in the front, his wing-tip,
two-tone shoes polished to perfection. After greeting her he listened for a few moments.

"All right. Bye." He turned to his wife, her hands on her hips. "I'll run you over to Wheezie's and you can catch a ride with her. Mom needs me for a minute to fix her back door."

"For Pete's sake," Juts exclaimed in such a loud voice that Buster barked. "She needs you every minute. Why can't your father fix it?"

"Because he's at his lodge meeting tonight."

"Well, Chessy, she can't shut her back door. Big deal."

"She's afraid the wind will tear it out of the doorjamb and she'll have bigger repairs."

"Oh, balls."

"Come on, I'll run you over to Wheezie's."

So mad she couldn't talk, Juts stalked to the Chevy Roadster convertible built in 1933, which Chessy had bought used. He lavished attention on the bottle-green car until it sparkled as if on display in the showroom.

Juts slammed the door so hard the heavy machine rocked. She had never been invited to set foot in Josephine Smith's house— her mother-in-law's revenge for Chester marrying beneath him. Juts hated every minute Chester spent with the woman.

Chessy quietly slipped behind the wheel, placing his straw boater on the seat between them. The soft tan nap upholstery wasn't even worn thin.

Yoyo and Buster stared mournfully out the front window as the car backed down the driveway.

"You won't get to Dingledine's until ten o'clock. I know your mother. First you'll fix her back door and then she'll want you to check the boiler and after that she'll want the blades sharpened on the lawn mower because Rup is too creaky to bend over for that long."

"Here we are." He forced a smile as they coasted up to Louise's house, which was around the corner. "In the nick of time."

Louise, Paul, Mary, and Maizie were climbing into the car.

Without so much as a good-bye, Juts again slammed the door. Chester waved to the Trumbulls and backed out.

"What's news?" Louise asked, using the old phrase.

"Mother Smith needs her son."

"Oh." Wheezie squeezed next to her husband so Juts could fit in the front. The girls giggled in the backseat.

"Never marry a man until you take a hard look at his mother." Juts called over her shoulder, "Hear me, back there?"

"Yes, Aunt Juts," came the singsong chorus.

"Daddy, what did you think when you first met G-Mom?" Mary asked.

"I do wish you wouldn't call her G-Mom. It makes her sound like a gangster," Wheezie grumbled.

"I thought," Pearlie said, smiling as he recalled that distant day, "she was the nicest, kindest lady I had ever met—a lot like my own mother."

Pearlie's mother died before the girls were born. Although that was seventeen years ago, he still missed her.

"What a sweet thing to say." Louise patted his arm.

"Mom, what did you think when you met Mrs. Smith?" Mary pursued the subject.

"Oh—"

"Don't fudge, Wheezer," Juts said.

"I thought," Louise measured her words, "that Josephine Smith had a very high opinion of herself and a low opinion of the rest of us—but then I'd known her since I was tiny. She never has spoken to a Hunsenmeir."

As Julia predicted, Jo found plenty of chores for her son. Chester fixed the door and then checked a leaky faucet in the back bathroom, replacing a washer. When she nudged him toward the old stable in the back, now serving as a garage, he balked. Chester did not believe in raising his voice, least of all to his mother. She railed about loose morals, about the proliferation of alcohol in so-cial life, about the Dingledines, who charged way too much for a

puny azalea, and about Julia Ellen, who wantonly displayed herself
while dancing. She reminded her eldest that he couldn't dance, so
what was the hurry?

"Mother, I'm late already."

"You don't listen to me. Not a word I say."

"I do."

"You came over Easter for exactly one hour. One hour for
your own family."

Knowing there was no way to please her, he kissed her on the
cheek and left. She stood in her doorway protesting even as he
rolled down the street.

The party was in full swing. He joined Maizie at the table because everyone was dancing but her.

"Hi there, girlfriend." He beamed at her and she beamed
right back at her big, blond uncle. "Are you sitting this one out?"

"Uncle Chessy, only my daddy has asked me to dance." Her
little face fell with the telling.

"Is that so?"

"Won't you dance with me?"

"Honey, I can't dance. I've got two left feet."

Tears welled up in her hazel eyes. "Nobody likes me."

He put his huge arm around her small shoulders. "That's not
true. I like you. I think you're the prettiest girl here. You're still
young and there aren't many boys here your age. In fact, I don't
see a one."

"I'm fourteen."

She had turned fourteen on April 1.

"You're getting bigger every day." He noticed the rounded
face, the once-chubby limbs that were becoming angular. Maizie
was set for another growth spurt. He wondered what his children
would have looked like if he'd had them.

"Uncle Chessy, I wish you would learn to dance."

He laughed. "You and my wife." He nodded in the direction
of Juts out on the wooden dance floor. Japanese lanterns swayed

overhead. A swarm of men buzzed around Juts. She possessed terrific rhythm and a beautiful feminine body. Men couldn't take their eyes off Juts dancing.

Maizie cried in earnest now. "I'll never have a boyfriend. I'll never have admirers like Aunt Juts."

"Honey, yes, you will. Now you buck up. The prettiest girl at the dance can't be crying. People will worry."

She sniffled, "And you know what? Mary is dancing with everyone." She boo-hooed loudly. "She says Mom told her she had to dance with more boys than just Extra Billy so she is, and she's not bringing any back to me."

He kissed the top of her head and rocked her a little with his arm around her shoulders because he had no idea what to do or say.

A lovely young woman approached the table. She leaned over and addressed Maizie.

"I couldn't help but overhear you. Come on the dance floor with me. I'll teach you some new steps."

Chester stood up. "Hello, I'm Chester Smith and this is my niece, Maizie Trumbull."

"Trudy Archer. I just moved here from Baltimore." She smiled a dazzling smile. He guessed she was twenty or maybe twenty-two.

"Welcome to Runnymede. We're no bigger than a sigh"— he smiled—"but we pack a lot of life into this place."

"I can see that. Do you mind if I take Maizie out on the dance floor?" She paused a moment. "I'm opening a dance studio on Hanover Street. I trained in Baltimore with the Fred Astaire studio."

Maizie was already on her feet. Chester nodded that it was fine, and Trudy walked the girl over to the side, showed her a few basic steps, then twirled her around. Maizie was thrilled. Extra Billy strolled by. He kept his eye on Mary valiantly dancing with everyone to please her mother. Chester motioned for him to come over.

"Sir?" Extra Billy squared his broad shoulders.

"I'll help you if you'll help me."

"Yes, sir." Billy respected Chester. Most men did, and not just because of Chester's heavy musculature but because, as the boys said, he never lost his shit.

"I'll help you with the Meade statue if you and your friends will dance with Maizie. She's at that awkward age and she's been crying her eyes out." He stopped a moment. "And you know, Bill, it might help you put a foot right with Louise Trumbull. In fact, let the night wear on a bit and then you really ought to ask Louise to dance and tell her she looks like Mary's sister."

Extra Billy smiled. "Yes, sir. Thank you, sir."

As Trudy led Maizie back to the table, Extra Billy offered her his arm. "Maizie."

"Oh, wow." She squealed.

Trudy smiled as Chester again stood up. "Please join me. My wife won't come back to the table until the party's over. I always thought she could dance with Fred Astaire." He indicated Julia Ellen.

"A real natural." Trudy appreciated Julia's untrained talent. "You don't dance?"

"Not me."

"You look like an athlete to me."

"I can throw a ball, I guess, or hit one, but Miss Archer, I'm pretty clumsy otherwise."

"If you come to the studio I'll give you a free lesson." He hesitated, so she pressed. "Wouldn't it be wonderful to sweep your wife into your arms and surprise her? I bet she'd love it."

Chester stared back into those intent, disquietingly green eyes and found himself saying, "Uh—I couldn't take advantage of you like that, miss, but I think I would like to dance. I'm afraid everyone will laugh at me."

"One free lesson. And I promise, I *promise,* or you get your money back, that no one will laugh."

"All right."

"Tuesday at six-thirty?"

"See you then, Miss Archer."

"Oh, please, call me Trudy. Miss Archer makes me sound like I'm going to target practice." She rose and he stood again. She tossed him a radiant smile over her shoulder. He sat down, wondering why in the hell he had made a fool promise like that.

Maizie came back when the dance was finished, but before she could sit down, Billy's best buddy, Ray Parker, reached for her. "Come on, Maizie, I need a girlfriend."

"Oh, gee, Uncle Chessy, this is swell," she gushed, then twirled off.

As he was instructed to do, Extra Billy asked Louise to dance. Stiff at first, she didn't refuse. That would have violated the S.C.C.—Southern Conduct Code. Paul, weary from dancing, joined Chester at the table.

"Cold beer." Chester shoved a fresh beer at a parched Paul.

Paul gratefully knocked back the beer. "Celeste Chalfonte may be in her sixties, but she wore me out."

"She's something."

Pearlie noticed Louise in the arms of Extra Billy. "Will you look at that? That boy's got guts."

"That boy is probably going to be your son-in-law, so we'd better figure out how to get along with him."

A shadow crossed Pearlie's face. "I think you're right. What would you do?"

"Well, he's young, rebellious, but he's not mean-spirited, he's not lazy. I'd teach him the business if he married my daughter. Course, it's easy for me to offer advice, Pearlie, I don't have a daughter."

"You will," Pearlie reassured his brother-in-law, whom he had learned to love. He knew this was a sensitive subject. "There's something to what you say. If I take him in the business, assuming they do get married, I can keep an eye on him. I don't think anyone paid much attention to the boy."

"Guess not."

The Bitters family bred like rabbits and then left their kids to fend for themselves.

The dance ended and Extra Billy squired Louise back to the table. A secret smile played across her face. He bowed to her and left.

"That was something," Pearlie commented.

Wheezie, trying to sound proper and put out, said, "I had to dance with him."

"I'm glad you did, honey." Pearlie supported her decision, slyly noticing she seemed decidedly youthful.

Walter Falkenroth walked over. "Paul, I want your wife," he joked.

"She is popular." Pearlie smiled as Louise took a quick sip of soda and followed Walter onto the dance floor.

Paul returned to Chessy. "Extra Billy had the sense to ask my wife for a dance. He may be smarter than I thought."

"Yep." Chessy smiled.

17

A cool, heavy mist clung to her cheeks. The headlight of the train glowed, diffuse in the silver moisture, then passed as the streamlined Pullman cars, painted dark green, stopped at the station siding.

Doak Garten, the young porter, waited off to the side, his cart filled with Ramelle's expensive luggage. This train would take her to Washington, D.C., where she would transfer to another train, which would snake through the South, giving her a few hours to disembark at New Orleans for coffee and jazz. The lushness of the South would give way to the browns, mustard-yellows, and brick-reds of the Southwest. Finally the journey would end in Los Angeles, languidly reposing between the San Gabriel Mountains and the Pacific Ocean.

"I'll write you every day." Ramelle kissed Celeste.

"You can be the Marquise de Sévigné of Los Angeles." Celeste returned her kiss.

"All aboard!"

Although the steps were high, Ramelle gracefully hopped up, then leaned down for one more kiss. Doak handed her luggage up to the conductor, his square kepi askew.

Finding her compartment, she sat by the window, her gloved hand raised in a farewell. As the steps were lifted onto the train and the conductor waved down to the engineer, she pressed her lips to the windowpane, one last kiss.

Celeste waved back and then the train pulled out. She stood there watching the red taillights disappear into the thickening silver until one long mournful whistle blast bid the final good-bye.

At seven in the morning the temperature hung in the forties. Shuddering, she put her gloved hands into the pockets of the Norfolk jacket.

She walked into the scrubbed station. "Doak, I nearly forgot my manners." She found him behind the office window. "Where's Nestor?" She inquired about the ticket dispenser, station manager, janitor, and general all-around man.

"Doughnut run. Yost's would go out of business without that man."

She discreetly pushed a folded twenty-dollar bill under the window. "Another cool day."

"Makes spring last longer." He pushed the bill back under the window. "Miz Chalfonte, that's too much."

"It will make up for all the times I forget to pay you."

"You never forget to pay me, Miz Chalfonte. You never forget anybody that ever done you a favor."

"Put it in the bank, then. Keep the tellers busy."

He knew there was no sense arguing with her. "Yes, ma'am, and I thank you kindly."

Walter Falkenroth hurried in. Celeste stepped aside after exchanging hasty pleasantries. "Doak, I'll see you."

She walked outside. Old Patience Horney, feebleminded and two years older than God, squatted at the front door with her hot soft pretzels and a little mustard jar.

Celeste bought a pretzel for the same reason everyone did: to give Patience money and because they were good, although at this early hour Celeste wasn't in the mood.

"Celeste, dearie, I tell you that Brutus Rife is still in love with you. He'll never get over you." Patience turned her good eye to Celeste; her bad one was milky.

She referred to a man dead for twenty-one years.

"He'll just have to." Celeste smiled.

"You're the most beautiful woman ever walked through Runnymede. Plenty says you're the most beautiful woman ever walked through Maryland."

"You're very kind, Patience." Celeste hadn't the heart to tell Patience that she was in her early sixties and Patience herself had to be pushing eighty.

"Wish I'd been born beautiful." Her toothless mouth collapsed into a concave smile.

"You are beautiful, Patience." Celeste pressed money into the gloved hand. "Now you have a good day."

"Yes, ma'am, yes, ma'am. You give the Major my regards, now." She remembered Celeste's father.

"I will, Patience."

Celeste walked out to the small parking lot. In her youth she had read constantly. She had wanted answers. She never did find the answer to one of her questions: why Patience sat at the train station.

For a searing moment she thought she would sob. The anguish of the world washed over her, or was it Ramelle's departing? She didn't know. Was it the thought that Doak and the other young men would eventually be sucked into this monstrous evil across the Atlantic, or was there evil enough at home? Were Al Capone and Pretty Boy Floyd small-fry versions of Hitler and Mussolini?

She sniffed. The first delicate fragrance of lilac haunted the air. The buds remained closed, yet that unmistakable sweetness lingered.

She felt young. She felt no sense of her age except for the decades of memories. This anguish would have felt the same at twenty. Emotions have no history.

She wondered if she needed a romance, one last fling, one discreet pursuit. *One last quest. A quest is a pursuit,* she thought, her hand reaching for the chrome door handle. *What is to pursue, for what could be worth having that would flee you? Whatever is worth having is within, and if you find it, others will come to you. Pursuit is antithetical to gain.* She opened the Packard's door and slid in the seat, put her hands on the wheel, and stared at the tracks. *Well—what's inside of me?* She smelled the fresh hot pretzel, snatched it off the seat, the thin wax paper crinkling as she picked it up.

She bit into it, chewed, then announced, "A hot pretzel," and burst out laughing.

18

Long golden shadows rolled over Runnymede Square. On the south side of the square, the flickering light on the faces of the statue of the three Confederate soldiers gave them expression. One fired his rifle, one carried the standard, and the third was falling to his knees, wounded. The standard-bearer reached down, his hand under the stricken man's armpit, trying to keep him on his feet. Behind them the cannon loomed, its barrel pointing at the Bon-Ton department store on the corner of Hanover Street, the Yankee side of the square.

The extra sunlight on the summer side of the spring equinox stretched the days, adding a languor punctuated by laughter as more people stayed outside. The dogwood, mint-green buds soon to open in a rash of white or pink, speckled the beautiful square, laid out and planted before the American Revolution.

The Corinthian columns of Runnymede Bank and Trust, situated on the southwest corner of the square, loomed an imposing, glossy blue-white. Houses of money, redolent with dignity and the old Latin word *gravitas,* rivaled churches in holiness.

As Chessy walked across the square accompanied by a jaunty Buster, the people he had known nearly all his life were closing up their shops, winding up colorful awnings, locking doors. The greengrocer always left aging oranges, apples, and pears outside on the stands for the poor each Tuesday night. A fresh shipment would arrive Wednesday morning.

A steady stream of people filed into Cadwalder's for a hamburger or a soda. Some would linger for the first showing of the movie just down the street. Young men, a blush of peach fuzz on their cheeks, would ask to carry home girls' books.

He had lived in this area his entire life, nearly thirty-six years. The web of interconnecting lives and generations glistened golden in the sunset. The more he had lived, the more he felt those connecting strands between people.

Chester Rupert Smith thought much and said little. This was a habit acquired early in a house where Josephine Smith pontificated hourly. His middle brother, Joseph, looked and acted like their mother, domineering and talkative. The youngest brother, Sanford, had some ambition but was easygoing.

All his life, Chessy had bent under the weight of the accusation that he lacked ambition and that he should have put his intelligence to better use. Getting and grabbing held no appeal for him. He felt his life was in a constant state of richness. He wasn't unwilling to share that richness, but he didn't believe anyone else wanted to hear about it.

Not a day dawned that he didn't have some new idea or insight. The fact that not one of them was commercial seemed no great sin to him. He'd grown accustomed to disappointing his mother and his wife; Juts possessed enough drive for both of them. But he didn't disappoint himself. He was content to let life unfold in all its squalor and grandeur.

Junior McGrail, resembling a sloth in good shoes, stood at the base of George Gordon Meade's statue with her friend Caesura Frothingham.

"Good evening, ladies." Chessy tipped his hat.

"Good evening, Chester," they replied.

"George looks much improved, don't you think?" He smiled.

"We saw you, Harmon, Extra Billy, and those riffraff friends of his over here last night pulling General Meade upright. What really did happen to our glorious hero?" Caesura thought anything in a Union uniform glorious. This created problems.

"Perhaps he drank too much."

Caesura pinched her lips. "Not General Meade."

"Ah, well, too late for the old boy now."

"You know what happened," Junior said, her tiny Yorkshire terrier tugging on her pink leash toward Buster, who wagged his docked tail.

"As soon as this corner of the base is repaired, all will be well, so it doesn't matter what happened."

"You ought to talk to the Trumbulls, Chester. No good will come of Extra Billy keeping company with Mary."

"Now, Junior, that's none of my business." He put his hands in his pockets, jingling the change. "Ladies, you all enjoy this soft evening. I've an appointment." He again tipped his hat.

As he walked away, Caesura whispered, "What do you expect of Mary Trumbull? She lives in a house with painted statuary of an explicit anatomical nature!"

Junior concurred. "Mmm. Something's not right there. Why, it's akin to living in a den of vice. Pearlie's artistry calls attention to women's bosoms in such a disquieting manner."

The twosome shrieked with laughter.

Chessy threaded through the shop clerks pouring out of the Bon-Ton. Small as the town was, the Bon-Ton enjoyed good business because Baltimore was an hour away to the southeast on bumpy roads, Hagerstown was an hour to the west, and York was forty-five minutes to the northeast. Gettysburg, only twenty minutes away, was all battlefield—no shopping there except for a brisk market in used ammunition.

Four doors down from the Bon-Ton, on the west side of Hanover Street, was the Rogers Building, erected in 1872. The second floor housed the new dance studio, and a top hat and cane were painted on one of the windows facing the street. He opened the door and climbed the maroon-painted stairs, Buster bounding ahead of him.

Trudy Archer stood at the top of the stairs. "Mr. Smith, I'm glad to see you. Come on in. Who's this?"

"Buster."

"Well, I'll give Buster a free lesson too."

When Chessy stepped through the open door, the first thing he noticed was the beautiful maple floor. "I had no idea this was up here."

"Me neither, until I got all the paint off. I assumed it would be oak." She dropped the phonograph needle on the shiny black record. A Cole Porter song floated across the room. "Ready?"

He swallowed. "Sure."

Buster sat, his head cocked, watching his master attempt the box step.

"One two three, one two three." She smiled up at him. "You've done this before?"

"Never."

The record finished, she put another one on the player, then picked up Buster's front paws and danced a few steps with the terrier, who hopped along. "Very good, Buster."

Chessy laughed.

Trudy worked with Chessy for one hour and he even mastered a glide step. Although stiff and unsure of himself, he wasn't as clumsy as he thought.

At the end of the hour she patted Buster on the head and thanked Chester for dropping by.

She smiled. "If you listen to the music it will tell you whatever you need to know."

"You're a good teacher." He had his good Borsolino hat in his hand. "You know, I would like to learn. I'd love to surprise Juts. Is it expensive?"

"Five dollars a month for a one-hour private lesson once a

week. There are group lessons for less, of course, but then I'm afraid word would get back to your wife and spoil the surprise."

"How about if I try for one month? We'll play it by ear."

She smiled at his pun. "Deal."

He reached in his pocket and gave her five dollars in ones. That was good money but he felt excited. He could dance.

As he strolled back out on the street he thought how wonderful it was to move to music and how Trudy Archer seemed clean and new, lustrous.

19

Juts dumped out the contents of a can of mixed nuts on the kitchen counter. She fished out the almonds, filberts, and cashews, leaving the lowly peanuts.

She wore her genuine Orioles baseball cap, which she had secured when she drove down to Baltimore to bargain for slightly used beauty-salon equipment. Never one to miss a baseball game, even at the high-school level, Juts hovered over the Orioles dugout in the splashing sunshine, begging one of the boys to part with a baseball hat. As Juts wasn't hard to look at and had more charge than 220 volts, the catcher gave her his cap.

The morning paper, folded over to reveal the Curl 'n' Twirl grand-opening ad, proved handy for Yoyo, who never could resist the crinkle of paper.

Louise had insisted they also take out an ad in the evening paper, the *Trumpet*. That paper hadn't arrived yet so she whiled away her time reading the classifieds in case she had missed something earlier.

The shop was as ready as it would be. Chessy had built the cabinets and the little back room. Pearlie and his crew had added the gloss of fresh paint. There wasn't anything to do but worry now, and since Louise had worried enough for a woman of one hundred years, Juts saw no reason to duplicate her sister's efforts.

The Hunsenmeirs hired away Toots Ryan, Rillma's mother, from Junior McGrail. They offered Toots seven more dollars a week and she grabbed at it. Fair business practice, but Junior howled "Foul play."

Chessy turned ashen when Julia boldly announced her coup. In order to pay back $398 the sisters were sinking deeper and deeper into the red. She told him to stop grexing and groaning. "It takes money to make money," she quoted him.

The thump of the paper hitting the door sent Buster scrambling. She let him out. He picked it up, proudly bringing it back to her.

"Good boy."

Before she opened the paper she returned to the kitchen to carefully scrape the peanuts into the can. She covered the top, setting it back on the heavy wax-paper-covered shelf. Then she flipped open the paper. In cursive script like a formal announcement was the ad for their grand opening. She stepped back to admire it.

Then she turned the page, where she was assaulted by a half-page ad for Junior McGrail's Runnymede Beauty Salon for Discriminating Ladies. A bold banner declared, "Ladies, don't be fooled by cheap imitations."

"I'll snatch her bald." Juts dashed for the phone. She dialed Louise.

"Hello."

"Mary, get your mother on the phone."

"Hi, Aunt Juts, what's up?"

"Look at page four of the *Trumpet,* that's what's up."

Mary called out, "Hey, Maizie, go and get the paper."

"Get it yourself."

"I'm on the phone with Aunt Juts. You better do as I say."

Julia heard the trudge of feet, a door slam, a door slam again. "Mary—Mary—"

"I've got the paper now."

"You could thank me." Maizie pouted.

"Thank you, Maizie," Mary said.

"Where's your mother?" Juts demanded.

"Out in the garden with Doodlebug."

"Go show her the ad on page four. Right now, Mary, and don't hang up the phone."

"All right."

Julia heard the receiver rock on the table and then in the far distance, "What!" The sound of a hurried footfall followed.

"Julia, I can't believe she would stoop so low!"

"I can."

"I was gardening to soothe my nerves before tomorrow and this—well, I don't understand how Junior McGrail can consider herself a Catholic."

"I don't understand how anyone can consider themselves a Catholic," Juts snidely said.

"Julia—" Louise's voice warned. "We have to respond to this, this attack."

"And give her free advertising? Not a chance."

"Well—there is that." Louise sat down on the phone stool. "Guess she's still hotsy about Toots."

"If she'd treated her better, Toots wouldn't have left." Juts spoke the plain truth. "Too bad her daughter's in Washington.

Whenever Rillma is around, the boys are around. I'd like a crowd."

"We'll get a big crowd. What else is there to do on a Thursday?"

"Yeah, the Strand doesn't change the movie until Friday. Anyway, competition is the life of trade. I think we're doing Junior a favor. After all, we're focusing people's attention on their hair and nails. She'll benefit from our advertising if she's smart. Or she'll get better, right?"

"I don't know about that."

"How much longer can she keep showing Marie Antoinette's radio cabinet?" Julia giggled.

Junior crammed her salon with fake French antiques. She was big on gilt. Her huge radio cabinet, a frightful sight, had been hand made, she said, in Paris, France—as opposed to Paris, Kentucky—and fashioned from valuable debris of Marie Antoinette's. She also claimed to receive visitations from the murdered queen, checking on her radio, no doubt. Junior gave tarot readings in the back, even though Father O'Reilly declared it pagan superstition. Those tarot readings were Junior's main draw, because her hairstyling consisted of a spit curl on the forehead and two for sideburns. She might branch out and give someone a finger wave, but you were just as likely to end up with hair that looked like frayed fuse boxes.

"Are you nervous?" Louise lowered her voice.

"No."

"I am. If we flop I think my husband is going to put me on an allowance and God knows what else."

"We aren't going to flop," Juts reassured her. "I have my lucky baseball cap, remember?"

"You just got that thing."

"Doesn't mean it isn't lucky. Now relax. What's the worst that can happen?"

"We go broke. Our husbands leave us. My children are shamed by a bankrupt mother. I suffer from angina and palpitations—"

"Nothing ventured, nothing gained. Drink a hot toddy and go to bed early."

"Alcohol never touches my lips, you know that."

"For medicinal purposes, Louise. Like tobacco, it's soothing. So if you will make yourself a hot toddy, you'll sleep like a baby and be ready for tomorrow. We're going to be on our feet all day, you know."

"How do I make a hot toddy?"

Juts shared her recipe.

"Well—"

"I'll see you in the morning."

Knowing she had talked her sister into what Wheezie wanted in the first place, Julia repaired to the pantry, grabbed a bottle of whiskey, and made herself a bracing whiskey sour.

When Chessy came home from work that night he grabbed the can of mixed nuts while Juts made him a whiskey sour and one for her, which she pretended was her first.

He twirled his forefinger in the nut can. "It's all peanuts. False advertising." He slammed the can down on the counter.

"I know. It's awful," Juts said as she handed him his drink.

20

Junior McGrail believed more is more. Staggering under the weight of bangle bracelets, large dangling earrings, and many wraps of roped beads around her fleshy neck, she marched down

Frederick Street looking neither to the left nor the right. This took great discipline because the crowd spilled over onto the street like colored jelly beans.

The opening of the Curl 'n' Twirl had exploded into a block party. The mastermind behind the frolic, Pearlie Trumbull, had motored over to the Budweiser distributor and bought seven kegs of beer.

When Chessy asked whether he could afford it, Pearlie told him they couldn't afford not to do it. Chessy, nursing along his old Dodge work truck, cruised back with heavy whiskey casks cut in half and crammed with ice, sodas, and mixers. He bought them from a big distillery down in Baltimore on the dockside. Noe Mojo, the husband of Louise's dear friend, Orrie, and a hardworking man of Japanese descent, went along with Chester to help him load the casks.

To add a whiff of sin to the party, Chester bought some of the finest moonshine this side of the Mississippi, made in Nelson County, Virginia, and sold on the sly by Davy Bitters, Billy's older brother. Those Blue Ridge Mountain streams produced exceptional shine but one had to be careful. If you drank too much your knees would lock up on you.

The boys had the bottles of moonshine stashed in various glove compartments, trunks, plus a few hip flasks for the daring.

With the exception of Junior, the town turned out in force. Even Caesura Frothingham showed up. She said it was to gather information for poor, dear Junior.

Junior pretended she was on her way to the Strand, but since the show didn't start for another hour everyone knew that was a lie. Besides, she only had to walk across the square from the other side to reach the Strand.

"Junior, come on," Juts motioned, never one to hold a grudge. Then, too, she had tested the moonshine.

"Never." Junior glared at Caesura and continued in her progress.

Orrie Tadia Mojo sniffed in Louise's ear, "The tragic queen."

Thanks to Mary and Maizie, the kids from South Runnymede High gathered around, as did many from North Runnymede High.

Juts had even hired a small band.

Trudy Archer whispered in Chessy's ear, "Why aren't you dancing?"

"I'm not ready yet."

"You've had three lessons, four including the free one."

"I'm too—" He shrugged. "I'll get there. You have to be patient."

"Am I not doing a good job?"

He patted her on the shoulder. "You're great. When I'm ready—well, I'll know. Now you go on and grab some of these guys. Edgar Frost is a good dancer."

She smiled and moved toward the lawyer she'd met a few days ago.

The three ancient unmarried Rife triplets, the sisters of Brutus—Ruby, Rose, and Rachel—appeared, escorted by much-younger men. They could be distinguished by their attire. Ruby wore Mainbocher, Rachel wore Hattie Carnegie, and Rose had just discovered Sophie of Saks. Given the war, no one could go to Paris, and while it ravaged Europe the conflagration was a blessing to American fashion designers. Ruby's milliner was Lilly Daché, Rachel adored John Fredericks, and Rose pounced on a rising star in the hat firmament, Tatiana, countess du Plessix.

The La Squandra sisters, as they were known behind their backs, were tolerated not because they spent money but because they were so patently useless. It was rumored that they couldn't draw their own bathwater. Certainly one couldn't blame them for the sins of their deceased brother and father.

Too tired to stand for long, they lounged in the barber's chairs Juts had bought.

Fannie Jump Creighton, between boyfriends, squeezed by

them when Rose declared, "Fannie Jump, do you think the girls can flourish? You know how dreadfully they fuss."

Fannie paused and admired the sleek hat with curving yellow feathers. "They'll be too busy to fight."

Celeste emerged from the private room, a seraphic smile on her face. She edged toward Fannie.

"Celeste, Celeste, darling!" Rachel held out her gloved hand and in a flash of lucidity blurted out, "I want you to know I never minded you killing Brutus. Even though he was my brother he was a brutal son of a bitch."

The buzz was so loud in the room, only Cora and Fannie overheard this statement.

"Will you hush, little girl," Rose hissed at Rachel.

Ruby blinked her big china-blue eyes as though reentering the world. "Well, she did it, Rosie, everyone knows she did it."

Cora stepped in. "Who knows how such things happen? He had many enemies and 1920 is so long ago."

"Me!" Rachel pouted. "He sent away my gentleman caller."

"Your gentleman caller was a gold digger," Rose growled. "If Brutus hadn't sent him packing, I would have."

"Jealous," Rachel triumphantly replied. "But Celeste, darling, I never cared a bit that you shot him."

"Now, Rachel, don't accuse me without the facts." Celeste had in fact killed Brutus those twenty-one years ago for many reasons, not the least being his reign of terror in the town. She never admitted it and never would. "As for your gentleman caller, he was before my time, but I heard he was very handsome."

"Oh, he had the softest hands, hands like a girl." Rachel sighed like a coquette.

"Ha!" Ruby exploded, before lapsing back into silence. Celeste pushed her way through the bodies, Cora and Fannie right behind her.

"Useless as tits on a boar hog," Cora mumbled.

Popeye Huffstetler, cornered at the front door by Caesura Frothingham, seized the chance to get away by grabbing on to Celeste, a good foot taller than his puny self.

Caesura called out, "Popeye, you aren't being much of a reporter. You haven't found out who smacked into George Gordon Meade."

"Robert E. Lee," Celeste answered her.

"You think you are so witty, Celeste Chalfonte." Caesura reached for another beer, which was being handed to her in a sherry glass so she had to refill frequently.

"Caesura, let's celebrate this wonderful opening. I think it's good that you came over."

"I came over to spy for Junior."

"Have another sip," Cora suggested.

"Believe I shall."

"Junior is out there marching and countermarching. She's doing her own spying." Fannie harrumphed.

"I am not speaking to you."

"Good." Fannie pushed by Caesura to reach the street.

Julia Ellen danced with all the boys from the two high schools. Louise was as happy as anyone had ever seen her. She pointed her finger at Mary a few times, warning her against slipping into the shadows with Extra Billy.

The party rolled into the velvet twilight. Flavius Cadwalder, encouraged by his son and the moonshine, told the Hunsenmeir girls that he knew what a hardship the debt was. If they fell behind he'd work something out with them. Everyone cheered and solidified the goodwill with more spirits.

Jacob Epstein Jr., a high-school buddy of Extra Billy's, passed out on the curb. The men lifted him on the flatbed where the band performed. He was out cold for every song, once emitting a low moan during "Red Sails in the Sunset."

Junior grew tired of her ceaseless parade so Caesura joined

her and they walked back to the north side of the square. Junior had to assist Caesura who, tipsy, lied and said she had sprained her ankle.

The miracle was that Julia Ellen and Louise didn't have one single battle, not one. Everyone knew it couldn't last.

That Sunday, both sisters visited their mother at Bumblebee Hill for supper.

A weak knock on the door lifted Juts out of her seat at Cora's dining table.

"Oh, honey, sit down," Chester said, but she was already out of the room.

She opened the front door to face an old man, perhaps once handsome, now hunched over.

"Is Mrs. Hansford Hunsenmeir at home?" he gasped.

"Yes. Would you wait a minute?"

She walked back to the dinner table and whispered, "Mom, there's some old geezer at the front door. You'd better talk to him in a hurry because he looks to die on the spot."

Cora folded her napkin and walked to the door.

Juts, Chessy, Louise, Pearlie, Mary, and Maizie heard muffled voices and then a sob. Both Chessy and Paul hurried to the door.

Baffled, they walked with Cora as she helped the old man, crying, to the table.

"Girls, this is your father."

21

"That man is not my father." Louise folded her arms across her chest.

"Well, if he's not your father I guess he's not mine either," Julia said.

Chester and Pearlie sat in Louise's two big armchairs with the heavy wool covering that looked like carpet and scratched in warm weather. Mary and Maizie were supposedly in bed.

The kids crept to the top of the stairs to listen. So far they'd managed to keep quiet.

"Why don't you two sit down? You're making me dizzy." Pearlie, his long, angular face somber, pointed to the sofa.

"I can't. Walking around helps me think."

"Better walk around a lot, then," Julia half joked.

"This is no time to be lighthearted. An imposter comes into our midst. He'll eat Momma out of house and home—"

Chessy interrupted, "He won't eat much, Wheezie. He's on his last leg."

"What about medical bills?" Louise, focused on money, had visions of a huge stack of white paper impaled on a long nail. Across each sheet was a red rectangle with "Bill" in the middle. It wasn't a vision, it was a waking nightmare.

"And then there will be the cost of the burial and the casket—you've got to be rich to die." Louise paced faster.

"You could hang him on a gibbet." Chester kept a straight face. "I could build one in a day."

"Yeah, you could put the gibbet in front of Junior McGrail's. I bet that would turn customers away."

"Think of the dogs, though," Chessy said deadpan.

"Will you two shut up." Louise plopped on the sofa. "This is serious. It's terrible."

"Momma's such a soft touch, she'll take care of him no matter who he is. He can't be our father. Hansford Hunsenmeir was a handsome man with a black handlebar moustache."

"Except it wasn't black, not really. It photographed black."

"How do you know?"

"I remember him—sort of." Louise sighed. "Mostly, I remember Momma crying."

"Thirty-four years is a long time. I don't think any of us would look like our photographs," Pearlie observed.

"Why not? Celeste Chalfonte does," Louise replied.

"She is the exception that proves the rule," Paul said.

"Her hair turned silver—that's about it." Chester ran his hands through his own blond curls; his hairline was receding slightly. He didn't like that one bit.

"Well, whoever he is, he insulted me before he even sat down at the table. He said, 'You must be Louise.' I said, 'Yes,' and then he says with that pathetic excuse for a moustache wiggling, 'You must be forty now.' "

"Oh, Wheezer, for Christ's sake, you are forty."

"I am not. I most certainly am not and I don't know why you insist upon such misinformation."

"If I'm thirty-six, you're forty." Juts stood her ground.

"I am not forty! And as for you, he looked at you and wanted to know where your children were. I may be closer to forty than you are but at least I'm a mother!"

"Louise, calm down."

She whirled on her husband. "Calm down? What would you

do if some horrible man blew through the front door and said he was your father!"

Pearlie clasped his hands in front of him. "I would trust my mother to know her husband."

"Whose side are you on?" Louise shrieked.

"Yours, honey, but if Cora Hunsenmeir says that fellow is Hansford, then he is."

"How would she know? She hasn't seen him for thirty-four years either." Louise, anger ebbing because she knew Pearlie was telling the truth, sank into her seat.

"He's right." Julia bounced down next to her sister, who turned her shoulder away, still miffed for being fingered for forty.

"Juts, I think you are too easily swayed."

"Ha." Chessy laughed.

"Easily swayed or not, what are we going to do?"

Chester's rich baritone surprised them. "We're going to do what Cora wants."

Tears glistened in Julia's eyes. "But Chessy, I don't want that nasty-looking man to be my father."

"Me neither." Louise put her arm around Julia's shoulders, their spat instantly forgotten.

"Now, girls, we've got to make the best of it. Chess is right. This is up to your mother."

"Momma can't resist a stray. She's got four cats—"

"Five," Julia corrected.

"Five? When did she get five?"

"She found an abandoned kitten with a broken leg."

"Well, you know what I'm saying. We've got to protect Mother from herself." Louise sounded very mature when she said that.

"Well, practice your Christianity, then," Pearlie told her.

A voice piped up from the top of the darkened stairs. "It is more blessed to give than to receive."

Louise shot up off the sofa, halting at the bottom of the stairs and clicking on the light. No one was at the top. "Mary, I know your voice."

"She's asleep," Maizie called out.

"Shut up," Mary whispered.

"Mary, I wasn't born yesterday."

"We know," Juts called from the living room.

That made Chessy and Pearlie laugh and then the kids started giggling in Mary's room where they'd hidden.

Louise's pout dissolved into a chuckle. Then she threw her head back and roared.

"Mom," Maizie called out, "I'm hungry."

"It's ten o'clock at night."

"Hey, let's have hot-fudge sundaes. I've got lots of peanuts at my house." Juts would kill for ice cream.

"I've got peanuts," Louise said.

"Mom—*please*." Maizie's request sounded so plaintively sweet.

"All right."

Julia heated up the sauce, Paul scooped out the ice cream, and Mary set the table with Maizie's help. Chester opened a fresh can of mixed nuts.

"I'm getting cheated."

"Huh?" Paul turned to Chessy.

"My mixed nuts are just peanuts."

" 'Cause you're living with a nutcase," Louise pronounced. "She picks out everything but the peanuts. I hide my mixed nuts so she can't find them."

Chester, like an innocent, faced Julia Ellen. "Honey, do you do that?" He edged close behind her and nuzzled her neck. "I always thought I could count on you."

"The only thing you can count on these days is your fingers." Juts popped a huge Brazil nut in his mouth.

22

"I thought he was dead." She raised her voice. "He should be dead."

Chester, surprised at his mother's vehemence, neglected to hang his hat on the hat rack. This would be a short stay. He couldn't stand his mother when she soured. He had realized years ago that he loved her but he didn't like her.

Josephine continued, "I told you when you married that hellion she would never set foot in this house. No offspring of Hansford Hunsenmeir will ever walk through my door." She caught her breath. "And now he's back. You'd think he'd have sense enough to stay where he was."

"Maybe he came home to die."

"Fast, I hope."

Chester had caught his mother off guard with the news. He knew she disliked the Hunsenmeirs, but this was more emotion than he'd witnessed since he announced his engagement.

"Mother, since I don't know why you hate him I can be but so sympathetic."

"All you need to know is he offended me. Your place is with me."

"What did he do?"

"That's none of your business!" she snapped.

"Whatever he did, why stay angry at Cora, Juts, and Louise?" he quite logically replied—a mistake.

"Because I feel like it! Cora Zepp threw herself at Hansford. It was disgusting."

"That had to have been quite some time ago." He rolled his hat brim between his thumb and forefinger.

"Not to me, it isn't."

"Mother"—he attempted to cajole her—"when I'm your age I hope my memory is as sharp as yours."

"Memory is everything. It's your whole life."

"I guess, but haven't you ever noticed how someone—Pop, say—remembers something one way and you remember it another?"

She stared at him with her steel-gray eyes. "Your father would forget his head if it wasn't attached to his neck."

As she had purposely missed the point, Chester's mouth twitched in an involuntary smile. He put his hat back on. "I'm sorry I've upset you. I thought you ought to know before someone told you on the street."

"Where are you going?" A flash of disquiet illuminated her face.

"Back to the store." He opened the back door. "Bye, Mother."

"Chester."

"What?"

"How did he look?"

"Uh—old. He can't breathe too good."

"I'll bet Cora was shocked."

"You might say that. He cried when he saw her."

"I hope he chokes to death."

"I'll be seeing you." Chessy shut the door behind him.

Josephine stared at the pretty tablecloth on the kitchen table, its scalloped edges embroidered in silk thread. A blue salt-and-pepper-shaker set, along with a sugar bowl, graced the middle.

She yanked at the edge of the tablecloth, sending the shakers and bowl crashing to the floor.

23

As months passed, neither Julia nor Louise would call Hansford Hunsenmeir "Father," but they tried to be courteous. Slowly they began to see aspects of his character that had merit. For one thing, he didn't tell them what to do.

So far he had offered no explanation for his thirty-four-year absence. Cora didn't ask. He spoke little because breathing was difficult for him, although he perked up under Cora's care.

The Curl 'n' Twirl was the place to congregate. Not that Juts or Louise could cut hair worth a damn, but Toots made up for that. What Juts and Louise could do was paint fingernails, gossip incessantly, and make people laugh. They even had a water fight while washing Lillian Yost's hair, and Lillian, instead of fuming, filled a cup of water once her hair was done and dumped it on Julia's head.

A big blackboard with lots of colored chalk in the wooden tray hung on one side of the wall. Paul had artistically lettered "Gossip Central" on top. Everyone could stop in and write what happened that day—things like Wheezie taking a drink out of the garden hose and getting a centipede in her mouth. Births, anniversaries, birthdays, and party dates were scribbled across the board as well as funny sayings.

Cora came in one day and wrote, "If you want a helping hand, it's at the end of your arm."

Louise, in a pious fit, would sometimes write down a biblical passage.

The kids gathered around because Mary and Maizie told them their mother would give them free Cokes. The Curl 'n' Twirl got more haircuts out of those free Cokes, which cost Louise and Juts a nickel apiece. Even the animals congregated there, thanks to the antics of Yoyo and Buster.

Older ladies continued to patronize Junior McGrail, who on Saturdays retaliated with a day of culture. That meant her son, who resembled a hairy ape, squatted in the storefront window playing the harp. It ran in the family because Junior's brother played the harp too.

Celeste journeyed to Washington frequently and her first stop on her return was the Curl 'n' Twirl. She always brought Toots news of Rillma. Rillma and Celeste's nephew, Francis, were ensconced in a small room in the State Department Building. Celeste figured her nephew was in some form of military intelligence but she didn't know what. He didn't volunteer much information and she didn't press. She knew the Army and the Navy were quietly building up—one had only to drive past an Army base to see that—but the papers wrote very little about the buildup, which was, to her mind, an ominous sign.

Cora surmised that Celeste was having an affair in Washington, but she didn't know with whom. Celeste never said a thing.

Ramelle returned in the fall but Celeste's trips to Washington continued. Sometimes she took Ramelle with her. Cora figured sooner or later she'd find out what was going on.

The summer seemed unusual because of the squadrons of butterflies and the Orioles finishing at the bottom. Joe DiMaggio got a hit in fifty-six consecutive games, which electrified every-one, just as Whirlaway's Triple Crown victory did, Eddie Arcaro up. The fall was unusual because of the large number of ring-necked pheasants. The cornfields were full of them.

As 1941 coasted toward winter, the Hunsenmeir sisters made a dent in their debt to Mr. Cadwalder. Extra Billy, a bit toned down—in front of Louise and Pearlie, anyway—continued to court Mary. Louise appeared somewhat mollified. Not that she didn't hope for a suitable boy to appear, a match commensurate with her grandiose ideas of the future. She continued to pray to the Blessed Virgin Mother and to make occasional trips to Diddy Van Dusen, who was reportedly beginning to think she was the Blessed Virgin Mother.

Juts was the first one to unlock the shop door. She brewed some chicory coffee as a treat for the customers, piled up plates of cookies, cakes, and doughnuts, and wrote the date in red chalk—November 26, 1941—on Gossip Central. Since it was Wednesday she knew the shop would be wildly busy. Tomorrow was Thanks-giving and ladies wanted to look their best.

24

Mary's eyes looked like round, red lizard eyes, the kind that let the lizard see in two directions at the same time. She collapsed in the middle barber's chair at the Curl 'n' Twirl and cried even more.

The wild turkey, testimony to the taxidermist's art, shared the front window with glazed pumpkins and squash. People waved as they walked by. The Closed sign hung in the window, as it was six-thirty. The day had been so busy that there hadn't even been time for a coffee break. Maizie was out grocery shopping with her father, a good thing, because Louise, clean out of patience, would have knocked her flat if she'd opened her mouth during this latest set-to. It was going to be a wearisome Thanksgiving.

"I love him, Mother!" Mary sobbed anew.

Juts scrubbed out the washbowls as Louise swept the floor. Mary, immobilized by her misery, did nothing except be miserable, at which she excelled.

"Will you stop slobbering." Wheezie thunked the back of the chair with the broom. "If I hear the word 'love' one more time I will cut out your tongue."

Mary howled in anguish.

"Ah, Louise, don't cut out her tongue. Just tape her mouth shut." Juts's hands sweated inside the heavy red rubber gloves. She was vain about her hands.

"Aunt Julia, I thought you were on my side." Mary's nose dripped along with her eyes.

"I am on your side, Mary. That's why I have to agree with your mother—fifteen is too young to marry. You can marry Billy later."

"When? She'll do anything to break us up." This was followed by a moan that could wake the dead.

"He has no prospects, no blood, no—nothing." Louise swatted with the broom again.

"You don't know him, Momma."

"I don't want to know him. You've let a handsome face turn your head. Marriage is more than that." She paused, leaning on her broom. "What a pity Ramelle didn't have a boy instead of a girl. That would be a match made in heaven."

"All you care about is money."

"Exactly," Wheezie spat right back at her. "And when you grow up and have to pay your own bills it will finally sink into your thick head that I'm trying to do the best for you. A poor husband is not happiness, believe me. That love stuff wears off after a while and you'd better have more than that or you're just another dumb woman who followed a dumb man!"

"I hate you!" Mary jumped off the chair and ran for the door.

"Mary," Julia called after her, "come on back here. You two are like banty roosters. There's got to be some middle ground."

"Not with her," Mary half squealed.

Louise bellowed back, "Listen here, little girl, if you think you can marry behind my back I can get it annulled in a heartbeat, so put that in your pipe and smoke it."

"You don't understand. You just don't understand." Mary blubbered again.

"Sit down, both of you. I'm tired of this wrangling. For Christ's sake, you're giving me a headache." Juts pointed at the two chairs on the ends. She stood in front of the middle chair, her back to the counter and the mirrors. "Now, here's how I see it and I want you both to keep your big traps shut." She pointed at Mary. "You are fifteen years old. You can't do a thing about your age."

Mary butted in, "Why not, Mom does."

"You little—" Louise leapt up to go over and smack her but Juts pushed her back in her seat.

"That's enough out of both of you. I mean it." They settled back down like ruffled hens in their broody boxes as Juts continued. "Mary, Extra Billy will still be here when you turn sixteen in January. What's the rush? You can marry him when you graduate from high school."

"Julia Ellen!" Louise bellowed. "Have you lost your mind?"

"No, I have not. Louise, she's in love. She's going to marry this kid whether you like it or not. Now, she can either run away and scare the bejesus out of all of us or we can make the best of it and have a decent wedding here at home with enough time to plan it. She skipped a grade, so come June she's out of high school and on her own."

"You're telling me to make a silk purse out of a sow's ear," Louise shouted, the veins standing out on her neck.

"Mother!" Mary objected to being called a sow's ear, although that wasn't what her mother was saying, exactly.

"I am telling you to accept the inevitable. Hell, Louise, it might even be a good marriage."

"Don't make me laugh." Louise slammed her fist on the arm of the barber's chair.

"Will you be laughing when an out-of-wedlock baby appears?" Juts pointed a finger at her sister.

"What? What!" Louise shot out of the chair to stick her face in Mary's face. "Are you—?"

"No!"

"Don't you lie to me, you hussy."

"I am not lying to you." Mary wanted to smack her mother, but since she was pregnant her voice betrayed her.

"Julia, is she lying to me?"

Juts shrugged eloquently. She really didn't know, but she suspected as much.

"I don't want to be a grandmother," Louise wailed. "I'm not old enough to be a grandmother."

"All right, then, we'll pass you off as Mary's sister—her much-older sister," Julia sarcastically replied.

"Will you shut up!" Louise, nostrils flaring, wheeled on Juts. "You've been feeding Mary this pap about love and sharing with a man and oh I could just puke. You don't share with men, Mary. You don't even think about it, my dear daughter—you tell men what to do. You organize their lives for them. You grab the paycheck out of their hand before they can spend it. You say what they want to hear. You let them think your ideas are their ideas. It's a lot of work running a man but you have to do it because they are so goddamned dumb!" She shocked herself by using the word "goddamned."

"I don't want to love like that," Mary determinedly said.

"Juts, I lay this at your door. You and your mooning over Chessy. He's barely got a pot to piss in." Louise pointed her finger in her sister's face. "You're full of those cockeyed ideas."

"We live in a nice house." Juts held on to her rising temper.

"You wouldn't have a thing if it weren't for my castoffs—or Celeste's. It's a sure bet Mother Smith wouldn't give you a moldy loaf of bread."

"Louise, I am taking into account the fact that you are overwrought—"

"Overwrought? I am ready to *kill*." She inhaled slowly, then blew out the air with violence. "You're not a mother. You can't understand how I feel."

Julia had heard that one too often, but this time she wasn't going to take the bait. She didn't know if her niece was in trouble or not. She didn't want Mary to run off, though. Nor did she want the kid to have to battle her mother the rest of her life. Louise needed to bend to keep her daughter's love and keep her family together. Juts had lived for fourteen years as wife to a man whose mother made certain, every day, that she was found wanting. It wasn't a great feeling. At first you ignored it. Then you got angry. Finally, you went dead on that score, but the bad thing was that you started to go dead about other things, too, other people. It spiraled out of control, that numb feeling.

"Louise, you're a good mother—"

"Well, thank you," Louise mocked.

"Momma birds push babies out of the nest. Mary's ready to fly from the nest. Everything you taught her will stay with her. Don't worry so. She's picked a boy you don't like. But Wheezie, he's good-hearted—" She caught her breath. "—I hope. Half the time the kid didn't get enough to eat and you know that's the truth! That little boy started working for food when he was seven years old. If you don't know anything else about him you know he's not lazy. He's found Mary and she's found him. Let the Lord work His wonders. After all, He brought them together."

Involving the Lord was Julia's masterstroke.

Louise puckered her red lips. Nothing came out of them, not even a slow hiss before speaking.

Mary, too, was speechless.

Finally Louise recovered her voice. Although her sister had reached her with a compelling argument, she had to know the truth. In a calm voice, she asked, "Mary, before I can make any decision, I have to know. Are you pregnant?"

Mary burst into tears. Louise had her answer.

Juts patted Mary's hand. "It's okay, kid. You're not the first."

Louise, deflated, began to cry. "Oh, Mary, how could you? After all I have taught you."

"That won't help now." Julia faced the two women, who were exploding in tears. "All the training in the world can't change Mother Nature." Before Wheezie could marshal her moral objections, Juts continued. "Mary, you weren't wise. You have to recognize that you did something that can't be undone. Even if it all turns out right, you have changed your whole life without letting us all sit down and think it through—your future, I mean."

"I know," Mary bawled. "But I love him." A gust of emotion overtook the tears.

"Louise?"

Pale, Louise croaked, "I can't believe she'd do that to me."

"She didn't do it to you, Sis. She did it to herself. How much did you think about other people at fifteen? The kid's in a jam. Like it or not, we're her family. We have to help."

Steadier now, Louise asked her daughter, "Does he know?"

"Yes. He asked me last week to marry him."

"Last week!"

Juts held up her hand. "He did the right thing. Let's not quibble about time."

"I didn't know how to tell you." Mary sobbed anew.

Julia, in a clear voice, said, "Give them your blessing. Give her a proper Catholic wedding. Pearlie will have to counsel Billy on his obligations. Chester can help too. That's between men. Between us, we can welcome him into the family."

Louise fought back the tears. "I don't want her to get hurt."

"She's going to get hurt anyway. She might as well do it on her own terms."

"What do you mean, Aunt Juts?"

"She means Billy will run around on you."

"He will not!"

Julia held up her hands for silence. "I said no such thing. I don't know what will happen. All I know is every now and then Life sticks his boot up your ass. You live through it. Louise, don't put words in my mouth. Mary, if your parents do this for you, then you have to finish school before getting a job."

This prospect was not appetizing but Mary nodded in agreement.

A long, long silence ensued. Outside they could hear the crunch of feet as people walked past the store. Every now and then Julia waved at someone.

Finally, Louise half whispered, "Well, Mary, it is your life. I've had my chances. I guess you have to take your chances."

Mary scrambled over to her mother and hugged her. Then they indulged in a joint cry.

Juts, tired after this rake and scrape-up, cut the overhead lights. She thought being an aunt was hard work; being a mother must be hell, and yet look at them now.

25

"Mom, I can't find my bouquet." Maizie frantically wrung her hands.

"You will find it!" Louise ordered.

"But Mom, I can't remember anything." The young girl, hair in a shiny pageboy, leaned against the church room wall.

"Don't wrinkle your dress. That dress cost almost as much as your sister's bridal gown. I don't remember prices being this high when I got married."

"She gets to wear your veil. That ought to save some money," Maizie replied, the first signs of teenage rebellion brewing.

Ignoring this, Louise, worn out and fresh out of patience, grilled her younger child. "Where have you been in the last twenty minutes?"

"I went to the bathroom."

"Well, did you leave the bouquet in there?"

"I don't know. There's always someone in there."

"I'd start there."

"What if it isn't there, Mom?"

"Then think of the other places you've been." Louise checked her watch. "And work backward."

"All right." Maizie wobbled off in her high-heeled shoes toward the bathroom.

"Everything looks perfect in the church." Juts hurried past

the retreating Maizie. "Aunt Dimps is up at the organ with Terry Tinsdale—just in case."

"Father O'Reilly said if we didn't use our own church organist it would break her heart." Louise exhaled. "Personally, I don't think Terry Tinsdale can carry a tune with a bucket. And now Maizie can't find her bouquet. I think she'll break her ankle thanks to those high heels."

Juts came over and put her arm around her sister, who was so frazzled she could barely draw breath. "Everything's going to be fine, Sis."

"It better be, because there's nothing else I can do about it." Louise's head snapped up again. "Celeste's car! I forgot to pick it up this morning."

"Done. It's sitting right out in front of the church."

"Where's Momma?"

"Plopped in the front row."

"What about fur-face?" Louise said sourly, referring to Hansford.

"He's there, too, with a pink rosebud in his lapel."

"Juts, Juts, I forgot the satin cushion for the rings!"

"Father O'Reilly has it and he had the satin cleaned, just like you requested. Now, take a deep breath and count to ten. This is going to be a beautiful sunrise wedding. Your husband looks as handsome as the day you married him. He's upstairs with Mary. She needs a rope to keep her from floating into the sky, but Pearlie's in charge up there. The best thing you can do is to give yourself a few minutes of rest."

What Juts didn't say was that the speed of the wedding had tested her organizing skills as well as Louise's. The fact that Mary insisted it be at sunrise added to the exhaustion. She wanted an original wedding.

Louise's eyes filled with tears. "Juts, I want Mary to be happy."

"Then smile, because she is today. The future will take care of itself."

"I guess." A ragged intake of breath garbled the "guess." "Are Billy's people here?"

"His mother. His father hasn't been home for three days, so she says. Chessy is with him, saying whatever men say to each other in a situation like this."

"Chessy's a good egg." Louise folded her hands together, trying to compose herself. "I guess we aren't the only people in Runnymede with a worthless father." Juts didn't reply, so Louise continued. "What time is it?"

"We've got about ten more minutes."

"I really should see Mary one more time."

"Look!" Maizie burst in waving her bouquet.

"Where'd you leave it?"

"With Mary."

"How's she doing?"

"She's giggling a lot. Ha-ha," Maizie sarcastically said. "And I still don't see why I have to be on the end of the line. I'm her sister."

"Your bridesmaid is your best friend, Maizie. We've been over this." Louise glared at her. "The way you two carry on you're lucky to be in this wedding at all. And for another thing, you are the shortest person up there. You have to be on the end."

"Who was your bridesmaid?"

"I was," Juts answered.

"See," Maizie said, a touch too loud.

"Maizie, my wedding was very different from Mary's wedding. For one thing, it wasn't slapped together at the last minute. You shut up and play your part or I'll yank you out of that bridesmaid's line faster than you can say 'Jack Rabbit.' "

Maizie bit her lip, turned on her heel, and stalked out.

"Oh dear God, let me live long enough to be a burden to my children. I want to destroy their furniture, break their plates, interrupt their sleep, and contradict them morning, noon, and night. I want to cost them money."

Juts laughed, then Louise had to laugh at herself. Juts checked her watch again, "Well, mother of the bride, let's go down the aisle and sit. My feet hurt."

Louise, motionless for a minute, blinked, then nodded. The sisters walked out into the vestibule and then, shoulder to shoulder, strolled down the center aisle as the congregation stood to honor the mother.

Back in the groom's room, Jacob Epstein, in his rented morning suit, together with Extra Billy's two brothers in their rented clothes, nervously blinked, paced, and breathed deeply. Billy's broad shoulders filled his gray tailcoat.

The groom cleared his throat. "Mr. Smith, I really do appreciate you being here with me."

Chester smiled. "Billy, that's the fourth time you've thanked me. I'm happy to be here."

"Guess I'm a little jumpy."

"Billy"—Chester put his hand on his shoulder—"in about twenty minutes' time the ceremony will be over and you'll be a married man. Everything changes. I think when we get married we're thinking a lot about the physical part, but it takes more than that to make a partnership."

"Sir," Billy agreed.

"I think if I had three lifetimes I'd never understand women. They are peculiar." Chessy smiled at the big young man in front of him. "But you've got to pull it together, talk to each other, and overlook the little niggling things that get under your skin. And one more thing—tell her you love her. Sometimes we think they know it, but for whatever reason, women need to hear it more than we do." He held out his hand. "I wish you all the luck in the world."

"Thank you, Mr. Smith." Billy shook his hand as the organist played the groom's cue.

"I'll walk you to the aisle."

He led the fellows to the aisle to the right of the altar. "Billy, count to five to give me time to get to my seat. Okay?" When Billy nodded, he winked at him. "You picked a wonderful girl." Then he quietly slipped down the side aisle.

As the music ended, Billy and his groomsmen silently filed out in front of the altar. They stood ramrod straight.

The bride's march boomed. Mary appeared in the vestibule, her father next to her, fighting back his tears. He kissed her quickly through her veil before they started down the aisle. Maizie brought up the rear, dreaming of her own wedding some-day. Billy turned when he heard the bride's march, and the sight of Mary, dazzling in her white bridal gown, brought a smile of pure joy to his face. No one in the congregation that day would ever forget the look on Extra Billy Bitters's face. It truly was a love match.

Louise cried in her lace handkerchief. Juts put her arm around her, the tears welling up in her eyes, too. Why, she didn't know. Maybe hope pulled the tears up, the hope that somehow these two would survive together, survive the curveballs life throws at you, and survive their own shortcomings.

Even Chester cried.

Juts glanced across the aisle, noticing that Millard Yost dabbed his eyes. The she remembered a poster he had put up in every storefront window in Runnymede when his Irish setter ran off.

LOST

SEAMUS, FAT IRISH SETTER

NEUTERED, LIKE ONE OF THE FAMILY

Her shoulders heaved. Louise hugged her tighter, thinking the sacrament was touching Juts to her deepest core. Then she noted her younger sister's face.

"Stop it," Louise whispered in a hiss.

"I can't." Juts nearly choked.

"I am going to name my first ulcer after you." Louise jabbed

Juts so hard with her elbow that an audible *oomph* could be heard behind the sisters. People assumed both were overcome with emotion. In that, they were correct. Fortunately, conventional sentiment obscured just what those emotions were. People see what they want to see.

Juts felt Chessy's strong hand take hers and gently squeeze. She pulled herself together but she knew she'd never be able to think about this wedding without thinking about Seamus, the fat Irish setter.

The bride and groom drove around the square on their way to Baltimore for their honeymoon. Extra Billy turned on the radio when they were about five miles out of town. He pulled a U-turn, heading back to Runnymede on that frosty December 7 morning.

PART TWO

26

It's funny what sticks in the mind after a seismic shock, sticks in the mind like leftover cotton fluttering on a picked boll.

The shop was always closed on Sunday and Monday, so Julia and Louise walked Buster and Doodlebug around the square. Even the dogs were subdued. The post office on the north side was behind the sumptuous City Hall Building on the square. Built of granite with Doric columns, whereas City Hall had Ionic columns, the post office loomed. Two enormous braziers, half a story high, flanked the steps. Even though pale winter light filtered through the glowing clouds, the flames in the braziers were lit. A line of young, middle-aged, and even old men stretched down the Emmitsburg pike; another line curled around City Hall almost to Hanover Street.

The sisters, arm in arm, stared with mouths agape. Billy Bitters, a worn scarf wrapped around his neck, patiently waited. As soon as he'd heard the news on the radio he had turned the car around and headed home. The honeymoon would have to wait. He was surrounded by Ray Parker, Jacob Epstein, Doak Garten, and other friends. He smiled and waved at the Hunsenmeirs. Juts waved back. Louise nodded. It was bad enough that he had married her daughter. Now he was going to leave her.

They walked over to the South Runnymede post office, a more modest affair of white frame with a long porch and green shutters. The American flag flew at half-mast, as did the flag of Maryland, an exceptionally beautiful red, black, and yellow state flag, quartered with the coat of arms of Lord Baltimore. The post office faced Baltimore Street. One line of men snaked west along the square, with stragglers queuing up in the alleyway between the library and the P.O. Yet another line stretched east clear down Baltimore Street. Paul Trumbull and Chester Smith, side by side, stood in the line down Baltimore Street.

Juts left Louise and ran. It took Louise a second until she saw her husband standing there in the cold. She, too, ran toward him.

"Chester, don't do this. You're thirty-six. You're too old."

"Honey, go home."

"You can't go to war. I'll starve!" came the plaintive wail.

"You won't starve."

"They won't take you. I'm telling you, you're wasting your time."

"Julia Ellen, this is no place for you."

"Why not? There are even some women in the line."

"Well, uh—two people from the same family can't enlist," he fibbed.

Meanwhile Louise harangued Pearlie. He was quite firm with her.

Finally the tearful sisters left. Since they were halfway through paying off their debt, they wandered into Cadwalder's, only to find Flavius Cadwalder in tears, too.

"Girls, excuse me." He wiped his eyes.

"Where's Vaughn?"

"He was in front of the post office at six this morning in the freezing cold." Pride as well as worry shone on his face. "Vaughn has enlisted in the Army. He was the very first person to sign up today."

"Well—" Juts thought a moment, and then said, "You raised a wonderful son. He'll be a fine soldier."

He pressed to his face one of the thin white cotton towels used for wiping glassware.

Louise reached over the counter and patted his shoulder. "Flavius, everything will be okay."

He wiped his eyes. "Wheezie, nothing will ever be the same. The world's gone crazy." He sniffled. "Here I'm forgetting myself. What can I get you?"

"We don't really want anything. We don't know what to do." Louise's lip quivered. "Our husbands are standing down there in line, too, and they're enlisting behind our backs." Louise started to cry.

That made Julia cry and Flavius, as well. The Yosts came into the store. Pretty soon everyone who came in was crying. People were shocked, confused, and deeply worried.

Lillian said, "Ted Baeckle won't take Chessy or Pearlie. Don't fret."

Ted Baeckle was the Army recruiter. When Germany invaded Poland on the first of September, 1939, Juts, as a precautionary measure, visited Ted, begging him not to let Chester sign up should he try to enlist.

Ted replied that she shouldn't worry. The United States wasn't at war. If they went to war he'd sideline her husband. However, that was two years ago and she was plenty worried.

"You know during the War Between the States they took men who were in their sixties and boys who were twelve." Juts dabbed her eyes. "How do we know it won't happen again?"

"We're not that desperate," Lillian stated.

The door swung open. Doak Garten came in. He smiled at them. "Navy!"

"My God," Louise exclaimed, then forced a smile. "You've done the right thing, Doak, we're just all—I don't know what we are."

"Miserable," Julia, chin on hand, answered.

Just then Ray breezed in. He and Doak slapped each other on the back. This was a big adventure to them.

Louise called out to Ray, "Extra Billy still in line?"

"Yes, ma'am, Mrs. Trumbull, and he's going to enlist in the Marines."

"He would," she grumbled.

Julia, under her breath, whispered, "Louise, you can be hateful. The boy could get killed, you know."

"Don't be dramatic, Julia. He's too thickheaded to train. He'll spend the war in the brig." She wanted to add, "And what am I supposed to do with a crying Mary and a crying baby?"

Louise couldn't have been more wrong.

27

"You know how strongly I disapprove of war, no matter what the provocation," Mother Smith declaimed. "Thank heavens Ted Baeckle exhibited judgment."

Chester, hands clasped behind his back, surreptitiously glanced at the clock. "Yes, Mother."

"Why did I raise you if you mean to persist in immoral activities? War is immoral."

"Ted made me second in command of the Civil Air Patrol. I guess it's better than nothing. Celeste Chalfonte is head of it, of course. She'll whip everyone into shape." Chessy sighed.

"Part and parcel of war." Jo Smith stuck out her chin.

"I'm not going to sit on the sidelines after what happened at Pearl Harbor."

"Thou shalt not kill. You can't amend the Ten Commandments. They are the Ten Commandments, not the Ten Suggestions." Not given to a sense of humor, Josephine Smith didn't realize that she was funny. "What are you smirking at?"

"Nothing, Mother."

"Your brothers had the sense not to try to sign up."

"Bulova will be involved in war manufacturing, so Joseph's contributing to the war effort." The minute the words were out of his mouth he wished he could call them back. You never won an argument with Mother Smith.

"Don't try to hide behind Joseph," she snapped.

"Mother, I have an appointment."

"I don't recall you having appointments on Tuesday evening."

"Well—I do."

"I suppose that wife of yours put you up to trying to enlist."

"No. She didn't want me to go. This may be the only time you and Juts have agreed on anything."

Her *harrumph* was a sign of distaste.

"Give Dad my best."

She followed him to the door. "What is that father of Julia's doing? Is he sitting around like a bump on a log, useless?"

"He does odds and ends around the house. He can hardly breathe."

"Won't last long," she said with relish. "The wages of sin, I expect."

"The wages of too many cigarettes and breathing all that dust in the Nevada mines, Mother." Chessy was counting to ten. "When he left here he headed for the mines. He's trying to make amends."

"He should have stayed underground." She pursed her lips. "Your wife has a cigarette buttoned to her lip. If there's lung weakness in the family then she'll come down with it."

His mother was talking even as he started his car motor. Finally she shut the door to keep out the cold.

He parked behind the dance studio. All the streets in Runnymede had alleyways behind them, which facilitated deliveries and also helped drivers detour around bad traffic.

He ran up the stairs and opened the door.

"Hi, I'm sorry I'm a little late. My mother can talk."

Her eyes were sorrowful even as she was smiling. "That's okay. I had a lesson that ran late. I bought some new records last week." She paused. "I heard you enlisted." She dropped the needle on the record, and "I Don't Want to Set the World on Fire" played.

"Nah." He took her in his arms, ready to warm up. "I'm not that brave."

"I saw you standing in line."

"Where were you?" He twirled her around.

"Yosts'. I ran in to get a doughnut and just talk, I guess. This is all so terrible and it frightens me so. Anyway, I saw you standing there with Pearlie. The Yosts were so upset that when I left, they closed up the shop for the day."

"Everybody is shook."

"Did you sign up?" Her voice lowered.

"Ted won't take me. He said I'm an old man."

"You're not old at all." She gazed up at him.

"Well—anyway, Ted made me second banana of the Civil Air Patrol. At least I'm doing something."

"I'm glad you're not going."

His eyes brightened in amusement. "You must like having your feet stepped on every Tuesday."

She didn't reply. As the lesson wore on she added sweeps and swoops to the waltz, a dance both of them enjoyed. Chessy was losing his inhibitions and becoming a good dancer.

After each lesson they usually sat for a few minutes and chatted.

"Are you all right? You seem a little low."

She folded her hands together, leaning forward. "What if the Japanese sail to the West Coast with their aircraft carriers? They could bomb San Francisco and Seattle. It'll take a long time to rebuild our fleet."

"I guess we've got some ships left in places like San Diego and Newport News. They'd have a naval battle before anything like Pearl Harbor could happen again. The Navy will fly reconnaissance missions every day. At least I hope they do."

"What if the Japanese success makes the Germans think they can attack us? You know, people say submarines have been sighted off Baltimore Harbor."

"The British couldn't sack Baltimore, and the Germans won't be able to do it either. The state of Maryland may be tiny but we're tough." He smiled. "Don't worry, Trudy. Tomorrow's worries may never arrive." He laughed. "Now my mother, she can worry, and Julia's sister, Wheezie—there's another one. They worry enough for the rest of us. Relax, because Josephine Smith and Louise Trumbull are worrying enough for you, too."

This made her laugh, so that her pretty features were ever prettier. "You're right. I wish I were as smart as you are."

Now he laughed. "Trudy, you're the only woman who ever called me smart." He stood up. "Well, time to go home. I'll see you next Tuesday." He paused a moment. "I'm getting a kick out of this. You're a good teacher. I never thought I could learn to dance."

"Thank you." She put her hand on his arm. "I know you wanted to go to war but I'm so glad you'll be protecting us here." She reached up and kissed him on the cheek.

He felt her lips burning on his cheek the whole way down Hanover Street.

28

What do you make of it?" Harper Wheeler, the South Runnymede sheriff, asked Millard Yost, the baker who was head of the volunteer fire department.

"Arson. Didn't even try to cover up the evidence." Millard pointed to rags and gasoline cans scattered about.

"That's a hell of a note." Harper spat on the water-soaked ground already turning to ice in the bitter night air.

"Yep." Millard watched his men roll up the hoses.

Chessy screeched into the parking lot of Sans Souci, Fannie Jump Creighton's nightclub, which stood next to the meat warehouse that had been the arsonist's target. The firetrucks of both North and South Runnymede's volunteer fire departments filled the parking lot. Although the fire took place on the south side, each fire department assisted the other, state lines be damned.

Chessy hurried over to help Pearlie, his face red as he hauled hoses. "Damn, this would happen on my week off."

Pearlie grunted. "Couldn't do a goddamned thing."

"You kept it from spreading to Fannie's. That's something." He noticed Fannie, wrapped in her expensive beaver coat, sitting in her Buick. "She sound the alarm?"

"Yeah, got everyone out of her place, then cut off the power. She tried to cut the power over here but it was already too far gone."

"You don't need me. I'll visit Fannie."

He rapped on the window. She rolled it down. "Fannie, you okay?"

She nodded grimly.

He got in the passenger side as she rolled up the window. The meat-warehouse cat, Matilda, wild-eyed but unsinged, burrowed in Fannie's voluminous coat.

"Do the Mojos know yet?"

"Haven't told Orrie, and Noe's in Washington."

"Oh." Chester hesitated. "What's he doing down there?"

"He didn't want to stand in line here because he was so ashamed of being Japanese. So he went to Washington to ask our congressman to sign him up for the Army. Noe contributed heavily to his campaign, as you know."

"Jesus!" Chester rarely swore in front of a lady. "Oops—sorry, Fannie."

"I say worse than that."

"*He* didn't bomb Pearl Harbor. Why should he be ashamed? I wish I'd known. I never gave it a thought."

"Someone did." She stared in the direction of the ruined plant.

"Who could do something like this?"

"Who knows what people think anymore? Noe's Japanese-born, I guess that's enough."

"He's one of us." Chester crossed his arms over his muscled chest.

" 'One of us' means white, Anglo-Saxon, and Protestant, with a few Catholics thrown in for seasoning."

"Ah, I don't think that way."

"Neither do I, Chessy, but plenty do. He's a target. They bombed us, we'll burn one of their own. Kill two birds with one stone—sort of. The Rifes own the warehouse. Noe just rents it."

He quietly watched the figures in their big fire helmets. "What next?"

"God only knows—if He cares." She stroked the cat's smooth head. "At least Matilda's safe."

"And you, too." He sighed. "I was on my way home and saw the red ball in the sky." He checked his watch. "Bet Juts is wondering where I am."

"She'll understand." Fannie sighed deeply. A puff of cold breath floated toward the windshield in the acrid air. "Guess I'd better go tell Orrie. She's already having fits because Noe's enlisting. This will really set her off."

"He speaks Japanese. That makes him pretty valuable."

"I'll swing by the T.P.—what do you think?" She had picked up Juts's name for Louise's residence. "Orrie will be needing Louise."

"Good idea," Chester agreed.

"You know, I had a funny feeling something like this would happen. Ever since Fairy Thatcher disappeared in Germany back in thirty-seven, I've never felt right about the world. She's dead, of course. I know perfectly well she's dead. To be a rich woman and fall for that socialist crap—poor sweet thing. She never did have the sense God gave a goose. I expect the S.S. shot her, or someone in a spanking-new uniform put her down. I don't know, Chester. I'm an old woman. The world's gone crazy, it seems to me."

Gallantly, he protested, "Fannie Jump, no one will ever call you old—and the world has gone crazy. I think Fairy knew it before we did."

"Well, she died for it. If the Germans wouldn't listen to their own kind they weren't going to listen to an American tell them the Nazis were evil." Tears welled in her eyes. "Celeste and I sit and talk sometimes. People have changed. *This* country has changed. It's not just that we're getting old and cranky . . . you can smell the violence." She stopped, then grumbled, "Here comes that goddamned nosy Popeye. Can you imagine the kind of woman that will marry him? She'll—"

A tap on the window interrupted her. She rolled it down.

"Mrs. Creighton, I forgot to ask you the exact time you noticed the burning smell."

"About eight-thirty."

"Thank you. Hello, Chester. Do you know anything?"

"I'm dumb as a sack of hammers, Popeye, you know that."

He peered over his spectacles. "Well, then how did you know there was a fire?"

"I saw the red glow on my way home so I headed in this direction." He reached over to pet the frightened cat. "Heard the sirens, too."

Popeye flipped the pages on his stenographer's pad. "Let me double-check this." He smiled at Fannie. "You saw a car pull away about the time you smelled the fire?"

"Popeye, I told you. I saw an old Ford, a Model A, and the license plate was painted over."

"Hmm."

"Why didn't you enlist?" A hint of malice laced her voice.

Unperturbed, he replied, "Flat feet."

"How convenient," she acidly remarked.

"You could join the Civil Air Patrol," Chessy said mildly.

"Being a reporter's a twenty-four-hour job. A free press is the backbone of a democracy, so I'm playing my part."

"I'll just bet you are." Fannie glared up at him.

"Any idea who would do such a thing?" Popeye focused on Chessy.

"A real shit-ass."

"Now, now," he chided, "you know we can't print that."

"Don't, then." Chester felt a ball of anger rising in his throat. "Whoever did this ought to be horsewhipped in Runnymede Square. Noe Mojo can't help being Japanese-born any more than I can help my people being English. He's a good man. You know, Popeye, Noe's not a rich man. He can't cover these losses."

"Rifes own the building." Popeye scribbled some more.

"They may own it, but we don't know the arrangement. What if Noe is held liable? He'll go bankrupt."

"I'll call Zeb Vance. Thanks for the lead."

Zeb Vance owned an insurance agency in town.

"Suit yourself," Fannie said. "Popeye, I'm cutting this interview short. Orrie needs me."

A light went on in his eyes. "Oh."

"Yeah, and if you follow me and try to take pictures I'll bust your face in. Might even be an improvement." She turned on her motor, gunned it, and left Popeye standing in the parking lot.

29

The Curl 'n' Twirl was somber the next morning.

Juts and Louise hadn't the energy to pick on each other, much less on anybody else.

As friends came in for their appointments, they mourned recent events. Who would set a deliberate fire in a place like Runnymede?

Theories abounded, several women insisting the culprit had to be a thrill-seeking teenager. The most disquieting opinion was Celeste Chalfonte's. She suggested a situation like Pearl Harbor gave lazy people the opportunity to extract revenge. The act only appeared political.

"What do you mean, exactly?" Juts held the nail-polish brush steady over Celeste's long, aristocratic fingers.

"Noe is a success. The arsonist is not. The arsonist is the worm that turned."

"So you think it's one of us."

"Not one of us in this room—but yes."

Julia shuddered. "What an awful thought."

Louise was making up a bleaching solution for Ev Most, who would deny it if asked. Ev, Juts's best friend, had just endured a six-month ordeal in Clarksburg, West Virginia, caring for her husband's dying mother. The suffering soul finally went to her reward. "When old Brutus was alive we could blame every tragedy on him."

"The current crop of Rifes would rather suck blood than spill it." Celeste leaned back, her eyes half closed. "Brutus was at least a formidable enemy. No—this is some small, inconsequential person who now feels very powerful indeed." Then she asked, "When does Noe's train arrive?"

"Seven-thirty," Louise replied. She had already told everyone that Orrie had taken the news like a trouper, rejoicing that Matilda was alive.

"Ladies, we should make an effort to greet that train."

Many other people shared Celeste's sentiments. When Noe disembarked at the station, his friends and well-wishers were there along with the inevitable Popeye Huffstetler.

Noe informed the irritating reporter that he had been accepted into the Army and would most likely be assigned to cryptographer duties, decoding messages from the enemy.

"How do you feel fighting against your country?" Popeye asked.

Noe, calm in the face of stupidity, replied, "This is my country."

"But aren't you angry? Someone burned down your business."

Noe shrugged. "I'm angry, I'm sad."

"Who do you think did such a thing?" Popeye persisted.

"Will you shut up?" Chessy pulled Noe away.

Walter Falkenroth was in the group, but he had an ironclad rule never to interfere with his reporters. He did, however, cast Popeye a disapproving stare.

Orrie held up until she embraced her husband, then she cried like a baby.

"All our hard work," she sobbed.

He whispered in her ear, "It's all right, baby. We're still young. We'll build back up after this war is over."

Extra Billy, his arm around Mary, kissed her cheek.

"Billy, do you know anything about this?" Mary asked her source of wisdom.

"I don't, but I'd sure like to find out."

A mist covered her eyes. "I can't believe you're going to leave me."

"I'll be back." He kissed her again.

Zeb Vance pushed his way up to the front. "Noe, I want you to know Julius and Pole Rife are working with me. We'll get this sorted out. Don't worry."

"Thanks, Zeb."

"I'm shipping out in six weeks. If we don't have the *i*'s dotted and the *t*'s crossed, Priscilla Donaldson in my office will take over the case. She'll do a good job." He shook Noe's hand and joked, "Guess you girls will have to get along without us."

Mary's loud crying pierced the silence. Then other women started crying, too.

Father O'Reilly raised his hand in a benediction. "Friends, let's pray together."

And so they did, each one knowing it would be the last time they would all be together.

30

Wearing her ankle boots with the fur lining had helped keep out the cold at first, but Juts had been on her feet shopping all day. By now her toes were blue.

Louise, Toots, and Juts each took one day off work to do their Christmas shopping. Juts thought she'd taken care of everyone—she'd bought Yoyo a big catnip mouse and Buster and Doodlebug chews—then she realized Hansford needed a present. She hadn't warmed to the sick man, but she couldn't ignore him—not at Christmas.

As for her customers, she gave each one a free manicure. That way no one could say she played favorites.

She knew that as she fell asleep tonight she'd remember somebody she'd forgotten.

As she passed Senior Epstein's jewelry store she spied Chester. She scrunched down, peeking around the doorjamb. He was buying gold shell earrings. She loved earrings!

A few desultory snowflakes circled down from a leaden sky. The packages were getting heavy. Chilled to the bone, Juts sat down on a bench in the square, wishing she could be a pigeon sitting high up in a branch, watching the people below.

A huge wreath was laid at the statue of the three Confederate soldiers. The snow in their eye sockets made them look blind. An even bigger wreath, compliments of Caesura Frothingham, adorned George Gordon Meade. The snow fell harder. The lights of the shops twinkled through the deepening gray and white.

She felt for one fleeting moment how precious this place was to her, and she knew that across the Atlantic Ocean an English-woman she would never meet loved her own little town just as much. But Juts was safe and sound. The Englishwoman was not. She felt as though her heart would burst with sorrow for all the women in the world. They had yet to wage one war but they sure suffered and died in them.

Small halos of red, yellow, green, and blue surrounded the colored Christmas lights in the shop windows. She stood up, shaking off the snow, and headed for the Bon-Ton, her last stop.

All the swirling snow, the colors, the sharp cold, the sound of tires with chains on snow, the occasional honk of a horn, the bark of a dog tired of waiting for its master outside a shop...such sounds made up her Christmas.

Juts wasn't a philosophical woman. She took life as it came. She didn't know where her life was heading, only that it was get-ting there faster than she had anticipated.

She thought of her life as bumper cars on overdrive, a pinwheel with naked ladies on it, candy bars and crapshoots, Longhorn steers and red-hot poker games, cartwheels at sunrise and a hint of sad-ness at sunset. She recalled the smell of Buster's fur when he came in from the rain and Yoyo's funny little habit of retrieving crinkled-up paper. She thought of Chester's laugh, the smell of gasoline and new-mown hay, and now the moist scent of falling snow.

For the first time she wondered what her mother's memories were. If this was what made a life—impressions—then what were Cora's?

She pushed open the revolving door at the Bon-Ton and stepped inside, looking in childlike wonderment at all the big support columns wrapped in red-and-gold paper. Each wooden counter was decorated with red-and-gold streamers with a Santa on the top center, except the different Santas were dressed in the uniforms of the Army, Navy, Marines, Air Force, and Coast Guard. The mannequins wore the uniforms of the Allies.

Someone bumped into her from behind.

"I'm sorry," Juts said and stepped out of the way.

Aunt Dimps, also laden with packages, replied, "Julia Ellen, why don't you bring Yoyo in here and see what she can do with the decorations?"

Juts laughed, then thought how lucky she was to live in Runnymede . . . even if she did have to share it with the likes of Josephine Smith.

31

Mary folded in half a sheet of medium blue paper and carefully slid it into the airmail envelope. Her mother would wail at the extravagance of airmail. That would lead to recounting Mary's other foolish expenditures. She took the precaution of tucking her letters into her book bag and dashing to the post office before school.

A light rap on the door made her quickly place her chemistry book over the envelope.

"Come in."

"It's snowing again. Want to go down to the pond? We could ice skate."

Mary glanced out the window into the darkness. "Mmm, I don't know."

"Oh, come on, Mar, the fire department set up big torches so we can see. Everyone's going. Isn't that swell?"

"You go on."

"Bet you were writing Billy again. Say, if you come skating with me you can tell him all about it. He's a good skater."

Needing to be begged, Mary weakened a little. "Well . . ."

"You can tell him who was there, what they wore, who fell, and how much you miss him."

"I can't live without him. I think about him every minute of every day."

Blankly Maizie nodded.

"You don't understand," Mary said crossly.

"Uh—gee, Mary, that's not fair." Maizie pulled open a drawer.

"Hey, those are my socks."

"If you're not going I need them."

"Use your own damn socks."

"I'm telling Momma that you're using foul language. If you skated you'd be in a better mood and you wouldn't need to curse." She removed her ankle socks as she dropped on the corner of the bed.

"Put those back!" Mary bounced out of her chair to grab the socks.

Maizie put them behind her. "Uh-uh."

"I didn't say I wasn't going. You jumped to conclusions."

Maizie sat on the long socks. "Read me your letter and I'll give you back your socks—only if you're really going to skate."

"Ha." Mary snorted. "I'm not reading you anything."

"How am I ever gonna know what it's like to be in love?"

Mary, dying to share her newly discovered emotions, surreptitiously picked up her chemistry book. "Only parts of it. I'm not reading all of it."

"Okay."

" 'Dear Bill' "—she cleared her throat—" 'Everything is gray without you . . .' "

Maizie interrupted. "It's always gray in wintertime."

With a superior air, Mary shrugged. "You have no sense of—poetry." Mary folded her letter. "I'm not reading any more to you."

"Oh, come on. I'll sharpen your blades."

Mary flipped open the page, the paper making a light rattling sound. " 'I think about you when I see the sky. I think about you when I see mistletoe. I think about you when Doodlebug barks—all the time. I think . . .' "

Fifteen minutes later Mary finished reading her torrid epistle.

"How romantic." Maizie dreamily fell back on the bed.

Mary swiftly leapt from the chair and snatched one of the socks exposed underneath Maizie's buttock. "Gotcha."

"Here." Maizie threw the other one after, sitting up. "What does Billy write?"

Mary pulled out one letter from Parris Island, South Carolina. The handwriting was an oversized scrawl. " 'Dear Mary, the D.I. chews my ass. The chiggers is awful. I hate this place. Love, Bill.' "

Waiting a moment, Maizie swung her feet to the floor. "That's it?"

"Men aren't good at writing letters." Mary defended her laconic husband.

Showing surprising maturity, Maizie said, "At least you know he's thinking of you. Come on, let's go to the pond."

32

Tobacco flecks dotted Hansford Hunsenmeir's bluish lips. Despite his breathing difficulties, he craved that soothing nicotine. If he was going to die he might as well die on his own terms.

He sucked on his cigar, and a gray-blue line lazed up to the ceiling in Celeste's kitchen. Hansford, a small mountain of tack in front of him on the big wooden table, possessed nimble fingers. O.B. Huffstetler, Celeste's stableman, had fallen behind on his chores, this being one of them. The young man was exhausted by his six-month-old infant, a boy they had named Kirk but called Peepbean. Peepbean, born with leather lungs, put them to good use throughout the night. No one had warned O.B. or his wife that infants are hazardous to your health as well as your personality.

Neatly laid out to his left were the leather-repair tools, while on Hansford's right were pieces of rich English leather in Havana brown. Nobody made better tack leather or better steel for bits than the English.

"Julia, do you remember the time you saved up pennies and nickels?" her father asked. "You couldn't have been three yet but you knew money was something special, so you saved and saved every time someone gave you a penny for ice cream. Then you marched right across the square to the Bon-Ton and bought yourself a little iron elephant bank with an upraised trunk. Louise laughed at you because you spent all your money on the bank and had none left to put into it. You cried and cried. I gave you a penny to put in your bank and you stopped crying. Then Louise cried because she said I loved you more than I loved her. So I gave her a penny and she shut up. You offered your bank for her penny's safekeeping." He rested his cigar in a big ashtray as he set to work on a torn throatlatch. "She refused because she said how could she tell her penny from your penny."

"I don't remember about Louise's penny." Juts reached for a laced rein where one of the laces had broken. She, too, was good with her hands. "I still have the bank, though, and it has that first penny in it—for luck."

"The damnedest things pop into my mind." He reached for waxed thread. "Maizie wants a dress for a Christmas party. Louise won't buy it for her. How about I give you the money and you buy the kid the dress. Louise won't like it, though."

"Louise will get over it." Julia noticed a flame-red cardinal darting in a holly bush by the garden. Celeste's kitchen was her favorite room in the entire grand house. "I feel sorry for the kid. She's playing second fiddle to Mary forever. She's asked to her first big party. She and Mary are so differently shaped she can't wear Mary's old clothes." She exhaled through her nose.

He punched the thread through a hole he'd made with an awl.

Cora came in and put up the teapot. "You two are nesty."

"Maizie's party dress," Hansford said with no further explanation.

Cora nodded at her younger daughter. She had heard three sides of the story already: Louise's, Maizie's, and now Juts's. Maizie had been invited to a dance and had found the perfect dress, green velvet with white fur trim, at the Bon-Ton. Juts had watched her try it on and told her it looked beautiful. But the dress was thirty-one dollars and Louise had refused even to discuss it.

Celeste, wearing a silk kimono in a deep, rich navy blue, pushed open the swinging door.

"I need something hot."

"On the stove."

"Mmm." She inspected the pot.

"A watched pot never boils," Cora told her.

"I know." She smiled. "Naturally, you all will remain silent about my wearing a Japanese article of clothing."

"Better than lederhosen," Juts cracked.

"My legs would get cold." Celeste joined them at the table and rooted through her tack. "It's always something, isn't it? I've broken two martingales—actually, I didn't break them, Rambunctious did—and, oh thank you."

Cora put the teacup in front of Celeste and then served Hansford, Juts, and finally herself before sitting next to Celeste. "Maizie's fit to be tied."

"She can't go to the party naked." Celeste laughed.

"Louise will pitch a hissy." Hansford shook his head.

"According to Louise *she* is the only mother in the world. None of the rest of us know anything. She even crosses you, Momma," Juts said.

Cora smiled. "Louise gets the big head." She added, "Even if you all buy Maizie that party dress, Louise will take it back. You know it for a fact."

"Yeah. Hateful, mean, and bossy—those are the facts."

"Spoken like a true little sister," Celeste noted. "I was one myself."

Hansford took another drag from his cigar. He was watching Juts closely. "She's like your mother," he observed to Cora, chuckling.

"Well—Momma sure had a sense of humor."

"Bepe was nutty as a fruitcake." Hansford called Harriet Buckingham by her nickname.

"*I'm* not crazy. Louise is crazy. I'm perfectly sane."

"Isn't memory convenient?" Celeste said.

"Just a minute here, Hansford, Bepe was not tetched at all." Cora rattled her teacup, her hands delicate even though she'd put on weight over the years.

"She dropped a net over your father at Pauline Basehart's and drug him right out in the street. Sure caught those girls off guard. I tell you, it was a spectacle."

"Never mind. That was long ago."

"Who was Pauline Basehart?" Juts asked.

"The local madam," Celeste informed Juts.

"Mom!" Juts exclaimed.

"My father had a weakness for women."

"Weakness—it killed him. There he was in the middle of Hanover Street, naked as a jaybird, with Bepe beating his ass until his nose bled. He couldn't get out of the net and Pauline wasn't going to free him. She sent a girl to fetch Ardant Trumbull— that's Pearlie's great-uncle—who was sheriff then."

"I didn't know that," Juts exclaimed.

Hansford laughed. "Girl, there was a whole heap of living in Runnymede before you made an appearance."

"My father—" Cora shrugged. She didn't know what to say.

"He was no better nor worse than many, but Bepe fixed his wagon." Hansford shook his head.

"You think I'm like Bepe?" Juts asked.

"All over again." Hansford clapped his hands. "To the teeth."

"Old men live in the past," Cora rebuked him.

"At least I remember it. Harold Mundis's grandpa couldn't even remember his children when he was my age."

"The things I'm learning." Juts got up and poured everyone more tea. "Celeste, I'm dying of starvation. May I have one of your scones?"

"Put them on the table. We'll all enjoy them."

Juts admired the hand-painted china as she placed the scones in the middle of the table.

"We still haven't solved the Maizie problem."

Ramelle opened and shut the front door. They heard her stamping the snow off her feet.

"Anyone home?"

"We're in the kitchen," Celeste answered.

Ramelle walked in rubbing her hands. "It's getting frigid out there. Scones! Cora, you've outdone yourself."

Ramelle squeezed in next to Celeste and heard the entire dolorous tale of Maizie and the emerald dress she coveted at the Bon-Ton. Cora began making more tea.

"Why can't she wear one of Spotts's dresses? Maizie's about her size now, don't you think?"

"Grand idea," Celeste declared.

They marched upstairs to the huge cedar closet. The effort of climbing the stairs exhausted Hansford. Breathing hard, he sat on a Regency chair. Many of the dresses were out-of-date, but one lovely chiffon, almost a flame-red, was perfect.

"Maizie will look like Christmas itself," Ramelle said.

"What if Louise says this is charity?" Juts felt the sheer fabric.

"I'll take care of that," Celeste volunteered.

As they walked downstairs, Julia said to Ramelle, "Louise is forever harping on how being a mother is different. She's always saying I can't understand. You're a mother. You don't seem any different to me than before you had Spottiswood."

"On the outside, no; on the inside, yes. I had to put someone else first."

"Oh," came Juts's weak reply.

Cora held on to the finial at the bottom of the dark mahogany steps, waiting for Juts. "Don't fret so about it. You'll never have a baby if you think about it all the time. Gets your innards worked up."

"She's right about that." Celeste put her arm around Juts's shoulders.

"I put Chessy first. How much different can it be?"

"Chessy's not helpless," Ramelle offered.

"Wanna bet?" Juts replied.

"All women think all men are helpless without them," Celeste said. "Truth is they do fine without us. They might not have as much fun, but they'll live."

Cora disagreed. "A woman can live without a man; a man can't live without a woman."

"What do you think, Hansford? Speak for your entire sex."

"Well, a man might be able to live without a woman, but life wouldn't be worth living. I've seen men die of loneliness in those mines, yes, I have." He changed the subject back to Juts's dilemma. "Girl, if you want a baby, then you should have one."

"I don't know if I can." Juts swallowed the words.

"You can," Celeste said with authority. "After all, the doctor didn't find anything wrong with you. It's Chester you've got to get to the doctor."

"Men are peculiar about those things." Hansford coughed; it took him a few moments to get his breath back. "If he won't go, Julia, there are children out there needing a home. You think about it."

"I don't know if Chessy will raise a child that isn't his."

"Have you asked him?" Celeste usually took the sensible approach, so people's tender emotions were left out of the equation.

"No." Juts's voice grew fainter.

"Well—ask him."

"I can't. I'm afraid." Julia's chin trembled.

"Maybe you can find some subtle way to bring up the subject," Ramelle said soothingly.

"A child that's unwanted will be illegitimate. Mother Smith would have a cow—"

Celeste interrupted. "Mother Smith is a cow."

Julia smiled weakly. "Chessy won't go against his mother and she won't want someone that's not her own blood."

"I think you're right about Mother Smith, but maybe you underestimate your husband—after all, he married you," Ramelle said.

33

C hessy was surprised when he arrived for his dancing lesson and found Trudy had two other couples there, friends from Baltimore. She said this was her Christmas present to him. He'd gotten too used to dancing with her—he needed to dance with other women.

After a few false starts he discovered that if he gave a strong lead the lady would follow.

After the lesson the group stayed to chat. Since the next week was Christmas, Trudy was booked at dances every single night, either as an escort or to help things along. The Sisters of Gettysburg, the Daughters of the Confederacy, the Kiwanis Club, the Elks, the Sons of Cincinnatus, the Pilot Club, the North Runnymede Country Club . . . everyone was throwing parties.

Before leaving, Chessy gave her a small present wrapped in gold paper with a red ribbon.

"Don't open until Christmas."

"What a sweet thing to do!"

"Merry Christmas, folks." He waved to the couples as he opened the door to leave.

Trudy followed him into the hall. "I have a present for you, too."

He smiled. This was the second surprise of the evening.

She dashed back into the studio, emerging with a narrow box about thirty-six inches long. The bow was a big centerpiece almost like a paper chrysanthemum, with curly tendrils. "Merry Christmas, Mr. Smith."

He laughed at the formal address. "Do I have to wait until Christmas to open it?"

"No, but if you don't it means you're undisciplined."

"All right, then." He stepped down onto the top step. "I'll save it."

She leaned forward and kissed him on the cheek. "Merry Christmas."

He wanted to say something but blushed instead, turning to hurry down the stairs.

34

Mary appraised her sister. The chiffon dress draped perfectly on Maizie. Mary wasn't the least bit jealous.

She'd received a postcard reading, "Miss you. Your Billy." From this terse communication she divined red-hot oceans of love.

The snow shone blue in the twilight. The house lights splashed gold over the snow. Maizie, in a frenzy of anticipation, kept asking, "Is he here yet?"

Louise answered, "You've got an hour to go, Maizie."

"Momma, my hair will fall by then."

"No, it won't, but if you don't sit still you'll wrinkle your dress."

"When does Aunt Juts get here?"

"When she gets here. She stopped by church. It's food-basket night."

"When do we do that, Mom?" Mary wondered, although her mind was in South Carolina at Billy's training camp.

"Tomorrow. This would be easier if all the churches coordinated their baskets to the poor on the same day. Your aunt ties the bows on most of them since she's so good at it. Maizie, sit still!"

"Mother, time is so slow."

"Just wait until you're my age. It'll fly fast enough."

Doodlebug wandered in looking for food or company, preferring the food.

"Maizie, have you written your thank-you to Mrs. Chalfonte yet?"

"How can I write her a thank-you before I've gone to the party? I have to tell her what happened."

Louise pulled a sheet of paper and an envelope out of the little secretary in the corner. "At least address the envelope. I know you. You'll put off writing and I'll be embarrassed."

"No, I won't." Maizie sat down at the secretary.

She wrote, "Mrs. Ramelle Chalfonte."

Before she could add the address, Mary held the end of the pen. "Wrong."

"What's wrong?" Maizie frowned.

"Mom, she has to write 'Mrs. Curtis Chalfonte,' doesn't she?"

Louise leaned over Maizie's shoulder. "Oh, Maizie, you know better than that."

"Better than what?" Maizie, on edge, was getting irritated.

"You address a lady by her married name. You wouldn't write 'Mrs. Ramelle Chalfonte' unless her husband was dead."

"Mother, Ramelle doesn't care."

"Whether her husband is dead or not?" Mary teased.

"You know what I mean." Maizie slapped the pen on the secretary. Ink spritzed across the leather pad.

"Idiot!" Louise grabbed the pen. "If you get any on that dress I'll never be able to fix it."

"I'm sorry." Maizie hung her head. She pulled another envelope from the slot and wrote the correct form of address. "There."

"Now, tomorrow morning, first thing, you write her a thank-you. I mean it."

"I will."

"How come Ramelle married Celeste's brother?" Mary idly asked.

"Because she couldn't marry Celeste," Maizie answered flatly.

"Maizie, where do you get such ideas?" Louise was scandalized.

"It's no secret." Maizie shrugged.

"Know-it-all. You have no idea of the relationship between Celeste and Ramelle. Nobody knows what goes on behind closed doors."

"G-Mom does." Maizie defiantly stuck out her chin.

"G-Mom ought to shut her trap." Louise sighed.

"Mom, nobody cares," Mary said.

"You stay out of this." Louise pursed her lips, Christmas-red today. "Maizie, will you stop wiggling. You are going to ruin that dress. If you spill one drop of soft drink on that dress I will wring your neck until your eyes pop. Do you hear me?"

"I hear you."

Juts stuck her head in the back door and gave the twoey whistle.

Maizie hurried to the kitchen. "Aunt Juts, what do you think?"

"Prettiest thing I ever saw." Juts tossed her scarf over the chair. "Psst." Juts palmed Maizie a tube of lightly colored lipstick. "Don't let your mother see it."

"Thanks." Maizie's petite nose wrinkled in delight.

"And don't try to put it on without a mirror. Takes years to perfect that trick."

A rumble outside, then a knock on the door, announced Maizie's date. Angus wore a red bow tie and cummerbund with his rented tuxedo. Louise welcomed him.

"Here." He handed Maizie an orchid corsage.

"Would you like me to put it on?" Mary offered.

Angus nodded and Louise waved to his father, driving the Oldsmobile.

Juts handed Maizie's coat to Angus. He held it for her, everybody exchanged polite farewells, and Louise leaned against the door when Maizie traipsed down the drive.

"I have aged ten years since last Christmas. Two daughters. Double the trouble. Why me, Lord?"

"Because you pissed Him off," Juts said.

"That's not funny." Louise stood at the window and waved some more until the car disappeared around the corner.

Mary, not ready for a litany of her misdeeds, bowed out. "I'm going upstairs to study."

"Don't lie to me. You're going upstairs to write Billy another novel. That boy will go blind reading your letters. I can barely read your handwriting."

"It helps if you wear glasses." Juts was hungry.

"I don't need glasses."

"Is that a fact? I've noticed you holding the newspaper as far away from your face as you can get it."

"Everyone does that."

Mary tiptoed upstairs.

Louise trailed Juts to the kitchen, where Juts reached into the icebox, helping herself to her sister's cheese. They sat down at the table.

Louise's eyebrows knit together. "You know, I feel bad. I called Maizie an idiot tonight."

"She won't remember. She's too excited."

"Julia, sometimes I say things and I don't mean them. They just fly out of my mouth."

"I know."

"What's that supposed to mean?" Louise got her back up.

"It means I know—I do it myself."

"But I wonder, what will Mary and Maizie remember? Are they going to remember me as this mean mother? They just prey on my nerves sometimes and I think if I hear their voices or the word 'Mother' one more time I will scream. And then something ugly pops right out of my mouth."

"Everybody does that."

"Pearlie doesn't."

"Men don't count."

This made Louise laugh. "That's a new one. Especially from you."

"You know what I mean. They're raised differently. They keep more stuff bottled up. They probably think as much hateful stuff as we do, but they don't say it."

"I don't know about that. Paul can miss the most obvious things. Really simple things, like forgetting to tell the girls they look pretty. That's not a good example, but you know what I mean."

"Chester does that, too."

"There's a part of their brains missing. I don't know exactly what it is but I know there's a blank space up there. I get afraid that Paul is saving everything up and then, *boom*." Louise threw both her hands up in the air. "That's what happened to Hansford."

"Yeah, he went up like a rocket and came down like a stick." Juts paused a moment. "Do you really think Pearlie could be storing up anger or jealousy or something and one of these days he'll explode?"

"I don't know."

"He seems pretty levelheaded to me. Quit worrying. You've got too much on your mind. Lay it by."

"I'm forty. I'll admit it to you," she whispered. "You know anyway, but I wish you wouldn't say things in public about my age. Just wait until you get there. I won't pick on you."

"Promise?"

"I promise. But here I am at forty and I feel like I'm supposed to know something, except I don't know what it is." Louise turned up her palms in supplication.

"Maybe there isn't anything to know, Wheezie. Maybe we make it up as we go along."

"No. There has to be some reason."

"I don't think so. Life is a crap game, two bits a shot. When you're cold, you're cold, and when you're hot, you're hot."

They sat for a while, then Louise said, "I'm afraid life is passing me by."

Juts got up and hugged her sister. "No, it's not. Life can't pass us by. We are life."

35

Each Christmas, carolers sang their way to the square, moving in four groups down each main artery: Hanover Street, Baltimore Street, Frederick Street, and the Emmitsburg pike. Those who could commandeer sleighs, hay wagons, carts, gigs, phaetons, or any other horse-drawn conveyance lorded it over those on foot. Blankets for people and horses, wicker baskets bursting with food, jugs filled with libations of varying intensities, plus apples and carrots for the horses, were crammed into the carriages.

Cherubs, usually accompanied by a mounted adult, sat their ponies astride. Many houses in Runnymede had stables in the rear built from the same materials as the main house.

With so many people parading through the crunchy snow, it was a wonder anyone remained at home to serenade. The small brick houses, the lonely frame ones, and the grander stone ones had big bay wreaths on the doors and mistletoe hanging in archways; candles in the windows awaited the singers.

Every year Mary Miles Mundis lashed her husband, Harry, to spray paint a tree white. For days afterward he walked around town with speckles of white paint on his face and hands. Then Mary Miles, called M.M. by everyone, hung enormous shiny red balls on each branch along with red garlands. The tree excited comment and inspired competition from Junior McGrail and Caesura Frothingham, her neighbors on either side. They, too, bullied husbands, sons, workers, and friends into spray painting trees white. Junior graced hers in the emerald-green of Ireland; after all, she was a McGrail, even if by marriage. So Caesura adorned her tree in royal blue balls with golden garlands, very Union.

Julia Ellen festooned her tree with everything but the kitchen sink, whereas Louise, considering herself the Dorothy Draper of Christmas trees, wrapped a deciduous tree in white cotton and then hung multicolored balls, cranberry strings for garlands, and a big angel on top plus tons of tinsel.

Celeste, having the highest ceilings in Runnymede, sported the biggest tree—it needed guy wires to hold it up—except for the one smack in the center of Runnymede Square.

O.B. Huffstetler had been grooming Celeste's matched pair of saddlebreds. She loved driving them because they reminded her of the grand hackneys she had seen in Rotten Row in Hyde Park as a small child. Glorious as the standardbreds from Hanover Shoe Farms were, she would make pilgrimages to Kentucky to pick up saddlebreds for driving. These two mares, matched bays, were named Minnie and Monza. Minnie had a star on her forehead and Monza had a stripe down her face.

As the sun set, the activity became more feverish in the little barns and big stables surrounding Runnymede.

Two long surcingles with bells of different sizes were draped over Minnie and Monza. Their breast collars rang with bells. The rosettes where the browbands met the crowns carried small bells, as did the back straps to the cruppers. Two silver bells also hung on either side of the sleigh. Celeste was driving, Ramelle seated next to her. Julia, who loved to drive, snuggled in next to Chester and Louise. Pearlie sat opposite them.

Mary and Maizie, far too grand to be seen with their parents, were singing with the group walking down the Emmitsburg pike.

Celeste and company were moving up Frederick Street.

Cora and Hansford met Martel Falkenroth, Walter's father,

and a boyhood friend of Hansford's. Martel drove a sleigh he had bought from the Amish about the time of the Spanish-American War.

As various groups assembled at their respective meeting places, the squeals of children could be heard all over the Mason-Dixon line.

The carolers stopping by each house were plied with food, drink, and cheer. Often the inhabitants would bundle up and join them so that as the voices moved ever closer to the square, the sound grew stronger.

Maizie, who had been the hit of the party, didn't just emerge from her sister's shadow, she catapulted from under it. Surrounded by friends, many of them boys and therefore especially useful in relations with the girls, Maizie glowed with excitement. Mary, artfully shedding a tear over Billy when speaking to her friends, didn't notice this transformation at first. However, as the party moved eastward on the pike, she finally realized her little sister was the belle of the ball. It seemed impossible to her that this worm could have blossomed into a butterfly. Mary caught herself. Maizie wasn't a butterfly, she was a moth. She, Mary, was the butterfly. Maizie could be one of those pretty moths, though. Then again, what good did it do to be a butterfly if no one noticed?

As they came within a block of the square, the Frederick Street carolers could hear the other carolers as they moved down the various roads. A tingle shot down Juts's spine as she heard their distant voices floating up from the three other directions. She remembered the first time she had heard this as a child. At five she'd been allowed to go caroling, but, pooped out, had to be carried on her mother's shoulders. She thought the night was magic then and it was magic now. Big chunks of stars glittered in a crystal-clear black sky. The moon, surrounded by a large pulsating halo, smiled down on them. The shepherd's-crook streetlamps, bent over like angels, cast a warm glow over the packed snow.

As the groups entered the square, each burst into "Adeste Fideles," trying to outdo one another as they proceeded to the huge symmetrical tree. Sitting under it was old Patience Horney, tone-deaf, caterwauling to her heart's content. She had her pretzel cart beside her.

Big Digby Vance, the band director at South Runnymede High—called Tubby behind his back and Tonneau by Celeste—stepped forward and held up his baton. Everyone quieted.

" 'Adeste Fideles,' " he said.

Hundreds of voices in sync boomed out, " 'Adeste fideles, Laeti triumphantes—' "

Little Barbara Tangerman screamed as her pony bolted. She was in no danger, but the pony had had quite enough—not so much of the singing as of Barbara. Bucky Nordness, astride his good pal, Target, took off after her. It was a good thing he'd stayed mounted. Everyone else had dismounted, holding their horses' reins. Bucky caught Toothpaste in front of the Bon-Ton, where the pony had stopped to admire the big store window decorated with Santa and his reindeer. Barbara Tangerman, dumped in the snow, sniveled but was none the worse for her adventure. Toothpaste, enchanted by the reindeer, didn't want to follow Target. Lured by apples, he finally gave in.

As they sang "The First Noël" and "God Rest Ye Merry, Gentlemen," Julia noticed that some of the men were already in uniform. Those who had served in World War I and reenlisted thanks to special skills wore their uniforms. The young men soon to leave envied them.

Rillma Ryan, home for the holidays, sang with the Baltimore Street crowd—causing a sensation among the men just by breathing.

As Juts drank in the whole cocktail of happiness it was hard to believe that someone in this group or in one of those cozy houses had burned out Noe Mojo's business. She put the incident out of her mind, but it would pop back again like a headache. She decided she never would understand people. This chased away the headache.

Other reminders of the war would creep into her conscious-ness. She wondered, How were they celebrating the holiday in Paris? Or London? And what of Berlin—did they go about their Christmas festivities believing they were in the right? After all, they started the damned war. Why march into Poland or Czecho-slovakia? Did Hitler really think the Western nations wouldn't fight?

Were the German people told the truth? Maybe they didn't know over there.

A chill shot up her spine. *Maybe we don't know, either. Are we told the truth?*

If Popeye Huffstetler is an example of the free press, God help us, she thought to herself.

Then she thought of the huge poster in the post office. It showed people gossiping in an armaments factory while, behind them, a ship hit by torpedoes was sinking. "Loose Lips Sink Ships," read the warning.

The carolers had started on "It Came upon a Midnight Clear," Juts's favorite carol.

Even Mother Smith, on the other side of the tree, seemed to enjoy herself.

Maizie asked Cora if she thought people were singing carols in Germany.

"I expect." Cora handed her a red-sugared doughnut made specially by the Yosts for this occasion.

"I don't get it." Maizie blinked.

"What, sweetheart?" Cora watched Tubby's baton.

"They're like us, then."

"More or less." Cora readied for "Good King Wenceslas."

Maizie sang along with her grandmother. Adults made life complicated. If she ran the world there wouldn't be any wars, Maizie was sure of that.

After the caroling, people exchanged favors, kisses, hugs, food and drink. Bitter cold was fended off with inner fire. For one evening, domestic squabbles were set aside, financial troubles forgotten, cracked romances ignored, and old enmities muffled. Christmas Eve in Runnymede was about as close to heaven as a body could get.

Juts floated home on a cloud until she opened the door to her house and beheld her decorations shredded, the presents under the tree clawed to pieces, and the balls, as high as Yoyo could reach, smashed in glittering colored pieces on the floor.

This proved conclusively that cats do not have Christmas spirit. They might not even be Christians.

36

Christmas supper at Cora's, everyone ate like pigs.

Juts held up her glass. "Here's to 1942, Louise. We'll have paid off Flavius by May."

"Free and clear." Chessy clinked his glass to his wife's.

"Here's to an end to this war before—well, you know." Mary raised her glass.

Everyone drank and chattered, exchanging gifts. Juts oohed and aahed at the beautiful gold bracelet Chester gave her. She assumed the earrings she'd liked had gone to his mother, the bitch. They'd look better on her.

Trudy had given Chester a gentleman's walking stick. He

unwrapped it while at the store. Chester had given the gold shell earrings to Trudy. He wasn't sure it was proper to give her earrings— maybe he should have given her perfume—but the earrings looked like her.

Pearlie stood up. "I'm going to pick up Patience Horney."

"You are?" Louise smelled the wonderful fragrance of cherry wood in the fireplace.

"All her people are dead now and she's alone. I just this minute thought of it."

"Really? Did Rollie Englehard die this year?" Juts was losing track of time. "Was it this year?"

Rollie was Patience's last surviving cousin.

"I think he did," Cora replied.

"Be right back." Pearlie grabbed his hat and coat. Chessy followed him.

Twenty minutes later they returned with Patience, so happy she babbled. It made the others teary, not just because they were glad to make her happy, but because Patience's situation could be any one of theirs someday. Nobody ever knew what might happen. And it happens so damned fast.

37

Mary Miles Mundis declared she had second sight, a nifty concept since most people don't even have first sight: People see what they want to see.

Chester, not a man seeking arguments in order to display his intelligence, casually let such ideas go in one ear and out the other. He was one of those men who drive their wives to ask constantly, "Did you hear a word I said?" Not that Chessy pondered second sight, but if he'd paid a bit more attention to himself and others he would have known what was hurtling around the corner like a trolley car out of control. Maybe he could have ducked.

He left the hardware store at five to see his mother. Josephine, rolling pie dough, shook her rolling pin at him. "You're late."

Black-eyed peas bubbled in a pot on the stove because New Year's, commencing the following night at 12:01, she had to eat black-eyed peas for luck. Mother Smith first boiled them, then let them simmer on low, low heat, every now and then adding more water and molasses.

He didn't reply, but went down into the cellar to check the furnace. The coal-delivery man had left the doors to the coal chute open, so the frigid air was pouring in. He shut the doors and then shoveled coal into the furnace. He dusted himself off as he walked up the wooden stairs, which reverberated with each step. "Tommy left the doors open."

"That boy." She shook her head. "He'll never be able to take over his father's business."

"He's enlisted. Maybe when he comes home he'll be ready."

"Tom West enlisted?"

"Army. Ted Baeckle told me he scored so high on the entry tests that he'll be going to officers' training school after boot camp."

"That's a surprise."

"I don't know, Mother, maybe Tommy West is a square peg in a round hole. Someone else can run West and Co."

"That's ridiculous. Where do you get these ideas? Juts?" She squinted.

"You know, Mother, I've been thinking a lot lately. I surprise myself." His tone of voice was crisp. "I realize that I can't make you happy and make Juts happy. If I do something for you, she's upset. If I do something for her or agree with her, you're upset. I've decided I'm going to please myself. At least one person will be happy." He walked out the door.

It was snowing again so Chessy drove slowly to the dance studio and parked, as always, in the alleyway. He took the stairs two at a time and threw open the door. Trudy was wearing the lovely gold seashell earrings.

"Let's dance." He laughed, swept her in his arms, and kissed her. She returned the kiss with passion. It was a sure bet that Chester Smith's 1942 was going to be different from 1941.

38

Yoyo snuggled on the afghan drawn around Juts's legs as she flopped onto the sofa in front of the roaring fire. Buster, head on paws, stretched out on the floor in front of Juts because Yoyo wouldn't let him on the sofa.

"I told you to wear a hat when we went caroling."

Louise's admonition at this moment was not appreciated. "You say that every day there's a drop of moisture in the air, Louise. Don't take credit for being right one time out of thousands."

"You're not a good sick person." Louise handed her a hot tea. "Come on, Juts, drink a little of it."

"New Year's Eve, one of my favorite nights in the whole year, and I'm home sick. This is as bad as the time I got measles at Christmas."

"That was 1909!"

"So?" Juts squiggled farther down in the afghan, kicking the newspaper on the floor.

The headline of the *Clarion* read "Dusseldorf Bombed."

Wheezie picked up the paper and properly folded it. "Guess the Germans are getting back some of their own."

"You'd think they'd have the sense to realize if they're going to bomb London then the English will fly over the Channel and bomb them." She sat up a little straighter and reached for the tea. "Can you imagine, Wheezie, being high up in the air with people shooting at you from the ground and other planes coming at you to blow you out of the sky? I can't imagine it, really, and the cold air when those bomb doors open." She shivered.

"I could be on the ground but I couldn't be a pilot or a sailor." Louise folded her arms across her chest. "I want the ground under my feet at all times. Hey, where's Chessy?"

"Civil Air Patrol, emergency meeting. He's learning Morse code and semaphore."

"If the Japs bombed Pearl Harbor off aircraft carriers, why can't the Germans do the same thing?" Louise asked.

"Do the Germans have aircraft carriers?"

"I don't know, but they have submarines." Louise stared into the fire.

"Guess I should let him go to the party with you and Pearlie, huh?"

"Well, he can't dance. He'll just sit around and watch the rest of us."

"He can drink and throw confetti with the best of them." Juts's laugh turned into a cough.

Buster barked, hearing the car turn down the block before

the human ears could pick up the tread sound. Within a minute Juts and Louise heard the car and saw the lights, which were soon switched off.

Chessy pushed open the back door, his arms full of groceries. "Hey."

"Hi, Chess." Louise walked into the kitchen to help him with the bags. "The patient is"—she lowered her voice—"crabby."

"You're talking about me," Juts yelled from the living room. "I know you are."

Chester tiptoed into the living room, face solemn. "We were talking about you." He shook his head. "Tuberculosis. Won't be long."

Louise sang a hymn from the kitchen, where she was putting away groceries.

"You wouldn't think it was funny if you were sick on New Year's Eve," Juts pouted.

Louise brought in orange juice and a bottle of gin as well as little party hats and streamers. "Whoopie!"

Juts smiled. "Chester, did you think of this by yourself?"

"Yep."

"I'm going to make mild orange blossoms because you're sick. You'll get drunk as a skunk if you aren't careful." Louise measured out the gin, pouring it into a tall glass tumbler, then she added the orange juice and gently mixed the concoction. Finally she poured the bright liquid into martini glasses, which Chester brought out for the occasion.

"Does this mean I'm going to get drunk and you're going to leave me?" Juts imploringly asked her husband.

"No, it means we'll have our own party." He put on a hat.

Louise put one on, then bent down to fix up Buster, who shook his head and tried to work it off. He finally did. Yoyo eyed Louise with suspicion. Louise didn't try to put a hat on her.

Juts picked out a purple hat with a little tassel on it, bright green. "Junior McGrail's colors," she joked. She held up her glass. "Cheers."

"Cheers and a happy, healthy New Year." Louise lifted her glass, which she didn't drink from because she was sticking to her story of not drinking alcohol. Occasionally, she'd forget but tonight was one of her virtuous nights.

"Louise—" Juts motioned for her to drink.

"No, I think I'll pour a glass of orange juice."

"You won't be needing this, then." Chester knocked back her drink.

A honk outside sent Louise to her feet. "All right, Sister, you have a happy New Year, get better."

"I'll be good enough to work on Friday, don't worry."

"Okay."

"Happy New Year, Chester." Louise kissed him on the cheek, bent over and kissed Juts, then zipped out the door.

"You aren't going?"

Chester shook his head no, then added, "Wouldn't be any fun without you."

"Really?"

"Really." He turned on the old radio. They sang along, whipped around their noisemakers, which made Buster bark. Yoyo ignored the whole undignified procedure. Chester didn't feel like an unfaithful husband. It was curious, but somehow he loved Juts more than he had before.

At midnight he walked out with a big pot and ladle to bang in the New Year. She hollered "Happy New Year," and then promptly fell asleep.

39

Except for Pearl Harbor, the war still seemed far away, but each time Juts scrambled across the slippery walks in the square, or hunched her shoulders to ward off the cold as she bought more doughnuts from the Yosts, she saw fewer and fewer young men.

Albert Barnhart, Lillian Yost's younger brother, was the last to enlist. He joined the Coast Guard. He kidded the sisters Hunsenmeir by saying he did it so he could get a free haircut and Lillian could get her nails done.

Not wishing to seem less patriotic than that fat load on the other side of the square, Juts and Louise had run a big, expensive ad in the *Clarion* and one in the *Trumpet,* too, announcing free haircuts for servicemen and manicures at half price for the wives, mothers, sisters, and girlfriends of same. The place was mobbed.

Celeste, under heavy pressure from both mayors, agreed to head up the Red Cross, which meant endless fund-raising. Chessy, in response, assumed more duties for the Civil Air Patrol. His Tuesday-night dance lessons continued. He occasionally walked Buster to Trudy's little apartment but he couldn't make a habit of that.

The Civil Air Patrol attracted Louise, Fannie Jump Creighton, Lillian Yost, Agnes Frost, and the entire BonBon family over the age of eighteen. Digby and Zeb Vance and O.B. Huffstetler were the only men. Chessy had to train Runnymede's two sheriffs as well. Celeste pressured her connections in Washington for the latest in training films.

Training proved more rigorous than the volunteers had anticipated. Juts and Louise easily mastered Morse code but Lillian Yost had a hell of a time with it.

Turned out in their Army-surplus uniforms from the 1914 war, they drilled with wooden rifles until blistered. Fannie Jump bitched that drilling was absurd. Their job was to identify aircraft and lead civilians to safety in the event of bombing. In a fit, she threw down her wooden rifle. Chester, in his deepest baritone, told her to pick it up. She did and marched some more. Seeing Chester bark out that order to Fannie impressed everyone.

The patrol members concentrated fiercely during the film sessions. They watched German, Japanese, and Italian planes. The films showed each side of the machines, the underside and the topside.

Posters of silhouettes of planes as seen from the ground were tacked onto the walls of their small office in the Lutheran church. Chessy gave pop quizzes on what they learned, including enemy insignia, the black cross with white lines for the German aircraft and the red sun on the Japanese aircraft.

Each night two people pulled duty. Day duty was much easier because one could see the aircraft. Chessy, overrun with women wanting to contribute, discovered he was respected by people. They wanted to work with him. He was surprised and pleased.

Despite all their training, identifying a plane in the night sky by shape alone was difficult.

Chester found a big antiaircraft gun and an antiaircraft light in a salvage yard outside of Philadelphia. From the Great War, they still worked. The arrival of the antiaircraft equipment was a triumphant moment for Chessy and his CAP's. A heated argument flourished in the basement of Christ Lutheran's, where the meeting took place, over whether to place it by the fire tower or set it up in Runnymede Square. Louise wanted the antiaircraft and light gun in the square because it was easier for her to walk there, although she declared it would be a reminder to everyone that a war was on.

Caesura and Agnes wanted it by the fire tower, closer to their homes.

Finally, Digby stood up, lifted his band baton, and asked for silence. He suggested using a crane and lifting the antiaircraft light into the fire tower; that way the two CAP's would be together, which would help if the worst happened. He felt certain that an enemy plane would zoom down on the light, trying to knock it out, so the gun had to be there also. If the operator was injured the other CAP could take over.

Louise argued her program was better. If an airplane went after the tower, both CAP's would get it. If the troops were divided, maybe one person would survive. She also pointed out that the fire tower had a roof, which would shut off part of the light beam.

Chester finally quieted the group by telling them that if a plane flew over, it would most likely be a reconnaissance plane. Their task was to report it immediately to Col. Frank Froling at the armory in Hagerstown.

Louise hollered out that it might be more than reconnaissance—after all, look what had just happened in Hawaii. And what was the CAP doing in the armory?

Patiently, Chester explained that special phone lines in the armory were connected to Baltimore and to Washington. Given the jolt the country had just endured, the Civil Air Patrol was well organized, even if HQ was in an armory.

Louise still wanted the big light in the square. The feuding rolled into the night. Digby Vance, tired and disgusted, suggested they let Colonel Froling make the decision.

Chester said no because then the colonel would lose confidence in them. They had to settle this themselves. At one in the morning they reached a compromise: They would build a new tower with no roof in the vacant lot behind St. Paul's Episcopal Church. While that was being built, the light and gun would be placed in the center of the square, straddling the Mason-Dixon line. The big air-raid siren stayed in the fire tower while the new tower was being built. Chester prayed the new tower would be quickly completed and fortunately it was. Everything was then put in the tower.

40

Monday's hustle and bustle was damped by the news that Singapore had fallen to the Japanese. General Percival, without water, food, gas, or ammunition, surrendered. As people huddled at the counter of Cadwalder's or squeezed into a booth for breakfast, they wondered how they could become mobilized fast enough to stop the Japanese steamroller and the German juggernaut. The *Clarion* estimated that sixty thousand British and Imperial troops had been captured, while the *Trumpet* put the figure at a more modest fifty thousand. Everyone wondered what would happen to the captured men.

Julia Ellen and Louise, worn out from Civil Air Patrol duty that frozen night, sipped coffee, ate grits, eggs, bacon, and biscuits, and slowly warmed up.

"I'll be glad when spring gets here," Juts moaned. "My Orioles have to be better this year." Juts didn't like to stay on the subject of the war for long.

"Nothing can be as bad as last year," Flavius offered from behind the counter. "Birds sank to a new low."

"So many of the ballplayers have enlisted," Harper Wheeler chimed in.

The night owls on their way home to bed and the early-morning birds coexisted at Cadwalder's every morning at five-thirty. O.B. Huffstetler came in and sat next to Harper.

"Morning, Sheriff."

"Morning, O.B. Don't guess Miss Chalfonte is going to ride today."

"Nope. Monday's our quiet day."

"When you gonna give me a ride in that big-ass station wagon?" Juts called from the booth.

"Anytime."

"Goody. You can carry us home."

"Juts, that's pushy."

"I know, but..."

"Don't mind a bit." O.B. smiled. "Hop in."

"Sheriff," Louise called.

"Yessum."

"Nothing on Noe's file?"

"Now, Louise, I can't discuss certain aspects of the case."

Juts piped up. "You ought to talk to Hansford. He's got nothing to do but repair tack, talk, and think. The thinking's what surprises me."

They settled back to their food. Louise read aloud from Walter Winchell's syndicated column as Juts ordered more biscuits and grits.

Junior McGrail trooped in.

Trudy Archer dashed in, bundled up in a long chocolate-brown coat with dyed rabbit-fur trim. The men sat a little straighter at the counter. She threw off her hat, fluffed her hair, and unbuttoned her coat. She slipped in between Harper Wheeler and Junior. Good thing she was skinny.

"Hi."

"Hi, there. What will it be this morning?" Flavius asked, a big smile on his face. He looked like his son when he smiled.

"Over easy..."

Harper purred, "That's what I like to hear."

Juts called out from her booth, "Don't listen to him. All talk. No action."

Harper laughed and Trudy turned to see the Hunsenmeir sisters. "Good morning."

"How's the dance school?" Louise politely inquired.

"Coming along."

"I wish you could get my Chessy to dance." Julia idly glanced up from the sports page. "He breaks out into a cold sweat at the prospect."

Trudy smoothly replied, "I'd be happy to teach Chester. I'm sure he has talent."

"I'm still searching for it," Juts joked.

She noticed Trudy's earrings, just like the shells she had seen Chessy hold in his hands when she inadvertently passed Epstein's before Christmas. She wondered if Trudy had bought them or if a beau had given them to her. Well, she liked the bracelet he had given her for Christmas but she'd had her heart set on those earrings. She wondered if Epstein's could get another pair, except she couldn't afford them anyway.

"Here." A cup of coffee was pushed in front of Trudy.

"Good morning, gang." Senior Epstein unwrapped his wool scarf from his neck. "Can you believe the Japs took Singapore?"

Senior, an outgoing man with a booming voice, had begun referring to himself that way when his son was born. He was one of those men impossible not to like. As he greeted everyone and slid onto a counter stool he ordered French toast. His wife had passed away from leukemia three years earlier and Jacob took most of his meals in restaurants. He was just starting to look at women again and he liked what he saw in Trudy Archer.

As he chatted with Louise and Juts about the Civil Air Patrol he noticed Trudy's shell earrings. He quickly shot a look at Juts's ears. No earrings. The shell earrings were most definitely on Trudy's scintillating lobes. He saw Juts's bracelet when she dropped her arm for a moment to eat; the gold links slid out from underneath her sweater. In an instant he grasped the situation, since those were the only gold shell earrings he'd had in his store before Christmas. His face turned crimson.

"Senior, are you okay?" Harper, ever ready to practice his life-saving techniques, noticed.

"Sure, sure," the dark-haired man mumbled.

When they left Cadwalder's, Louise leaned toward her sister. "Did you see the way Senior stared at Trudy? Mmm, mmm."

Juts nodded. "You can hide the fire but what are you going to do about the smoke?"

41

Buster circled three times and dropped at the foot of the bed. Yoyo had already secreted herself under the covers so that when Juts jumped into bed, her feet icy from the cold floor, a healthy set of fangs lightly nibbled her toes.

"Yoyo, I hate it when you do that."

Chessy called from the bathroom, "Can't you see the lump under the covers?"

"I'm not looking for groundhogs in my bed." Juts shivered. "Yoyo, you come up here."

This request was met with a defiant meow. Juts pulled the covers over her head and crawled down to the cat. She didn't want to throw the covers off because it was too cold. A howling wind had brought the winter chill into every crack in the old house.

Chester emerged to behold a mountain under the covers. "Juts, what have you been feeding the cat?"

Yoyo didn't think this was funny. The bottom of the bed pleased her not only because it was warm but also because Buster couldn't crawl under the covers. His whine as she disappeared under the sheets was music to her ears.

"She won't come out of here. She wiggles away when I get close, the sneak."

Chessy opened the top drawer of the dresser, a stash for catnip, keychains, loose pennies, and tie clips on his side; bobby pins, hankies, and fancy barrettes on Juts's. He opened the lid of a small horn box. He rattled the lid off the box. Yoyo stopped moving; she considered her options, which were to endure Juts's clumsy attempts to extricate her or to leave voluntarily and enjoy catnip. She chose the latter, squirting out from under the covers.

"There you are, you rascal."

Buster opened one eye, jaundiced with jealousy, and sighed.

Chessy crumpled a few pungent catnip leaves on the end of the bed while Yoyo watched, whiskers twitching in anticipation. When the last leaf hit the bedspread she launched herself into the intoxicating treasure.

Chessy slipped under the covers to watch Yoyo's antics. Exhausted by her ecstasies, Yoyo flopped on her side, tail slightly flicking, and exhaled with a pure, intense pleasure before closing her eyes.

"It must be wonderful to be a cat," Chester said.

"That cat, anyway." Juts snuggled up to his big warmth. "Honey, who is on duty tonight?"

"Lillian and Caesura, I think." He glanced out the window, opaque with frost. "It's colder than a witch's tit out there."

"Wheezer and I about froze last night and tonight's even worse . . . not that I don't wish some small suffering on Caesura, but maybe not an entire night of it . . . after all, she's no spring chicken."

Chester got out of bed and slid his feet into his worn leather slippers. "Pearlie is on duty at the firehouse. I'll give him a call."

When he returned to bed she asked, "What's the scoop?"

"He'll go out and check on the girls every hour. I know we've got that heater up there . . ."

Juts interrupted. "You have to sit right on top of it to feel anything. I hate those kerosene fumes."

"Me, too, but it's the best we've got."

"I was okay until my hands and feet finally turned blue. We were so cold we couldn't even fight."

His eyes twinkled. "A cold day in hell . . ."

"Huh?"

"Nothing. Hon, there's just not much I can do about the weather. I don't remember winter being this damned cold. Maybe I'm getting old."

"No you're not. You're six months younger than I am."

"I don't know what we are. We aren't young anymore. We aren't middle-aged, exactly, and we sure aren't old."

"It is strange, isn't it?" She waited a moment, then swallowed and cleared her throat. "Chess, I want a baby."

He stayed quiet a moment. "I do, too, but it just hasn't worked out like we'd planned."

"Well . . . I went to Doc Horning. He said my organs are healthy. I want you to go."

"I hate doctors."

"We're running out of time. I'm thirty-six."

"Yeah . . ." His voice trailed off.

"Do this for me. You don't have to tell anyone . . . like your mother. Anything she produced is perfect, which means you. But there's got to be something not quite lined up, you know what I mean? Honey?"

"Uh."

"You put things off. Just go, Chester. Even if the news is bad, we'll know what to do."

"What can we do?"

"Adopt."

"I don't know about that."

"I want a baby and I don't care how I get one."

"I care."

"Then go to the doctor."

"I wish your sister would shut up," he mumbled.

"The last thing to die on Louise will be her mouth. But she has nothing to do with this."

"Sure she does. She rubs your face in it every chance she gets. Even I'm getting sick of her real-mother routine."

"Anyway, I need a baby so Louise doesn't get the farm all to herself," Juts only half joked.

Chessy rubbed his chin. "Your mother would never give Bumblebee Hill to Louise alone. Don't worry."

"What if Hansford went along with the idea? His name's on the deed."

"He won't. He doesn't much like Louise. Her special pleading about passing it on to their grandchildren cuts no ice."

Juts giggled. "She is pretty awful to him. Yesterday she said his beard looked like an old bird's nest. Right in front of everyone, too."

"Where was that?"

"Shop. He came by."

"It's a good thing your sister lives in a town where everybody knows everybody and their peculiarities."

Juts shook her head. "I'm not peculiar. Louise is. I'm normal." He laughed. Then she asked again in a soft voice, "Chester, give me your word that you'll see Doc Horning before the month is out."

He sighed. "I promise."

42

Mother Smith allowed herself to be driven down to Runnymede Square. She was born in an age when coachmen wearing livery hung on to the backs of carriages. She had heard once that ladies, daring ladies, drove their own carriages in London's Hyde Park, but she certainly wasn't going to do it.

Mother Smith conceived of herself as a duchess condemned to live in a democracy, and a convalescent democracy at that. FDR, serving his third term, put paid to Washington's admonition that two terms was enough for any president. Her illusion coalesced over the years until it gained the consistency of concrete, which often seemed the consistency of her intellectual capabilities as well. Her family, the Holtzapples, had neither great wealth, great talent, nor great land. A few proved agreeable fellows and ladies but by no stretch of the imagination were they a distinguished family. Nor were the Smiths, a plain-living Dunkard

family into which she married in 1889, although they had contributed an undersecretary to Millard Fillmore. Rupert, a handsome man, as were his sons, had a good contracting business but
he wasn't wealthy. Mother Smith believed when she married
Rupert that over time she could change him, lead him up to her
standard of living. The years disabused her of this notion as well as
her love for Rupert.

People her own age remembered that Josephine Holtzapple
had always had a high opinion of herself, and it gained further altitude as she aged. She had no friends, appearing not to notice.
She lived for her family, which meant her sons were prisoners to
her tyrannies; two escaped and Chester stayed home, a glutton for
punishment. Although he let her barbs and bullying roll off his
back, there were times when, caught between the iron will of his
mother and the lopsided unpredictability of his wife, he felt like a
hot horseshoe flat on an anvil.

Today was one of those times.

Staring up at the watchtower behind St. Paul's, her muskrat
coat wrapped tightly around her, she scowled. "Why subject
yourself to this hardship? Even if the Germans attacked us they
wouldn't bother with Runnymede."

"The *Hindenburg* flew over." He reminded her of the last, fa-
tal flight of the giant zeppelin, which cruised over Runnymede as
it waited for winds to abate in New Jersey, where it was to be
moored.

"Chester, don't argue with me." Feeling the cold, she walked
back toward the car, taking short steps.

"If we had better lookout stations in the Pacific we might
have had warning of the Japanese attack. We might have had time
to get our ships out of Pearl Harbor."

"Might have, could have, should have, would have . . . I still say
there is no earthly reason for you or anyone else to climb up that
tower and sit in the cold waiting for what—bombers?" She
stamped her foot as she waited before the passenger door.

Chester opened the door, helped her in, then walked around and slid behind the wheel. "How about if I leave you off at Aunt Dimps's? I have an appointment. I could pick you up, say, three-thirty."

"Where are you going?"

"Dr. Horning."

"Are you sick?" Alarm crept into her voice.

"No. It's time for a checkup."

"You look healthy to me."

"I am, but I guess I'm at an age where I shouldn't take anything for granted."

"Fiddlesticks, you aren't even forty."

"Where do you want me to drop you, Mother?"

"Not at Aunt Dimps's. Just because we attended school together doesn't mean I want to hear Bach on her piano. I suppose I could visit your father. He's come down with a cold but insists on going to work."

"Juts had a cold for the longest time."

She ignored this, folding her arms across her chest. "Start the car, Chester."

"Okay." He turned the key, then pulled out into the hard-packed road, his chains singing as they bit into the snow.

"Is something wrong? I watched Johnny die. If something's wrong I want to know." Chester's older brother had died when Chester was six. John had been Josephine's favorite. She rarely mentioned him, but his photograph was next to her bed.

"I'm not dying. I'm going for a checkup."

"Juts is behind this. I know it." When he didn't reply, she shifted to the offensive. "Tainted blood. It comes down the Zepp line, I can tell you—and the Buckinghams had a wild streak, too, as everyone knows. Of course, that incident with Otto Tangerman..." Dropping her voice, she paused. "I mean Otto's father, Gunther, well, that was unforgivable." She stared ahead as though Chessy would remember something that had happened before he was born.

"Uh . . . which one, Mother, there have been so many incidents."

"That's my point, the tainted blood."

"But what happened to Gunther Tangerman?"

"Cora's father, Hans, stole the body from Gassner's Funeral Parlor, put him in his Union uniform, and hauled him up on George Gordon Meade's statue. I told you this," she grumbled, then continued. "Had him riding behind Meade with his arms around the general's waist. It gave everyone a startle the next morning. Old Priscilla McGrail fainted dead away at the sight. Hans never got over the Cause, as he put it, even though he and Gunther were friends."

She referred to Gunther's having fought for the Federals while Hans fought for the Confederacy.

"What did Major Chalfonte say?"

"That Gunther sat a horse better dead than alive. Oh, it was a terrible shock." She folded her gloved hands. "Where are you taking me?"

"To Dad's, unless you have a better idea?"

"Did I tell you to bring me here?" Puzzled, her eyebrows shot upward.

"No, you mentioned he had a cold."

"Oh . . ." She pondered this. "I guess I did, didn't I? Chester, I don't want to see Rupert. He's out of sorts. Maybe you'd better take me home."

"How about if we go to the Bon-Ton? I bet one of those white sales Julia talks about is on."

"I don't need any sheets."

"Maybe the clothes are on sale, too."

"I have no time for modern fripperies that show everything. When I see women with a few threads pulled over their bodies I wonder what's left for their husbands to look at, I really do. Young people today have no sense of decorum."

"We could go to Cadwalder's for lunch."

"Gives me gas pains."

"Okay, then. I'll take you home." He moved slowly, because even with chains he didn't trust the traction. "Mother, Julia wants a child."

"I've heard that before."

"She's worried about her age. She's worried if we wait she'll be too old to have a baby."

"Your wife is a child herself. She couldn't possibly discipline a child."

"She was pretty good with Buster when he was a pup."

"Oh, Chester"—her voice rose in mock amusement—"babies and dogs are not at all the same. Your Julia Ellen is not fit to be a mother. You, on the other hand, would make a wonderful father."

Nothing like getting kissed and socked at the same time. Chester replied evenly, "Children change people. I think Julia would be responsible."

"Tainted blood. Listen to me. What have I been telling you?"

"What about Hansford's side?" He tacked to the wind.

"Nothing good can ever come of Hansford or his blood." She snapped her mouth shut like a turtle.

Chester realized that members of a generation knew one another in ways the younger generation couldn't fathom until they, too, were older. He'd never thought to ask his mother or his father about Hansford because no one had even known Hansford was alive. Once he showed up, the questions slowly bubbled in Chester and other people, too.

"Mother, what do you think happened to him all those years he was away?"

She stared out the window. "He got what he deserved, that's what happened to him."

"What do you mean?"

"Nothing."

"Maybe you knew him better than I thought." Chester gave her a rare dig.

"What's that supposed to mean? I did not teach my sons to be rude."

"I'm not being rude," he calmly said. "Just curious."

"Curiosity killed the cat." She paused. "Is yours still attending services at Christ Lutheran?"

"No. She prays at home now."

Mother Smith turned her head to stare at her son. He had such a good sense of humor, and since she had none there were times when he was a mystery to her, not that she'd admit it. Part of her armor was in announcing to her sons and husband, as well as anyone else unfortunate enough to get caught in her crossfire, that she knew her sons inside and out.

They reached the house. The blue spruce out front, covered in snow, could have graced a postcard.

He walked her up to the front door. "Mother, if Julia and I can't have children—"

"Don't say that. It's her, not you."

"It doesn't matter. It takes two to tango."

"I do wish you wouldn't use slang in front of me."

"If it turns out"—he patiently stuck to his subject—"that we can't have children, we're thinking of adopting. Would you accept an adopted child as your grandchild?"

"Never."

43

Do you think Louise will ever remove her Civil Air Patrol white helmet? Perhaps it's grafted to her head." Celeste inhaled a Montecristo No. 3 cigar, a habit she hid from everyone but Cora and Ramelle.

Cora laughed and continued scrubbing the intricate pattern of Celeste's silverware with a toothbrush dipped in tarnish remover. "The good thing about the war is it gives my girl something to think about besides Mary."

"I don't suppose she has much choice but to ease up on her—" Celeste took a drag, then added, "I take that back. She could raise recriminations to new heights."

"She doesn't shut up, if that's what you mean."

"In a sense." Celeste picked up a heavy fork and rubbed it with a green cloth.

"That's my job."

"Idle hands do the Devil's work." Celeste smiled and picked up another fork. "How's Hansford today?"

"He's down with O.B. at the stable. He says they're going to refurbish the tack room, except that word 'refurbish' worries me."

"Me, too. I think it means dollars."

"No." Cora shook her head. "He'd hike on up here to tell you if'n money was needed."

"Do you like having him home again?"

Cora shrugged. "There's things about him I remember as the same, but other ways he's some old man I don't much know."

"I don't suppose anyone is so strange to us as ourselves when we were young. He must remind you of yourself when you were young."

"I don't know as I considered that."

"Haven't you ever thought about who you were when you were young?"

"No."

"Cora"—Celeste exhaled a perfect blue ring of smoke, which lazed upward—"you amaze me."

"Why think about myself—then or now? I am what I am."

"You don't think time changes people?"

"Yes—what good does it do to worry it?"

"I'm not worrying—just turning it over in my mind the way we used to turn over arrowheads when we'd find them as children. Every little chip was a source of fascination and delight."

"My mind doesn't work that way." Cora smiled, hands on hips. "Sometimes my mind doesn't work at all. Like I say, sometimes I sits and thinks and sometimes I just sits."

"And sometimes I think too much." Celeste whistled a snatch of a tune, then asked, "Well—are you thinking about anything?"

"Mary. The war. Seems like our country gets into these messes every twenty years or so. We raise up a new generation of men and they get killed off."

"Yes, I think about that, too."

Cora dipped the silverware in a bowl of warm water after scrubbing it. "Juts worries me."

"Julia?" Celeste's voice rose in surprise.

"She finally got Chessy to see Doc Horning. She's been there twice in the last few years. She's hunky-dory. What if Chester's not right?"

"Ah—that does present a problem."

"Juts is determined to have a baby."

"Perhaps she could accomplish this without the assistance of her husband." Celeste smiled wryly.

"That would be a fine kettle of fish, wouldn't it?"

"There's more than one way to skin a cat, to use the old phrase."

Cora shook her head. "I don't think my girl would do that. Every year this wanting a baby notion gets stronger."

"I love Juts, but she is spectacularly unsuited for motherhood, that altar upon which the ego is daily sacrificed."

"You lost me with the altar but I'd say she has a lot to learn."

Celeste laughed. "Juts is the quintessential little sister: rebellious, self-centered, and somewhat adorable."

Cora smiled. "Those two girls like to drive me to drink when they were little. I thought, 'Oh, they'll grow up one day and all this tussling and hustling will stop. They'll be best friends.' " She lifted up a dripping spoon. "They're still tussling and hustling."

"It is *amazing,* isn't it? Out of each other's sight they behave as relatively normal people. Put them together and they're six and ten all over again. That episode last year in Cadwalder's was the limit."

"Over Juts not being a mother. See, that's what worries me."

"I thought it was over Julia reminding Louise she was forty." She tapped her finger next to her nose for a second. "Oh, Lord, her forty-first is around the corner, isn't it? *And* she'll be a grandmother soon. And Juts will be—"

"Thirty-seven on March 6. If only Louise's birthday was in front of Juts's, she could lie better." Cora shook her head ruefully.

"You know what will happen, Cora? Someday Mary will be forty and Maizie will be thirty-nine and Louise will tell everyone she's forty-five."

This set them off into peals of laughter, these old friends who had lost count of the years between them. Although born on opposite sides of the tracks, they'd known each other all their lives. In time, the material differences eroded in significance. Only character remained.

"What do you think about adopting a baby?" Cora asked.

"Me?" Celeste was startled.

"Julia."

"So—this is serious."

"Appears so."

"I hope the baby has a sense of humor—it's going to need it."

"I'll be there to help."

"Julia wants to be the center of attention. For all of Louise's religious mania, which recurs like malaria, she is the more responsible of the two. Juts isn't happy if she hasn't upset the applecart, but usually it winds up being her own applecart."

"I know." Cora smiled, thinking of her younger daughter. "She was a kicker even when I carried her."

"What about Chester?"

"Any man that can put up with Josephine for a mother has hidden strengths. He'll be a good father."

"You know, Cora, I never thought of that. He probably is stronger than we give him credit for. He's usually so quiet."

"Well, how can he get a word in edgewise? But he'll come around, just wait and see."

"Then he'll have two children—Julia and the baby."

"She'll muster up."

"Juts—no, she won't." Celeste shook her head.

"Wanna bet?"

Celeste's eyes brightened, her shoulders straightened; nothing like a wager to get her blood up. "You want to bet me that Julia Ellen Hunsenmeir will mature enough to make a good mother? How many years do I have for this bet?"

"One. One from the time the baby arrives."

Celeste slyly smiled. "What are we betting?"

"Your John Deere tractor, the old one. Attachments, too."

"Cora!" Celeste laughed. "You've been thinking about this for a long time." Cora nodded yes and Celeste tacked on, "Of course, this may come to naught. There may not be any baby."

"She'll get a baby even if she has to steal one. Just you wait."

"Well, how much time, really, are we discussing here?"

"You think Louise hit the hernia note when she hit forty? Wait for Julia Ellen. Oh, Lordy." Cora pointed her finger, something she rarely did. "She'll have that baby before she's forty, and I mean it—if she can't have one or adopt one, she'll lift one."

Celeste crossed her arms over her chest, bit her lip, and thought. "The John Deere. Well, what do I get if I win?"

"Two months—my work—free."

Celeste reached across the nook table to shake hands. "Deal!" She couldn't wait to write Ramelle about this!

44

Pearlie filled in for Lillian Yost, who had picked up a bad chest cold. He crouched next to the small kerosene heater while Chester scanned the deep skies with his binoculars. A laminated chart of enemy aircraft as seen from the ground rested against one wall of the tower.

Huge, inky cumulus clouds were rolling in from the west.

"Another one coming." Pearlie lit a cigarette and offered Chessy one.

"Ever try anything other than Luckies?" Chessy asked. He was a Pall Mall man, himself.

"If I did, I wouldn't tell you." He tapped the pack so an extra cigarette slid farther out than the first.

Chester hunkered down next to Pearlie to light his cigarette off of Pearlie's. He dragged deep. "Funny how you get used to a brand. Julia and her Chesterfields... She started smoking them when she was twelve. You can't get her to try anything else and if I forget to bring home a pack after work, I'm in trouble. She's started playing poker with Fannie Jump Creighton for cigarettes. Says she'll win lots and save money."

"Won't be long before Fannie's got her playing for dimes and then dollars."

"She says it makes the time pass."

"Makes the money pass, too," Pearlie snorted.

"I wasn't taking bets on that shop. I figured you and I would be working for the Rifes sooner or later."

"Me, too." Pearlie stared up at the winter sky, half of it clear, with stars like big chunks of ice, and the other half looking like a black cauldron. "Imagine flying into something like that."

"I'd like to give it a shot," Chessy said.

"I saw one war. I don't need to see another."

Pearlie had lied about his age, enlisting in the Army at fifteen, shipped to France within weeks. His memories of the country were of mud, shelled towns, and bloated corpses. "I learned to love American cigarettes. Those French things are like sucking on corn silk, and if you really want to puke, try the Turkish weeds."

"Too young for the first and too old for this one—hell." Chessy spit out a fleck of tobacco. "I don't think I'm too damned old. I'm stronger than I was when I was twenty."

"Smarter, too. You tell a twenty-year-old to go over the top, machine-gun fire flying every which way, and he'll go. At your age you think twice about it."

"Doesn't mean I won't go up and over," Chessy said.

"You know, politicians are claiming victory before we're even over there. I fought the Germans. They're tough and they're smart. You might get your chance yet, Chessy."

"Think it's going to be that bad for us?"

"Yeah, I do."

"Don't you think Germany's got to wear down?"

"If they conquer enough territory they can replenish their supplies. They can win the whole shooting match. The secret is gas. No kidding. If they can protect their fuel supply, they've got a chance to take home all the marbles."

"What about the Japs?"

"Not a prayer. The Pacific war isn't our first priority and we'll still skunk them."

"You're a lot smarter than I am. I don't pay much attention to the world out there. I know I should, but—" He paused. "I've got enough right here to keep my mind busy." He ground out the stub. "I have been reading my maps, though. If the Germans have any kind of aircraft carriers they can hit us wherever they want. Or they can take Newfoundland—"

His brother-in-law interrupted. "Not a good idea. They couldn't hold it, not even long enough to build air bases."

"Then Cuba."

"Yeah, that would work if they want to commit a big enough force to do it. But yeah, that would work."

"They say Argentina's for Germany even though she's playing neutral. That's a rich country."

"Rich and far away." Pearlie held his feet toward the heater. "Funny what happens to your mind when you read maps and start thinking like a general. You begin to think those countries in their different colors are like Fannie's poker chips. You're going to pick them up and put them in your pocket. And all the thousands—millions, even—of people clinging to that poker chip, you start thinking they're ants."

The first snowflake lazed down, a warning of what was to

follow. The men pulled the tarp over the top of the tower. It was rolled up like a window blind, but horizontally instead of vertically. So many Civil Air Patrol volunteers had been coming down with colds because they were drenched in rain or covered in snow that Chessy had rigged up the tarp. This way, if airplanes did brave bad weather, the second you heard them you could roll back the tarp and turn on the searchlight. The second man could crank the siren. They sat down next to the kerosene heater again. Snow fell more thickly now. As the wind picked up, the tower swayed slightly.

"Shit, Chessy."

"She'll hold."

"First you try to freeze me to death, now I'll go down buried in a mess of timber, a big searchlight for my headstone."

"Nah, we can roll the light off so it crashes into St. Rose's."

Pearlie laughed. He paused a long time before he said, "You've been lucky, buddy."

"Huh?" Chester's blond stubble was growing out.

"Tuesday nights with your mother." He paused. "And the occasional swing by the firehouse to make it look good."

The glow illuminated Chester's surprised face. "I do see my mother on Tuesdays."

"That's not the only person you're seeing."

Chester clamped his jaw. When he finally spoke, his voice was so low you could almost hear the snowflakes piling up on the tarp. "No. I've been taking dancing lessons. I want to surprise Juts."

"You will."

"Come on, Pearlie."

"I'm not an idiot. I'm not a judge, either. Things happen. I'm just telling you, you've been lucky. Your wife and your mother can't stand the sight of each other, so they won't compare notes, but that doesn't mean there won't be a slip-up along the line."

"I said I was taking dancing lessons."

"Jesus, Chester." Pearlie glared at him.

A low sigh, a moan, escaped Chester, who now felt the cold acutely. "I don't know how I got into this."

"I do. We're both married to women who would rather give orders than take them." Paul grimaced, then relaxed into a smile. "I could kill Louise. If I had a nickel for every time I wanted to wring her neck, I'd be richer than all the Rifes put together, but—" He shrugged. "I've got two great kids. I'd die for those girls. I never knew I could—" He stopped because he couldn't describe his love for his children. "And I love Louise even when I hate her. Crazy."

"I never thought it would be like this—life."

"My problem is, I never thought." Paul looked his best friend in the eye. "I'm thinking now. I'm thinking for my family. I'm thinking I can't protect my daughters if they marry the wrong men. I can't even protect my wife if we do get bombed. And I'm thinking for you, man. You think we're in the middle of a storm now—shit."

"What am I going to do?"

"Do you love her?"

Chester put his head in his hands. "Yes."

"Damn."

"It just happened. She thinks I'm the best thing since sliced bread. I can't hurt her, Paul, I can't."

"Everyone gets hurt, not just her. If you give her up now, it won't be as bad as if you wait—unless you want to divorce Juts."

He forced a smile. "She'd kill me."

"Do you still love her?"

"Yeah—but it's different."

"That wild first stuff, it's like some kind of dope. I couldn't keep my hands off Wheezie when we started out. It changes. But I love her. We've walked a lot of miles together. I can't imagine living without her." He put his gloved hand on Chester's shoulder. "You've got to take charge. Like I said, I'm no judge. If you had a squeeze in Baltimore or York, maybe you could get away with it, but Runnymede?" He shook his head.

45

The bright nail-polish colors offset the dull gray outside. Juts favored brilliant reds for herself. Many of her customers liked pastel shades, or even mauve. She always suggested mauve for the ladies who blued their hair. Toots, talented with color, had yet to turn anyone out with that lavender shade so favored by Junior McGrail and her generation. That didn't prevent Louise and Juts from doing it, though. Some ladies even liked it.

Junior McGrail died and her son, Rob, went all to pieces. He soon let Runnymede Beauty Salon for Discriminating Ladies go to pot. In Rob's defense, he evinced little desire to blue, bleach, and curl. Digby Vance found him a post as assistant band director, which steadied him.

Aunt Dimps rented the salon, transforming it into a flower shop. Prudently, she used the Dingledines as a supplier even though they were a touch more expensive than if she'd gone to the flower auctions at Baltimore. But they threw a lot of local business her way.

Gossip Central was filled with news of sons and husbands and boyfriends at boot camp. Vaughn Cadwalder graduated at the top of his unit. After that there were ripping items like "Orrie doesn't understand how anyone can drive in Washington, D.C. Noe accepted a commission as a captain and works morning, noon, and night." Lastly, in peach chalk in the lower right-hand corner, were scribbled announcements: "Fluffy has six beautiful kittens. Free to good home. Patsy BonBon."

"I am so sick of winter I could throw up," Mary Miles Mundis complained. "Harold puts on fifteen pounds every winter. The buttons pop off his shirt and if I tactfully suggest he curtail his appetite he says look who's talking. I don't think I'm fat."

Juts massaged M.M.'s hands with a soothing lotion, since people's hands and lips cracked in the dry air of their homes. "You've never been fat."

Mary Miles beamed. "Neither have you."

"That's because you never carried a baby." Wheezie joined the conversation while she trimmed Aunt Dimps's locks. "I got big as a house and it took me a whole year to shed it off. I don't know when I've been so miserable."

"Oh, I can think of a few times," Julia dryly suggested.

"Because of you," Wheezie fired back.

"Well, I remember one Fourth of July parade when you two almost set the town on fire." Mary Miles laughed.

"That was so long ago I forgot all about it." Louise airily dismissed the subject.

"Funny, we didn't." Aunt Dimps giggled. "That was 1912 and Donald and I were courting." Donald was Dimps's deceased husband. He died in a train wreck, a spectacular pileup north of Philadelphia.

"It couldn't have been that far back." Louise sidestepped the year.

"Yeah, according to you, you weren't born in 1912." Juts kept her eyes trained on Mary Miles's thumb.

"People who live in glass houses shouldn't throw stones." Wheezie tilted her chin upward.

"Don't start spouting these little sayings. It was 1912 and Idabelle McGrail, Junior's mother, was in front of our float playing 'America the Beautiful' on her accordion. Her son and grandson get all their musical talent from her."

"Poor souls," Mrs. Mundis muttered.

"She scared the mule pulling our float," Juts fibbed.

"Ha. You set the float on fire, Julia Ellen." Louise remembered the incident vividly, though she chose to fudge the year.

"Hey, I wasn't Miss Liberty. You held the damned torch. You dropped it. I was a little tugboat in New York Harbor."

"A little tugboat who knocked Liberty off her base." Aunt Dimps laughed. "Scared the mule when the float caught on fire and he tore through the parade. Oh, God, I never will forget it. Donald grabbed me and pushed me out of harm's way. He couldn't stop the mule. And old Lawrence Villcher—remember him? head of the North Runnymede Fire Department—turned the white engine around and Increase Martin—they still used fire horses— he turned the South Runnymede engine around, and the blast of water stopped the mule and put out the fire." She licked her lips. "Cleanest mule in two states."

"And you swore in public." Julia wanted to deflect her misdeed, no matter how distant.

"I don't curse, Julia," Louise frostily replied.

"You did that day."

"Memory plays tricks on people." Louise was doing her rise-above-it number, which only goaded Juts.

"At least I have one."

"My mind is sharp as a tack."

"Yeah, and just as pointed." Juts suppressed a giggle.

Louise held a wet flip of hair between her finger and middle finger, scissors poised in midair, which gave her a mildly threatening quality. "You're not going to make me mad. I have enough on my mind without fooling around with you."

"Good." Juts was disappointed. She felt like a mix-up.

Mary Miles gazed off in the distance, straining to remember. "Wasn't that when your mother met Aimes Rankin?"

"Gee, I don't know."

"It was," Louise affirmed.

"Well, how's Hansford coming along?" Aunt Dimps jumped from one man to another in Cora's life, which made sense to the group.

"Healthier. He ought to go out and work," Louise replied.

"He does seem better. It's about time to trim that beard of his." Juts, having prepared Mary Miles's nails, now selected the color. "What about Cherry Tart?"

"No. Too dark. I need a pick-me-up."

"Try whiskey," Aunt Dimps suggested.

"Dimps, I didn't know you drank." Louise pretended to be scandalized.

"I don't. Others drive me to it."

"Me, too." Juts pulled out Victory Red, a good color for the times.

"Me, too," Fannie called out from the back room, another card game in progress.

"That's good." Mrs. Mundis leaned back in the chair, appreciating Dimps's comeback.

"Hansford was an educated man. Geology." Dimps was about twenty years older than Juts, Wheezie, and Mary Miles Mundis. "I was in my teens when he left but I know my mother used to say there wasn't enough to hold him here. And she said that no matter how good a woman Cora was, it would be hard for a college-educated man to have a wife who was—" she stopped for a moment, her face beet-red, and softly said, "not educated."

"Not educated. Hell, Dimps, Mom can't read or write." Juts hit the nail on the head.

"No, but Cora's smarter than any of us." Dimps righted her conversational ship. "Still, I wonder if Mother wasn't right."

"That's not what I heard." Mary Miles cleared her throat. "My mother said it was because of Josephine Holtzapple."

"What?" Both sisters spoke at once.

"Yes. You never heard that?" Mary Miles was surprised.

Aunt Dimps, frowning, pointed her finger at Mary Miles's reflection in the mirror. "You all were too little to know anything. Besides, that's water over the dam, or is it under the dam?"

"Over." Toots had been silent this whole time; actually, she'd been dozing in the chair, as she had a half hour before her next customer arrived. She opened her eyes.

"What do you mean, it was Josephine?" Juts held Mary Miles's right hand.

"My mother said that Josephine was in love with Hansford. They say she was a beautiful woman in her day."

"Bet she was a bitch then, too," Juts grumbled.

"Haughty." Dimps wished Mary Miles had shut up.

"How come we don't know this story?" Louise fluffed Aunt Dimps's hair, searching for scraggly ends.

"The younger generation isn't interested in the older generation. You can't even imagine us young."

"Dimps, you aren't old." Julia smiled.

"Fifty-eight, and with all the padding I've picked up, I look every day of it. Any more and I'll be the fatted calf." She patted her tummy.

"You look just fine." Louise concurred with her sister. "But what is Mary Miles talking about?"

"You have to remember that this is ancient history," Dimps said, "and I was pretty young myself. They say that Josephine fell in love with Hansford, but he wasn't in love with her."

"Was he married to Momma?" Juts was intensely curious but tried to appear nonchalant. It didn't work.

"Yes. He loved your mother, really, I think he did. I think he still loves her. Your father was a devil-may-care young fellow. Just the type to inflame the heart of someone as proper as that damned Josephine, who hadn't been married to Rupert but so long. Hansford was long on looks and short on responsibility, I guess."

"But you said he didn't love her." Louise snipped another lock.

"He didn't." Toots spoke again. "I kind of remember. I was in grade school then. Anyway, whatever happened, Hansford left. People said he would have left anyway. Restless."

"Did he have an affair with her?" Juts wasn't one to beat around the bush.

"No," Dimps quickly answered.

"Well..." Mary Miles paused. "Nobody really knows except that he walked out flat. Just—" She made a flyaway motion.

"Put your hands back here, M.M.," Juts commanded.

"And Josephine broke bad after that. She was always a snob but after that she became insufferable."

"I'll ask him," Juts said.

"Let sleeping dogs lie," Dimps warned her.

"You said it was ancient history," Juts replied.

"Not to them, it isn't. Don't make one of your messes, Juts," Dimps told her.

"Why is everyone picking on me?"

"Because we know you only too well." Louise thoroughly enjoyed her sister wiggling on the hot seat.

"My mother-in-law is a whistling bitch," Juts said. "I wouldn't mind giving her a little back."

"Leave her to heaven," Aunt Dimps recommended.

"God is too slow."

"Julia!" Louise appeared shocked. She wasn't, really, but she believed everyone present considered her deeply spiritual. Nobody did; they thought she liked the pomp and ceremony of high mass.

"Well, Louise, it's the truth. I see people getting away with murder. God sits on his big celestial butt and nothing happens. I mean, why doesn't he kill Adolf Hitler? If I can see evil, why can't God?"

"People have been trying to answer that question since the beginning of time." Toots heavily lifted herself out of the chair. She was sleepy and needed to move around to wake up.

"These mysteries are too great for our minds to understand." Louise had no answer, but this sounded profound.

"I don't believe it." Juts pouted.

Mary Miles said, "Maybe God made the world and then left it. We bored him."

"Then why do I bother praying?"

"Juts, you never pray unless you want something," Louise chided her. "It's like shopping with you."

"You don't know what I pray for."

"I know you," Louise responded.

"No philosophy has ever been able to answer the big questions—and neither will we. You live on a wing and a prayer, girls." Aunt Dimps winced when Louise twisted a roller in too tightly.

"I have a philosophy. Birth leads to death." Juts put cotton balls between Mary Miles's fingers so she couldn't close them and wreck her polish job.

"You're a crab today." Louise glared at her. "Rest your mind and shut your mouth."

"I am not crabby. I'd like to know what happened between our father and my mother-in-law."

"Well, I expect you'll just blunder right in and ask," Louise growled.

"Here comes Hansford, Juts. You've got your chance."

He opened the door and smiled. All eyes were upon him. "Hi, girls."

"Hi," Toots finally responded.

"Have I come at a bad time?"

"No." Louise didn't look up.

"Hansford, you just sit a minute and I'll get to you." Juts rolled the manicure tray to the side.

"Do you want me to move, Julia?" Mary Miles asked, aquiver with expectation.

"Uh-uh. Toots's chair is open for the next quarter hour and this won't take long. Toots, okay?"

"Sure." Toots walked into the back room to make fresh coffee.

"Come on." Juts pointed to the chair and Hansford gratefully sank into its comfortable contours. She studied his beard from every angle. "Some people see a long beard and think wisdom. I think: fleas."

The ladies exploded with laughter, as much from tension as from the fact that Julia Ellen was herself again.

46

The cool, slick cards felt familiar in Juts's hand. Ever since childhood she had loved playing cards. She used to imagine herself dressed as the queen of diamonds, a jack as her servant, a king as her husband. She had a wonderful memory for which cards were out and which ones remained in the deck. Although four years younger than Louise, she could beat her at fish, war, and hearts by the time she was six, which used to provoke screams of protest, fistfights, and tears. Louise hated to lose.

Yoyo was curled asleep in her lap and Buster snored under the card table. The old wall clock ticked in the kitchen; the house was so quiet she could hear it even though she was sitting in the living room, an afghan around her legs to ward off the chill.

Rarely did she get a quiet night to herself. Usually Louise, Mary, Maizie, or Chessy needed something, and if not, then a friend would call or drop by. Juts loved being around people, most especially as the center of attention, but occasionally she enjoyed her own company. This was one of those times.

She was self-centered, to be sure, but she had enough sense to know the world did not revolve around her, much as she wished it did. Sugar, coffee, and gas were being rationed, a reminder to her and everyone that small sacrifices had to be made so other people could make larger ones. Last week, the Battle of the Java Sea had brought home those sacrifices. On February 27, the previous Friday, a small Allied squadron of ships engaged the Japanese fleet protecting an invasion convoy. Outnumbered, the Allies took the fight to the Japanese. By March 1, the Allied force had been obliterated. The evacuation of Rangoon seemed sure to follow.

As she smacked down her cards in a line of seven for solitaire, one of her favorite games, she imagined being on the deck of a destroyer, torpedoes crashing into the sides, the smell of smoke and flame everywhere, a ship listing badly, men screaming, guns firing, and the sickening knowledge that you were going down, all hands on deck. She wondered if fear took over or if you became so infuriated that you decided you would take as many of the enemy with you as you could.

She didn't want Death to be certain. She hoped he would sneak up on her. She didn't want to see his face. Those poor men at the bottom of the Java Sea stared Death in the eye.

She moved the red four of diamonds over to a black five of clubs. This was going to be a long hand.

She banished thoughts of death from her mind, bending over

her cards. She thought about Hansford. She had asked him point-blank what happened with Josephine Holtzapple.

"Nothing."

She couldn't pry another thing out of him, and Cora's response was, "Let bygones be bygones."

She pulled out the ace of spades and the ace of hearts. She hadn't even needed the cards in her hand yet. A good game was shaping up.

Yoyo turned on her back, reached up with a paw, opened her eyes, then closed them, purring loudly.

"Last time I played solitaire you jumped on the table and ruined the game."

Yoyo only purred louder.

Juts pulled out the king of hearts after transferring a card off the piles. She placed him at the far-left space, which had just become vacant because she was able to move a black seven onto a red eight.

Chessy seemed distant lately. She attributed this to his recent appointment with Dr. Horning. She was nervous herself. She felt incomplete without a child. All the worse that Louise hammered away at her over it. Juts had thought marriage could complete her. Much as she loved Chessy, she found marriage wasn't the great be-all and end-all she had dreamed of when young.

She had yet to find the wife who didn't think for her husband. Some women had to work around their men, others had to sabotage them. Still others spent days, weeks, and months luring their husbands into believing some thought was their own, when it was really planted by the wife. It was exhausting. At least with Chester she could give a direct order.

She wondered if men were incapable of thinking ahead or if what they thought about was completely different from what women thought about. She thought about paying off their home, putting aside money for a rainy day—except she never did—and then she thought about her friends, her enemies, and finally clothes. Clothes made the woman. She absolutely believed that and was convinced Louise would never be taken seriously by important people because she wore too much costume jewelry. Caesura Frothingham wore too much jewelry, to be sure—major jewels before sunset. Really, how lurid. But Louise would travel to Baltimore and back for a clunky bracelet. It helped if the earrings made noise, too.

Today, at the shop, her necklace, bracelet, earrings, and pin had created such a racket that Georgette Dingledine told her to take them off while she worked on her head. With a forced smile, Louise swept the bracelet off her wrist—and snapped the elastic in the process, sending little bits of painted wood and metal flying over the floor. That put her in a mood.

Juts couldn't remember one time when Chester had paid attention to clothes. She had to drag him into the Bon-Ton for a jacket or a tie.

In fact, she couldn't remember any man who cared about clothes. Even Millard Yost, who always looked natty, was dressed by Lillian.

What did she talk to her husband about? Chores, money, townspeople, and their schedules. She thought that was enough, but maybe she needed to make an effort to learn about stock-car racing. Both Chester and Paul adored the races. Watching cars go around in circles made her dizzy, but they could wax forth on the subject for hours.

Maybe if she learned about stock cars she'd become more alluring to him. She had heard stories about men's sexual desires being reignited with such tactics. Maybe that was why they didn't have a baby.

She won the hand of solitaire as he came in the back door. Buster scrambled up to greet him.

"Hi, honey."

"Hi." She turned her cheek so he could kiss it. "You know, I can double-clutch."

He blinked. "You can?"

"I can take a corner on two wheels, too. I think I ought to enter the ladies' stock-car races."

"Juts, you hate stock-car races."

She stared at her cards, now in four neat little piles. "Well— what do I have to do to be—uh—sexy to you?"

"You are sexy to me."

"Black slip?"

"You don't need a black slip." He smiled. "What set you off on this tack?"

"I don't know." She gathered up the cards, straightening them out by tapping them against the tabletop. "You've been far away."

"Oh, honey, I've got a lot on my mind."

"Yeah, I know, and I never seem to be there."

"You are." He reached down and kissed her on the lips.

47

Gas rationing didn't affect Mary Miles Mundis's desire to show off. She tooled around town in a new 1941 Pontiac V-8 Torpedo sedan coupe in creamy burgundy with a tan pin-stripe and tan interior. Harold bought the car in Baltimore for a good price because it had been sitting on the lot since the end of

1941 and the dealer, paying interest on his inventory, wanted to move it. Gas rationing killed car sales, and the automakers converted their factories for the war effort. No new cars.

Of course, Mary Miles Mundis just drove the Torpedo around town. There wasn't enough gas to drive long distances in it, which was fine with her. The main point of the automobile was not to provide transportation but to excite the envy of her friends. In this she richly succeeded.

"Would you look at that? Just swanning about." Louise slapped a comb against her thigh. "I'd look better in that car than she does. Her hair's the wrong color."

"She'll dye it to match," Toots Ryan said.

Wistfully Juts followed the progress of the beautiful machine as she stood next to Louise and Toots in the front window. "Must be great to have all that money."

"She's not that rich. She wants us to think she's rich. Harold's a contractor. His finances must be like a roller coaster."

"Chessy says what with the war and all, Harold will make a fortune. He's in there bidding for government contracts all over the state of Maryland, and since we're so close to Washington he goes down there to oil palms."

"You gotta hand it to Harold Mundis, he has ambition," Toots noted.

"I'd be happy if Pearlie showed a bit more spunk," Louis complained.

"Well, we know my husband has none, never will. He says once you hire other people, your troubles really begin." She watched Mary Miles hit the brakes, and the taillights glowed bright red. "Of course, what are a few headaches for all that money?"

"We do all right. I don't think we have headaches," Louise remarked. "We've almost paid off Flavius."

"Women have sense." Toots flicked her tongue over her teeth. "Men waste time puffing up for one another. I declare, they spend more time trying to impress one another than they do us."

"It's a man's world." Louise sighed.

"Yeah, that's why we're having another war," Juts sharply responded. "I don't give a damn who runs what. I mean, if you can do the job, do it. Why it's divided into men-do-this, women-do-that makes no sense to me. I've got more drive than Chester. I love him to death but he's not Mr. Get-Up-and-Go. Right?" They nodded their heads and she continued. "I could go out and fight for government bids same as Harold Mundis but I couldn't even get my foot in the door."

"You don't know anything about construction." Louise popped her balloon.

"No, but if I did, it still wouldn't do me any good."

"That's the whole point of marrying well, Julia. You never have figured that out. It doesn't matter how smart a woman is. If she's not married to the right man she can't make him a success. All your ambition is never going to light a fire under Chester Smith. I told you that in 1927."

"Richard doesn't breath fire, either," Toots said. Her husband worked on the loading dock for the *Clarion*.

"You can't help your heart." Juts stoutly took issue with Louise.

"Help it. *Ignore* it. Men are like streetcars, there's always another one coming round the corner." She paused for dramatic effect. "Love is the least of it—really." Her voice dropped low.

"For you."

"I love my husband, but if he hadn't had prospects I wouldn't have married him." Her lips compressed. "I had the example of Momma. I wasn't going to marry a do-nothing man."

"Sounds to me like Hansford did too much," Juts wryly replied.

"We'll never know. They're all buttoning their lips, aren't they?" Louise sarcastically said. "Oh, who cares, anyway. I don't care. Just a bunch of old people sitting around remembering stuff. About all they have is memories."

"Louise, nobody knows what the future holds. It's easier to look backward." Juts folded her arms across her chest.

"That's the truth." Toots nodded. "Rillma says sometimes she wonders if Washington will be bombed. You just never know."

"Men must be falling all over her in Washington." Louise, for a fleeting moment, wanted to trade places.

"She's met a fellow from the Free French army. He's handsome, she says. Bullette. Pierre? Louis? I don't remember. Says he works around the clock and that Francis is a good boss. He reminds her of Miss Chalfonte. 'Do it right or don't do it at all.' "

"Here she comes again." Juts laughed as Mary Miles glided by.

"How many times has she come down Frederick Street this morning?" Louise craned her neck. "If she's coming down our street you know she's going out Baltimore Street, cutting back in the alley, coming down Hanover Street, and then going out the Emmitsburg pike. She's going to make sure every single person in this town sees her."

Juts waved just in case Mary Miles was looking in—which she was. She had to swerve to get back on the road. "Funny how spring arrived overnight," Juts said.

"Spring and her new Pontiac." Louise erased the old news on Gossip Central. "Guess I'll put up that Mary Miles has a new car."

"Better not," Toots advised.

"Yeah, let her do it herself," Juts agreed. "Boy, it's deader than a doornail today. Fannie Jump even canceled her card game. Spring fever, I guess."

"Is anyone coming in?" Louise asked.

Juts walked over and ran her finger down the time line of the big appointment book. "Not a soul. I say we take the rest of the day off. I've got spring fever, too." Juts smoothed out the pages of the book. "Let's go someplace."

"Go where?"

"I don't know. Anywhere."

"We don't have a car."

"All we need to do is stand on the corner and Mary Miles is bound to cruise around again. We'll hitch a ride."

"She won't want Doodlebug and Buster in the car."

Juts stared down at the upturned faces. "Oh, hell, let's go for a walk."

They admired the daffodils peeping up at the base of the Confederate memorial. They marched straight down Hanover Street, determined to work up a big appetite for lunch. Buster barked, turned circles, and sat in front of the entrance to Trudy Archer's dance studio.

"Isn't that the cutest thing. He wants to dance." Julia Ellen laughed. She whistled for him and he followed her down the road with a backward glance at Trudy's door.

48

A paper moon, a bottle of scotch, and a large green jar of bubble bath sat on Trudy Archer's table. Chester had given her the moon and the scotch. The bubble bath was her own idea.

After dance class on Tuesday night, he would leave her apartment, only to sneak back on foot. Sometimes he brought Buster—his excuse for taking a walk. On those nights when Juts was in the air-patrol watchtower he would come late at night, when Runnymede's houselights were turned off, and leave before sunrise. He knew everyone's CAP schedule, which helped in his subterfuge. If he was really lucky he would catch a ride past the watchtower with one of the firehouse boys, since Trudy lived on the Pennsylvania side of the line. Then he'd hop out one or two blocks away in pitch-darkness and hurry to her tidy apartment.

Chessy's knock—a-shave-and-a-haircut—on the back door sent Trudy to her feet. She opened the door and Chessy hastened inside along with Buster.

"I'm so glad you're here." She put her arms around his neck and kissed him, then led him by the hand into the bathroom, where a tub filled with iridescent bubbles promised an unusual evening.

Chessy had come tonight with the intention of breaking off the affair. Each Tuesday he geared himself up to tell her this had to end, but each Tuesday he'd melt in her presence. This Tuesday proved no exception.

He discovered that when he was with Trudy he didn't think of Juts. However, when he was with his wife he often daydreamed about Trudy, her supple body and green eyes. Because Trudy was new to him he thought about her more. He knew he loved Juts, although she irritated him so much sometimes he'd get a headache. His bond to her was as much loyalty as love. Juts put up with the never-ending insults, direct and indirect, of his mother. Then again, worldly success eluded him, and she endured having to count every penny, which, given his wife's expansive nature, had to be hard on her. She cooked, cleaned, and gardened, performing the typical wifely chores in her energetic fashion. Apart from telling him what to do and how to do it, he found no fault with his wife. Much as he desired Trudy, he didn't see how he could walk out on someone who kept up her end of the bargain. It just wasn't done in Runnymede.

As he slid into the tub and Trudy handed him a glass of scotch, he put his worry out of his head.

You only live once, he thought to himself.

49

Sheriff Wheeler and Sheriff Nordness were cooperating fully over the torching of Noe Mojo's meatpacking warehouse. Each department carefully sifted through the physical evidence and then questioned potential suspects.

At first, Harper Wheeler had agreed with the general consensus that the crime was a kids' prank fueled as much by alcohol as by gasoline. Harmon Nordness kept his mouth shut. Not that he didn't think young men galvanized by Pearl Harbor weren't capable of such an act, but somehow the evidence suggested someone more sophisticated than a kid soaking rags in gasoline cans.

Their joint work yielded questions and few answers.

Harper sat in a ladder-back rocker in front of the big fireplace at Bumblebee Hill. A soft twilight flowed over the rolling hills, but the night temperature dipped into the forties. The fire warded off the chill.

"Cora, thank you for this hot coffee. You make the best coffee in Runnymede."

"Well, thank you, Harper. If you boys don't need me I'll be in the kitchen." She was determined to sand and paint the small table that sat by the window. Deep hunter-green would be perfect and she thought she might add a yellow pinstripe on the edge with a small curl in each corner.

Harper clasped his hands together as if in prayer. "Hansford,

I've run into a wall. Don't expect you'll be able to help, but you're the last person in South Runnymede for me to question." He plunged right in. "Where were you when the meat plant burned?"

"Here—in the house with Cora."

"I didn't mean to imply that you did it."

"No offense taken. Anyway, it's your job to suspect everyone."

"Yeah—I reckon."

"Do you know the history of that building, Sheriff?" Hansford slyly asked a question of his own.

"Sure do. Cassius Rife built it before the War Between the States, and then when he died Brutus kept it running."

"As a coffee mill." Hansford coughed, holding a crisply ironed handkerchief to his lips.

"Yes."

"Coffee's like the stock market, it has cycles. A man can make a fortune or lose one on a harvest in Colombia. I expect Cassius made another fortune."

"I thought it was just a coffee mill, you know, where they grind the beans and bag 'em."

"Oh, it was, it was. But he brought the green beans in by the railroad car. There's a siding there."

"Siding's been unused since the late thirties."

Hansford leaned back and put his feet up on a small woven-straw hassock. He left room for Harper's feet. "Cassius built the mill long before I was born—February 13, 1869, if you need to know. Anyway, when I was a boy the place was hopping. All of Runnymede floated in the aroma of fresh-roasted coffee beans. Sure beat living in Spring Grove, I can tell you." He laughed, mentioning the small town on Route 116 northeast of Runny-mede, in which a paper mill spewed out the odors so peculiar to cooking pulp. "The business boomed until 1929 and then the old man was gone anyway. He died in, oh"—he raised his voice—"Cora, when did Cassius Rife meet his Maker?"

"Had to be around the time Julia Ellen was born. Maybe a little after 1905."

"Well"—Hansford shrugged—"let's say somewhere between 1905 and 1908. Anyway, I was still here when he died, so 1908 will take it on the outside. Brutus took over the mill, the canning factories, and of course, the munitions plant. He sold off the coffee mill in one of those dips in the market."

"He sold it to Van Dusen in 1915."

"Carlotta's husband. He looked good in an Arrow shirt." Which was Hansford's way of saying there had not been much inside the shirt.

"Then Brutus bought it back five years later, for a tenth of what he sold it for, since Van Dusen had a box of rocks upstairs." Harper smiled. "Nothing illegal about that."

Hansford closed his eyes, then opened them. "Brutus knew that going in, Sheriff. Believe me. There's no such thing as a Rife can't smell a profit. After all, they've been making money from death—think about it. They see money in places we never look."

"I don't think Pole and Julius are that smart." Harper referred to Napoleon Bonaparte Rife and his surviving brother, Julius Caesar Rife, who ran the conglomerate together. A third brother, Ulysses S. Grant Rife, had died by his own hand, and the oldest brother, Robert E. Lee Rife, born in 1899, had moved to San Francisco, where he ran the Stagecoach Bank. As it was, Julius and Pole spent as little time in Runnymede as possible, preferring the enticements of New York City.

"Here I've been poking around in the past with my little pick, just pulling nuggets out of the vein." Hansford slowed his voice, lulling Harper, who underestimated the man.

Harper replied, "The insurance payment is contested because we can't find whoever started the damn fire. Julius and Pole are breathing down my neck. You'd think they had enough money."

Hansford shrugged. "I look at everything through a miner's eyes. You got to dig deep on this one, Harper, and I mean dig."

"I'll bear your advice in mind. Thank you, Hansford." Harper stood up.

Hansford held on to the arms of the chair and pushed himself up. "Are the Rifes trying to get money out of Noe?"

"No."

"That's unusual. Like I said, you ought to dig deep and notice if anyone poor suddenly has money."

"I'll bear it in mind, as I said." Harper shook his hand and left . . . not fully understanding what Hansford was implying.

50

Days come and days go. Sometimes one will stick in the brain like chewing gum on the sole of your shoe. April 29 was that kind of day for Julia Ellen. Hitler and Mussolini were meeting in Salzburg, and much as Juts pretended to be interested in current affairs, she was a lot more interested in her own.

Louise was taking pride in Maizie, who was becoming very popular at school. At fourteen her awkwardness could be painful, but since her peers suffered the same predicament they didn't notice it about one another. Not only was she popular with the girls, she was popular with the boys. She also danced attendance on her sad sister.

Mary, a pretty girl, asked Maizie how she had become so popular. Maizie replied, "I listen to everybody and don't interrupt."

No doubt she had learned to listen because her mother, her aunt, and Mary fought for airtime, but she didn't say that.

Juts painted the big window boxes out front of the shop, hung baskets, and arranged flowers between appointments. Buster dug up one lovely tub of pale pink tulips, receiving a spanking for his efforts. Both sisters worked hard that day, fueled by the fact that they had one more payment to Flavius Cadwalder before they would be out of debt.

By the time Juts dragged home she felt out of sorts. She lay down on the sofa, intending to read the *Trumpet,* when Chester came home early.

"Hi, hon," she called out.

"Hi," he answered from the kitchen. "Got off early. Want a drink?"

"No, I'm so tired it would put me right out."

She listened as he cracked ice cubes, appearing with a scotch.

"I'm bushed." He sat opposite her on the sofa.

"Don't take your shoes off. That's worse than mustard gas."

He crossed his feet at the ankles, his shoes nearly touching her face. "We build fighter planes but can't fix stinky feet." He swallowed a bit. "Hey, what if we go to a movie tonight?"

Pooped as she was, she could always find the energy to go to a show. She fluffed up her hair while Chester finished his drink.

They made it just in time.

After the show, a soft mist curled around Runnymede Square.

"Who's in the tower tonight?"

"Caesura and Pearlie."

"How'd he get roped into that?"

"I was short a man so he pitched in. It's pretty out tonight, isn't it?" The Corinthian columns from the bank loomed out of the mists as they strolled by.

"A little damp."

He put his wife's arm through his. "My tests came back finally." She walked quietly and he said, "I'm the bad guy here. It's because of me we can't have children. Not enough sperm. Doc Horning said it was maybe 'cause of the mumps I had when I was a kid."

Julia said nothing as they kept walking. They stopped to admire the display in the Bon-Ton window, a golf outfit highlighted against a realistic green, the pennant hanging with number 16 on it.

Her first response when she did speak was, "Did you tell your mother?"

"No. I wouldn't do that."

"I don't guess I'm surprised, Chessy." She squeezed his arm. "Something had to be wrong. After all, we've been married long enough to get lucky—don't you think? I mean, it's not like we didn't know, it's just now we really know."

"Yeah."

"We can adopt."

"That's—let's take it as it comes, Julia. My family won't accept an adopted baby."

"So?" she belligerently replied.

"Don't you think that will make it hard on a kid?"

"Life *is* hard."

"You're losing me."

"Life is hard. The kid will find out early. That's how I see it. If we love the baby, then he will have a head start in life. We have to do the best we can. I don't give a rat's ass what your mother thinks about anything. She's never cut me slack since day one. We need a baby, Chester. If we don't do it soon we'll be too old to raise a child—too set in our ways."

"Honey, let's give this a little time."

"How much time?" She was right in his face now.

"I'll know."

"What kind of answer is that?"

"It's the only answer I have. Jesus H. Christ, Julia. I feel awful. This is all my fault. I need to get my feet under me."

"It's not your fault. It's something inside your body."

"If feels like my fault." He jerked his head up. "I'm not saying no. I'm saying I need to . . ." He shrugged. Emotional descriptions eluded him. He felt plenty but he said little.

"All right." She was matter-of-fact, as though this were a bargain between them. "Let's hope you know before I run out of patience."

He put his arm around her as they crossed the street and walked into the square, the mist giving George Gordon Meade a runny nose.

51

The boys who enlisted after Pearl Harbor had all completed basic training. It was only a matter of time before most of them would be posted overseas.

Rob McGrail and Doak Garten missed the Battle of Midway, which infuriated them, for it was a decisive American victory according to the newspapers, although by now people took the war news with a grain of salt. They may have been small-town, but they weren't stupid.

The S.S. commander in Czechoslovakia, former Olympian Reinhard Heydrich, had been assassinated. The occupying forces announced they would destroy an entire Czech village, Lidice, in retaliation for killing a man even the Germans themselves didn't like. The British were being handed their ass in the desert as the Germans roared toward Tobruk.

A restlessness infected Americans. They wanted to fight now. The tedious process of training men, gathering sufficient materials, and getting them across the Atlantic and Pacific dragged on.

People danced longer, laughed louder, and partied harder than before. They thumbed their noses at death by celebrating life. Julia danced the most. Chester still had not surprised his wife by dancing. Louise discovered parties, not that she had avoided them before, but now she entered into the spirit of them because she said it was good for morale. She was really doing it for the boys.

This particular June 15, Runnymede Day, celebrating the Magna Carta, fell on a Monday, so people enjoyed a long weekend. The pageant took place in Runnymede Square, where it always had, and most inhabitants dressed in thirteenth-century costumes, which meant lots of brightly dyed bedsheets wrapped in silken draper cords. Digby Vance played King John while Millard Yost was head of the barons.

Local breweries supplied kegs of beer, the Coca-Cola dealer donated sodas, and the Rifes paid for free hot dogs. Spoon races, three-legged races, and gunnysack races filled the afternoon once King John got his comeuppance.

Chester winked at Trudy Archer but steered clear. Celeste and Ramelle won the three-legged race against all comers, even the kids. The sight of Celeste Chalfonte hopping along unraveled her opponents.

With the soft fall of a long twilight the band played; adults and children danced under gently swaying lanterns. Julia Ellen and Louise were on tower duty at nine, but they hung around until the last sliver of light.

As they climbed the ladder up to the top the music sounded ethereal. Juts sang along as she swung her leg over the side of the sturdy tower. Louise, being the elder, believed she was in charge; she checked and double-checked the enemy-aircraft silhouettes leaning against one side of the tower. Juts double-checked the big searchlight, antiaircraft gun, and siren.

"You've got those memorized cold."

"Doesn't hurt to refresh my memory," Louise smugly said.

"How much did you have to drink?"

"I don't drink."

"Oh, yeah, I forgot," came the sarcastic reply as Juts sat down.

"How much did you have to drink?"

"A beer." Which meant at least three. "But don't worry. I drank it at six. It's worn off by now."

"When you climb up and down that ladder to go to the bathroom I'll know this is just another Juts fact." Louise called any fib a Juts fact.

Julia leaned over the tower to watch the dancing below. She tapped her foot to the beat. The scarlets, royal blues, burnt oranges, yellows, and purples of the costumes sparked her imagination. This really could be a square in medieval England.

"Think dead people had as much fun as we do?"

"No, they're dead." Louise fiddled with her binoculars.

"That's not what I mean. I mean, when the people who signed the Magna Carta were alive, do you think they had as much fun as we do?"

Louise stood next to her sister to observe the music and frolic. "I don't know. They had the One True Church, so they weren't tempted by false prophets."

Disgusted, Julia, a tepid Protestant but a Protestant nonetheless, said, "I bet they didn't think of the church when there was dance music. I bet they didn't worry about half the crap we worry about. And I was reading somewhere—maybe the 'Your Health' column in the paper—that they had fewer cavities than we do because they didn't have refined sugar. Their sweets were made with honey. Sugarcane came with the New World. So there."

"What did they do when they got sick? Died. That's what."

"So? So do we—it just takes longer. You know what else I think?"

"I can hardly wait." Louise spied Maizie dancing with a classmate, yet another of the numerous BonBons.

"I believe we grow all our lives—"

Louise interrupted. "Junior McGrail certainly did. Took two chenille bedspreads to make her robe that time."

"I remember. Anyway, if we don't keep growing we shrivel up."

"Juts, you had more than one beer."

"Two, but let me finish."

"Let you finish? You'll talk all night."

"I will not, Louise, but I want to tell you this. I think the dead keep growing, too. If our souls depart our bodies, then the soul can keep learning, so if I want to talk to Mamaw I can, and it affects her as well as me." Juts mentioned their deceased grandmother.

Since this was close to blasphemy, Louise, on dogma alert, remained silent for some time. "I don't know about that. I'd have to ask Father O'Reilly."

"Think for yourself."

"I do," came the curt response. Irritated, Louise put the binoculars back up to her eyes. "I don't believe my eyes."

"What?"

"Chester is dancing."

"Oh, he is not." Juts paused a moment. "Not unless someone poured twelve beers down his throat. He can't dance." She reached up for the binoculars but Louise shrugged her off because they both heard a droning in the sky. Louise scanned the night skies.

Julia babbled on. "Had to be someone else, not Chester." She craned her neck to peer into the velvet darkness. "Louise—"

"Julia, shut up!" Louise searched for the plane. "There he is!"

"It's one of ours."

"Shut up!" Louise trained the glasses on the plane, looking for telltale insignia. A big white number was painted on the side, as well as a white circle with a white star inside. "It's a Boxcar. Wonder what he's doing here?"

"Thought he'd drop in on the party." Juts wanted those binoculars. "Maybe the weather's bad where he came from."

"Could be." Louise dropped the binoculars. They hung around her neck.

"Let me." Juts reached for them and Louise flipped the strap over her head.

Juts didn't bother to check out the airplane. She zoomed right in on the dancing. "He's not dancing. He's sitting next to his mother, the bitch."

"He was dancing with his mother."

"Boy, he must be loaded."

"Looked okay to me."

"Maybe she held him up. She thinks she's been doing it for thirty-six years."

"I'm telling you, he was dancing with his mother."

Juts didn't believe her. She changed the subject, which was what she always did when she wanted to avoid an argument or slide away from criticism. "I've a mind to ask the old battle-ax what's the deal with Hansford? Wouldn't you like to see her face?"

"No. I don't care."

"Ah, Wheezer, come on, he's our father."

"Some father."

Julia shrugged. "I don't guess we ever know what goes on inside someone else's head. Maybe he had good reason."

"His excuses don't hold water. I don't see why you waste time on him."

"Because he's the only father we've got, whether he's a good one or a bad one, and when he's gone, that's the end of that. We'll never know whatever it is he learned from life."

"You're on a learning kick."

"Some people learn from books. I learn from people."

"And what have you learned so far?" Louise challenged her.

"That everyone has their reasons, no matter how crack-brained they may be. People really think they're doing the right thing. Adolf Hitler thinks he's doing the right thing."

"That's ridiculous. You're telling me that Hitler doesn't know right from wrong."

"He knows. He thinks he's right."

"I don't believe it. Some people serve the Devil."

"I think some people serve themselves—it's the same difference."

Louise wrinkled her nose. This was a new thought for her, and her first reaction was always to stiff-arm something new. However, she mulled it over. "I don't know."

They sat together, listening, the laughter curling up from below. Tears trickled down Julia Ellen's rosy cheeks.

Louise noticed. "Juts, what's the matter?"

"I don't know."

"Are you sick?" Louise got cross. "I know you drank too much. You always babble when you do."

"I did not." Juts stopped crying. "I feel funny, that's all."

"If you get sick up here in this tower I am not cleaning it up."

"I'm not sick!" Her eyes flashed. "I feel blue, kind of. Louise, you can be a real turd sometimes, you know that? I don't pick on you when you feel blue or have the mean reds."

"I don't get the mean reds." Louise tucked up her chin.

"The hell you don't."

Ignoring this, Louise said, "What's going on?"

"Chester hasn't said a word about a baby since the results

came back from Dr. Horning. He said he needed time, but how much time?"

"It's only been—well, a few weeks. Don't pressure him."

"I haven't said a word." She wiped her eyes. "Wheezie, maybe he doesn't love me anymore. If he loved me he'd know this means the world to me."

"He loves you. Being a father doesn't seem to be as important to men as being a mother is to us. Leave him alone."

"You think?"

"Men are like children, Juts. I don't know why you can't get that through your head. You treat them like a friend, and you can't. Chester is a big boy so you think for him, manage him— you know."

"God, Louise, that's so much work. I want a husband who can go and do for himself."

"Never happen."

"Pearlie seems to do all right."

"I make his appointments, I keep his books, run the house, I figure out big purchases—he's too impulsive—I lay out his clothes each morning. What does he have to worry about? Not one thing. All he has to do is get up in the morning and go to work. It's never going to change, Julia. Women have been organizing men since B.C."

"No wonder we're exhausted."

In the depth of the night the only music left was provided by Patience Horney, who availed herself of the free beer. She lay sprawled on her back in the middle of the square singing "Sweet Marie" at the top of her lungs. Occasionally she varied this tune with a heartfelt rendition of "Silver Threads Among the Gold."

Finally both the sheriffs converged upon the square. Half of Patience belonged to Pennsylvania and the other half belonged to Maryland. Patience was probably the only drunken person in the history of the United States to sleep smack on the Mason-Dixon line. After a fulsome discussion as to where she should continue her slumbers, the North jail or the South jail, the two men reached a compromise and carried her home.

Staying awake pushed every Civil Air Patrol watchman to the limit. Sometimes Juts dozed off, then Louise would rouse her and vice versa. Neither woman noticed Chessy slip off with Buster after the party broke up. The only bad thing about neither Chessy nor Juts being home at night was that Yoyo went on a rampage. Usually Chessy could get home in plenty of time to repair the damage.

At about 0400—Louise had taken to using military time—both sisters slept, sitting down, leaning against the side of the tower. Louise opened her eyes first. She heard a strange sound. She stared up at the sky and saw Prussian-blue cumulus clouds curling over her head. She knew there were airplanes up there—not one or two, but a squadron.

She shook Julia. "Juts, Juts, wake up!"

"Huh."

Louise, on her feet, tried to catch sight of the planes coming closer now. She strained for a glimpse of anything through her binoculars but the clouds played peekaboo with her.

Juts scrambled up, strained to hear the sound, but it didn't sound like engines to her, although there was something up there, sure enough.

"Hit the lights," Louise commanded.

Julia hurried, rolled back the canvas, and turned on the great searchlight, but it took a moment or two to warm up. "Shit, this sucker's heavy." She trained it straight up in the sky.

"Can't you move it around—over there."

"Stop giving orders!"

"I'm the senior officer here," Louise spat at her.

"Oh, balls."

"If those are enemy aircraft up there you'll have a lot to answer for!"

That settled Juts's hash. Reluctantly obedient, she grunted and groaned as she swung the big light upward toward the noise.

"Stukas!" Louise shouted.

The black silhouettes in a V, high up, could have been the lean German dive-bombers used to devastating effect.

"The motors sound funny."

"It's the altitude—Julia, stay on the planes."

"I lose them in the clouds."

"Stay on them! I'll crank the siren."

"Shouldn't we be certain before we blast everyone out of bed?"

"Better *we* blast them out of bed than the Germans."

"Okay." Julia steadied the light, her shoulders straining as she tried to tip the beam at a higher angle.

Louise turned the big wooden handle on the siren and the low wail, a sound of terror the world over, shrieked through the summer night.

"Louise! Louise!" Julia shouted, but Louise couldn't hear her over the earsplitting howl. "It's Canadian geese!"

People poured out of their houses in nightgowns and pajamas, pastel robes for the ladies as the siren split the night's silence.

Juts tapped Louise on the shoulder. She stopped turning the handle for a moment. "Canadian geese!" Juts shouted.

"Impossible." Her disbelief had some foundation, for those beautiful flyers usually migrate north in spring, returning for the fall.

Juts kept the beam on the geese, who soared in and out of the huge clouds. "Look for yourself."

Louise watched as the V formation flew directly overhead. "Oh, my God." She dropped her glasses. "Julia, Julia, you can't *tell* anyone."

"Jesus, Louise, we can't have people thinking it's the Germans. It will get all of Maryland in an uproar."

"You can't do this to me!" Tears rolled down Louise's cheeks. "Canadian geese," she cried out loud.

"Come on, Wheezer." Juts thought and said, "Tell them it's German geese." She paused. "Anyone can make a mistake."

"Not one this big." Louise picked up the binoculars. "Oh, no." Then she swung them down to look at the people. "Oh, God!"

People staggered out of back doors, shot out of front doors. A few, perhaps still feeling no pain from Runnymede Day, leapt out of windows.

Caesura Frothingham, in her nightgown, exposing more of herself than anyone needed to see, was screaming, "We'll be killed," just as Wheezie fired the antiaircraft gun in the air to pretend she was attacking the enemy.

Mother Smith pointed to the sky as Rupert knocked her down on the ground.

Verna BonBon, surprisingly calm, checked every house on her street. If she didn't hear sounds of danger, she wasn't going to lie down on dew-soaked grass.

After firing the perfunctory round, Louise again scanned the uproar with her binoculars. A tinny note crept into her voice. "Juts—Juts, look."

The minute she handed her sister the glasses and pointed, Louise realized she'd made a horrible blunder. She should have kept this new knowledge to herself. Too late now.

Juts trained the glasses on the people below, then picked out what caught Wheezie's eye. Chessy was running down the street from the North Runnymede side, Buster running with him. About half a block away she saw Trudy Archer standing in a lace nightgown, watching him run. Juts handed the binoculars back to her sister and lunged toward the big light. With all her strength she swung the beam from the skies down to the streets below, sweeping over Lillian Yost, hair in pink curlers, illuminating Runnymede's finest in disarray.

"Have I got him?"

"Bullseye!"

"Dead to shit," Juts said through gritted teeth.

"You'd better swing that thing back up in the sky."

"I want him to fry."

"He will, but if you don't swing that back up, Julia, we will, too."

Juts, bracing herself by putting one foot against the tower wall, heaved the hot light back up into the sky. The sound of honking receded while screams below picked up volume.

The first person to the base of the tower was Fannie Jump Creighton, who had never gone to bed. Or more accurately had never gone to sleep. The young man at her side couldn't have been a day over eighteen. On closer inspection it proved to be Roger Bitters, two years younger than his brother, Extra Billy.

"What is it?" Fannie yelled up.

"Stukas," Louise yelled down, "flying at about ten thousand feet, I'd guess."

"Okay." Fannie ran toward the firehouse to get a phone. Harmon, doomed not to sleep tonight, stopped when she waved him down. She tucked her head in the window and told him what Louise had reported. He called it out on the police radio. Prudently, he kept his headlights off.

Bewildered people stood in the middle of the streets. Caesura remained crouched by her car, taking no chances. The amount of white cream slathered on her face would have absorbed flying debris with no ill effect to her.

Louise, with presence of mind after her initial gaffe, cranked the air-raid siren and gave the all clear.

As soon as she finished, Harper climbed into the tower. "What happened?"

Louise opened her mouth but it was so dry no sound came out.

Juts quickly filled in, "A squadron of German planes, at about ten thousand feet."

"Could you recognize them?"

Louise nodded. "Stukas."

Julia hastened to add, "We were lucky people didn't turn their lights on once we sounded the alarm. The blackout saved us." She heard a clamber below her and peeped over to see her husband hauling himself up the ladder. She picked up a thermos jug, aiming it right at his head. "You son of a bitch!"

Harper looked over the side. "Juts, he couldn't help being asleep. Now, you calm down. The sight of an enemy squadron is enough to shake everyone. Good job, ladies."

Louise smiled weakly but Julia had a mission: She was going to kill her husband.

She reached for the binoculars. Louise pulled them away from her. Juts took off her shoe, hitting Chessy square on the head.

"Julia," he called, hanging on to the ladder. "I can explain everything."

"Explain it to God." She pulled off her other shoe.

She put two and two together with alarming speed: the shell earrings and Chester's dancing with his mother.

A crowd had gathered below. Louise grabbed her sister by the elbow. "You have to understand. Julia is a fighter. She's furious she didn't get to fire the antiaircraft gun like I did. Aren't you?" Louise couldn't think of a better story.

Juts blinked. "Uh—" She focused on Harper. "We had 'em, Harper. We had 'em in our sights but the clouds messed us up!"

Chester neither ascended nor descended. People shouted from below. He turned his head, calling to them, "Hold on. Just wait a minute."

Harper leaned over, cupped his hands over his mouth, and shouted, "German planes. It's all right now. Go on home."

"How do we know there won't be more?" Millard sensibly replied.

"We don't." Louise leaned over the side as Pearlie raced up to the tower base with Mary and Maizie. "But we're not their target."

Popeye Huffstetler, sensing his big break, a wire story with his byline, shouted out so many questions from below that Louise finally yelled, "Popeye, I will answer all your questions but not until I make a full report to the head of the Civil Air Patrol. You all go on back home." She looked straight down at Chester. "You'd better come along with me. Don't you think?"

"Yes."

She turned to Juts. "You need to make a report, too."

"I will." Juts's lips quivered. She didn't know whether to sob or kill.

As they made their way down the ladder, elbowing through the crowd to Harper's waiting squad car, Julia wouldn't let Chester touch her. Popeye followed in his 1937 Chevy.

Louise dutifully made her report to Hagerstown, waking up Colonel Froling. Then she and Juts answered Popeye's insistent questions. Buster patiently sat by his mother's knee. Chester stood behind the women. Louise had managed to whisper to Pearlie what happened with Chester so Pearlie stood by Chester—just in case. He sent Mary and Maizie home.

Millard Yost took over in the tower along with Roger Bitters, who volunteered to stay. The tower couldn't be left empty at a time like this.

By five-thirty in the morning the reports had been completed.

"Let me take you home, honey." Chester reached for Julia's hand.

She shied away from him. "I'll walk. I need time to think."

"I'll carry you home," Louise said. She glared at Chester. "We'll meet you there." For everyone else's benefit she said, "We're exhausted and I'd be a liar if I didn't tell you we were scared."

As the group parted for them, Juts breathed deeply and said, "I feel like the running gears of hard times."

The story, along with pictures of the Hunsenmeir girls, went out over the UPI wire service, AP wire service, and Reuters. The next day Juts and Louise were so besieged they locked their doors.

Popeye, whose story was picked up by a wire service, was in tabloid heaven.

52

The drama of infidelity rarely unfolds privately. Like a slow hiss in a punctured tire, the news leaks out. Mother Smith, while publicly maintaining the sanctity of marriage, managed to secrete a few comments on why men stray. Something must be amiss with the wife. Privately she gloated over Julia Ellen's grief.

She was even snide when visiting her son one day while Juts was shopping. Walking around the backyard, noticing the garden, Rupert asked his son, "What's she growing in there?" Josephine smugly replied, "Sour grapes." Chester, as usual, remained silent.

Louise, stunned at her sister's decline, sympathized. Sympathy gave way to encouragement, which devolved into hectoring. "Snap out of it."

Juts couldn't.

Cora paid special attention to her younger daughter and even Celeste, usually aloof from such domestic swamps, worried about Julia, saying to Cora, "Her mind is oppressed with care. She's turning in on herself. There must be something we can do."

"Time heals all wounds," Cora replied.

"Time wounds all heels," Celeste responded, then wondered if Chessy really was a heel. Since she thought monogamy a lovely pipe dream, she preferred not to dwell upon it. But Julia believed in faithfulness with all her heart and soul, a belief now painfully apparent to everyone. People usually underestimate Juts because of her rebelliousness and partying ways, but she felt things deeply, and this time she couldn't hide it.

It was as though her intelligence was paralyzed. She got up, cooked breakfast, went to work, came home, played with Yoyo and Buster, but life moved neither forward nor back.

Hansford had a long talk with Chester, who repented of his ways. He broke off the relationship with Trudy, and he cried because he feared he'd lost Juts forever. She stayed with him but she didn't trust him.

His mother hinted he should leave. He couldn't. He had betrayed the person who loved him most and had stood by him since the day they collided in front of the altar.

Even though his men friends allowed as how these things happen, he couldn't shake his pressing guilt nor his fear at the sight of his wife's body. She was wasting away.

He took her to the movies. At one three-hanky picture she sobbed so hard he had to take her out of the theater. People pretended not to notice. By morning that story was all over Runnymede.

Trudy Archer sank a bit herself. She loved Chester, no matter how hopeless the situation. In time, she began to date Senior Epstein. The jeweler was so thrilled to have female companionship that he cared little about her fallen-woman status. Business at the dance studio sure picked up. Half the men in town came around. Perverse as it was, the women then joined their husbands out of raw fear. Marriages that had been extinct volcanoes suddenly erupted. Without knowing it, Trudy put the fire back into many a union.

Extra Billy noted Julia Ellen's thin frame and downcast eyes when home on leave before being shipped out to the Pacific theater. Mary, too young to comprehend why her aunt was shattered, made a point, at her mother's urging, of spending a precious hour with her husband visiting Juts. Mary had been worrying herself nearly as thin as Julia. She was smart enough to know that Extra Billy's posting meant he'd soon be in the thick of the shooting match.

Two years passed and Juts moved from intense grief to numbness to anger. She began to enjoy exercising her stale power over her husband. After all, she was the pure victim and he the embodiment of male sin. Chester accepted this as part of his punishment. Juts gained back a little weight. She didn't look so cadaverous. Many attributed her renewed health to the fact that Trudy married Senior Epstein in June 1944. Jacob junior sent a telegram from the French border wishing his father well. It was the last anyone ever heard from him.

Many other young men from the border town enlisted the moment they graduated from high school. Others skedaddled to York or Baltimore, lied about their age, and enlisted while only sixteen.

Zeb Vance was hurt in a training accident stateside. Ray Parker, a tank gunner, was killed in combat near the German border. Tom West lost part of his lower jaw charging a machine gunners' nest. The worry drew people closer together. Few were free from anxiety.

Rob McGrail wound up in the Navy band, which infuriated him. He wanted to fight, a surprise to those who knew him as a fat, lazy kid. Military life whipped him into shape, and gave him a breath of fresh air amid masculine companionship. Rob turned out to be handsome. But he chafed at tinkling on the glockenspiel for dignitaries.

Doak Garten was assigned cook duties on a submarine. Segregation existed below the sea as well as above it, but Doak, an unusually self-possessed young man, kept bitterness at bay. He was proud to serve his country and he rode out the depth charges as well as any other man on the sub. He may not have won equality but he won respect. It was a beginning. He came home on leave once, promising his family that when this war was over he was going to amount to something. They told him he already did.

Vaughn Cadwalder, breveted to a lieutenant in combat, had been wounded twice. A bullet passed through the fleshy part of his calf. He let the doctors sew him up, leave a drain in, and he returned to his unit. The next time he was hit in the shoulder, the bullet lodging in his clavicle. The medics cut out the lead, bandaged him up, tied up his arm, and he walked out again against protests from the doctors. Vaughn discovered he was a born warrior. Even when the Germans shot both legs out from under him, crippling him, he continued to crawl toward the machine gunners' nest. His platoon took the nest. Vaughn was awarded the Silver Star.

Joe BonBon fought in Italy. His few letters home were filled with wonder at the beauties of the country and the utter imbecility of its leaders.

Edgar Frost copiloted B-17 bombers over Germany. He made captain. He hated the war, he hated dropping death down on people he couldn't see, but even more he hated Hitler and what he had done to a country Edgar had visited while a junior at the University of Maryland. If this was the only way to fix the mess, so be it.

It was as though Runnymede collectively held its breath for its sons and lately its daughters. Vicky BonBon joined her brothers in the Army. She, too, was posted to Europe. Spottiswood Chalfonte, sick to death of being a glamour girl in Hollywood, chucked it all to become an Army nurse, and served in the Philippines. What she saw of the war was the wounds, inside and out.

The tide had turned in 1944. The Allies, after taking beating after beating in 1941 and 1942, even in 1943, pushed back the Axis powers.

Although citizens in Runnymede and Spokane and Pueblo—as well as in Medicine Hat or Rostov-on-Don or Keswick, in Auckland or Melbourne, wherever there were Allies—knew their side was winning, each soul feared the deaths yet to come. The tide had turned but it was still a tide of blood.

And so the small casualty of a woman's honor seemed tiny indeed, even to the woman herself. Rillma Ryan, by mid-March, had known she was pregnant without benefit of marriage. She refused to divulge the name of the father, although the name Bullette was whispered. Rillma couldn't make up her mind what to do. She was happy, frightened, and terribly confused. Her mother, along with Celeste Chalfonte, took the train to D.C. Rillma wanted to keep the child, but Toots and Celeste advised against it. She'd have to marry fast and risk a life of unhappiness with the wrong mate or navigate the world as an unmarried woman with a child. That was a sure ticket to poverty. Or she could move west and make up a story about a father killed in combat—but sooner or later, even in the most remote part of the world, the truth comes out.

Rillma, still wanting to keep her baby, finally surrendered when Celeste reminded her, "You once told me you would do anything for me. Do you remember that?"

"Yes," a surprisingly composed Rillma replied.

"Then I wish you to give the baby to Juts. Chester has agreed to adoption."

Only then did Rillma give way. But she agreed to Celeste's terms. The curiosity of it was that no one wondered why Celeste Chalfonte had taken charge of the situation. They were accustomed to Celeste in command.

And so Juts became a mother at last. Chester prayed the baby would heal their wounds. He sought counseling from Pastor Neely because he feared that his infidelity would render him unfit for the heavy responsibilities of fatherhood. Pastor Neely only replied that if that were the case, there'd be few fathers in Runnymede.

Louise, torn about accepting an illegitimate child into the family—who would become a first cousin, after all, to Mary's little Oderuss—also sought guidance. Father O'Reilly told her the sin belonged to the parents, not the child, and with this blessing she enthusiastically supported the idea of the nameless baby becoming a Hunsenmeir, so to speak.

Cora and Hansford merrily painted a room in Julia's house, rooted out old baby garments, and prepared for the arrival. They painted the room a pretty pale yellow, figuring that would do nicely for a boy or a girl.

Mother Smith smoldered with contempt. Even Rupert grew disgusted with her, not that he was keen on the idea of a bastard carrying the Smith name.

The cherub arrived in a small, discreet hospital on November 28, 1944. A tiny girl. It was a rainy, cold day and a bittersweet one; the previous evening, Celeste Chalfonte, bullheaded and bored with waiting for the baby, had decided to ride and pop over fences despite the gathering twilight. She broke her neck and died instantly. She never saw the baby she had shepherded toward adoption. Despite the shock and grief, Ramelle assured Louise that she would step in as the baby's godmother.

Juts cried twice, out of loss for Celeste and out of joy for the baby.

But November 28 was to prove a memorable day, freighted with events and meanings only the years would unravel. Rillma Ryan snuck out of the hospital in the middle of the night, running away with her still-unnamed child.

In fury and despair, Juts, Chessy, Louise, and Toots began the search for the infant. Rillma, finally coming to her senses, slunk home three weeks later and reported she had left the baby in a Catholic orphanage in Pittsburgh. Everyone pooled their gas-ration coupons and Chessy and Louise drove there to fetch the baby. They pretended to be married; she'd caught him in an affair—that was their story—but was willing to claim his child.

By that time, Julia, through so many ups and downs, had caught pneumonia and had to stay home with Buster, Yoyo, Mary, Maizie, and Pearlie in attendance.

On the way back from Pittsburgh, a whopping blizzard struck with white fury. The infant weighed five pounds, one reason the good sisters were glad to release her. All across the great state of Pennsylvania, Chessy and Louise would pull into gas stations, farmhouses, wherever there was light, to get milk and warm it for the infant. Not one person refused them and many gave them gas coupons to make sure they would get back to Runnymede.

Once in Runnymede they immediately took the infant to Dr. Horning. Exhausted, Louise burst into racking sobs when the doctor begged them not to take the baby to Juts. Why let her love something that was sure to die?

Chester, dark circles around his eyes, hands shaking, took the baby from Dr. Horning and vowed, "This baby isn't going to die. You tell me what I have to do."

And so for the next six months, Chester Smith got up each night, every three hours, to feed the scrawny thing a special formula. Julia Ellen recovered in a month and she, too, fed the baby around the clock. They never complained about the lack of sleep. Sometimes they'd both get up at the same time, even though one should have seized the chance to sleep. They liked to hold the girl together. Finally, by May 8, Nicole Rae Smith, called Nickel by everyone, was so fat she looked like a sumo wrestler. She was healthy enough to be carried in her daddy's arms to celebrate V.E. day with all of Runnymede. People cried, shouted, and drank. Surely it would be a better world now.

And Julia Ellen returned to the land of the living. Julia, her Chesterfield stapled to her lip; Julia, who shot from the hip; Julia, who tweaked authority and danced until dawn; Julia Ellen was finally a mother.

PART THREE

53

The lilac bushes drooped low from the colorful masses of butterflies perched on the nourishing blossoms: red-spotted purples, their electric blue fanning over the black wingtips; yellow and black swallowtails, like elegant dancers swooping over the fragrant pale purple blooms; a huge Thaos swallowtail, a band of purest yellow horizontally slashed across the black wings from tip to tip. Angelwings, more subdued in color but not in conformation, hovered so close to Nickel's tiny ears that the puffs of air from their wings tickled her. The air was alive with sulphur butterflies, blues of every hue, skippers, and cloudywings, hairstreaks, buckeyes, whites and marblewings, checkered wings, goatweeds, and tiny butterflies the color of milkweed.

Each time the two-year-old reached for a butterfly, with a flutter it eluded her grasp. Yoyo, by now rather fond of the two-legged intruder, sprawled on her side under the lilac bush. Too lazy to catch a butterfly, she enjoyed watching them swirl as the tip of her tail wagged as if in a breeze. A bold orange monarch zipped by her nose. Yoyo nonchalantly slapped at it and missed.

Yoyo and Buster were the child's two best friends, with Louise's Doodlebug a close third. She played with other toddlers: her cousin Oderuss, two years older; little Jackson Frost, two years older; Robert Marker, one year older; and Ursula Vance, also one year older.

Nickel walked at a very early age. Her coordination was extraordinary. However, she spoke little, which worried Juts so much she took the child to the doctor, who declared her throat and vocal cords were intact; her mental powers, for her age, appeared superior. He concluded that Nicole Smith didn't have anything she wanted to say. In truth, she played so much with Yoyo and Buster that words were irrelevant.

She certainly mastered "No," which she pronounced vigorously whenever Juts or Louise pushed her toward something that held no interest for her, such as dolls. Nor did she want to eat baby food from jars, offered for her gastronomic pleasure. To make matters worse the child loathed milk. Julia Ellen feared she would become dehydrated, because once they weaned her off her special formula she wouldn't drink anything but water. So Juts put Coca-Cola in her baby bottle and Nickel gurgled with glee. While other mothers criticized Julia for her unorthodox methods, she replied, "Fine, you handle her."

A few attempts at bending the baby's will to their own quickly dissuaded Mary Miles Mundis, Frances Finster, Lillian Yost, and other professional mothers from fooling with the curly-haired girl. Lillian had lost her firstborn to a fever in 1943 but she bore a perfect little boy a year later, and she and Julia spent a lot of time watching their tots, so close in age, crawl around together. Millard junior, called Mill, was a sweet little baby with flaming red hair and more freckles than a pinto.

Although Nickel liked tiny ones her own age, she gravitated toward animals and occasionally adults. She had a disquieting way of sitting motionless and silent, her big brown eyes following every movement of the grown-ups.

She loved Cora but fussed at Hansford; his beard scratched. She adored Ramelle and would clap her hands together whenever the willowy gray-haired beauty appeared.

She ignored Mary and the now-rebellious Maizie but she toddled after Pearlie and Extra Billy. She smiled when Louise gave her a dog biscuit. Nicky would flop on the floor and try to chew the biscuit like Buster or Doodlebug. She got Oderuss to eat a biscuit, too, which did not endear Nicky to Mary. Patiently, the dogs would wait for her to become bored with her trophy, or for Oderuss to drop the dog biscuit and leave it, and then one of the dogs would snatch it. If the baby cried, Buster, to everyone's amazement, especially Yoyo's, would drop the biscuit back at Nickel's feet.

Aunt Dimps declared the child was going to grow up to be an animal trainer. Ramelle would carry Nickel into the stable, put her on a horse's back, and hold her. Nickel showed no fear. Ramelle declared the child was going to be as good a rider as Celeste. Louise said Nickel would become a writer, which made everyone laugh, since Julia Ellen hated writing even a grocery list. The only book in the Smith house was the Bible, which Julia ignored. Cora told everyone that Nicole would be whatever she wanted to be. She had a mind of her own.

The one person who abstained from these prophecies was Mother Smith. She refused to see the baby, nor would she allow Chessy in her house with an illegitimate child. Rupert appeared to have no interest in this subject one way or another but he was smoking more than normal and slipping in a few extra scotches. Chester called upon his mother every Tuesday, dutiful as always, but he never visited the house at any other time despite her entreaties and occasional furies. Mother Smith grew increasingly embittered but since she had cultivated no true friends in this life, no one cared.

Two soldiers passing through Runnymede on leave in 1945 fell in love with the town. Pierre and Bob, as soon as they were mustered out of the service, bought the Curl 'n' Twirl from the Hunsenmeirs. Juts put her half of the money into savings bonds for Nickel, the only time in her life that she showed prudence. To everyone's surprise, Louise splurged and bought her own automobile. Pearlie nearly died. When he rode in the passenger seat he feared he truly would. Louise's Buick coupe, a handsome British racing green, excited her as few things in life had.

Juts, tired from running after Nickel one afternoon, collapsed in the white deck chair. Louise pulled up in the driveway. She gave the twoey whistle.

"I'm in the backyard," Juts replied to their childhood signal.

Buster rushed out to greet Doodlebug. Yoyo stayed put. No dog was worth that much effort.

Louise, purse over her arm, shoes, bag, gloves, and hat matching, traipsed into the backyard, exclaiming, "I've never seen anything like it," as she beheld the cloud of butterflies.

"Me neither."

"You've got to take a picture."

"I'm too tired to get the Brownie."

"I'll get it." Louise scurried into the pantry, where Juts kept the small black box camera. She returned to snap photos of Nickel reaching for butterflies and rolling on the grass with Buster and Doodlebug. In one picture, which she hoped would be good, the child was jumping in the air, the big zebra swallowtail just out of reach, its wings outstretched to the full as it headed for the papaw tree behind the lilac bush.

Juts clapped her hands in rhythm. "Dance, Nicky, dance for Aunt Wheezer."

Nickel stopped chasing butterflies and turned to face the adults. She put her hands on her hips.

Louise, also cajoling, sang, "If I knew you were coming I'da baked a cake." Juts sang along.

The child lifted her hands over her head and danced a little jig, Doodlebug and Buster yipping and yapping on either side of her.

Yoyo, disgusted at such display, remained immobile under the lilacs.

After her dance Nickel flung herself on the ground and cooed, "Kiddie cat."

Yoyo yawned.

Nickel carefully crawled over to the cat and lay with her head on her hands in imitation of Yoyo, whose furry head rested on her front paws.

Louise snapped away. Then she, too, sat down, putting the camera on the low white wooden table. "The energy. Where do they get it?"

"I don't know, but I could use some. If we didn't have schedules—I mean, if we could follow what our bodies want to do—I bet we'd be more like they are."

"I wonder." Louise kicked her shoes off. "Maizie's recital comes up the end of May. Now, you won't forget it."

"No."

"She's plenty full of herself, I can tell you. Maizie has, uh, focused on music now after that little incident at the convent school." The little incident was that Maizie set fire to her room and got expelled. Louise chose not to dwell upon it. "Oh no. She wants to go to New York City now, and play in the symphony. With all those Yankees. I told her she'd be miserable and slink home by Weeping Cross."

"They may be Yankees but they're musical Yankees, so if she makes the grade, more power to her."

"I don't want my daughter that far away in a big loud city."

"Well, Baltimore isn't exactly dead quiet."

"Baltimore is civilized. There are families there."

What she really meant was that there were people with proper bloodlines going all the way back to Lord Baltimore, a claim Louise made herself. She neglected to mention the Hunsenmeir genealogy, which led directly to a Hessian soldier, a mercenary who, tired of King George, liked the look of Maryland and went AWOL.

"There are families in New York. After all, there's the Colony Club, the Knickerbocker Club and—"

Louise cut her off. "It's not the same."

"Sure it is."

"No, it's not. Many of those people made their money in mercantile pursuits." Louise dressed up her vocabulary to enhance her own social standing. "And furthermore, many are descended from war profiteers even worse than the Rife rat pack."

Juts waved her hand. "Whatever you say."

"Don't get like that. I hate it when you get like that. Bloodlines are important." She sniffed. "And New York is full of Jews."

"So?"

"Julia, what if Maizie took up with a person of the Hebrew faith? It just wouldn't do."

"Jesus was a Jew."

"Oh, that's poppycock. There is One True Faith, One True Church, and only One Way. Sooner or later you will repent the error of your ways. And Jesus wasn't Jewish. He was a Christian."

Juts sat upright now, tiredness vanishing in anger. "What'd you do, go to confession this morning? We go through this holier-than-thou shit once a week now. For about two hours you believe you are without sin."

Louise folded her arms over her chest. "I'll not discuss it."

Juts smelled a rat. "Louise, what have you done?"

"Nothing?" Her voice lilted up in the air like one of the butterflies.

"Louise—" Juts dragged out her sister's name. "Louise Alverta—I know you."

"Nothing." Louise shook her head, hugged herself tighter.

"An affair?" Juts hoped for something exciting.

"How could you even think such a thing?"

"They do happen." Julia's voice dropped, hope vanishing.

"You should know."

"Hey, I didn't do it!"

Wheezie considered that her comment was a low blow. "You're right. But Julia, you have sex on the brain."

"I do not. I like to hear about it. Doesn't it fascinate you how people get mixed up with one another?"

"No," Wheezie lied—a fat whopper, too.

"Go on."

"Certainly not."

"Like you don't care that Rob McGrail hangs out with Pierre and Bob all the time. One of the boys."

"Just because they're sister boys doesn't mean they're *that* way."

"All right then, Mary Miles Mundis takes a tennis lesson every single day. Don't you find that peculiar?"

"One a day?"

"That tennis pro is a helluva lot better looking than Harold, even if Harold does have more money than God."

Louise leaned forward, dying for gossip, but realized her eagerness would prove Julia's point. "I hardly ever think of such things. Your mind is in the gutter."

"Oh la!"

"I'm going home." But she didn't move a muscle.

"Why'd you come here?"

"To see my sister."

"Yeah, sure." Juts looked around. "Where's Nickel?"

"She must have wandered behind the garage. She's not here."

"Well, she went in the house, then."

"She's too little to reach the doorknob."

"Wherever she is, Buster and Doodlebug are with her."

Wheezie got up and walked around the house as Juts looked over the neighboring backyards. She returned. "Juts, I don't know where she is."

"She couldn't be far. Those little legs only go but so fast." Julia ran to the front sidewalk and there in the middle of the street played Nickel. "Nicky," she shouted, "stay right there," and she tore off.

"Tell her to get out of the street!" Louise sprinted after her sister.

Juts reached the child and scooped her up in her arms as the dogs bounced around. "Nicky, don't go without telling Mommy—and don't ever go in the street."

Louise, scared, face flushed, reached them. She wagged her finger. "Don't you ever do that again!"

Nickel wagged her finger right back at her aunt.

"Juts, you've got to discipline this child *now*."

"Don't defy Aunt Wheezie, kid." Juts reached in her house-dress pocket for a cigarette. She lit one for herself and gave another one to Nicky to play with.

"No, Julia, you've got to smack her. I tell you like I tell Mary with Oderuss. Be strict. Be consistent. Nicky wandered off. She's being defiant. She could have been killed!"

"I'm not going to smack her unless she does it a second time."

"You're raising a hellcat. You don't know the first thing about mothering," Louise, still shaken, complained as they walked back to the house. "But then what should I expect?"

"Just what does that mean?"

"Well, you didn't carry the baby. It's different when they grow inside of you." Louise swung the cudgel she still possessed.

"Bullshit."

"See, a real mother wouldn't swear like that in front of a little one."

Julia, face reddening, cursed through her teeth. "Shut your goddamned trap."

"I beg your pardon." Louise's voice was hollow.

"You'll beg more than my pardon. You raised your children your way and I'm raising my child my way. And don't you ever pull this growing-inside-yourself stunt on me again or so help me God, I will knock all those gold fillings right down your throat."

"Don't be so touchy."

"If you'd think before you opened your mouth you wouldn't get in half the messes you do." Juts bumped Louise with her shoulder, forcing her sister to shift her weight.

"People who live in glass houses—"

"Shouldn't throw stones."

"A bird in the hand—"

"Is worth two in the bush. Birds of a feather—"

"Flock together."

"A rolling stone—"

"Gathers no moss." Wheezie smiled, as they pushed open the picket-fence gate. She studied Nickel, who didn't look like a Hunsenmeir although Rillma Ryan was related to Cora on the maternal line, the Black Irish line, actually. It crossed her mind that it might be an odd experience for a brown-eyed child to grow up in a home where the father was blond with gray eyes and the mother had honey-brown hair and lustrous gray eyes also. When her girls looked at her they could see themselves, sort of, but Nickel wouldn't have that sensation. In Louise's mind that had to matter. It never occurred to her that the child might feel freer because of not having just such ties and expectations.

"Louise, being a mother is a lot harder than I thought, but raising a child has nothing to do with blood." Juts, drained after her fright, didn't have the energy to lambast Louise for her natural-mother slam.

"Don't you see that everything you do now pays off later? You can't let a child run around—"

"I took my eye off of her for one second."

"That's all it takes. Look at what happened to Talia BonBon." Talia's little boy had drowned in a swimming pool the year before. Her attention had been diverted for just a few moments. Everyone had blamed her, too, which made it even more awful. "I don't want you to have any more heartache than you've already had. She's a determined little thing and she needs a strong hand. They're like animals, Julia, you've got to take control of them or they'll ruin your house, spend your money, and leave without so much as a thank-you. My God, look at the whole Bitters clan. I think Extra Billy is the only one who's tried to make something of himself and he's still plenty rough around the edges. You've got to be firm."

Juts replied, "Sometimes I think you have all the pearls without the string."

54

The hay swayed green in the fields. Spring, again early this year, helped everyone's crop get off to a good start, and farmers predicted that if the weather held, they'd get three cuttings, rich cuttings.

Chester belonged to the don't-count-your-chickens-before-they're-hatched school of life. In the evenings he was finishing a tack room for Harry Mundis, who wanted to live like an English lord. Of course, the real English lords had lost so much in two world wars that many of them shivered in cold houses to save money on their heating bills. Harder still, some were beginning to break up the great estates. But Harry was making a bloody fortune, first in fulfilling government contracts during the war, then in tearing down those same buildings after the war and selling the stuff to contractors. Nothing illegal about it so long as he identified the materials as used, which he always did. Since money was tight after the war, many a person was happy to get bricks, timber, siding, and gutters at a reduced price. The steel he stockpiled.

For the Mundises to catapult from their former station to rivals of the Rifes and Chalfontes in splendor aroused admiration, envy, and even bewilderment. Mary Miles was among the bewildered. She wanted her old friends, her old habits; she even liked her old house better. Not that she didn't like having money; she did, but she saw no reason to put on the dog—except when it came to new cars. She loved cars, as did most people in her generation, born before the internal-combustion machine. They were mesmerized by them.

Chester knocked off work as the sun's slanting rays cast long golden shadows. He drove through the square, stopping to double-check at the hardware store. Trudy was locking up her husband's jewelry store. He looked in the other direction. Since that painful night of the air raid he had only spoken to her to end the affair.

For a long time he felt like a dead man. Everyone's attentions had been focused on Juts. No one paid attention to his grief. He had no doubt that Trudy, too, felt dreadful for a time—and hated his guts. When she married Senior Epstein he felt both jealous and relieved. Jacob, a good man, would no longer be lonely and Trudy would have a solid husband.

Chester had never imagined the marriage vows would be so hard to keep. He vacillated between being ashamed of himself and believing he wasn't so horribly wrong in trying to grab more happiness out of life. He didn't bargain on that happiness causing equivalent sorrow.

Whatever else, he loved his little girl. He opened the door, Buster rushed up, Juts called out from the kitchen, and Nicky ran up to him as fast as her legs would carry her. "Daddy!" It didn't exactly sound like "Daddy" but he knew what she meant.

"How's my scout? How's my best girl?" He kissed her and

swung her around. She squealed. Buster watched with interest. He kissed her again and put her down but she hung on to his leg. So he walked into the kitchen with the two-year-old plastered to his leg. "Have you ever seen such a big bug?"

Juts laughed. "Your big bug was a naughty girl today."

"Oh?" He shook his leg to more delighted squeals.

"Walked down to the corner and sat smack in the middle of the road, and Chessy, I swear—Louise can be my witness because she was here—I took my eyes off her for about a skinny minute."

"Did you do that?"

Nickel shook her head no.

"Scared me so bad I had to come in and take two aspirin. I've still got the headache, though. She needs a leash."

Chester reached down and picked up Nicky. "You're not a big bug. You're a doggy. How about if I get you a leash to match Buster's?"

She nodded yes to that, then put her arms around his neck and laid her cheek next to his.

Chester had never known love like this existed. He only knew that being a father had changed his life forever. He finally felt like a man. He avoided conflict when he could, but if he couldn't, now he met it square on. This fact did not escape notice by his wife, mother, or his friends—nor did his radiant happiness whenever anyone happened to mention Nickel's name: Chester, fastest draw in Maryland, whipped out a photograph of his daughter, the most wonderful, the most beautiful, the smartest little girl in the universe. She was also, occasionally, the baddest. And she brought him and Juts back together.

"No playing in the road, scout."

She stared at him with solemn eyes. "Uh—" Her conversational skills hadn't advanced far enough for her to say why she wanted to go into the middle of the road.

"How about chicken corn soup for supper?"

Juts thought a minute. "Well, it's kind of warm for that, isn't it?"

"I don't care, honey, you know me. I'll eat anything that doesn't eat me first." He put Nickel on the ground but she stuck right to him.

Julia put her finger up alongside her nose, a curious gesture, borrowed from Celeste Chalfonte. "I'll fry some chicken and—" The phone rang, distracting her. "Damn, my hands are wet."

"I'll get it." He listened for the two rings, their signal on the party line, then hurried to the landing and picked up the phone. He listened intently for a moment. "We'll be right over."

"Juts, Hansford's—" he considered his words, "collapsed."

She dried her hands on a dish towel and threw it over her shoulder, quickly turned off the stove, and stared at Nickel. Juts didn't know what to expect when they got to her mother's. What did "collapsed" mean?

"Maybe we'd better not take the baby. I wonder if Ramelle would watch her."

His voice soft, he said, "I don't think there's time, honey."

They drove to Cora's. Afterward Julia had no memory of the trip at all. She felt as if she were underwater but she didn't know why. She thought she didn't care about Hansford. Seeing Louise's car already there reassured her, yet frightened her also.

Chester carried Nickel inside. Her eyes widened. She sensed the emotion. He handed the baby to Mary, who was sitting with Extra Billy, little Oderuss, and Maizie in the parlor, and followed his wife into the small bedroom. Hansford, propped up in bed, struggled to breathe.

Cora dabbed his brow with cool cloths. Juts sat on the other side of the bed while Louise stood at the end, facing him.

The racking sound of his labored gasps for air reverberated in the room. Despite his pain and hunger for air he was alert. He held out his hand to Julia Ellen, who took it and burst into tears. He patted her hand.

"Don't worry, Pop," she cried. "You'll be all right."

He smiled at her. It was the first time she had called him Pop.

Chester stood alongside Juts. Paul took the bowl of water to the kitchen and brought back another one with ice cubes floating in it. Louise remained rooted to the spot.

"The children!" Hansford gasped.

Louise snapped to at last, fetching Mary, Maizie, Oderuss, and Nickel.

Maizie knelt by her grandfather's side, next to Cora. He touched her head as though anointing her. Mary wouldn't kneel but he reached for her hand and she gave it to him. Oderuss hid his face behind his hands. When Nickel started to whimper, Chester lifted her from Mary. Hansford motioned for the baby, and Chester got down on one knee, the baby perched on the other knee so Hansford could reach her. He touched her smooth cheek.

"PopPop's going bye-byes." He smiled at her sad face.

"No!" She startled everyone with the volume.

"Sh-sh." Chessy bounced her on his knee but she'd have none of it.

"No! PopPop stay." She burst into tears. She may not have liked PopPop's beard and his odor of chewing tobacco, but she liked him.

For the first time tears rolled down Hansford's cheeks, disappearing in his beard, which Cora had carefully combed. He shook his head, his eyes cast over his family. He had squandered his life. He had abandoned Cora, Louise, and Julia. His return, drenched in need and suppressed sorrow, had taught him how much real love was worth but also how some fences could never be mended. And now it was too late to tell someone else, some other man fleeing from claustrophobic responsibility. Not only must a man have the courage to stand in battle, he needed the courage to stand at home. Hansford's greatest fear as a young man had been entrapment in this go-nowhere town. He'd feared missing out on the world. Instead he had become trapped by his own selfishness and missed out on love.

"Hansford, let me carry you to the hospital," Chester said.

Pearlie whispered to Chessy, "There isn't time."

Hansford pointed to Louise but she wouldn't come closer.

"Louise, for the love of God," her mother implored.

"Who truly owns this land?" Louise asked coldly.

Hansford pointed to Cora.

"Louise"—Cora spoke firmly—"make peace with your father lest it rest heavy on your heart for the rest of your days."

"My father?" Louise's voice dripped with poison from that old wound. "My father would have taken care of us, Momma. What about the times there wasn't enough to eat?"

"Celeste never let us go hungry."

"You didn't go to work for Celeste right off."

"This is no time for that kind of talk. Relieve his suffering and forgive him. Someday someone may have to forgive you, Daughter." Cora wrung out the cloth.

"I guess I'm not as good a Catholic as I thought." Louise turned on her heel and left.

Mary and Maizie, horrified, quickly kissed Hansford's hand and followed their mother.

"I'm sorry," Pearlie said to the man shrinking before his very eyes. "She's upset. She doesn't mean what she says."

Cora grabbed a dry cloth to wipe his cheeks and beard. Hansford blinked and reached for Pearlie's hand. Pearlie squeezed it, then let go of Hansford's hand.

Pearlie joined his wife in the parlor. He had his hands full with her.

Hansford reached for Julia's hand. "Forgive—?" was all he could rasp.

"I forgive you, Pop. I wish you hadn't left us. But I forgive you."

He squeezed her hand again, then released it. He smiled at

her, then he reached for Chester, who held the baby in one arm. He held Hansford's hand in the other.

"She . . . needs . . . you." Hansford pointed to the baby with his other hand. He made stabbing motions with his finger, trying to communicate further.

"I'll do my best, sir. I'll die for them both if I have to." Chester started crying, too.

Hansford smiled again and spoke his last words. "Live . . . for . . . them."

Then he sat bolt upright with a burst of energy. He reached for Cora, who held him with all her might as he surrendered his spirit to whatever adventure beckoned beyond.

"Safe journey," Cora sobbed.

Juts and Chessy left her alone with him for a few moments. Juts walked past an angry, choking Louise, already justifying herself. Juts paid her no more mind than if she were a goat barking. Chessy followed after his wife, clutching Nickel, who was crying again.

The sun was setting and near the house a redheaded woodpecker tapped into a bark alive with juicy insects, one last meal before packing it in for the night.

The idea flashed across Juts's mind that the woodpecker was signaling in Morse code, *Hansford Hunsenmeir is dead. Juts lost her father—twice.* She shook her head and buried her face in her hands, overcome with sorrow. She reached for her husband and he was there.

Late that night, after the undertaker had come, after Wheezie had screamed and hollered at everyone, after Cora had composed herself with remarkable dignity, after Mary and Maizie had accompanied their mother home, after Juts had finally fallen asleep and the baby was dreaming in her little bed with slats on it and Yoyo snuggling up to her, Chester walked the floors.

No peace came to him. He finally clucked to Buster, threw

on a coat over his pajamas, and walked outside, up one side of the tree-lined street and down the other.

He thought about life. When he was a boy he dreamed of heroic physical exploits, glory in war, and fast cars. He still dreamed of fast cars but he was mature enough to know there is no glory in war and heroic exploits are few and far between. A steady refusal to cave in to despair or self-indulgence now seemed heroic to him. Doing your job seemed heroic to him. Caring for those who need you seemed heroic to him. He would live on this earth and then die and, like Hansford, be forgotten when those who knew him also died. As a youngster that knowledge would have seemed terrible to him. Now it was just a fact. Fame, fortune, and power, those fantasies of youth, were not to be his. Life wouldn't be a daily diet of large victories. It wasn't like that.

He walked and walked, Buster by his side, and said aloud as the morning star appeared brilliant and clean, "Life isn't like that—it's better."

55

Showers of white cascaded over Juts's back fence. The crape myrtle bloomed. She struggled to put up a sturdy white trellis of four-inch squares against the garage. Nickel ran around the yard pursued by Buster.

The far end of the trellis leaned forward.

"Nicky, come to Momma."

"No." Nickel ran faster.

"I need you to help me."

The word "help" captured the child's attention. Small though she was, the idea of being useful appealed to her. She ran over.

Juts pointed to the far end of the trellis. "Can you lean against the wall?"

Nickel walked over and flattened herself bellyfirst against the wall, which meant she pressed the trellis to it.

"That's good. What a strong girl you are." Juts quickly tapped in a holding nail on her end, then hurried over to tap one in where Nickel stood. "Thank you." She popped open the stepladder and climbed to the top, where she tapped in another nail. Then she carried the stepladder to the other end, repeating the process. When she'd climbed down she admired the trellis. She could picture seashell-pink tea roses trailing over it. Or did she want ruby-red roses? Then again, yellow made her smile. "The hell with it, I'll plant them all."

A heavy footfall, a squeal from Nickel, and joyous barking from Buster alerted her to Cora's arrival. Cora had put on weight these last few years. She breathed heavily.

"Momma, why didn't you call me? I'd have come over and carried you here."

"With what car?" Cora fanned herself. In her generation fans were fashionable as well as useful.

"I'd have borrowed Wheezer's."

"In a pig's eye. Hello, my wild Indian." Cora reached down to kiss Nickel and then to pet Buster.

At the sound of her voice, Yoyo climbed down from the red maple tree. She waited a few moments. It wouldn't do to run. Then she sauntered over and rubbed the old lady's leg.

"That cat." Juts laughed. "She loves you. How about a Co-Cola or lemonade?"

Juts ran into the kitchen and returned with a huge pitcher of lemonade on a tray. Nickel carried the napkins. She walked over to her grandmother. Cora pretended to inspect the different colors. She picked red. Then she put it back and winked. She picked out a green one because she knew Nicky wanted the red one.

When Nickel sat down for her lemonade in a tin cup, Cora placed the red napkin on her lap. "Red's your color."

Nickel giggled.

"Julia, you have a green thumb. Always did. Louise has a black thumb." She half smiled. "But Louise can organize."

"She likes to tell people what to do. Here, Momma, put your feet up." Juts put her drink on the table and brought over a painted milk carton. "Don't you find your feet swell on such a hot day?"

"If I swell any more I'll burst like a balloon." She held the wet glass to her forehead. "A stinker."

"Dog days." Juts called to the terrier now under the crape myrtle, "Don't you think, Buster boy?"

Cora inhaled and exhaled, closed her eyes, then set the glass down. "Summer—fireflies and fishing, thunderstorms and rainbows. Did you know that it takes both rain and sunshine to make a rainbow?"

"Yes." Juts knew her mother was working toward something.

"Life's a rainbow. I never knew how much I loved life until I got near the end of it."

"Momma—" Juts was alarmed.

"Oh, settle yourself. I'm not sick but I'm old, honey. Most of my living's behind me. It went by so fast. I get up in the morning and my knees hurt and I don't know why. Then I look at myself in the mirror and see this old woman's face. I have to laugh. I wake up every morning expecting to be twenty with two little babies running around Bumblebee Hill. Guess I'm selfish. I don't want it to ever end."

A big lump stuck in Juts's throat. "Oh, Momma, you've got good long innings left."

"Well, I hope so." She drank, then held out her hand to her daughter. "Enjoy every minute, honey, and enjoy her. Well, I visited Edgar Frost last week and I signed over the house to you and to Louise. We fixed it up so I can live there until I die and he didn't charge me a penny. I don't remember him being so tall before the war."

"He was pretty tall."

"Guess it's me. I think they all came back changed. Those that came back."

"Vaughn amazes me."

"Yes."

Vaughn Cadwalder, legs amputated below the knee, asked for no sympathy and got around surprisingly well. Everyone said how lucky he was that he still had his knees because he could strap on wooden legs and use canes. That was one way to look at it. The doctors kept tinkering with the fit of the wooden legs. They were often painful and caused ulcers on his stumps. He didn't complain. For moving fast he used a wheelchair.

"Momma, I love Bumblebee Hill—but I love you in it, and I wish you wouldn't talk this way. I mean, you could have waited to deed over the house and the fifty acres."

"Wait for what? By the time I know I'm leaving, it will be too late." Julia remained quiet and Cora continued. "I'll tell Louise this evening. She's over in Littlestown. Has she said anything to you?"

"About what?"

"About the way she treated her father?"

Nickel raised her legs straight out. "Uppie-do. Mamaw, uppie-do."

"Nicky, hush."

"That's all right, Julia, she's been sitting so quiet that I thought she was a little mouse." Cora spoke to the child. "Darlin', if you want to play you go on ahead. Mamaw and Mommy are chewing the rag here."

Nickel glanced at her mother.

Juts confirmed Cora's suggestion. "Why don't you get your truck?"

"No." Nickel bounced off the little chair. She walked over to the trellis and imitated her mother, inspecting it, walking to one end and then the other. She made hammering motions.

Juts returned to her mother's question. "Wheezie doesn't say anything. Usually she runs her mouth a mile a minute but about Hansford—"

"Carrying around those feelings is like carrying a stone. I don't know why I didn't see it."

"Louise believes things are black-and-white. You know that. Hansford left us, so he's flat wrong. Maybe things hurt more when you're little. I don't know, Momma, 'cause I hardly remember."

"You weren't much bigger than Nickel." She finished her glass. "Has Josephine Smith come round at all?"

"No. She won't even let her in the door, not that we try. Chessy goes over every Tuesday, stays his two hours, and comes home. His brothers sneak by when they come to visit her, which is less and less. What a hateful woman."

"Leave her to God, Julia. Otherwise you'll carry around a heavy stone, too. People who are ugly act that way because something's bleeding inside."

"I don't care if she hemorrhages to death."

"Turn the other cheek."

"Momma, I can't. I'm not that good a Christian—course, I never pretended to be."

"I do think if the Lord wanted us to be better people He might have made the rules a little easier." Cora smiled. "But we can try. If you can't forgive her then put her out of your mind."

"I can forgive how she treats me, I suppose. Not that I want to, but to do Nicky like she does. . . . I want to run her over with that tractor Celeste willed you. Yeah, I'd like to bushhog the bitch."

"Now, Juts." Cora shook her finger at her daughter and wisely didn't tell her why she was really downtown.

56

It was a long walk to Josephine Smith's in scorching heat—five o'clock steamed hot as noontime. Cora hadn't told Juts where she was going when she left her house. Fortunately, the expansive maples, oaks, elms, and locusts that lined the pretty streets of Runnymede shaded the sidewalks.

By the time she arrived at the prim black door to the Smiths' she had to gulp for air. The front door was open, the screen door was shut. Cora opened it, reached inside and lifted the shiny brass knocker, and rapped.

"Who's there?" Josephine's voice floated out through the screen door. She stopped in her tracks once there. "What are you doing here?"

"Paying you a call." Cora sweated in the glaring sun.

"I told you I'd never speak to you again."

"That was before the turn of the century."

"This is 1947. You don't look any better to me now," Josephine barked.

Ignoring this remark, Cora patiently pushed on. "That was

such a long time ago. Whatever our troubles were, let's not push them onto the young ones."

"I don't. I couldn't stop Chester from marrying Julia."

"That was long ago, too, Josephine. They married in 1927. I'm talking about today."

"Today?" Josephine echoed with a snort, obviously believing she had done nothing recently.

"Your son loves his little girl—"

"She's not his little girl." Josephine's voice dripped venom. "She's Rillma Ryan's bastard and we all know it. The whole town knows it."

"Rillma fell in love with the wrong man at the wrong time. That ought to ring a bell."

"Just what are you implying, Cora?"

"That the child is blameless. That Chester is a happy man and the only thing missing is you. You should accept the baby."

"She's not a baby. She's two and a half. I've seen her—"

"From a distance."

"Cora Zepp"—Josephine addressed her by her maiden name—"you just go on your way. I'll not have a bastard as a grandchild."

"Well—Nickel was born a bastard. In your case you had to work at it."

"You get out of here!"

"You broke bad, Josephine. I feel sorry for you."

"You get off my property or I'll call the sheriff."

As Cora walked away she stopped at the sidewalk, which was county property, and yelled back, uncharacteristic for her, but she was as hot as the day now. "He never loved you, Josephine, and it was your own damn fault."

That did it. Josephine practically ripped open her screen door. She flew down the sidewalk and stopped at her property line. "Get out!"

"This here sidewalk belongs to York County, Pennsylvania."

"Get out! He did love me. You stole him back."

"You pushed him away. When he crawled back here you could have made peace. We could all have made peace. You wouldn't even talk to him."

"He was a broken-down old leech and he got what he deserved."

Cora, a welcome breeze ruffling her skirt, felt very calm now. "In the end, Josephine, we all get what we deserve."

"I'm glad he's dead." Josephine certainly didn't want to hear that she might get what she deserved. She already had. She was unloved, isolated, barely tolerated by her sons and her husband. Clearly, Rupert took his marriage vows seriously, for better or for worse. . . . He'd gotten worse.

Cora drew herself to her full height, which couldn't have been more than five feet two inches, but something about her made her appear larger and Josephine seemed to shrivel in comparison. "He repented his sins. He died thinking of others before himself. He died a man. You loved him once. He was worth it."

"You never loved him."

"Not so's you'd notice." Cora half smiled. "But I loved him."

Josephine felt weak in the knees. Her anger was transforming to some terrible pain that she'd kept at bay for half a century. She pushed the emotion back but it boomeranged on her with a force that knocked her flat. "He forced himself on me," she whimpered.

"No, he didn't. You've told that lie to yourself so many times you believe it. Hansford didn't need to force himself on any woman and well you know it."

Stricken, Josephine's mouth hung agape. As though struck from behind with a .38 slug, she dropped to her knees.

Cora ran up and put her hands under her arms and lifted her up. Josephine moved her lips. No sound. She looked like a fish.

"Come on, Jo, it's hot out here. Let me get you inside."

As Cora dragged her bitterest enemy toward her own front door, the phone lines were already humming. Caesura Frothingham, cruising by in her fancy car, glimpsed the drama, and Frances Finster, across the street, had seen it all.

Josephine struggled to put one foot in front of the other. Cora helped her inside, then found the kitchen and poured her a cool drink. Josephine, hand to throat, hunched over in Rupert's easy chair.

"Here, a little swallow will help."

Hands trembling, Jo, the once-pretty woman, grabbed the glass, water dripping on her chin. She hesitated, then drank a little more. A tinny squeak—like an unoiled brake—was the only sound she made as she handed the glass back to Cora, who put it on the table.

"Jo, we're old but there's a lot of life left. It's easier to be happy than unhappy. God didn't mean for us to be unhappy."

"I died those long years ago," Josephine whispered.

"Well—you're struggling to be born again." Cora tried to hand her the glass, which Josephine refused, as she was feeling better. "I always thought that's what Jesus' coming back from the dead meant. Not so much that graves are gonna open but that we can come back to life. Don't you know I've felt the way you felt?"

"You couldn't." Jo nearly strangled on her own voice.

"Maybe not for the same reasons, but just about every single person you pass and repass in Runnymede has felt in terrible pain or near to dead. They came back."

"Who are you to tell me how to live?" A sudden flare-up enlivened her.

"Nobody."

"Leave me alone."

"All right." Cora turned toward the door. "But if you can't come back, Jo, don't hurt the children, don't be cold to them. They need you."

"Nobody needs me!" Josephine exploded in rage and grief.

Cora quietly closed the door, glad to be in the sunshine, no matter how sultry.

Other things happened that summer. Cora laid into Louise about her hatefulness toward Hansford. She did that the same night she had confronted Josephine Smith. Louise blew up like a poisoned dog. She didn't want to share Bumblebee Hill with Julia. True, she was selfish, not that she'd admit it, but her argument was that Julia was a spendthrift and having to share property with her younger sister would be a hop, skip, and a jump toward bankruptcy. Cora said they'd have to learn to work together. After all, they'd done that when they owned the Curl 'n' Twirl. Louise's response was, only because she'd kept the books. So, Cora declared, keep them again. However, Cora extracted a promise from Louise that if she couldn't forgive her dead father she would try and forget. It did no good to carry hate about. Louise said she'd try.

Money was a problem for everyone except the very wealthy, such as Ramelle, the Rifes, the Falkenroths, and the spanking-new-rich Mundises. The cost of living skyrocketed over thirty percent. Returning servicemen, finally mustered out, couldn't find jobs even though women who had filled in during the war were being fired right and left.

Extra Billy, after struggling to farm on his own, agreed to go into Pearlie's business. Like many combat vets, he awoke night after night to hideous nightmares. Mary took a job with the telephone company but was pregnant again in no time.

Aunt Dimps hired Doak Garten, back from the Navy, to help her in the flower shop. People might have pinched their pennies, but funerals, weddings, anniversaries, and births dictated flowers.

Everybody was having babies.

Nickel, determinedly nonconversational, was now allowed to

visit Josephine and Rupert Smith on Tuesday nights with Chester *and* Julia Ellen. Word got out that Josephine spent many an afternoon in prayer and consultation with Pastor Neely. He advised her to listen to the words of Jesus: "Let he who is without sin cast the first stone." She struggled in her soul but did see the light. Not that it made her friendly or warm, but she had to crawl before she could walk. Nickel was even more silent at the Smiths' than at home. She sat in the corner and looked at the pictures in *National Geographic*. She wanted desperately to read. In the company of Yoyo and Buster, she would climb up, get the family Bible from a shelf, open it, and pretend to read aloud to the cat and dog. They were quite impressed.

57

T he change" became a subject of furtive, intense discussion among Louise and her best friends. Ev Most giggled with Juts over such a subject. Juts and Ev, classmates, weren't experiencing any symptoms yet. Having tiptoed over the forty-year-old line a few years ago, they were in no hurry to move along faster.

Hot flashes, unexpected flooding, crankiness, and confusion reigned among the slightly older set. Juts had never found female plumbing remotely interesting. If she didn't care about her own tubes and innards she certainly didn't care about someone else's. This did not prevent Louise from launching into exhaustive descriptions.

This particular Friday in September 1948, the Hunsenmeir sisters indulged in a food-shopping spree at the York market. Rows of succulent squash—pattypans gleaming white, yellow crooknecks, round green acorns—tempted them. Boxes of late blackberries, raspberries, and blueberries were so perfect they glistened. Marbled flanked steak, sides of ham, and juicy lamb chops rested on shaved dry ice divided by dark green parsley.

The Amish women wore head caps and aprons; the men nodded as the sisters approached their counters. Potatoes, corn, carrots, radishes red as rubies, okra, beans of every variety, and peas filled bushel basket after bushel basket. Nickel couldn't see over the counters but she could smell the produce. Occasionally a cat working at a booth would catch her eye and she'd stop to chat with it. Then Juts would notice the child was missing and backtrack until she found her, usually hunkered down petting the kitty.

"There you are. Sorry, Mrs. Utz, Nicky loves cats."

Mrs. Utz's broad face widened farther in a smile. "I do, too."

"You will come with me."

Nickel observed the commanding tone and also Aunt Wheezie hanging out at the corner of the aisle, waiting. She bowed her curly head, following her mother.

As they caught up with Louise, she launched into another report of her condition. "—as I was saying, there I was sitting at the table with Paul and all of a sudden—well, it was too much. No warning, no anything, and poor Pearlie—you know how men are about these things, I thought he'd faint. It's a good thing they don't have babies. They'd die from the sight of all that blood."

"Makes you wonder how they can stand war, doesn't it?" Julia said dryly.

"Yes. Oh, and I forgot to tell you. Frances Finster told me that when she was my age she had fainting spells."

"From all the formaldehyde at the funeral parlor."

"Julia, that's not true. Someday you'll go through this, too."

"If I do, you won't know about it."

"What's that supposed to mean?"

"That I don't want to hear about the change. Why talk about it?"

"Because it's a new experience. I like to share my experiences."

"You don't share them, you ram them down my throat."

"And what do you talk about? Julia Ellen Hunsenmeir. Julia Ellen Hunsenmeir. Julia Ellen Hunsenmeir."

Juts shrugged. "I'm interesting." She turned around. No Nickel. "Where does that child go? She's like a little weasel, she just slips away. I don't remember Mary and Maizie being like that."

"No." Louise's reply was clipped.

"I hate that tone of voice."

"My girls behaved like girls. They were obedient. And Mary's boys—they mind their mother. Nickel has entirely too much freedom. You don't discipline her."

"The hell I don't. She gets up at the same time every morning and she goes to bed at the same time every night and she eats her meals at the same time Chessy and I do. She's taught right from wrong as much as she can understand right now. She's not a loud kid. She listens pretty good."

"She wears jeans and T-shirts. That's not proper."

"Oh, for Pete's sake." Juts, exasperated, broke off the conversation to search for her daughter. She walked down the aisle. No Nickel. She walked back to the market's center aisle. No Nickel. She walked along the side where there was a small restaurant with oilcloth tablecloths. Nickel stood on a chair, hands on the table, and "read" the back side of *The York Dispatch* while an elderly gentleman read the front side. He wasn't the least disturbed by his visitor. His broad-brimmed black hat reposed on the wooden chair next to him.

"I'm sorry."

He glanced up. "We're enjoying each other's company."

Nickel pulled on her mother's hand, pointing to the headline with the other one. "Truman."

"Honey, come on. Aunt Wheezie is impatient today." She turned again to the gentleman. "Thank you for teaching her a new word."

"I didn't. She read it right off the headline."

"Truman." Nickel pointed to the paper again.

"She must have heard someone mention it." Julia smiled and lifted Nickel off the chair by her one arm.

"No." Nickel swung out at her mother with her feet.

Juts dropped her hard. "You do that again and I will give you a lesson you'll never forget, young lady." She nodded to the man, who had his nose back in the newspaper, and hauled off an upset but silent child.

On sight of Wheezie, hands on hips, waiting, Juts said, "She was reading the paper."

"Sure, Mike." Wheezie used an old expression between them that meant, "Not on your life" or "I agree" or anything you wanted it to mean, depending on your tone of voice.

"Nickel, Mommy thinks it's wonderful that you like words, but you can't go off without telling me." She turned to Louise. "I think she heard someone say 'Truman.' She kept pointing to the paper, saying 'Truman.' She's a curious little bug."

"Especially since you've never read a book all the way through in your whole life. But"—Louise inhaled, a whiff of superiority fraught with implication—"that's to be expected."

"What the hell does that mean, Wheezie?"

"Oh"—her thin eyebrows rose and her voice rose with them, in an air of phony nonchalance—"nothing."

"Balls."

"Julia, don't talk like that in public."

"Rounded objects." Juts forced a tight little smile. "Rounded objects like turdballs."

"Will you stop—and in front of your child, too."

"She's not going to say anything. It's hard to get two peeps out of this kid."

"You need another baby. She needs a sister or a brother."

"No," came a rather loud reply from Nickel.

"Don't contradict Aunt Wheezie, she knows what's best for little girls."

"I don't want to be a little girl."

This complete sentence stopped them both. "I beg your pardon," Louise finally said.

"Truman. I want to be Truman." Her legs were placed wide apart, her arms were crossed over her chest.

Juts peered down at this small animal. "I think she wants to be president." Then she burst out laughing.

"Don't encourage her, Juts. You're going to make a kegful of nails, if you do."

"Will you stop being so serious? If she wants to be president, by God, let her have her dream."

Louise smiled down, sickly sweet. "Nicky, girls can't be president. You can be a nurse. That would be nice. Lots of little girls grow up to be nurses. You would help people. Or you could play an instrument. Maizie plays the piano."

"No!"

Juts grabbed her hand. "Come on, kid, we've got a lot of shopping left to do. We'll settle this hash later."

As they walked past a booth with a big sign, Fletcher's Fruits, Nickel pointed up. "Fruit." Except it sounded like "Froo-ot."

Louise stared at her, a curious expression on her stern face. "How'd she know that?"

"I don't know." Juts shrugged. "I tell her stories all the time."

"She's three and a half years old. Children don't read until they're six."

"Well—I guess she's ahead of the game. Anyway, she'll be four in November."

Louise put her hand under Nickel's chin, staring into those brown eyes staring right back at her, not giving an inch. "Be quiet, Nicky. Sometimes it's better to not be so, uh, smart."

"Louise, leave her alone." Juts knelt down. "Nicky, you can read anything you want, if you really can read. I think Aunt Louise means it's not polite to point to things and call out a word. Now come on."

"That's not what I meant," Louise growled at Julia. "She's going to be out of place. You have to think about how she will get along with other children. She has a strike against her before she even goes out to bat."

"Children don't know about such things."

"They learn them fast enough from their parents."

"Do we always have to worry about what's a year down the road or ten years down the road? What will Lillian say, or Fannie Jump or Caesura, that ancient of days? What will Father O'Reilly think, and hey, the pope might get his nose out of joint. Tomorrow a hurricane might blow us off the face of the earth and if that doesn't do it, what about a flood as big as Noah's next springtime? If her little friends throw things up in her face, I guess she'll learn that some people are shits. And I hope she'll have the brains to hang with those that aren't."

Louise whirled on her. "You do a child no favors by letting her get ideas above her station. It doesn't do for a girl to be so obviously smart. You can be smart after you're married, not before."

"My God, she's not even four years old and you've got her married off."

"Someone's got to think ahead. You're like the grasshopper. I'm like the ant."

"Now we're insects."

"I know what's best. Didn't I tell you Chester Smith wouldn't amount to a hill of beans? You two soon won't have a car to drive, you'll have to push that old thing you've got. Didn't I tell

Mary the same thing? If Pearlie hadn't given Extra Billy a job, they'd be begging on the street. Didn't I tell her?"

"Yes, you sure did." Julia was getting mad.

"And didn't I tell Maizie not to go to New York? Not to even think about such foolishness? No, she didn't listen. Now what does she write me? That she wants to go back to school but not one associated with the church. What kind of request is that? What is that going to cost me? I know what's best." She paused. "She has to learn her place. Life is much easier when you know your place. She'll be another Rillma Ryan if you don't nip this in the bud."

As they passed luscious baked pies, Juts said low, "Well, Louise, what's your place?" She was so angry she didn't register that Louise had identified Nickel's mother right in front of the child.

"That's a silly question."

Menace laced Juts's voice. "You shut up about Nickel. You just shut up. Shut up about her place. She'll find her own place because, God knows, the world is full of people like you who won't give her one just because of something somebody else did!"

Nickel, tired of their fussing, left. They didn't notice.

"I didn't make the world, I just live in it!"

"Well, you're not doing a damned thing to make it any better."

"I, for one, do not believe people should engage in physical relations without benefit of marriage."

"Jesus H. Christ on a raft."

"Don't take the name of Our Savior in vain." Louise stepped toward a stall of calico aprons. "I need a new apron."

"You need a new mouth."

As Wheezie ignored her she noticed a pair of little shoes sticking out from under the draped fabrics overhanging the wooden stall. "Nicky?"

"She's not here." The reply was determined.

Louise stooped over and lifted a corner of a bright quilt. "What are you doing under there?"

"Thinking."

"Hi, Mrs. Stoltz, my little niece thought your quilts were beautiful." Louise forced a smile.

Mrs. Stoltz, as wide as she was tall, lifted the quilt from inside the stall. "I see."

"Sorry." Juts joined them, dropped to one knee, and held out her hand. "Let's rodeo, scout."

"No."

"Nickel, you get your butt out of there this minute or you'll regret it." The cigarette bobbed in her mouth with each clipped word.

"No."

Juts, pushed to the limit, although she didn't know why, pinched her cigarette between her thumb and forefinger and touched the glowing end to Nickel's arm above the elbow. Just a touch, but it produced the desired effect. The kid shot out of there—too fast for Juts to grab her. Nickel sped down the aisle.

"May the saints preserve us." Louise shook her head. She hadn't run since grade school. Louise thought running unfeminine.

"It's going to take more than saints." Juts trotted in the direction of her vanishing child. She called over her shoulder, "Don't just stand there like a bottle of piss. Move!"

"I won't be addressed in such a crude fashion." Grumbling under her breath, Louise moved over to a parallel aisle and walked briskly under the old hanging lights as she checked stalls to see if the child had ducked inside.

The two sisters met at the Taylor Hams stall at the end of the aisles. The huge stall ran horizontally across the major aisles.

Juts flicked ashes on the floor, then ground them out in the sawdust that spilled out from the Taylor Hams booth. "I don't know how she can move that fast."

"She's around here somewhere. Let's try the two aisles over there."

No booth revealed Nickel. To be on the safe side Louise asked the janitor if he had seen her. He said no but observed that kids played outside where the bushel baskets and other debris were tossed. He'd go out to clean up and there'd be maybe ten or fifteen of them in the alley. Juts walked outside in the soft September sunshine, a hint of fall in the air. She saw a squadron of children but not her own.

She rejoined Louise at the candy booth.

"I was sure she'd come here. Kids love candy."

"Wheezie, let's try the restaurant. She was over there before."

They hurried over, both more worried than they wanted the other to know. No Nickel.

Despairing, Juts dropped into a chair for a minute. "It's like living with a monkey. She runs and jumps and rolls around. She climbs and swings on tree branches. I get up in the morning and she's already up. She's pulled on her shorts and yesterday she had every cupboard door open, every single one, even the ones over the counter. She'd crawled up on the counter. Nothing was taken out, thank God, but every door open. She can sit for hours in the pantry staring at the labels on cans. She goes in my closet. She tries to put on my shoes. Last week she smeared powder and lipstick all over her face and she ruined Chessy's best bow tie because she was wearing that, too. Just wrapped it around her neck. My God in heaven, what do people do who have more than one child?" Before Louise could answer that her two were never like that, Juts shot her a hard stare. "This is your fault."

"My fault?" Wheezie's hand fluttered to her throat. Her nail polish matched her lipstick.

"You wanted me to have a baby."

"I what!"

"That's right, Louise. Every morning, noon, and night you hammered at me about how I wasn't a real woman because I wasn't a mother and you know how dumb I am, I believed you! I don't want to be a mother. It's hard work and I never get a break."

Louise, usually so quick to defend herself and deride her sister, paused, weighing her words. "Some days are better than others."

"Days? I'd settle for a good night's rest. She gets up at five-thirty in the morning. I hear her but I'm so tired from chasing after her the day before that I go right back to sleep."

"Well, at least she's not noisy."

"No, but she'll probably set the house on fire someday. She's into everything!"

"She'll grow out of that," Louise confidently predicted.

"I wish I'd never listened to you."

Louise leaned over her. "You're tired. She's a little fireball, I'll grant you that, but she is quiet."

"Quiet—she's practically mute. She hardly says three words together and I don't get it, because that kid is smart, Wheezie. Sometimes she's so smart she scares me. Those brown eyes watching me—I feel like I'm being watched by a tiger."

"She's learning. Why, when Maizie was little she followed me from room to room pointing at everything because she wanted to learn the names for chairs and lamps. You've got to remember, she's seeing the world for the first time."

"Well, I goddamned feel like I'm seeing it for the last. I don't know if I can live through this."

"Give her to Chessy for a day."

"She'd demolish the store."

"He can take her for half a day on Saturday or Sunday."

"Can't I give her back?" Juts forced an anemic smile.

"You don't mean that." Louise stood up straight. "There were days when I wanted to give mine back—of course, there was no one to give them back to, but I would gladly have wrung both their necks."

"You—the perfect mother?"

A wry smile played over Louise's pretty face. "Show me a

mother who doesn't dream of making her children angels even once in her life and I'll show you a barefaced liar."

"Yeah—but truthfully, I'm not up to this job."

"Nobody is."

"Then why'd you push me into it?"

"I didn't. Well—maybe I mentioned being a mother once or twice?"

"Once or twice—every day!"

"Hasn't she brought you and Chester closer together?"

"Yes, except now we never have time alone together. By the time we get to bed at night we're too tired to even talk." Juts ran her fingers through her hair, which showed only a hint of gray. "We've got to find her."

They walked out of the restaurant. Catty-cornered across the lofty market was a second-story balcony. Painted dark green, it hosted wooden rocking chairs and a ladies' bathroom. If a lady exhausted herself amid the asparagus she could climb the stairs, take a load off her feet, rock a bit, and pick up a thin rattan fan. A pile of fans was always on the table outside the bathroom. Juts lifted her eyes just in time to see Nickel spin a fan over to the top of the balcony rail. Now she was standing on the rail.

"Oh my God." Julia spun down the aisle like Jesse Owens.

Louise, baffled, noticed that people were gathering under the balcony. The circumspect, ladylike Louise perceived the object of their attention now dancing on the railing. "Holy shit," she breathed. She shifted her eyes to the right and the left, grateful that no one had heard her rude outburst. Then she hurried after her sister—to do what, she wasn't sure.

Juts screeched to a halt under the balcony. Nicky tossed fans down at her mother.

"Nicky, honey, don't do that. You'll hurt somebody."

Louise drew alongside and opened her mouth, ready to shout a warning. Nickel was dancing, grabbing a pole, and swinging around it. The kid seemed oblivious to danger.

Juts clapped her hand over her sister's mouth, smearing her with her own lipstick.

"Don't."

"Lady, is that little boy yours?" a middle-aged man, brows creased with worry, asked.

"That little girl is mine." Juts spoke to the crowd. "Don't scare her." She turned to Louise. "You go up the stairs. I'll keep talking to her while you grab her from behind. If she falls I'll try to catch her."

"Julia, she'll break your arms."

"You worry too much. Go on."

Louise tiptoed up the back stairway.

Juts smiled at the cavorting child. "Honey, you're just a little monkey. I bet you can't get down and sit in a rocking chair."

"I can."

"Let me see you."

"No," came the cry of defiance. Nickel found she liked being the center of attention. Having all those eyes focused on her was invigorating.

Louise softly crept up behind her and grabbed her around the waist, hauling her off the railing. Down below, people cheered.

"Nickel"—Louise was shaking—"you can't run off like that."

Pounding footsteps rang out on the wooden stairway. Juts reached the top, face flushed. "Nicky, you could have been killed."

"No." Nickel shook her head.

Julia took the child from her sister's arms.

"Well, we've had adventure enough for one day." Louise's whole body slumped. "I left my bags at Taylor Hams. I think we'd better collect our stuff and drive home."

"Okay by me." Juts squeezed the child before putting her down. "Promise me you won't run away like that, Nicky?"

Nickel nodded her head but without much enthusiasm.

As they walked out of the York market, Juts thought she heard Nicky say under her breath, "Rillma Ryan," but she convinced herself that she really said "Truman."

58

T reasure." Juts praised the old license plate Nickel found in the creek behind Cora's house. It was a scorching-hot day. "Let's get this paint off. There's black paint all over this thing."

"Nineteen forty-one." Nickel proudly pronounced the date.

"You're good with numbers, Nicky." Juts handed the license plate to the child, who held it under the pump while she pushed down the handle. In a few seconds the water gushed out, splashing Nicky, who giggled.

Juts took the dripping license plate from her hand and wiped it clean with an old rag. Cora always left a pile of rags by the pump.

"Momma, what'd you accomplish on your day off?" Juts asked Cora.

"Picked a peck of peas." Cora winked in Nickel's direction. "With help." As they walked back toward the sky-blue house on the hill, Cora added, "Rillma helped, too. She dropped by for a sit-down."

Juts stiffened. "Oh."

Cora wiped her hands on her apron. "Relax, honey."

"It's confusing. It will confuse—" Juts inclined her head in Nickel's direction.

"You're the one confused."

"I am not!" Juts threw the license plate down.

Nickel picked it up, wiped the dust with her hand, and watched her mother.

"We all got to live together, Julia."

"She's mine."

"Blood is blood."

"Don't you say that to me."

"Don't you sass me, Juts, I am still your mother."

Juts flung herself down on the porch step. Cora faced her daughter, but the sun, low and still bright, was in Julia's eyes so she shielded them with her right hand.

"A child's not a toy, Juts, you can't have her all to yourself."

"She's mine!"

"She's herself is what she is, just like you were yourself. Let things be. Let people be. If not, it makes for trouble. If not now—later."

"Trouble?" Juts sounded incredulous. "Trouble is everyone telling me how to be a mother. You say one thing. Louise says another. Jesus."

"Every mother hears that. I heard it from mine. Let it go in one ear and out the other."

Juts stared at Nickel, observing both of them. "Nicky, go wash your hands, then we're going home."

"No."

"Do as I say."

"No."

Juts jumped up, grabbed Nickel, and swatted her bottom. "Go sit in the car. Right now."

Nickel, license plate in hand, retreated to the car.

"Mother, she defies me. Maybe she wouldn't defy me if she were really my own."

"Makes no matter—and she is your own."

"Then why is everyone pointing out to me that she's not? I am not her real mother."

"I'm not saying any such thing, and I am *your* mother. Who you gonna listen to?"

"You're right—I'm so tired, Momma."

"Well, stop worrying so much. That'll rest you."

Later, when Chessy came home, Nickel ran up to him with the license plate. He told her that it was quite a find and he helped her tack it up on the front of her red wooden toybox.

The night was muggy. Chester sat down to listen to the radio. Juts busied herself in the kitchen, reorganizing her dish towels.

"Come on out here. I get lonesome for you."

Loaded with dish towels, she sat down next to him on the sofa. "They look like Switzer cheese." She poked a finger through a hole in the towel. "I can fix them." She noticed he had a far-off gaze. "Are you listening?"

"I'm sorry, honey. I had a thought?" His voice rose uncertainly on the last word.

"Jeez, I'd better call Popeye Huffstetler so we can get it in tomorrow's paper."

"Be right back." He tiptoed upstairs, followed by Yoyo. He jotted down the four numbers on the license plate. Then he bent over Nickel and kissed her on the cheek. Next he dialed Harper Wheeler. "Hey, buddy."

"Chessy, what's doing?" the sheriff said.

"Nothing. Will you do me a favor?"

"Depends."

"Nickel fished a painted license plate out of the creek up at Cora's. It's a 1941, Maryland numbers nine three one three. Can you find out who that belonged to?"

"Yeah. Might take a day or two."

"I've got a hunch about this—don't know why, but—well, I'll tell you once you find out."

"Sure 'nuff. Give my regards to the missus."

"Will do."

Juts had turned down the radio so she could listen. When he joined her she asked, "What's your hunch?"

"It's the damnedest thing, honey, but I feel like that license plate's got something to do with Noe's fire. Fannie Jump said she couldn't see the license plate on the car, it was painted over."

59

Maizie's piano recitals, for she had given many of them in her home state, were all successful. Musical talent proved insufficient for success in New York City. Her trip there was brutally brief. There were thousands like her flocking to the Hanging Gardens of Neon, each one bursting with talent. Nor did these hopefuls lack ambition. But an odd spark, something unteachable, separated the stars from the merely gifted.

This realization struck Maizie with the force of a bullet. She woefully gave up and boarded the next train to Runnymede. Within four hours, she stepped out onto the familiar siding, the faint smell of creosote hovering over the tracks, the stale-water smell from the steam. She thanked the porter for her suitcase and lugged it into the station.

It was as though she had never been in the Runnymede station before. The scrubbed floors, worn thin as half-moons at the doorjambs, the iron grating over the ticket windows, the public water fountain on the side wall between the ladies' and men's rooms—everything seemed smaller to her. She felt smaller, too.

She hadn't called her mother or father. No one knew of her dismal arrival.

Her head throbbed. She crept through the main room, pushing open the front door. No welcoming car awaited her, no chatter from Patience Horney, who worked her hot-pretzel stand the early-morning and the evening shifts. The afternoons Patience went home to sleep.

Luscious tiger lilies, blooming late this year, blanketed the bank opposite the parking lot. The *clickety-clack* of the departing train took her dreams with it. Maizie Trumbull, all of twenty-one, felt a failure as she trudged up the alleyway to the *Clarion* building. Her heavy suitcase dragged the ground. The *bumpety-bump* further dispirited her. She thought about calling a cab but didn't have the money. Of course, she knew every cab driver in Runnymede. All she had to do was ride up to her mother's door and borrow the cash. But she couldn't bring herself to admit she was flat broke.

She was so overwhelmed by what she thought she had lost, that she had no time to realize what she had found. A limitation can be as valuable as a victory if one learns how to use it. And Runnymede teemed with life, with music and drama at its own pace. Every hamlet, town, village, and city moved at a special pace, exhibited a personality. Maizie belonged here. She'd found her heart's home.

At that precise moment she took no solace in it. She sat down on her suitcase and had a good cry. Then she removed her clothing and ran around the *Clarion* parking lot. She gobbled like a turkey until Harper Wheeler rolled up in his squad car, summoned by Walter Falkenroth. Harper made her put her clothes on. He'd turn his back, she'd take them off again. Finally, he hand-cuffed her, half undressed, to the inside of the car door. She couldn't do much with one hand. All she could do was unbutton her blouse. She did manage to throw her shoes at him.

She screeched the whole way to Louise's door. Harper called ahead. To be safe he also called Pearlie in case she turned violent. He didn't want to hit a woman.

By the time he rolled into the driveway, Juts and Chessy awaited. Louise had called her sister, who in turn had called her own husband.

Maizie opened the door and swung her bare feet out. She shouted, "I'm home, you goddamned sons of bitches. I'm home and I hate everybody." She started taking off her clothes again.

Louise hurried over to restrain her. Maizie, with her free hand, slapped her squarely in the face.

"Don't you hit your mother." Juts grabbed her right hand as Harper unlocked the handcuffs.

"Maizie." A shocked Pearlie put his arms around his daughter's waist as she twisted and screamed.

Chester grabbed her arms. His reward was that she bit him.

"Louise"—Harper's voice was oddly tender—"I'll get Doc Horning over here right away."

Her face bone-white, Louise mutely nodded as Harper picked up his handheld transmitter. "Car Twelve, Car Twelve. Esther, find Dr. Horning. Now. Ten-four." He waited. "Doc, Harper. Can you get to Louise Trumbull's right away? Maizie's hard up. Better bring something to help her out. Speed. Don't worry about a ticket." He reached back into the car and hung up the hand-sized black transmitter on a small hook under the dash.

"I'm never going to mass again," Maizie announced, a note of triumph in her voice.

"Let's get her inside." Harper picked up Maizie's feet because she'd dropped to the ground.

Doc Horning arrived as the men were carrying her through

the front door. They held her tight while he knocked her out with a sedative. She screamed bloody murder when that hypodermic needle hit her. They carried her to the sofa. The drug worked quickly.

Louise was shaking so hard that Juts put her arms around her.

"Has she ever behaved like this before?" the doctor asked, his rimless spectacles sliding down his nose.

"No," Pearlie answered while Louise shook her head.

"No rebellious period? Hanging out with the wrong sort?"

"Back talk, but nothing more. Mary was the difficult one." Louise allowed Julia to walk her over to a chair. She also made no mention of the fire incident at the convent school but, of course, Doc Horning knew. Hard to keep something like that quiet over the years.

"Well, takes 'em this way sometimes. You make sure she takes these pills for the next two days." He handed Louise a small vial. "Bring her in to me Thursday if she's cooperative and I'll run a few tests on her. If she's not cooperative, with your permission, I'll take her over to Dr. Lamont in Hagerstown."

Both parents nodded.

"What's wrong with her?" Juts stuck right by Louise.

He folded his hands together and flicked them inward, cracking his knuckles, although he hadn't intended to do that. "I don't know. My hunch is she's in good health, just got a little confused. The mind can shut down like a machine on overload—you know how some things will shut down before they break? She'll most likely be fine. I suggest you don't prod her. Don't ask her questions. Just let her sleep and if she screams at you, ignore it. You know where to find me."

"Thank you," Pearlie and Louise said in unison.

Chester walked Harper out to the squad car as Pearlie accompanied Dr. Horning.

"Chester, you're bound to hear talk. Maizie took her clothes off and ran buck naked around the parking lot at the *Clarion*.

Walter Falkenroth's the one who called me. I leave it to you to inform Louise. May be less embarrassing coming from you."

"You think she's flipped her lid?"

"I don't know. The longer I live, the less I know and the more I see."

"Yeah, I know that feeling." Chester ran his hand over his brow, an unconscious gesture of worry.

"Oh, almost forgot. Heard from Baltimore. That old license plate? It was a company vehicle for Rife Canning. I rode on over there and asked Teresa to check through company files, which she did." He paused. "She said that was the plate for a 1938 Ford. She didn't recall the vehicle but there was a record for it."

"That was that?"

"As far as she was concerned. Not as far as I'm concerned. No one reported a car or a truck stolen back then. I can't imagine Napoleon or Julius Rife taking kindly to losing a vehicle like that. Tell you what I'm going to do, Chessy. I'm going fishing tomorrow. Want to come along?"

60

A light drizzle created perfect circles in the deep creek. Harper, Chessy, Pearlie, and Noe dragged fishnets. Chessy had Nickel with him since Julia was needed by Louise. Maizie behaved under sedation, but as the drugs wore off she'd begin to gobble like a turkey again. She did keep her clothes on because Louise took a switch to her. Mary, working at the Bon-Ton these days, promised to help after work.

Because of the unseasonable heat no one wore a raincoat. The drizzle felt good. Chessy, Pearlie, and Nickel trolled out of a little flat-bottomed boat. Sheriff Harper Wheeler and Noe Mojo moved faster; their boat had a hull bottom, and the outboard motor was bigger.

"Daddy?"

"What, honey?"

"Will the fish bite?"

"Not today."

"O.B. says rain's the best fishing." She quoted the stableman.

"He's right, but we're looking for a truck."

"Do trucks swim?"

Pearlie smiled. "Not this one."

"Oh." She dropped her hand into the cool water and watched the small waves.

Fannie Jump Creighton drove down the road to the small dock. She rolled down her window. "How long you been out here, boys?"

"Sunup," Noe answered.

"Why didn't you call me?"

"Haven't found squat. Why waste a nickel?" Harper Wheeler replied.

She checked her diamond-encrusted wristwatch. "About time for lunch. You want to come in or you want me to bring you something from town?"

"We'll be in. Just another minute or two." Harper shifted his pipe to the other side of his mouth. It wasn't lit, but sucking on it soothed him.

"Daddy?"

"What, honey?"

"There's a big fish over there." She pointed, the water dripping off her forefinger.

"That's nice."

"Look." She sounded cross, because he wasn't paying attention to her fish.

"Where?"

"There. Bet it's a giant catfish."

"Bet it's not." He waved to Harper. "Buddy, over here."

As Harper and Noe approached, the small waves slapped against the side of the flatboat.

"Over there." Chessy pointed.

Pearlie squinted. "Whatever it is, it's big."

"It's a whale," Nickel said authoritatively.

"Nicky saw it first." Chester praised his girl.

"Hard to see at all in the rain." Harper grumbled as the rain fell harder now.

"Why don't I drop over a hook?" Noe sensibly suggested.

He lofted the hook over his head, a circle, then delicately cast it into the deep side of the creek. A moment later he tugged. "Got something."

It took the rest of the afternoon with Harper commandeering Yashew Gregorivitch's tow truck. They pulled the rusty truck out of the creek. The words "Rife Canning" on the side had been painted over. The license plate was missing.

Fannie, mouth agape, stared as the truck was hauled up from its watery parking space.

"How'd it get down here?" she asked.

"Well, it was bound to drift some in seven years, even though it's heavy. Remember, we had all that rain the last couple of springs."

"You'd think someone would have seen it."

"Not if whoever drove it dumped it in the deepest part of the creek, which would be off Toad Suck Ferry." The old ferry station was about a mile and a half north of the meat plant and Sans Souci. No longer in use, the station was located in the widest part of the creek and the deepest water was around it.

Fannie slowly walked around the dangling truck. "That's it. I swear it. Sure a waste of a good machine, too, the walleyed son of a bitch." She remembered Nickel. "I'm sorry, Nicky. Aunt Fannie needs her mouth washed out with soap."

"Why would the Rifes have wanted to burn you out?" Harper fanned himself with his sheriff's cowboy hat.

"I don't know."

"Oh come on, Noe, you must have pissed them off." Harper was irritated that he still hadn't solved the motive behind the 1941 arson attack.

"I hardly even talk to the Rifes. Why would they have been mad at me, other than the obvious?"

"That's not it." Pearlie leaned against the tow truck.

"There's got to be a reason, dammit!" Harper put his hands on his hips. "People don't burn each other out for no reason."

"It was Pearl Harbor." Noe shrugged.

"Daddy, what's Pearl Harbor?" Nickel whispered.

"I'll tell you later."

She reached up for his hand, satisfied that he would keep his promise.

"You don't know for certain that it was the Rifes. It could have been an employee of theirs or someone who stole their truck and had a grudge against Noe. Or, well, maybe it really was Pearl Harbor. After all, that's what we thought at the time," Fannie said.

"If a truck had been stolen from Rife Canning, don't you think I'd have heard a squawk the minute it was missing?" Harper shook his head. "No, no, those two were in on this." Then he added, "Well, boys, we found our truck. Just what comes next is a point of solemn conjecture."

"Oh, for Chrissake." Fannie spit on the ground, an unladylike gesture but a fitting one, for Popeye Huffstetler was bearing down on them in his old car.

"That blistering idiot!" Harper slapped his hat hard against his leg. Chessy picked up Nickel, placing her on his broad shoulders. "Hansford used to say Popeye could screw up a wet dream."

The men and Fannie exploded in laughter.

"Daddy, what's a wet dream?"

"Uh—I'll tell you later, honey."

"You know, Hansford said something a little strange when I questioned him. What the hell did he say that time?"

Popeye pulled up, reporter's notebook in hand as he switched off the engine with the other hand. He was firing questions before he had both feet on the ground. When he caught sight of Pearlie he blurted out, "Louise wouldn't give me a quote about Maizie causing a disturbance yesterday. And—"

"Huffstetler, shut up!" Pearlie's face reddened.

"Hey, news is news and your daughter was exhibiting herself at the *Clarion* and—" He didn't finish because Pearlie socked him with a right cross.

"You print a word about my girl's troubles and I'll knock your teeth out, you stupid shit!" Pearlie advanced on the staggering Popeye, whose notebook and pencil lay in the sandy loam.

"Now Paul, you have to realize that everything people in this town do or say is news and I have a responsibility to the citizens to—" Backing away, he fell over a log.

Paul straddled him, fists doubled up. "I won't kick a man while he's down, which is more than I can say for you."

Popeye scrambled to his feet. "News is news," he repeated. "It's all over town. Give me your side of the story."

Pearlie lashed out with a left jab, his hands fast for an amateur. Popeye ducked and moved sideways.

Harper, in no hurry to intervene, ambled toward Pearlie. "Pearlie, let me handle this."

Chessy was now on the other side of Pearlie. "Come on, Pearlie. I'll carry you home."

"Paste him away, Uncle Pearlie!" Nickel clapped her hands with glee.

Pearlie, tears in his eyes, let Chester put his arm around him and guide him back to the car.

Fannie waited at the car.

Nobody heard what Harper said to the reporter but they heard Popeye's loud "Yes, sir."

The sheriff rejoined the group. "Noe, I told Popeye he can come when we dig around your plant. That suit you?"

"Since when are we digging around the plant?" Noe tilted his head, puzzled.

"Since I remembered what Hansford Hunsenmeir told me." He hitched up his belt and sauntered past, winking at Nickel.

61

I'm not crazy."

"I didn't say you were." Mary checked her small wristwatch as they strolled along the tree-lined street.

"If I'm that boring, just go home."

"Don't be tetchy. It's close to Billy's quitting time."

"Well, I am tetchy. Everyone's staring at me with goggle eyes. Okay, so I took my clothes off and ran around the parking lot. I didn't shoot anyone."

"No."

"Well—" Maizie noticed that Orrie and Noe Mojo had painted the shutters of their house dark green. Slanting rays of sunlight fell across the enticing green of the lawn. "When did they do that?"

"The week you were in New York. Billy painted it for them, making up for the times he comes to work late." Mary sighed. "Daddy gets on his nerves sometimes and he gets on Daddy's nerves."

"He's surprised everyone," Maizie stated, not indicating exactly how Billy had surprised people.

"Not as much as you have."

Maizie shrugged and turned on her heel to head back down the street.

Mary hurried to catch up, reaching for her sister's elbow. "I didn't mean to sound snippy. God, I hope I don't sound like Mom."

"No. She keeps jamming those pills down my throat. I spit them out when she leaves the room. Boy, they have a bitter taste."

"Nothing is worse than milk of magnesia."

"That's the truth."

A blue jay squawked overhead.

"I love this time of year. Billy and I like to walk out in the moonlight and smell the leaves turning."

"No one is ever going to fall in love with me." Maizie cast down her eyes.

"That's not true."

"Would you fall in love with a woman who took her clothes off and ran naked around the *Clarion*?"

"I don't know." Mary hesitated. "Why'd you do it?"

"Felt like it." She took a giant step forward. "You know what it is, Mary? I'm bored. Ever since I can remember, someone's been telling me do this, do that, say this, say that, don't get your dress dirty, wash your hands, don't talk with your mouth full, don't air your dirty linen in public, don't kiss on the first date, don't hang out with the wrong sort, blah, blah, blah—I hate it. I hate listening to all these old farts talk about the past. Is there one square foot of Runnymede that isn't drenched in somebody's memories?"

Mary, not an inquiring sort of person, was surprised by her sister's outburst. "Gee, I never thought of that."

"A thousand invisible threads are tying me down."

"If you don't have something tying you down, you float off." Mary nervously laughed.

"You have Billy and the boys."

"Yes . . . I just wish we had more money."

"That's another thing I'm sick of: money, money, money. Ever since I can remember, Momma has worried about money. And when she had that damned old beauty salon she'd tote up the money from the cash register every single day. Remember? She'd stuff nickels in red cardboard tubes and the bills in a canvas tote and hurry to the bank. Money, money, money!"

"You know how Momma is."

"She wants me to be just like her."

"She's like that with everyone. It's not you."

"Well, I'm sick of it."

"Maizie, you can be sick of it but you don't have to take your clothes off and you don't have to gobble like a turkey."

Maizie exploded with laughter. "I do that to drive her crazy. Scares her."

This stopped Mary in her tracks; she was scandalized. "That's mean."

"Payback."

"Why are you so mad at Mom?"

"I don't know."

"Forget it. Don't let her get to you."

"Easy for you. You don't live with her anymore."

"You don't have to live with her either if you get a real job."

"What in the hell am I going to do in Runnymede?"

"You could teach regular."

"I didn't go to teachers' college."

"Work for the Yosts. They need help in the bakery."

"Millard's a lech."

"He is?"

"Yeah."

"There's got to be something."

"You don't have a worry."

"I do so have worries," Mary protested. "We've got so little money I'm working part-time at the Bon-Ton."

"That's not what I mean. I mean, you know what you're doing. I don't know anything. I feel lost, kind of, even though I know where I am."

As they approached the house, Mary's step lightened. Billy's red beat-up truck was rounding the corner.

"What's he say about me?" Maizie sullenly asked.

"Nothing. Billy's not like that." Mary thought a moment, then said hurriedly before he reached the curb, "Whatever he saw over there in Okinawa . . ." She held up her palms, an involuntary gesture, and left the thought unfinished. "Small stuff, he doesn't pay attention to."

"Lose his wild streak?"

"He's full of energy but he's different now—"

"You're lucky."

"You will be too."

Maizie gobbled, then giggled.

"That's awful!"

62

Louise slept in a wicker chair on her screened-in porch. The *pitter-patter* of rain on wisteria vines climbing on posts framing the porch had lulled her to sleep. Doodlebug dozed at her feet.

Julia peeked in at her, Nickel by her side.

"Momma," Nickel whispered, "should I sing to her?"

The child, an early riser, would crawl into bed with Juts and Chester to awaken them with "Row, Row, Row Your Boat." She made up rhymes in her pleasant voice about Yoyo, Buster, birds, caterpillars, and horses, ending with "Morning, glory!"

"No."

"But Momma, why is she asleep? It's not bedtime."

"She's tired."

"Is Maizie tired, too?"

"Yes, Maizie's not quite herself."

"Is Doodlebug tired?" The Boston bull swept his ears back and front when Nickel mentioned his name.

"Yes," Juts, irritated, answered. She grasped Nickel's hand and led her away from the porch and into the kitchen. She'd made a gallon of potato salad, cole slaw, and biscuits for her sister. The food was cool enough to put in the refrigerator. Every time Juts visited she coveted Wheezie's new refrigerator. She was still using an icebox.

The sound of slippered feet announced Maizie.

"Time for another pill?"

"I'm not swallowing any more of that shit," Maizie defiantly replied, then noticed Nickel. "Sorry, Nicky. I used a bad word."

"I know a bad word."

"You do?"

"Doily."

"That's not a bad word." Maizie opened the refrigerator door and a light went on inside, the latest in convenience. She pulled out a jug of lemonade. "Anyone?"

"No, thanks." Juts leaned against the counter.

"Nick."

"No."

"No, what?" Juts said sternly.

"No, thank you."

"That's better."

"Maizie, the doctor wants you to take your pills until you've used them up. It won't be much longer."

"You're right, it won't." Maizie seized the pills, tossing them down the sink.

Juts reached her hand into the drain, too late. She controlled her temper. "I guess Dr. Horning will write another prescription. I'll call him."

"Don't. I'm not crazy. I took my clothes off, but I'm not crazy."

"I take my clothes off," Nickel stated.

Indeed, she did. On hot days Juts allowed Nickel to run barefoot in shorts and no shirt.

"Nicky, why don't you go"—Juts glanced out the window; it rained harder—"into the parlor. Aunt Wheezie has some pretty picture books."

"I know." She'd memorized each of them.

"Aunt Juts, I don't care if she's here. I'm not going to fly off the handle."

"The doctor said we shouldn't ask you too much. Build up pressure or something. I don't know."

"You know what happened?" She placed the empty lemonade glass on the counter. "I woke up and couldn't see anything. My eyes could see but I couldn't. Just a blank."

"I guess everyone feels that way sometime or another."

"I don't have a life, Aunt Juts." Her throat constricted. "Blank."

"Of course you do," Juts replied.

"You know what? I look at Mother and I think, 'Am I going to look like that? Am I going to act like that someday?' Blood tells. Scares me so bad I can't see straight. Nicky's the lucky one."

Nicky, head cocked like an inquisitive bird, observed her, brown eyes alert.

"I hope so." Juts worried, though. What if Nickel turned out like *her* mother or her unseen father? What if her own influence evaporated, leaving no more trace than a whiff of perfume?

"Aunt Julia, what's there to live for? I don't want to live and die in this one-horse town. I don't want to be like my mother or my sister. Guess I don't want to be like Dad, either. It's so small. Everything is so small."

"I figure wherever I am, that's where the world is." Julia meant it, too. "What happened to you up north?"

"What happened to me here?" Maizie ruefully replied. "Nothing. I guess I thought my life was going to be like a movie or something. Not this."

"Be patient," counseled she who rarely was.

"Why? For what? I don't even have a boyfriend. What am I going to do until Prince Charming arrives?" Her light blue eyes clouded over. "Mother wants me to be a nurse or a teacher. A nurse? I don't want to change bedpans, and take old men's pulses, or give strangers a bath. I don't want to touch people I don't know. Mother thinks it's respectable and I can play my piano in my spare time."

"What about teaching?"

"I'd kill those brats."

"Well, you could be a secretary or work in the Bon-Ton, if they're hiring, I mean."

Maizie shook her head.

"I want to be a cowgirl," Nickel chimed in.

"Hush, Nicky," Juts lightly scolded her.

"I can work!" Nicky proved belligerent.

"I'm talking to Maizie. You butt out."

Nickel put her hands on her hips. "I am too going to be a cowgirl!" Her eyes blazed. "Me and Maizie."

"Sure, Nicky," Maizie appeased her.

"See!" Nickel raised her voice.

"Will you shut up."

"It's okay, Aunt Juts. Let's get out of here. Go for a ride or something."

"I'll have to wake your mother."

"I'll do it." Nickel scampered in and cupped her hands around her mouth. "Gobble, gobble, gobble!"

Louise shot out of the wicker chair about as fast as Julia ran into the porch room. She grabbed Nickel by the elbow and smacked her hard on the rear. Nickel winced but didn't cry. Maizie doubled over with laughter.

"Don't you ever do that!" Juts wouldn't let go of Nickel's elbow.

Louise looked from Nickel to Maizie. "What's going on here?"

"It's catching," Maizie whooped.

"Oh, God, no." Louise's hand fluttered at her throat.

"Mother, get a grip. I'm joking."

"That's not funny." Louise, all offended dignity, turned on Nickel. "You're a naughty girl."

"Me and Maizie are leaving." Nickel wrenched her arm free from her mother's hand and stomped over to Maizie. "Let's go."

"Bye." Maizie took her hand, waved to the sisters, and headed for the door.

"Just where do you think you're going?" Louise sprinted to the front door.

"Let's go out to the packing plant," Juts suggested. "Chessy and Pearlie are out there. Maybe they found something."

"What if it's bodies?" Louise's lip curled.

"Neat." Maizie opened the door.

Louise whispered to Juts, "She seems better. Did she take her medicine?"

"No. She threw it down the drain."

"What!"

"Louise, let's worry about this later. She seems better. Accentuate the positive."

"Let me call Dr. Horning."

"Call him later, come on."

"Easy for you to say."

"She's not sick. She's really not."

"Come on!" Maizie yelled from outside; she and Nickel were already in the car. Nickel bounced up and down on the seat.

"Just a minute." Louise stepped outside, then whispered to Juts, "If she's not sick then what's wrong with her?"

"I don't have a word for it. She ran into a wall and now she's got to dig under it, climb over it, or blast right through it."

"Just what the hell is that supposed to mean?" Louise caught her breath, mad at herself for swearing. "Really, you get my goat."

"Better than your lamb."

Louise grimaced. "What'd she tell you?"

"She's trying to figure out what to do with her life. That's not so strange."

"She'll get married and have children, that's what she'll do with her life, and in the meantime she can earn some money. If she's a nurse she'll meet a doctor. That's the plan."

"Your plan."

"Well, Julia, someone has to think for her."

"Come on!" Maizie shouted, then maliciously added, "Gobble, gobble, gobble."

Nickel joined her.

"I ought to beat them both silly." Louise thumped out to the car. "Will you both stop that this instant!"

Julia hopped in on the passenger side. "Dead bodies, here we come."

Nickel cupped her hand and whispered to Maizie as they headed out the twisting road to the plant, "I'll close my eyes."

"What'd she say?" Louise lived in fear that she'd miss something.

"If there are dead bodies she'll close her eyes."

"What's she going to do about the smell?" Juts laughed.

Nicky pinched her nose with her thumb and forefinger, which made them all laugh.

No dead bodies were unearthed at the meatpacking plant. But a room reached by a tunnel had been dug up. Noe and his wife, Orrie, plus Fannie Jump Creighton, Harper Wheeler, Harmon Nordness, Chessy, and Pearlie stood in the cool brick chamber.

Juts walked in. "This is as big as a gymnasium!"

The space was piled from floor to ceiling with cannon balls, grapeshot, cannisters, and cartridges. It was an arsenal.

Louise and Maizie walked in, their mouths hanging open.

Nickel ran to her dad.

"Look at this." Fannie pointed to the left side of the room.

All the ordnance was stamped C.S.A.

"Now look over here." Harper guided the ladies.

The ammunition was stamped U.S.A.

"That son of a bitch. What they said about him was true! He sold to both sides during the war," Juts blurted out. "If only Celeste were here to see this. Her father despised Cassius Rife."

"Maybe they're having it out in the great beyond," Harper Wheeler joked.

"But why worry about this now? Why burn the place down?" Louise asked.

"Who knows?" Harper shook his head. "Insurance. Pearl Harbor provided them with perfect timing. What greedy bastards. They have so much but they wanted more."

"I called Julius. He said he doesn't know nothing about this chamber," Harmon Nordness informed them. "Not doodley."

Since the Rifes lived on the Pennsylvania side of the line, Sheriff Nordness was the one to make the call.

"Maybe Brutus knew and didn't tell his sons or only told one." Pearlie started to think about it "Nah, they both knew."

"Yeah," Chester said. "They probably found some of the old man's papers."

"Who cares now?" Julia stared at the stuff.

"We do," Fannie Jump said. "We all do. We grew up hearing stories about how Cassius made his millions, but no one could ever prove it. It was like being a blackbirder, it was so bad back during the war, that's what Celeste's daddy used to say. Here it is eighty years later. That's not such a long time. It'd be like selling arms to Hitler and Roosevelt at the same time."

"What's a blackbird?"

"A blackbirder," Fannie corrected Nickel. "That's a person who brought slaves over from Africa by boat. Way, way back before this war even. Usually they were sea captains from Boston or New York. They got very rich."

Nickel smiled. She liked to learn things but she was often confused. Did this mean that a blackbird was a person? Did a person turn into a bird if she was bad?

"I need a smoke." Harper Wheeler led everyone back out of the room through the tunnel, which was constructed with intersecting arches.

Maizie walked over to him. "Sheriff, I'm sorry I caused you trouble."

"Don't you give it a second thought. All forgotten."

As they emerged back into the rain they ducked into the back part of the packing plant, which wasn't as badly burned as the front. Harper jovially instructed Noe, "Guess you'll have to put in the call to Popeye."

Noe smiled. "No phones here."

"Got a dispatcher in my car," Harmon Nordness said.

"Make you a bet," Harper said to Noe.

"What's the bet?"

"Bet you that Julius Rife has already hired him some slick fellow from New York City to talk to Popeye for him."

"That's no bet. That's a sure thing," Juts said.

Louise, Maizie, and Pearlie, happy to see his younger daughter so improved, drove home in their car.

Chessy, Juts, and Nickel piled into theirs. Julia wanted to drive over and tell her mother everything that had happened.

The windshield wipers swooshed. Nickel flattened her nose against the window. "Gobble, gobble, gobble."

"You stop that!" Juts reached over the seat to swat her.

63

Indian summer lingered, its sweetness thickened by the knowledge that winter would follow. Ring-necked pheasants filled the cornfields, and quail tottered about in low cover; foxes ran everywhere. Juts remembered, when she was Nickel's age, having once been taken on a shoot with her uncle, long ago deceased. He bred English setters, magnificent gun dogs, and he brought down three pheasants that day. It made Juts cry to see them fall out of the sky, but she didn't refuse to eat them once on the table.

Seasons triggered memories for her more than specific dates. Songs did it, too. "Red Sails in the Sunset" reminded her of her troubles with Chessy over Trudy. Whenever that song was played she'd snap off the radio.

The brilliant leaves this fall fascinated Nickel, who picked them off the ground to save them. Already she could identify poplars, bright yellow; sugar maples, flaming red; and most varieties of oak, which ranged from a pure yellow to electrifying orange to brown. The willows, yellow now, dropped their leaves over the old well in the backyard. She'd climb effortlessly, her bare feet seeking a place to wedge themselves, and once up she'd sit in the lowest branch. She'd listen to the leaves rustle and once to a mockingbird perched on a limb above her.

The more Nickel grew, the less she wanted to be with her

mother. Her favorite word was still "no." She'd rise with the sun and rush to breakfast. Sunny-side up eggs delighted her. Then she'd put on her shoes, shoestrings flopping, and carefully walk over to Juts; she didn't want to trip. She'd ask for her shoestrings to be tied and then she'd bolt out the door, not returning until lunchtime or until she was called in.

Julia had thought she would become the center of her child's world. When Nickel was an infant, she belonged only to Juts. But with each passing day Nickel wanted to belong to the world. She wasn't a cuddler. She never ran up and threw her arms around Julia's neck. She'd take her hand, but that was about it. She'd kiss her good-night. She wanted to play with animals, any animals, and once she picked up a tiny copperhead to show her mother. Julia, usually calm in a crisis, simply told Nickel to put the snake back where she found it because its mother would be worried. Nickel immediately obeyed. A direct command would not have worked with this child.

But Juts felt lonely. Nickel didn't need her, and she wanted to feel needed. Oh, the child needed food, clothing, and shelter— that and any book she could get her hands on, but she didn't seem to need Juts. It preyed on Juts's mind.

Maizie's nervous condition scared her, too. Maizie had bounced back, although she still lacked direction. Louise, ever the taskmaster, told her she wasn't going to support her; Maizie was strong, healthy, and bright enough to support herself. This made Maizie cry and Louise panic. However, she didn't back down on her demand that Maizie work. In Runnymede the worst insult was to be tabbed a layabout.

Juts wondered what kind of work Nickel would find. So far the only career that came to mind was veterinary medicine. She didn't know how she and Chester could send a child through college, much less vet school. Well, it was a long way away.

Today the light breeze sent the creamy clouds sailing across an azure sky, perhaps the prettiest day of the fall so far. Juts leaned on the fence rail at Celeste's stable. O.B. Huffstetler put Nickel on Rambunctious and his son, Peepbean, now seven, rode General Pershing. Nickel, too small for a saddle, rode bareback. Already she surpassed Peepbean's skills on a horse.

O.B., who valued horsemanship above all else in this world, was as disgusted with his son as he was delighted with Nickel.

Ramelle, walking with a cane these days because she suffered from disc problems in her lower back, stood next to Juts under a huge chestnut tree, which shaded part of the ring.

"Rambunctious is the kindest fellow with a child on his back, but he's a pistol with an adult. He used to so enrage Celeste that she'd expand her vocabulary of abuse. In fact, she could have written a thesaurus of abuse."

"I miss her." Juts sniffed the scent of leaves. "She loved fall."

"Sometimes I think she's near. Sounds funny, doesn't it?"

"Not to me." Julia believed in spirits but kept her mouth shut about it.

"Nickel will make a rider, you know."

"She's a bug."

"When Spotts was Nicky's age she decided she was the queen of England. Remember that? She wore a tiara that whole year."

Juts shook her head. "She was going to be an actress, that's for sure."

"Getting tired of it. I think she liked her war work more than acting. She said for the first time in her life she felt useful."

"I know what she means. I loved working in the Civil Air Patrol."

"I'll never forget the night the sirens went off."

"Neither will I," Juts drily replied.

"Look, Momma!" Nickel held up her arms as Rambunctious trotted slowly.

"Wonderful," Juts called out, then said to Ramelle, "Did you like being a mother?"

"Not every day of the year. Actually, I loved it until Spotts turned fourteen. Then I would have gladly sent her to Siberia."

Juts flinched. "Yeah, Mary started to act up around that age, too. Maizie didn't, though."

"She's making up for it now."

"There's no way around it?"

"I don't think so, Julia, but you have some time before she contradicts everything you say, wears the worst things she can find, and lives only for her friends."

"I don't remember doing that."

"Oh, Julia." Ramelle burst out laughing, that silvery laugh that made her sound twenty-one again. "You never stopped."

In the ring, O.B. picked up Peepbean by his belt, as the boy had slid off General Pershing's back. He started to bawl. Nickel stared at him in disbelief. She wasn't sympathetic and unfortunately neither was O.B.

"Uh-oh." Juts noticed.

"That child will end up avoiding horses like the plague." Ramelle stepped out from under the chestnut tree and rapped her cane on the fence. "O.B., come here a minute."

As O.B. walked over, Nickel stood on Rambunctious's back, waved her arms, and shouted, "Momma, come ride with me."

"No."

Ramelle leaned over to O.B. as she stood on slightly higher ground. "Let's try a new tack with Peepbean."

"Tie him on."

"No. Forbid him to ride for a while. It just might work. If he has to do it he'll resist. If you pay him no mind he'll want to do it—I think."

"Momma, please!" Nickel shouted.

"Go on, Miz Smith. Try it. Pershing's the laziest horse God put on earth."

"I don't know how to ride."

"If you can dance, you can ride."

"Wrap your skirt around your legs or you'll rub yourself raw," Ramelle advised.

Juts, not a scaredy-cat, hopped over the fence and swung up on Pershing.

Nickel, thrilled that her mother was joining her, clapped her hands, which made Rambunctious take a step or two. Nickel stood on the horse's back like an acrobat.

Juts rode her horse alongside Nicky's. They walked around the ring and for the first time Nicky chattered like a blue jay. She told her mother all about Pershing's liking peppermints and that Rambunctious wanted apples but you had to cut them. She bubbled, babbled, and fairly screeched with happiness, so much so that Juts had to laugh at her.

"Momma, I love you," Nickel said at the end of their ride.

"I love you, too." Juts slid off and then caught Nickel as she launched herself off the horse's back, fully expecting to land on her feet or tumble and roll. The child had no fear. This both delighted and terrified her mother.

"Let me!" Nickel reached up for Rambunctious's reins; O.B. threw them down to her. He took Pershing and they walked the horses back to the stable.

"Do I have to brush Pershing down?" complained Peepbean, who was following.

"No," O.B. replied.

"I'll do it. Please, Mr. Hoffy." Nickel couldn't say "Huffstetler."

"All right." O.B. smiled. He'd have to drag out a tack box for her to stand on.

Ramelle and Juts lingered under the chestnut tree. Few chestnuts remained on the East Coast after a terrible blight attacked them at the turn of the century. But this one, far away from other trees, spread its long limbs, growing mightier with each year.

"She told me she loved me." Juts, still astonished, shook the horsehair off her skirt.

"They don't realize we have feelings. They know if we're mad *at* them or happy *with* them but they don't know we have feelings *separate* from them. I imagine you've felt unloved sometimes. I know I did," Ramelle said. Her insight into people was one of the reasons Celeste had loved her. Celeste's insights had generally run in a cynical direction.

"Mostly I've felt exhausted. This isn't what I expected."

"Believe me, Julia, if we knew what we were getting into, no woman in the world would give birth."

"I didn't."

"You know what I mean."

"What I wonder about is, am I missing something? Louise knocked me once by saying that since I didn't carry Nickel, I couldn't be as close to her."

"Louise is hardly the expert on motherhood."

"She thinks she is."

"Julia, Louise thinks she's the expert on everything. She's always been that way. I don't think giving birth makes you one bit closer to your children. Raising them is the true test."

"But she's a distant little thing. She just goes off, does what she wants."

"That's who she is."

"You mean, she would be that way even if I were her natural mother?"

"Most likely, she would. They come into this world with everything they need. They're formed. We influence them, but their characters are set. I've seen many a good child ruined by a hateful parent"—she paused—"and I've seen many a good parent ruined by a child." She inhaled the fall tang. "They are what they are. The question is, do *you* feel close to *her*?"

Juts rubbed her ear; her earring was pinching. "I do sometimes. I think Chessy feels closer to her than I do."

"Chester doesn't have to discipline her every day. Fathers get the easy part."

"I was beginning to think I wasn't a good mother. You've made me feel better."

"Every woman feels that. Don't be so hard on yourself."

"I'm either too hard on myself or too easy. I can't find the middle ground."

Ramelle smiled. "I have a suggestion."

"What?"

"Why don't you come out and ride with Nickel? If you share what she loves instead of trying to get her to love what you love—like O.B. there—you'll grow together."

"Well—" Juts considered this generous offer. "I would pay you for the use of your horses."

Ramelle's laughter lifted into the breeze. "And Celeste would haunt me the rest of my life. After all, the Chalfontes and the Hunsenmeirs belong together."

"All right." Julia brightened.

As they walked toward the barn, there was Nickel, on Celeste's old tack box, brushing Pershing's back. She sang to the horse, she sang to O.B., she sang to the sun, too.

"You're a good mother," Ramelle said.

Juts felt so relieved she nearly cried.

She had her doubts two hours later when, walking around the square, Nickel declared, "I know a new bad word."

"Oh."

"Turd."

"Nicky."

"Know what else?"

"I can hardly wait."

"Grandma Smith is the turd of all time."

Juts started to laugh. As a reward for Nicky's vocabulary they commandeered the counter of Cadwalder's and shared an ice-cream soda.

Vaughn restacked the aisles, lingering at the shampoo shelf. He was agile in his wheelchair.

After they finished, Nicky bounced over to the handsome man. "Will you give me a ride?"

"Sure."

"Nickel!" Julia reached to grab her.

He smiled up at Juts, his face old yet young. "I don't mind."

Nickel climbed in his lap. He pushed the wheels with his strong hands, giving her a spin around the store. Juts couldn't remember the last time she had heard Vaughn laugh.

64

Good Friday, a bleak day that April 15, 1949, depressed Julia Ellen as she and Nickel went to church. Louise, attending St. Rose of Lima's, had stirred up Nicky when the sisters parted at the northeast corner of Runnymede Square. Nickel demanded to know why Wheezie didn't go to Christ Lutheran with them. Louise, her face veiled in black mesh, intoned that she would gladly take Nickel to the One True Church.

The child, now four and a half, informed Louise that she attended Christ Lutheran, not the One True Church. This allowed Louise to expound on the errors of Protestantism as well as the peril of the child's soul.

Naturally, Nickel wanted no part of peril, temporal or eternal. Juts told Louise to shut her fat trap. Louise flounced off, with Nickel shouting, "I don't want pearl!"

Passersby thought Nickel was complaining about her uncle. Finally Juts, forcing a smile, hauled her ever-growing kid up the marble steps of the chaste, imposing temple of holiness and not a little wealth.

Once seated, Nickel started to squirm. Juts pinched her. The child glared at her but stopped. Then Juts bribed her with a Sen-Sen. As Nickel sucked on the gray breath candy she observed the parishioners. A few other children attended, but not many.

Bored, Nickel reached for a heavy red hymnal and began leafing through the pages. She mouthed the words in an exaggerated whisper.

Juts put her finger to her lips.

Defiantly, Nickel mirrored the gesture of her mother.

As always, on Good Friday, the drapes in the church were black velvet, and black velvet covered the lectern, the pulpit, the altar. No flowers or color of any sort enlivened the severely beautiful white interior.

The dolorousness of the occasion began to wear on Nicky. At three o'clock the organ hit a shudder and the black curtains were drawn.

"Momma!"

"Hush."

"Turn the lights on!"

"Will you hush."

"Turn the lights on!" A hint of fear sounded in Nickel's voice.

"Shut up!" Julia hissed.

"I don't like this!" Nickel pushed past her mother and ran down the aisle toward the door, which was closed. Donald Armprister, an usher stationed at the door, grabbed Nickel, since she couldn't push the door open. He dragged her toward Julia.

"No!" Nickel kicked him in the shin.

In her high heels Juts clicked down the aisle, grabbed her

angel, opened the door, and booted her into the vestibule. She closed the door behind her with a solid *click*.

Donald stuck his long, elegant face out the door. "Juts, do you need a hand?"

"I need a paddle."

He winked and closed the door again, plunging the congregation back into the blackness of Christ's crucifixion.

"Don't you ever do that again!" Juts fanned Nickel's behind, her petticoats softening the blow.

"I don't like the dark."

"And I don't like your attitude." Juts batted her once more for good measure.

Nickel wrenched free, heading back toward the inner door.

Juts raced after her. "Oh no, you don't."

"Then I'll go to Aunt Wheezie's True Church."

"You set one foot in St. Rose of Lima's and I will fry your face," Juts exploded. "Jesus never had a bad little girl like you."

"Jesus didn't have a little boy, either." Nickel pouted, her red lip protruding. "Maybe he didn't like children. Maybe he lied. He didn't want us to come unto him."

"Where in God's name do you get these ideas?" Juts threw up her hands in despair. "Outside, young lady. You've ruined the service for me and for everyone else."

"Did not."

Julia unceremoniously yanked her out the front door into the cool, gray day. "You've made a spectacle of yourself and a fool out of me. I don't know how I can show my face in there again."

"No one can see it. The lights are out." Like most children, she possessed a ruthless logic.

"It's Good Friday, Nicky, I told you."

"What's good about it, Mommy? I didn't like the dark, and the seat tickles."

"What do you mean, the seat tickles?"

"It does. When Aunt Dimps plays the organ it tickles."

Juts thought about this. "Well—I guess it does."

"It makes me have to go to the bathroom."

"Do you have to go right now?"

"Uh-huh."

"Can you make it to Cadwalder's? Because I don't want to take you back in there. Actually, the Bon-Ton is closer. Can you make it?"

"Yes."

They walked toward the big department store.

Nickel asked, "Why did Jesus die? If he was the Son of God he shouldn't die."

"He died for your sins."

"I don't have any sins." Nicky quickly defended herself.

"You most certainly do have sins and you chalked up a big one today."

The Bon-Ton was closed. A sign on the double doors read, "Reopen 4:30."

"Damn."

"Momma, I have to go."

Juts looked around. "Come on."

She dragged her into the park and told her to hurry up and go to the bathroom under George Gordon Meade's statue.

"Momma, there's dog doo here."

"Exactly. Now hurry up."

She dropped her cotton panties, bending over so as not to soil them, and urinated.

"I need toilet paper."

"Here, use a Kleenex." Juts dug into her purse and handed her a tissue. "Hurry up. I don't know who might see you."

The child did as she was told. "Am I going to get in more trouble?"

"No, you've made up for your scene in church by peeing on George Gordon Meade. He was a Yankee."

"Grandma Smith is a Yankee."

"That she is."

"Does Jesus love Yankees?"

"I suppose he has to, but we don't."

"Can God see everything we do?"

"Yes."

"Then God saw me pee on George Gordon Meade." Nickel furrowed her dark eyebrows. "I don't like that."

"I'm sure he was occupied by weightier matters."

They walked back home in the chilly air. The cat and dog greeted them rapturously. Juts happily changed into a comfortable housedress.

"Why does Aunt Wheezie go to a different church?"

"Because she's an idiot." Juts pointed her in the direction of the stairs. "Bath time."

"Z'at why Maizie left?"

"No, she left to go back to school."

"When can I go?"

"This fall. You'll start kindergarten and I'll be very happy." What Juts didn't say was she'd get a little peace and quiet.

"Will it be like Sunday school?"

"Sort of, but you don't have to pray and learn about the Bible. You'll learn to read—"

"I can do that," she bragged.

"You'll learn how to do it better."

Juts had maneuvered her into the bathroom and was unbuttoning her dress. She turned on the faucets after sticking the rubber stopper in the tub. It hung around the nickel-plated faucet by a tiny ball and chain. Yoyo stayed out of the bathroom but Buster bravely walked in. He knew the bath wasn't for him because he couldn't smell the flea shampoo.

Nickel held the sides of the tub, then lifted one leg over, her toes testing the water. She hesitated, then brought the other leg over.

"Do I have to go to Sunday school?"

"Why wouldn't you?"

"You said I ruined church."

"Forgiveness is part of being a Christian."

"I don't like that part."

"You have to practice all of it. You can't just pick and choose."

"You do. You take the parts you like."

"Just a minute here." Juts sternly smacked her with a bar of soap in her hand.

"You do. You don't forgive Grandma Smith."

This stopped Juts. "I'm trying, but it's very, very hard."

"She doesn't like us."

"No."

"Why?"

"Pure meanness, I guess. Anyway, that's why you have to go to Sunday school, to be a better Christian than I am." Juts cheerfully grabbed the tiller of the conversation, steering it in a calmer direction. "You like Sunday school."

"Most times." Nicky flattened her palms, then hit the water hard.

"That's enough."

"I'm tired of singing 'Jesus Loves Me.' "

"What brought that on?" Juts dabbed at her.

"Sunday school."

"Oh, right. Well, you like Ursie Vance and Franny."

Frances Finster's granddaughter was named for her.

"I don't like Ursie anymore."

"Why is that?"

"She said if I don't say my prayers I'll go to the bad place when I die."

"You say your prayers."

"I leave out the die part. I don't like that."

At bedtime, Nickel refused to say, "And if I die before I wake." She just would say, "I pray the Lord my soul to take."

"Don't worry."

"And Ursie is always stopping the teacher when she's telling Bible stories. She wanted to know what colors were in Joseph's coat. I hope she looks behind her and turns into a pillar of salt."

Juts wasn't pleased about four-and five-year-olds learning about Sodom and Gomorrah.

"Tell me that story."

Nickel sighed. How could her mother not know? "Lot and his wife ran away from bad people. And Lot's wife wasn't supposed to look back." She paused, concentrating on the details, then happily finished her story. "Lot's wife was a pillar of salt by day and a ball of fire by night."

65

Nineteen fifty was the year Wheezie discovered shocking pink. Festooned with shocking-pink plastic earrings, matching bracelet, and lipstick against a navy-blue sweater and skirt, she would occasionally offset this color scheme with lime green. She was also fond of pale pink and black. Julia retaliated by wearing yards of aqua and white.

Runnymedians, putting the war behind them as best they could, erupted in an explosion of music, building, big cars, and endless gossip. But then nothing could stop the gossip. If Hitler had won they would have gossiped about him and the German gauleiter sent to whip them into shape.

Nickel was in kindergarten and loved it. Chessy had reorganized the store and had hired an assistant. He had begun advertising too, and had bought the family a brand-new refrigerator because business was so good. He moved the icebox to the garage, using it for tool storage. Maizie's future remained cloudy and once when Wheezie pressured her about it said, "Gobble, gobble, gobble." Louise buttoned her lip.

Juts and Nickel continued their riding lessons. That and gardening were the two pastimes they shared, although it was not lost on Julia that Nickel preferred spending time with Chessy. She couldn't understand why the child would defy her but do anything her father asked.

Louise, ever the maternal expert, declared that girls stuck with their fathers, boys with their mothers. Other people echoed the thought and it certainly seemed true, because Lillian Yost's little boy screamed bloody murder when she took him to kindergarten for the first time. His eyes almost bugged out of his head, and his face went red, not a pretty sight, when it was time for his mother to leave.

Mrs. Miller, the teacher, told Lillian she had to leave . . . just leave, no matter how hard it would be. After all, the world does not shine on a mama's boy. The junior Yost pounded on the door, he kicked, he peed. Nickel pulled him from the door. "Shut up, bawl-baby." However much this sentiment endeared her to Mrs. Miller, it grated on Lillian Yost's last nerve when she heard the story. She flew all over Juts, who surprised everyone by not losing her temper.

Nickel and Peepbean Huffstetler fought at the stable, at school, anywhere. Three years older than the curly-haired girl, he could whop her. She'd get even on horseback. She literally rode rings around him, thereby ensuring further attention from O.B. and further hatred from Peepbean.

Juts had taken Nickel to see a Walt Disney movie showing in York. The projectionist, possessor of two brain cells, ran a newsreel that showed gangs of children foraging in the rubble of Dresden. A dead dog lay by the side of the road. The voice-over intoned about the suffering endured in the part of Germany controlled by Russia. Nickel sobbed over the dog and the children until Juts had to take her out of the theater. How could you explain to a five-year-old that other five-year-olds used to be the enemy? No matter how hard Juts tried on that cold January day, she couldn't condemn anybody's children, not even those of the Japanese, whom she still hated with all her heart.

She told Nickel that adults make wars and cause innocents to suffer. Nickel couldn't understand. For weeks afterward she asked everyone if she would die. And if there was a war, could she save Buster and Yoyo? Juts would find her rummaging through old copies of *Life* magazine at Mother Smith's; Josephine never threw out anything except kindness. Pictures of war fascinated Nickel.

Juts didn't recall being so concerned as a child during the Great War, but she had understood, finally, that Nickel was not a carbon copy of herself.

Juts, on hands and knees one afternoon, scrubbed the kitchen floor. Yoyo, grown plump, lazed on the countertop. Buster watched from the hall. The radio played "I Love Those Dear Hearts and Gentle People." Juts sang along, her soprano quite lovely.

Juts finished out the song: " '. . . that live and love in my hometown.' "

A light rap on the back window brought her to her feet. She walked on the balls of her feet to the back door.

"Rillma?"

Rillma Ryan, ravishingly beautiful now as she approached thirty, nodded.

"Hi, Juts."

"Come on in." When Juts opened the door, a rush of cold air followed. Buster barked at the visitor.

"I don't want to step on your wet floor."

"I'll mop up the prints. I didn't know you were coming home."

"I hadn't planned on it, but I earned a bonus at work so I thought I'd come see Mom and—the baby."

Raw fear seared through Juts. She liked Rillma. Everyone liked Rillma. But what if blood proved thicker than water? What if Nickel somehow recognized her mother and abandoned Juts? Then again, how could she refuse Rillma the common courtesy of inviting her in? After all, she had given Juts her child.

"Can I get you something to eat or drink?"

"Oh no, thank you. Is Nickel at school?"

"Kindergarten. She's only there a half day but I sure enjoy those three hours. Each week one of us takes turns walking the kids to school. It works out pretty good."

"Mom says she runs on twelve cylinders."

"That's the truth. Come on, let's go in the living room."

"I should have called, Juts, but I was afraid you'd say no. You know I won't do anything out of the way."

"I hope not."

"Mom said Louise is about to turn forty-nine and she's having a hissy."

Juts crossed one leg over the other as she sat in the deep chair. "She doesn't even admit to forty."

"I saw Mary briefly. She looks real good—a little tired, but good."

"She's happy."

"How's Chessy?"

"Same old guy. He loves Nicky. She's the center of his world." Julia paused. "I think he's the happiest he's been since I've known him, and that's saying a lot with that battle-ax of a mother."

"I know, Mom told me all about that, too. She said Cora marched right on down to Josephine's house and had a set-to and Josephine wouldn't see anyone or talk to anyone for days and then she snapped out of it."

"She endures Nicky. Nicky hates going over there but I told her once that we had to do this for Daddy, that no matter how much we didn't like Grandma, Daddy loved her. She was fine after that."

The front door flew open. "Buster, Yoyo!" The animals rushed over to Nickel. "Hi, Momma." She stopped hugging and kissing the cat and dog as she stared at the beautiful stranger. "Hi."

"Hi," Rillma replied. It seemed to Juts she was trying not to choke up.

"Nicky, this is Rillma Ryan and she came to pay us a visit."

Nicky bounded over—she never walked when she could skip or run—and held out her hand as she had been taught to do. "Hello, Miss Ryan."

"Hello, Nickel. You may call me Rillma."

"Neat name."

"My brother named me that."

Nickel couldn't remember a Ryan man about Rillma's age. By this time she knew everyone in South and North Runnymede. "Momma, how come I don't know Rillma's brother?"

Rillma replied, "He died of spinal meningitis when I was about your age."

"Did I do a bad thing?" Nickel, chagrined, asked Juts.

"No, honey, you didn't know."

Nickel threw off her coat and her scarf, dutifully taking them to the mud room off the kitchen. When she reappeared she smiled at the visitor. Although they had the same coloring and the same eyes, Nickel couldn't see it. She had the Ryan voice, too, but her high cheekbones, full lips, and athletic body were from the paternal side.

"Do you like school?"

Every adult asked this question.

"Yes, ma'am."

"Tell her what you like best," Juts encouraged her.

"Horses."

"No, your classes."

"Drawing. Mrs. Miller lets us use finger paints!"

"That's nice."

"Where do you live?" Nicky asked. The rudiments of making conversation were being taught to her by the Wednesday Tea ladies as well as her own family. Wednesday Tea was the precursor to junior cotillion and then cotillion, and attendance was mandatory for children whose parents revered good manners.

"Portland, Oregon."

"Oh." She had no idea where this place might be.

"That's all the way across the country on the Pacific Ocean."

"Oh." Nickel concentrated to come up with more to say. "Do they have horses in Portland?"

"Yes. The city is famous for its roses, though. It's right on a big river, which flows into the ocean. Maybe when you're bigger you'll visit it."

"That would be nice." She became quiet. She had exhausted her line of conversation and was dying to play outdoors even though it was cold. "Momma, can I put on my pants and go outside?"

"Yeah, sure." Juts lit up a Chesterfield after offering a smoke to Rillma, who refused.

"It was nice to meet you, Rillma. Do you have a little girl or a little boy I could play with?"

"No." Rillma smiled.

"Bye." She scrambled up the stairs to her room, followed by the cat and the dog. She changed in a flash and ran back down and out the back door.

The two women waited until the back door closed.

"She's getting better about slamming the door."

"She's a sweet kid." Rillma smiled tightly.

"She was born to be my baby." A rush of color flooded Julia's cheeks.

"She was."

"Anyone know out there in Portland?"

"No."

"No reason to."

"No. I don't even know if I'll tell my husband. That is, if I ever get married."

"A beautiful girl like you will get married."

"I don't trust men." Rillma's voice lowered.

"Who said anything about trusting them?" Juts exhaled through her nostrils.

"How can you love someone you don't trust?"

Juts shrugged. "You just do, Rillma. They can't help being what they are, any more than we can help being what we are—I guess."

"I put my foot in it, didn't I?"

"God, Rillma, this is Runnymede. Everybody knows everything about everybody. I survived. You survived. You just go on."

Rillma lowered her lustrous brown eyes to the floor and then raised them again. "I'd rather be by myself." She sucked in her breath. "You know how things flit across your mind? When all this was happening I thought my life was over." She paused. "But it all worked out somehow."

Rillma stood up and held out her hand to Julia, then hugged her instead. "Thank you. I was afraid you wouldn't let me in."

Juts held her cigarette away so she wouldn't burn Rillma. "You can write me. I'll write back."

"I will."

After Rillma left by the front door, Juts watched her walk down the sidewalk. Juts exploded into tears but she didn't know why as the graceful silhouette receded into nothingness.

66

You did what!" Louise paused, her fingers on the lace of a brassiere, for she was standing in the middle of Bear's department store on the square in York.

"I let her visit Nickel."

"You can't do that." In the next breath she said, "Does Chester know?"

"Sure."

"And he wasn't upset?"

"No."

She dropped the bra. "Then you're both of you out of your heads. Blood calls to blood. You're asking for trouble."

"Nicky couldn't have cared less. She was polite and then ran outside to play."

Louise hit the serious register in her voice, accompanied by a telltale shake of the head. "She has no business around that child. She gave her up. Nickel is yours."

"I didn't have the heart to turn her away. Anyhow, she can't take care of a child, and Chessy and I have legally adopted Nickel. There's nothing she can do."

"What if Nickel looks at her and sees herself?"

"Nicky doesn't look like Rillma."

"She talks in spurts, long silences and then boom," Louise

said. "That's unusual. Maybe there's something wrong. Maybe in-side she knows she's not blood."

"She talks about horses, Louise. You can be such an ass."

Surrounded by lace panties—pink, yellow, white, and danger-ous black—Louise and Juts got a hen-on. The customers at the lingerie sale hovered around the merchandise and the unintended entertainment.

"An ass, an ass? Who rode all the way to filthy Pittsburgh on borrowed gas-ration coupons to get your baby? Who wrapped her in a blanket and held her close during the blizzard? Who took turns driving with Chester? You are one brick shy of a load! You don't know anything about being a mother."

"Shut up," Juts threatened.

"Furthermore, you should never, ever have let Rillma Ryan see that child!"

"Stop telling me what to do." Juts slapped her with a brassiere.

"Free speech—this is America."

"For Chrissake, Wheezie, shut up."

Wheezie tossed her head as another bra flew at her face. "You're trying to deprive me of my rights as a citizen."

"No, I'm trying to shut you up! I'm sick of you."

Louise grabbed a handful of underpants and dumped them on Juts's head. One hung on her ear. Lingerie floated down like little silken parachutes. The floorwalker, a mincing twit in a brown suit, charged down the aisle.

"Ladies, ladies."

"Stay out of this." Juts threw a brassiere at him.

He pulled it off his face, his wedding ring catching the over-head light for an instant. Sales clerks deserted their posts to help him. Meanwhile, a crowd had gathered and women were scoop-ing up the silk goodies. Most intended to pay. A few did not.

The two sisters, pulled apart, were dumped out on the street.

A pair of pink underpants was lodged in Louise's blouse between the top and second buttons. She stormed down the street.

"Thief!" Juts pointed at the pink protrusion.

Louise stopped, saw the underpants, and turned around. She opened the front door of Bear's, grandly dropping them on the floor, then she headed across the square for George Street.

"You can find your own way home."

Juts, color high, tagged after her. "Gum flapper!"

"Don't be so childish."

A familiar face, though fatter now, smiled at them as Bunny Von Bonhurst came down the sidewalk from the opposite direction, waving at the sisters.

"Bunny." Louise, switching into social gear, forced a smile. "I haven't seen you in years."

Bunny, in a smart beige suite, hugged Louise and then Julia. "Why, I came on over from Salisbury to visit Rollie and the kids." Rollie was her son. "How are you?"

"I can't complain," said Louise, who usually did.

"You look good." Juts lied because she thought Bunny Von Bonhurst was fat as a tick.

"I hear you're a mother now."

"Yes, she's a handful."

"They all are." Bunny laughed heartily. "Say, I sure thought of you girls back during the war, when I read the article in the paper about the German planes. You must have been scared to death."

"We were," Louise truthfully replied, smiling reflexively.

"That was some night." Juts decided to add to Louise's distress. "Louise had the binoculars and we heard something. Naturally, we never assumed it could be the enemy, even though we were trained to look for them. Anyway, the clouds were big rolling ones so she had to really follow this high, faraway sound and then she saw them coming straight on in a V. My heart stopped."

So did Louise's, because she was sure that her angry sister would rat on her with an unvarnished account. "Really, Julia, Bunny doesn't want to hear the details."

"I do so!"

"Well"—Juts licked her lips—"Wheezie screamed 'Germans' and I swung the big light up on the aircraft, but they were really high up. Wheezie cranked the siren. It was the middle of the night. People ran out of their houses; Caesura Frothingham, you remember her—" When Bunny nodded that she did, Juts continued, "—hollered so loud she could have awakened the dead, 'We'll be killed!' then she ran around like a chicken with its head cut off until she finally dove under her car. A lot of good that would have done. And—"

"Julia, really." Louise checked her wristwatch in an obvious manner. "Bunny, I'm so glad to see you."

"You know what was odd about those Germans, though, was that they disappeared. Must have been heavier clouds farther west, or maybe they turned and flew back out to the ocean." Juts maliciously smiled at Louise and then sweetly smiled at Bunny.

"Pearlie always swore they came out of Newfoundland." Louise clipped her words.

"That's a long way away." Bunny wrinkled her brow.

"They didn't build aircraft carriers." Juts rubbed it in.

"They could have borrowed one from the Japanese. They were on the same side, you know." Louise stared daggers at her.

"Yeah, they had an Axis to grind."

Bunny giggled. "Juts, you never change."

"Unfortunately." Louise smiled stiffly. "Still my bad baby sister." She put her hand under Julia's elbow and pushed her right down the road, calling over her shoulder to Bunny, "You come on down and visit us. It's been too long."

Bunny waved. "I will."

Out of Bunny's earshot, Louise hissed, "If you ever even hint at what happened that night I will slit your throat."

"Then you'd better be real nice to me."

"I am nice to you. I am trying to avert a disaster down the road."

"When I want your advice I'll ask for it. Then again"—that malicious smile returned—"you are my big sister. You are having a birthday in the next minute and soon you'll be fifty."

"I will not!"

"That's right. I forgot. You were born in 1901. You'll only be forty-nine. Guess we have to wait another year for the Big One."

"I am not forty-nine."

"Well, that's funny, Wheezie, because I'm forty-five."

"You never were good at math."

They rode home in silence. Louise, warned, didn't want to further provoke Julia, but she was still so furious she didn't trust herself to talk. Juts hummed the entire way home, interrupting her musical reverie as they passed familiar sights on Route 116. She adored having Louise in her power. She even made her stop in Spring Grove so she could buy a Co-Cola, knowing the smell from the nearby paper mill would turn Louise's stomach.

When Wheezie pulled into Juts's driveway, Juts hopped out of the car, grabbed her few packages, and said, "I have a new philosophy—'Tell the truth and run.' Forty-nine!" She shut the door of the car and dashed to the house.

67

Everyone invited to Louise's birthday party had to keep up the fiction that she had only just nudged over the forty line.

Nickel, loving any kind of party, stood at the door taking coats. She threw them over the bed in Louise's bedroom. After the bed was piled high she threw coats over Doodlebug's bed because she figured it was the bed part that was important. The only bad thing about that idea was that Ramelle Chalfonte's mink coat got fleas.

Extra Billy and Mary acted as bartender and server. Mary carried around hors d'oeuvre trays. She couldn't believe how much people ate and drank.

Lillian Yost greeted Juts. "How about Natalie Bitters?" Natalie was a great-aunt of Billy's. "Strong as a horse and then—gone so fast!"

"Popeye Huffstetler wrote the obituary. He said, 'Natalie Bitters went to rest in the loving arms of Jesus.' " Juts giggled. "Well, that was a lie. Not even Jesus would want that bitch."

If Juts had watched her back she would have realized that Natalie Bitters's one friend in this life, Samantha Dingledine, was behind it.

"How could you say a thing like that?"

"She was about as attractive as goat pellets," Juts replied, having liberally sampled the libations as she helped prepare for the party.

"I'm leaving!" Samantha pushed for the door.

Louise, not wishing to offend Samantha because she had a great big house to paint and Pearlie had put a bid on the job, rushed over. "Ignore Juts. She doesn't have the sense God gave a goose."

"Goose or geese?" Juts's eyes narrowed.

Louise, sensitive to the hint, put her arms around Sam's shoulders while winking at Juts, hoping that would make them conspirators. "Loose lips sink ships."

"Are you talking to your sister or me?" Samantha wanted to know.

"Sorry, Sam. It's an expression Juts and I use to calm each other down."

As Louise approached the punch bowl, there was Nickel chugging a glass of punch.

"Put that glass down, you little lush."

"Huh?" Nicky, startled, faced her aunt, noticing that her red lipstick was a little smudged.

Louise grabbed the glass from Nickel's hand. Juts strode over to the punch bowl. "Wheezie, she didn't know there was one bowl for kids and one for adults."

"You might try disciplining her."

Nickel took in this exchange as Samantha Dingledine backed away. Then she hastily dipped another glass cup into the punch, which tasted delicious to her.

"I do discipline her!"

Louise didn't miss the second pass at the punch. She reached down and grabbed Nickel's wrist. "Don't you dare drink that punch."

"Leave her alone." Juts smacked Louise so hard on the back that her false teeth flew into the punch bowl.

Louise couldn't scream because everyone would notice she had no teeth. She was hoping no one had seen her teeth fly out, which of course many had. She fished in the bowl for them.

Nickel thought this was a great party game, so she dipped her hand into the liquid too. Her nimble fingers located the uppers.

"Here's your teeth, Aunt Wheezie."

Louise clapped both hands over the offered prize and hissed through her gums, "These aren't my teeth." She clomped upstairs.

"Momma, what'd I do wrong?"

"Not a goddamned thing. Why don't you help me clean out this punch bowl?" Julia picked up the bowl, careful not to slosh any punch. She carried it into the kitchen as Ramelle Chalfonte opened the kitchen door for her.

She poured the contents down the drain.

"Momma, why is Aunt Wheezie mad at me?"

"She's cross because she's an old bag." Juts scrubbed out the bowl.

Ramelle joined them. "Need a hand?"

"A foot, too," Juts joked. "Nicky, shake up the Hawaiian Punch, will you?"

Nickel grabbed the big can and shook it. Juts finished wiping out the bowl as Ramelle looked for a can opener or a church key.

"Here we are." She perforated two holes on opposite sides of the can. "I think we need two of these. Nickel, how about shaking up another one?"

"Okay." As Nickel shook and shook the blue can, she asked, "What birthday is this?"

"What she says or what she is?" Juts stopped herself. "Never mind, honey. Aunt Louise is thirty-nine. She's been thirty-nine many times. She will be thirty-nine when you are thirty-nine."

Nickel, oblivious to her mother's sarcasm, placed the can next to the punch bowl. She watched as Juts poured in a bottle of cheap vodka. When Juts turned to wipe her hands on a red-and-white dish towel, Nickel poured in a second bottle. Ramelle started to say something, then giggled behind her hand.

The two women called in Pearlie to carry out the heavy bowl.

The party picked up after that.

"Hey, Wheezie," Julia called to her when she reappeared, "drink to your birthday." She held out a cup.

"Now you know I don't drink."

The group stopped and people called out, "Come on."

"Enjoy yourself. It's your birthday."

"Well, just a smidgen." Louise knocked back the drink. As the night wore on she needed more smidgens.

Millard Yost danced close to Louise, very close.

Pearlie tapped him on the shoulder to cut in. Millard wouldn't let go. Pearlie tapped him again as the music filled the room. Millard still wouldn't let go. Pearlie then pulled him away from Louise but Millard, who'd partaken freely of the punch, reached for his partner and grabbed her bosoms, perhaps not unintentionally. Pearlie hauled off and decked him.

Lillian, mortified at her husband's behavior, stood over his inert form. "You can have him. I'm going home." She stormed out of the house, slamming the door behind her.

Chessy, a little high himself, said, "Let's move him, boys."

The men picked up Millard, depositing him in Maizie's old bedroom.

Nickel, past her bedtime, pulled on her mother's dress. "Momma, what's wrong with Mr. Yost?"

"He's snockered."

"How come he wouldn't let go of Aunt Wheezie?"

"Uh..." Juts thought a minute, then repeated something Celeste used to say: "The bonds of matrimony are so heavy it takes two, sometimes three, to carry them."

Nickel fell asleep upstairs next to Doodlebug, both of them

stretched out on the mink coat, but not before she told anyone who would listen to her that she was never going to get married.

Meanwhile, Louise hauled Juts into the kitchen, both of them unsteady on their feet.

"Now, Julia, you can't make jokes about my age."

"I haven't made one joke this evening."

"I don't trust you."

"I'm your sister."

"Exactly." Louise crossed her arms over her chest. "See, you have to realize that we sleep eight hours a day."

"So?"

"Eight is one-third of twenty-four. Right?"

"Right."

"I don't do anything when I sleep. My whole body and mind are at rest."

"Right." Juts leaned against the counter, glad for the support.

"Well, then, I don't really live for those eight hours, so they can't count toward my age. You can only count those hours when you know what you're doing. I am two-thirds of the age on the books. See?"

"Yeah." Juts was confused, but it sounded reasonable.

"Well then, Julia, I am really only thirty-two point three years old, but I can't say that because it's too difficult for people to grasp. So I just say that I'm thirty-nine. When my age catches up to thirty-nine I really will be thirty-nine because I've got six years to go. I know what I'm doing. You should listen to me."

68

The summer of 1950 sparkled with robin's-egg-blue skies and low humidity, a glorious contrast from the usual. The occasional sultry day brought out folks fanning themselves on their porches; old men in Panamas gathered at the square to sit under the shade of the cooling trees.

Juts, with an unenthusiastic Nicky tagging after, strolled through the park. Unlike her sister, who favored large flower-bedecked chapeaus, Juts was bareheaded. This gave her ample opportunity to demonstrate there wasn't a gray hair on her head. As she didn't resort to the dye pots, she was proud of this, doubly proud since a stunning silver streak was showing on Louise's widow's peak.

Mary Miles Mundis cruised by in a brand-new Cadillac, so big it hogged the two lanes. Mary Miles waved, setting the flab on her underarm to jiggling. Fattening up the family bank account had fattened up Mary Miles, as well.

"Momma, when's Mrs. Mundis's pool going to be ready?"

"Right soon."

"Will she allow children in it?"

"Only good children."

Nickel squinted up at her mother, clamped her lips shut, and cracked an imaginary whip.

Juts laconically told her, "You've watched too much Lash LaRue."

Lash LaRue, a popular cowboy star dressed in black, could snap a cigarette out of an enemy's mouth with his whip.

"Momma, is it true you served Daddy a dog-food sandwich?"

"Where'd you hear that?" Juts's gray eyes brightened. "Did my esteemed sister tell you that?"

By now Nickel had learned that the best way to get a reaction out of her mother was to tease out information. "I forget."

"You did not forget, you little shit, you've got a mind like a steel trap. Now you tell me who told you that or you can't go to Mrs. Mundis's pool party."

That did the trick. "Aunt Wheezer."

"Aunt Wheezer what?"

"Aunt Wheezer said you got mad at Daddy and fed him a dog-food sandwich with mustard and pickles and lettuce."

"I did no such thing." They reached the Confederate memorial statue to the glorious dead of the unsullied lost cause. "It was cat food."

Nicky burst out laughing. "Momma!"

"He never knew the difference." Julia pondered a moment. "Sugar pie, let me give you a piece of advice that may not mean much now, but you'll thank me for it later. Your father deserved far worse than a cat-food sandwich, but that was years ago." She lifted her eyes to Epstein's Jewelry and thought to herself that while the whole thing had happened years ago, it never went away. "If it's got testicles or tires it's gonna be trouble."

Spending time in the stable, Nicky knew what testicles were. "Oh" was her reply. She spied Louise crossing the square from the Bon-Ton, toting two shopping bags. "Aunt Wheezie!" She scampered across the shaded path to greet her aunt, whom she liked most days.

Juts caught up with them. "What you got in there?"

"Odds and ends."

"I bet everything in there is useful and you've been waiting years to purchase it."

"Don't start," Louise warned. "Why don't we sit for a minute?"

"Not on the north side. Let's cross the line." Juts walked back a few paces and flopped on a pretty wrought-iron bench. "Did you see Mary Miles Mundis's brand-new, as in two-minutes-old, Cadillac?"

"Not yet."

"You'll only have to wait a few minutes because she's cruising around town. She should be due for another pass at the square any minute now."

"It's red," Nickel piped up.

"A red Cadillac." Louise sighed. "Must be nice. Harold makes the money and Mary Miles spends it."

"You can't take it with you."

"Nickel, don't listen to your mother. Money burns a hole in her pocket. You must save."

"Yes, Aunt Louise." Nickel swung her legs back and forth, since they didn't touch the ground. The wrought-iron bench was cool on her bottom.

"What's this about telling my child I served Chessy a cat-food sandwich?"

"I thought it was dog food."

"That's not the point."

"I don't know," Louise hedged. "Just popped into my mind."

"Well, it didn't have to pop out of your mouth."

Louise, saved from further defense, caught sight of the red Cadillac stopping on the Emmitsburg pike, a flash of color between the sepulchral whiteness of the two city halls.

"She ought to give more money to the church."

"Balls," Juts snapped.

"Testicles," Nickel corrected her mother.

"No, balls." Juts lit up a Chesterfield.

"Your mother is relishing an uncouth moment," Louise commented dryly.

"You, of course, are so full of the milk of human kindness that you moo. Nary a harsh word escapes your perfect lips."

"I had something in this Bon-Ton bag for you. Now I'm keeping it for myself." Louise crossed her arms over her chest.

"What?"

"I'm certainly not going to give a gift to someone who insults me. My own sister!"

"That's what sisters are for." Julia smiled. "There she goes. I think she had the dealer remove the muffler."

They listened as the deep rumble of the huge V-8 engine permeated the square. Even the birds were silent.

"Can you imagine having that much money?"

"Yeah." A dreamy look came into Juts's eyes. She refocused on the shopping bag. "What'd you get me?"

"Don't you reach in there!" Louise smacked Juts's hand. She reached in and pulled out an egg slicer, a small gadget that had wires strung across it like a tiny harp.

"Hey, I can use this. Thanks." Juts kissed her sister on the cheek lightly so as not to leave a lipstick mark.

Nickel, quietly expectant, inched closer to her aunt on the bench.

"And this is for you." Louise brought forth a cowboy bandana.

"Neat!" Nickel immediately rolled it and tied it around her neck. "Thanks, Aunt Wheezie."

"Say 'Thank you.' 'Thanks' is for scuz buckets." Juts pointed a finger at the child.

"Thank you, Aunt Louise."

"You're welcome."

Mary Miles made another flyby around the square.

"How many miles do you think she gets to the gallon in that thing?" Juts blew out smoke.

"Luckily for her there's a station down on Baltimore Street."
Louise lusted after that car. "By the way, I almost forgot. The pool
party will be this Saturday. Everyone's invited."

"Peepbean, too?" Nickel asked.

"Everybody."

"Grandma Smith?"

"Her, too," Louise replied.

"I can't wait to see that fat load in a bathing suit," Juts said.

"Juts, Josephine Smith will never wear a bathing suit. She'll sit
under an umbrella. She'll complain of the heat even if it's a day like
today. She'll call for Rup to fetch her a lime rickey, which I know
full well is a gin rickey. She'll get bored after an hour and make
Rup take her home. Or better yet, she'll get Chessy to do it."

"I guess it's a good thing. She'd have to wear a tent."

The pool party, blessed with perfect weather, drew the whole
town. No one would miss it. And as Louise predicted, Josephine
Smith reposed under a large oak tree, fanning herself, drinking a
rickey, her feet on a small hassock provided by her attentive host.

As it was the beginning of summer everyone was white as
chalk, which made some of the guests look fatter than they were.
Mary Miles had picked up a pound or two, but at least her bulk
was well-proportioned. Also, her bathing suit had a little skirt
on it.

Juts, her beautiful figure still without a sag in it, splashed and
played around. Louise, too, was in good shape. Juts couldn't resist a
malicious remark to Louise concerning Trudy Epstein, who now
exhibited a little pot belly.

Juts had known that the Epsteins would be there. After all, the
whole county, practically, was invited. If she hadn't wanted to be
in the same place with Trudy, Juts could have refused to come.
She never would have done that, however. After all, she was going
to be the life of the party.

Nickel played with the other kids. She and Peepbean spit at each other. He pushed her down. Although half his size, she bounced up and knocked him sideways with all the force of her fists. O.B. stepped in before more damage could be done.

"That's enough. You don't hit girls."

Peepbean, rubbing his eyes to hide the tears, remarked, "She's not a girl. She's a bitch."

O.B. grabbed him by the ear. "You shut your trap!"

Nickel watched with obvious satisfaction.

Jackson Frost, almost seven and a half years old to Nicky's five and a half, put his arm around her shoulders. "Let's get ice cream."

Mary Miles and Harold filled tables with hot dogs, hamburgers, potato salad, cole slaw, baked beans, three-bean salad, pickled eggs, deviled eggs, cold hams, and fried chicken. The dessert table had big tubs of ice cream packed around with dry ice, everyone's favorite candy bars, and little peanut clusters that Mrs. Anstein made especially for the occasion.

Louise took up residence on a big air mattress. She paddled with both her hands.

Juts swam over. "Let me get up there, too."

"There isn't room."

"Take a swim and let me have it for a while."

"No. I don't want to get my hair wet. I went to Pierre today and it's just the way I like it."

"It's a pool party."

"That doesn't mean I have to swim." Louise closed her eyes. "Just let me float around up here. You know how many chemicals there are in pools. Might turn my hair funny."

Nickel watched as her mother dove under the air mattress and flipped it over. Louise rose to the surface, sputtering, while Juts swam away.

"Your mother's mean." Peepbean snuck up on Nickel.

"Shut up," Jackson warned him.

"You shut up."

"Peepbean, you're a real cootie." Nickel turned away from him to watch the scene in the pool. She was wearing her red cowboy boots, her bathing suit, and her bandana. Much as Juts tried to tell her this wasn't pool-party attire, Nicky would surrender neither the boots nor the bandana.

"I can't swim!" Louise hollered.

Mrs. Mundis turned up the radio, probably not to drown out Louise's cries. She wanted more music and she wasn't much paying attention to the drama in her pool.

Nickel ran to Chessy. "Daddy, Aunt Wheezie is taking on water." Nickel, hearing so much military talk because of the veterans, had picked up the phrase.

"Juts!" Chessy called to his wife, who was emphatically not paying attention to her sister.

"I'll drown!" Louise wailed.

"I'll save you." Nickel jumped in, boots and all, and sank like a stone. Soon the curly head popped to the surface. She dog-paddled toward her aunt.

"I'm drowning!"

"Not fast enough." Juts saw that her sister wasn't kidding. Worse, her hair was getting wet.

Juts put her arm under her sister's back, pushing her up. "Kick with your legs. Not me, goddammit," Juts said as she felt a thump on her thigh. She guided a struggling Louise to the air mattress.

Once she grabbed the side of it, Louise spit water at Juts. "You knocked me off."

"I'm sorry."

"You are not!"

A little yelp from Nickel alerted Juts and Chessy.

"Daddy, my legs are tired." And they were. "It's hard to swim in cowboy boots."

Chessy dove in, spitting water to either side, and grabbed his child. She put her arms around his neck. "Sugar pie, Daddy's got you."

"I can swim, I really can swim."

"I know, I know." He patted her back. "But it's not a good idea to do it in cowboy boots."

"Is she all right?" Julia called out.

"Yes."

"Well, I'm not!" Louise paddled to the side of the pool.

By now the partyers watched.

Louise clambered out of the pool and sank down on the coping, breathing heavily. "She's trying to kill me. She wants my half of the inheritance."

Julia ignored this, further angering Louise, still gasping for air.

Pearlie, pushing through the crowd, finally reached her and ministered to her. Mary made it to her mother's side as well.

Peepbean cornered Nickel near the dessert table. "What a dumb-ass you are."

Nickel shrugged. As Peepbean had just overheard an aside concerning Nickel's parentage he felt powerful. She brushed by him. He followed in her trail of water.

"Dumb. You're a dumb bastard."

Nickel didn't know exactly what "bastard" meant except that it wasn't a good word. "Shut up, Peepbean."

"You think you're so smart but you're a dumb bastard."

Extra Billy Bitters, just behind Peepbean, heard this. He didn't want this conversation to progress any further. "Peepbean."

Peepbean turned to see the towering blond man behind him. "Yes, sir?"

"Time for you to swim."

"Yes, sir." Peepbean walked back to the pool and slipped in.

Extra Billy walked over to O.B., told him what he had heard, and asked O.B. to see if he couldn't give Peepbean some fatherly advice. O.B., already disenchanted with his offspring, turned pale.

Billy patted O.B. on his narrow shoulder. "It's just...the kid shouldn't have to know—not now, anyway."

O.B. nodded. "She won't hear it from Kirk." Rarely did O.B. use his son's nickname.

Meanwhile, Nickel was madly unwrapping Baby Ruths. The adults, most of them, were still occupied with Louise. Nicky tossed the Baby Ruths into the pool.

"Honeybun," Harold Mundis bellowed as Peepbean swam around. "There's shit in the pool."

"Harry, there can't be. No one's had time."

Undaunted by this wisdom, Harold pointed to the offending candy bars. "Shit floats."

"Don't look at me!" Louise shouted. Her lungs recovered from her travail. "I was scared but I wasn't that scared."

Juts, oozing sisterly love and relishing the moment, purred, "Now, now, Louise, fear does that to many people."

"I did not defecate in Mary Miles's pool!" Louise sat upright, her eyes blazing.

"Well, someone did," Harold, not a sensitive man, observed.

Nickel piped up. "Peepbean Huffstetler."

Just then Peepbean surfaced from his underwater swim. He was showing off how far he could swim while holding his breath. All eyes were upon him. He smiled, held his nose, and flipped over backward, going underwater again. This time when he surfaced, a Baby Ruth bobbled in, eyeball level.

"Ugh." He pushed water at it, which sent that one away, but a few others headed toward him, tiny brown torpedoes. He yelled, splashed water everywhere, and swam to the side of the pool. He climbed out with everyone staring at him. They were too polite to point the finger, but everyone there just knew Peepbean Huffstetler had pooped in the pool.

69

The backs of Chessy's legs glowed, diaper-rash-pink from too much sun. He winced as he slid under the covers that evening.

Yoyo, languid across the end of the bed, observed his discomfort. She roused herself, stretched, then padded across the sheet, placing herself right by his hand. He petted her.

Juts, a jar of Noxema in hand, emerged from the bathroom. "Roll over."

"I don't think that does a damned bit of good."

"The menthol helps. Come on."

He rolled over and she pulled back the sheet. Yoyo moved to the pillow for a better view.

"You know what Extra Billy told me? I nearly forgot." He winced as the first white glob hit his calf. "He told me Peepbean Huffstetler called Nicky a bastard. Said he had a word with O.B. about it."

"That kid isn't wrapped too tight." Juts rubbed too hard.

"Juts—"

"Sorry."

"I think we've got to tell Nickel before she starts first grade. Everyone knows. Eventually the kids she plays with will know. I don't want her to hear it from them."

"September's a long way away."

"No, it's not. This is June. Time flies!"

"Oh, let's not tell her right now."

"We've got to do it before school starts."

Juts stopped smoothing on the cream. "Let her be mine for a little longer."

He twisted his head to see her. "She is yours, Juts. If you don't tell her, I will."

"No, you don't." Her voice rose.

"I'm not having some snotty brat like Peepbean—"

She interrupted. "He's mad at her because she rides so much better than he does. O.B. pays more attention to her than to his own son."

"I don't care why, I care when." He turned over, his legs tingling. "We need to sit down with her."

Juts screwed the cap back on the cobalt-blue glass jar. "Do you feel like she's yours?"

He blinked, then stammered a little. "She is mine. She's my baby. I don't care how she got here."

"Yeah." Juts rubbed the embroidered hem of the sheet between her left forefinger and thumb. "I don't see me in her at all."

"You aren't supposed to see you. You're supposed to see her."

"Louise looks at Mary and sees herself. I know she does. Maizie looks like Pearlie."

"What do looks have to do with it?"

"I don't know. Sometimes I see a little stranger."

He felt a bubble of anger rising in his throat and fought it down. "Well, Juts, maybe she looks at us and sees big strangers."

"Could be. . . ."

"What did you expect?"

"I don't know. More, I guess. Something. She's so goddamned independent. I thought she'd need me."

"She does."

"No, she doesn't, Chessy. She goes off by herself. She's—" She couldn't think of another word. "—independent."

"That's good. Look at how Maizie had to fight to get away from her mother. If those girls had been given more freedom maybe it wouldn't have been so bad, especially for Maizie."

"I don't know. I never thought Louise smothered them."

"I did."

"Men are different. You don't love children the way we do."

"Julia Ellen, that is the dumbest damn thing I've ever heard."

"Okay, then why is it so easy for men to leave their children?"

"Those aren't real men," Chessy shot back. "And you can't judge everyone by your father. Nickel's curious about the world and she's not afraid. Leave her alone, Juts. Be glad she's not some fraidy-cat."

"But I don't think she cares if I'm her mother or not."

"Of course she does." He sat up and put his arm around her. "She's a kid. She's not thinking about you, she's thinking about herself. Kids don't mean to be self-centered, but they are."

"I keep thinking something's missing."

"Nothing's missing. Really. Now, we've got to have a sit-down before school starts, Julia." He emphasized her name.

"Louise says the opposite. She says we should never tell. If we do, Nickel won't feel like our child."

"Louise is full of shit—for starters."

Juts placed the Noxema jar on the nightstand, then crawled in the other side of the bed. She turned on her side, getting a full view of Yoyo. She wiggled down to see Chessy's face as Yoyo's tail flicked over it.

"Honey, do you think I'm a good mother?"

"Sure."

"Really?"

"Yes."

She waited some more. "I wish Wheezie had stayed in the water longer."

"Huh?"

"Then everyone would have thought the Baby Ruths were hers."

"The look on Harry Mundis's face when he fished them out and discovered they were candy . . ."

"And Peepbean running around the pool shouting, 'I told you I didn't crap in the pool.' Jeez, it was worth the price of admission."

"Did you ask yourself how those Baby Ruths got in the pool?" He chuckled.

"Nicky. I know it was Nicky. Who else would think of such a thing?"

They exploded with laughter.

Chessy said, "She had him dead to shit."

70

The next morning, Juts was trimming back her wisteria, which threatened to take over the entire front porch, when Louise screeched into the driveway, slammed the car door shut, then charged up the front steps.

"How could you?"

"How could I what?"

"You humiliated me in front of everyone. I will never forget this. I may forgive but I will never forget."

"I shouldn't have tipped over the raft." Juts sounded contrite. She wasn't.

"That was the least of it. I lay there, lungs filled with water, fighting for air, then I had to defend myself against the idea that I'd defecated in the pool!"

"Wheezie, everyone knows you didn't do it."

Her long black eyelashes fluttered. "It was nip and tuck there for a while. The humiliation."

"Look at it this way." Juts tapped the end of a fresh pack of cigarettes, the cellophane smooth to her touch. "No one will ever forget the party or you."

Buster trotted around the corner, saw Wheezie, and bounced up for a pet. Nickel barreled up behind him.

"Hi, Aunt Wheezie."

"What's this I hear about you getting in a fight with Peepbean?"

"He started it."

"Nickel, he's slow in the head."

"Probably didn't get enough oxygen in the womb," Juts added.

Nickel put her hands on her hips. "Peepbean's a dingleberry."

"And what, may I ask, is a dingleberry?" Louise's eyebrows raised.

"A heinie hair with poop on it."

"Where do you hear such talk?" Louise was scandalized. Even Juts was taken aback.

"Jackson Frost told me Peepbean was a dingleberry. He *is*, too."

"Be that as it may, young lady, I don't ever want to hear that word out of your mouth again." Juts pointed her glowing red cigarette at Nicky.

"Why not? Momma, he called me a bastard and that's a nasty word, too. Why do I have to be nice? It's not fair."

Both sisters exchanged loaded glances. Louise gestured with her hand as if to say, "You first."

Juts sucked hard on her cigarette. "A Southern lady does not return rudeness for rudeness. You smile and walk away."

"Mom!"

Juts held up her hand. "I didn't say it was easy, but you earn the respect of everyone around you. Peepbean isn't worth fussing at."

"Do you know what a bastard is?" Louise prodded.

"No. But it's a bad word."

"Well, why don't we leave it at that?" Juts quickly said.

"If he hits me I'm hitting him back." She defiantly glared at her mother.

"You do have to defend yourself."

"You're telling her to hit him," Louise grumbled.

"No, I'm not, but kids are cruel. If she doesn't hit back they'll beat her to a pulp."

"She's not very big."

"I'm big enough to hurt someone." Nickel doubled her fists. "I'm not scared, either."

"That's obvious." Louise sighed. "I don't remember this kind of trouble with my girls."

"That was a different time." Juts was in no mood for a lecture on Louise's feminine daughters.

"It wasn't that long ago."

"Maybe not in years, but in other ways. The war changed everything."

Louise thought awhile. "Things are different."

Nickel studied their faces. "When I grow up I'll pound Peepbean to powder."

"That's hardly the answer."

" 'Turn the other cheek.' " Louise quoted the Bible.

"No."

"Nickel . . ." Juts frowned.

"No."

"It's in the Bible." Louise repeated a fact Nickel already knew.

"I'm not Jesus."

"Of course you're not, honey, but you must strive to live like Jesus." Louise's voice dripped saintliness.

"No."

"All right, Nicky, that's enough," her aunt said firmly.

"Jesus was crucified. I don't want to be crucified."

"Jesus died for our sins." Louise was positively unctuous.

"I don't have any sins."

"Of course you do. We are born sinful and unclean."

"I take a bath."

Set back by this intransigence, Louise bore down on the child. "We are born into Original Sin, Nickel. That is the word of God."

"I don't have any sins and I'm not turning the other cheek."

"Oh, Nicky, what would Jesus think if he heard you?"

She stared up at her aunt. "Jesus isn't here."

" 'Lo, I am with you always.' " Louise's voice lifted to the heavens.

"He's not here! He doesn't care about me."

"He does," Louise, shocked, blurted out.

Juts, amazed, watched and listened without speaking, a first for her.

Nickel stepped toward her aunt, ready to fight her, too. "If Jesus loved me he wouldn't let Peepbean pick on me."

"He knows you're strong enough to take care of yourself." This was a clever argument on Louise's part, but Nicky wasn't buying.

"Jesus let children die in the war."

"Not that again," Juts whispered, then spoke louder. "Nickel, I don't understand these things either. Why don't you work on your soap box? Okay?"

The child gave them both a long, hard look, then left.

Juts exhaled. "Goddamn, I wish she'd never seen that newsreel. That was months ago."

"The one with the dead dog?"

"And the gangs of orphans. What she remembers—" Juts shook her head.

"When we were knitting socks for the doughboys I don't remember thinking about the children over there. Did you?"

"No."

Louise shrugged. "Why is she building a soap box? Girls can't run in the derby."

"I know that."

"Well, the derby won't be for another year. It just happened."

As Louise's house was on the finish line everyone congregated there, and Nickel was vastly impressed by the competition.

"It keeps her busy. She likes to build things."

"She'd be better off sewing."

"She doesn't like to sew."

"Julia, you can't let children do what they want. You have to guide them."

"I am not in the mood for a lecture. Can it."

"Okay, okay. I will say, though, that Aunt Dimps doesn't sound like she's doing a good job as a Sunday-school teacher. Nicky is—"

"Louise, I mean it. I don't want to hear anything. I'm forty-five years old and *I* have a hard time believing in the Virgin Birth and the Resurrection. How come Jesus gets to come back but no one else does?"

"Don't even say such things. It's blasphemy."

"Christianity is not very logical, and if nothing else, Nicky is logical."

"Faith. You don't need brains."

"That's obvious."

This jab flew past Louise. She sat down on the swing, a tendril of wisteria at her feet. "Juts, I think you've got your work cut out for you."

"In all respects." Juts sat next to her sister. "As the governor of North Carolina said to the governor of South Carolina—"

Louise chimed in with Juts. " 'It's a long time between drinks.' "

71

A soul was in mortal danger. Louise came to the rescue. She gave Nickel a set of rosary beads, pearl-white, telling the child not to let her mother see them. She showed her how to say her novenas and Hail Marys. She volunteered to take Nicky out on walks or to the movies and then would instead sneak her into St. Rose of Lima's for a bracing mass.

Nicky, responsive to pageantry, adored the flickering votive candles, the icons, the paintings, the deep-rich colors of the vestments. *"Nomine Dominus, Filius, et Spiritus Sanctus."* She could chant her Latin along with Louise.

The conspiratorial nature of their expeditions appealed to both niece and aunt. Putting one over on Juts was a thrill.

"Don't mention this to your mother, now. Loose lips sink ships."

"We don't have a ship," Nickel replied.

Louise was again reminded that children know nothing of the past. "During the war we were worried about spies. There were posters all over that said 'Loose Lips Sink Ships,' which meant you were never to tell secrets because it might help the enemy."

"Is Mom the enemy?"

Louise drawled, "She's just a terribly misguided person."

"Did you worry about the enemy during the war?"

"Indeed I did. I was the one who saw the German bomber squadron on Runnymede Day . . . your mother was there, too. She didn't do much. I identified the enemy."

"Gee," Nickel exclaimed, filled with awe.

"Oh, yes." Louise nodded. "Now remember, pretend we're at war. Christians against the nonbelievers. Loose lips sink ships."

Juts, glad to be free of the rigors of loving motherhood, didn't question Nickel's jaunts. So long as Nicky said she'd had a hot-fudge sundae at Cadwalder's or she liked Lash LaRue better than ever at the movies, Juts failed to notice any spiritual improvements in her daughter.

Louise, like all the Hunsenmeirs, had been born to the Lutheran Church. It was during her adolescence that she had embraced the One True Faith. It was more than an embrace, it was a death grip. Since Louise wanted people to be better than they were, she was doomed to lifelong disappointment and bitterness. The Catholic Church enabled her to survive these disappointments, chief of which was her wayward sister.

Juts's habits preyed on her mind. When Louise made the sign of the cross at the dinner table, Juts would make the sign of the dollar. She'd trace an S in the air, dash her finger through it twice, and follow this with an extremely reverent "Amen."

Louise worried that Nickel would be corrupted by such entertaining blasphemies.

She missed raising children. She had loved Mary's and Maizie's antics, sayings, and questions up until age fourteen. At that point she thought God had come down and stolen her two adorable daughters, substituting two recalcitrant slugs.

Maizie had taken a summer job in Baltimore. Louise felt some relief that Maizie was returning to her old self.

Although she saw Mary almost every other day, she never felt that she spent time with her. It was rush here and rush there. She'd baby-sit for her daughter. She loved children but hated being known as a grandmother. She wouldn't allow the two little boys to call her Grandma. They called her Wheezie.

Nickel's enchantment with St. Rose's made Louise forget occasionally that she and her niece weren't the same blood. She was planning to take Nicky to high mass. So far, they'd only attended early-morning mass. High mass would do it. Nicky would be the church's for life.

She also gave Nicky a small black book, *The Key to Heaven,* instructing the child not to let Juts find it or the precious rosary beads.

Nicky hid them in the corner of her toybox after first wrapping them in her bandana. Since Nicky usually wore her bandana, Juts looked for it one morning, thinking perhaps the child had stuffed it in a pocket, dropped it, or forgotten it somewhere, although Nicky rarely forgot anything. She flipped up the lid of the toybox and saw the red bandana tied foursquare. She opened it up, spilling the rosary beads and *The Key to Heaven.*

"She'd better put her tail between her legs and kiss her ass good-bye." Juts stubbed out her ever-present cigarette.

She threw the bandana in the wash, then ironed it along with the other clothes. When Nickel came home she found her clothing neatly piled on her bed, the bandana on top of everything.

"Uh-oh." Nicky opened her toybox. *The Key to Heaven* rested on the chest of a worn teddy bear. She closed the lid. She wondered if she should slip out the back door and run to Wheezie or if she should pretend nothing had happened. As she sat on her trunk, pondering this crisis, she heard Juts's footfall. A long shadow fell by the door. Yoyo scampered in first, followed by Juts. Buster, on Nickel's bed, raised his head, then lowered it. Buster was slowing down.

Rosary beads twirled on Juts's finger. "Nicky, here's your necklace."

Nickel stared at the hypnotic twirling. She cupped her hands underneath it and Juts dropped it dead center.

"I'm not mad at you." Juts loomed over Nicky. "But I am ripshit at that religious-nut sister of mine. Come on." She grabbed Nickel by the hand.

They rode the bus to a joke shop out on Frederick Street. The faint aroma of mildew and alcohol permeated the premises. Musty, dinky, and dark, it was filled with items like fake ice cubes with flies in them, whoopee cushions, rubber snakes and spiders, and Groucho Marx noses, as well as sexual items hidden behind the desk. Stationed there, parked like a behemoth, was a distant cousin of Rob McGrail's.

"Momma, if I put this under Wheezie's seat she'll let out a real boomer." Nickel held up the whoopee cushion.

"That's too big to hide. I've got a better idea." She bought a large, realistic piece of plastic vomit and spent the trip home coaching Nickel on how to behave during her first high mass.

"Momma, why don't you like the Catholic Church?"

The maple trees swayed overhead. A light breeze was keeping the heat down. "The Lutheran Church is good enough for me and it ought to be good enough for you. Besides, one church is about as bad as another, so stick with the one you know. Louise thinks she's the Virgin Mary, and it's all Celeste Chalfonte's fault."

Nickel knew who Celeste was, if for no other reason than that she had died the day before Nickel was born, and people still talked about her. "Was Celeste Catholic?"

"No, she was Episcopalian, although just as happy going to the Lutheran Church. It's a long story. I'll make it short. Louise liked to play an old piano Celeste had—by ear, mind you, Wheezie is very musical. After a big fight because Celeste wouldn't give Louise the piano, Momma walked out on Celeste—she worked for Celeste, you know—Celeste weakened and finally gave the piano to Momma. Louise fell ass over tit. She played morning, noon, and night and was so revoltingly adorable that

Carlotta Van Dusen, Celeste's older sister, found her a place at Immaculata Academy and Celeste paid for Wheezie's education. That's how Louise became a Catholic. That piano."

"St. Rose of Lima's is pretty."

"Sure it is, but I'm not having any child of mine taking orders from some greaser in Rome."

"What's a greaser?"

"Oh—never mind. Now, do you remember what I told you?"

Nickel nodded that she did.

July 23 was the Feast of the Magi. The bones of Balthazar, Melchior, and Caspar were said to be in Cologne Cathedral, except that nothing much was left in Cologne now, and the Wise Men's bones were discreetly omitted from discussion. Then again, some stray schnauzer might have had a holy feast after the bombings.

The feast fell on a Sunday, so Louise fabricated a story about why she needed Nickel that Sunday even though it meant she'd miss church at Christ Lutheran. Juts pretended to believe her.

That Sunday when Louise picked up her niece, the plastic vomit was folded in Nickel's white patent-leather pocketbook, which matched her white Mary Janes. A white ribbon was tied around her black curly hair.

Nickel rehearsed every step in her mind. She was quiet, but then she was usually quiet, so Louise didn't notice. Also she was too busy saying, "I don't want to talk against your mother but—" after which she would launch into the litany of Julia Ellen's sins in the hopes that Nicky wouldn't repeat them.

Louise wore so much jewelry for high mass that she resembled a glamorous beetle, everything hard and shiny. She shepherded Nickel down the center aisle near the altar. The two sat at the end of the pew. Pearlie, backed up and working weekends, attended early mass, so it was only the two of them.

Mary Miles Mundis sat opposite them, Rob McGrail

immediately in front. Nickel returned everyone's smiles. They were all wondering, of course, why the child was in church with Louise rather than at Christ Lutheran with her mother.

The processional began, the music filling the beautiful, small church. Light flowed through the brilliant colors of the stained-glass windows.

Father O'Reilly walked down the aisle preceded by Peepbean, the acolyte, swishing the incense. An older boy, immediately behind Peepbean, held high the gold crosier. Behind Father O'Reilly walked the new junior priest, young Father Stewart.

Just as Peepbean passed the pew, Nickel yelled, "Your purse is on fire!" Then she threw out the plastic vomit.

She didn't throw it where Juts had told her to throw it, which was in front of Father O'Reilly. In her excitement, Nickel gave it a weak pitch and it splattered in front of Mary Miles Mundis. The sight of it made her sick as a dog.

Peepbean jumped to get out of the way, and in so doing he swung the incense bowl a little too high. He lost control of it and it flew off, whirling toward the altar.

Father Stewart, a quick thinker, sprinted from the procession to the vestibule to find the janitor.

"I'll kill her!" Louise exclaimed as Peepbean took a swing at Nickel.

"Peepbean wears skirts," Nickel taunted him.

The congregation was in an uproar as Louise yanked Nickel out of the pew by her wrist, holding her dangling for a moment, then dropped her as Peepbean rounded for another swing.

Father O'Reilly grabbed Peepbean as Wheezer hauled Nickel out of there.

"Did you think of this by yourself?"

"No."

The *click-click* of Louise's high heels reverberated through the marble vestibule. She pushed open the door with both hands. It swung back so hard it knocked Nickel off her feet. She picked herself up, opened the door, and stood on top of the steps, watching Wheezie hurrying down the sidewalk toward her car. Then she roared off, leaving the child standing there.

Nickel walked home. By the time she got there Juts was on her hands and knees trying to splice together the phone cords. Louise had pitched a fit and fallen in it, yanking the cords out of the wall. She'd yank her own out of the wall, too. Once, in the 1920s, she had wrecked a phone booth in the Bon-Ton. They had asked for her charge card back.

It took Louise five years of good behavior to get another card from the store.

Juts looked up at Nickel as she trudged into the house.

"Good job."

"Peepbean threw his purse at me."

"Ha!" Julia laughed after taking the precaution of removing her Chesterfield. "As you can see, your aunt Wheezie had a moment. At forty-nine, perhaps she's had too many of them." She laughed again, then held out her hand to Nickel, who sat next to her.

"Here." She turned around her cigarette, offering Nicky a drag. "You earned it."

Nickel eagerly lifted the cigarette to her lips and gently inhaled.

"Don't suck in too much. Okay, now let it out."

"Tastes funny."

"I love the taste. I bless the American Indian every day for cultivating this weed." Juts smiled and returned to twisting wires. She held out her hand for the cigarette, but Nickel took another puff.

"Momma, when I grow up I want to be just like you. I'm going to smoke Chesterfields."

Juts's laugh turned to a hum as she wondered what she'd have to do to top this one: a food fight in the Sistine Chapel?

72

The open can of paint sitting on the drop cloths dripped mint-green. Lillian Yost, due again and thrilled, had decided to paint the upstairs hallway mint-green. Millard indulged her every whim when she was pregnant, partly out of pride and partly out of guilt, he worked her so hard in the bakery.

Extra Billy Bitters dipped a wide brush into the paint. A vision of his life—open cans of paint, pink, blue, green, white, beige, eggshell, red—frightened him. His eyes glazed over, he held the brush a moment too long, and a big drop splattered on his shoe.

"Pop." He'd taken to calling his father-in-law that.

"Huh." Pearlie was cutting in woodwork.

"Is this it?"

"Huh?" Pearlie didn't look up.

Billy laid the brush on the wall in swift, controlled strokes. "What I mean is, when you came back from France . . . what did you do?"

"Started working for Bob Frankel."

"That was that?"

"Well, I was damn glad to be alive."

"Yeah." Billy's voice trailed off.

"You know, Billy, sometimes you can think too much. Sometimes I see the faces of my buddies . . . funny things. Like I knew this skinny Italian kid from Massachusetts, Vito Capeto, and we were eating fresh French bread, those long loaves. He compared French bread to Italian bread and I wish I could imitate him. Funny boy." He paused. "Guess I was just a boy, too." He exhaled. "Well, two days later we were in Belleau Wood and I slipped, fell facedown, mud up my nose, couldn't breathe. The earth shook. A damn sea of mud rolled onto me. I slid out, clawing for anything solid. Got on my feet and Vito was up in the tree branches, just like a rag doll. And here I am painting houses."

"Yeah." Billy, relieved, smiled at the older man.

"You know what else? I still don't know why I was fighting. The war to end all wars." Pearlie's voice had a mocking tone.

"Did you ever feel trapped?"

"Over there?"

"Here."

A long pause followed. "Sure. After Mary was born I had a rough time. I loved the little tot." He stood up to face his son-in-law. "But once the babies are on the ground you can't leave. You've got Oderuss and David. Boys need a father. You thinking about leaving?"

"No. It's just sometimes I can't breathe. I don't know why." He brightened. "I want to get in my truck, pick up the boys, and get drunk . . . go out and howl at the moon."

Pearlie gave a little howl and Bill joined him. The howling dissolved into laughter.

Billy abruptly stopped and imploringly asked, "What am I gonna do, Pop?"

"Make the best of it." Pearlie put his hand on Bill's shoulder. "You play the cards life dealt you."

73

Louise avoided Juts for three weeks, a record. She succumbed to the thrill of being a victim. She could shake her head, lower her voice, and intone how Julia Ellen was leading Nickel along the paths of unrighteousness. Filled with delicious anguish, the center of sympathy and attention, she told Orrie Tadia that Juts wasn't a good mother because she wasn't a natural mother. That pronouncement roared through Runnymede like prairie fire, everyone adding their own commentary to the issue. Some people agreed with Louise, others didn't, but everyone expressed some variation on the theme of the child's future, Juts's personality, and life in general.

The human tongue is like the rattler of a rattlesnake: People would be better off without it.

Mother Smith enjoyed this tempest thoroughly. Julia Ellen's reputation was being assassinated but Josephine's own hands were clean. Trudy Epstein didn't much mind, either, because her version of the past was that Chessy had truly loved her, only staying with his wife out of respect for social convention. Once she married Senior Epstein she shrewdly kept her mouth shut, but that didn't mean she didn't love hearing her friends trumpet her version of the story.

Mary Miles Mundis surprised everyone by saying, "We needed some excitement."

Ramelle heard about the gossip from Ev Most, who loved Juts but didn't want to be the one to break it to her. Ramelle then told Cora, working that day, who grabbed her purse and marched out the door. Ramelle hopped in the car to drive her over to Louise's. Cora rarely lost her temper, but she was so mad she couldn't see straight.

At the Trumbulls', Ramelle turned off the motor and waited.

Louise was sitting on her back porch, baskets of thread at her feet alongside Doodlebug. Needlepoint and suffering were her two comforts.

Cora threw her purse on the floor, looming over her daughter, who was so surprised at the sight of her mother that she held the needle poised in midair, royal blue thread dangling.

"Momma—"

"Sickness comes in through the mouth and disaster comes out of it. Shut yours."

"Huh?" She stuck her needle in the pillow but held the pillow to her chest.

"You'll kill Juts. You can't say she isn't a good mother because she didn't birth that baby. That's not right."

"It's true."

"You can't be saying that. It's cruel."

"She's cruel to me."

"Maybe so, but she's not cruel to your children or your grandchildren, and you're hurting Nicky."

"I am not."

"Everyone in town knows she's not Julia's child—"

Wheezie interrupted. "They always knew."

"Yes, but they didn't talk about it. Now they do. Nicky will notice those sideways glances."

"Well, that's Julia's problem. She should have told Nicky who she was a long time ago."

"And just who is she?" Cora folded her arms across her chest.

"Rillma's child."

Cora, enraged, came within a whisker of slapping Louise's face. Her expression scared her daughter enough that Louise held the pillow up to protect herself. Cora ripped the pillow away.

"She's Julia's baby. Don't you ever again say she's Rillma's."

"But Momma—" Louise felt queasy inside.

"Don't you 'Momma' me. Louise, you're fixing it so Nicky's got a harder fight. Everybody knows Juts gets notions. But not everybody thinks Juts is a bad mother. Plenty do now because of your fat mouth. You want to get even. Well, you did, but it's Nicky you hurt and she never did noways to you."

Wheezie's lower lip trembled. Cora picked up her purse. She left without another word.

74

Juts?" Louise called at the backyard gate. Getting no answer, she gave the twoey whistle.

Juts, paintbrush in hand, came out of the garage. "I'm in here."

Nicky, a smaller paintbrush in hand, heard her aunt Louise and stuck close to Juts.

Four wooden kitchen chairs dripped bright red paint onto newspapers.

"Redoing the chairs, I see," Louise said.

"They needed it." Juts prodded Nickel.

"Hello, Aunt Wheezie."

"Hello, Nicky, it's been a while since I've seen you."

"Yes, ma'am." Nicky returned to her task of painting the chair legs.

"I need to talk to you for a minute."

"Okay." Juts was suspicious.

"Alone."

"Nicky, I'm going into the garden with Wheezer for a minute."

"Maybe you should leave the brush here." Louise had visions of Juts ruining her dress with it.

Juts laid the brush across the can. They walked through the dark green grass of late August to a small bench under a rose trellis.

Louise started. "We need to hash this out."

"Yep."

"You first." Louise wavered.

"You're not making my kid a Catholic. You and I don't see eye to eye about religion and I resent you going behind my back and dragging Nicky to mass."

"Well." This was harder than Louise had anticipated because she believed that if everyone in the world were Catholic, all would be well. "It worried me when she questioned Jesus that day. I even talked to Father O'Reilly about it."

"She's a kid. Kids say all kinds of things. Remember the time when Maizie was four, she called Junior McGrail an elephant?"

Wheezie replied, "Well . . . yes."

"You go to your church. I'll go to mine."

"Agreed." Louise folded her hands together. "I got hot. I said some things around town I wish I hadn't said."

Juts cocked her head. "Like what?"

"Like you're a bad mother."

"Oh." Juts crossed her legs at the ankles. "You've said that be-fore."

"Yeah, I know, but I got so mad about the Feast of the Magi

mess that I said it to Orrie Tadia and a few others. I said you weren't bringing her up in a proper Christian home and I'm sorry I said it. Even the men are talking about it, and they usually just talk about one another."

"There's nothing I can do about it—but I sure wish you hadn't done that."

"I do, too." Louise started to cry.

After Louise left, Juts walked back into the garage. Nickel had finished two chair legs. She waited for her mother to paint the seats and the backs, since people would pay more attention to those than to the legs she had painted. This way if she missed a spot or it dripped too much no one would notice.

"Sorry, I was longer than I thought."

"See." Nicky pointed to her accomplishments.

Juts hunkered down, inspecting for drips. "Very good. Not one missed spot. You've got a little drip right here, though."

"I'll fix it." Nicky eagerly ran the brush over the spot, smoothing it out. "Momma, these will be pretty."

"Use it up, wear it out, make it do, or do without." Juts chanted the phrase she'd learned as a child. "Want some lemonade?"

"Sure."

They poured lemonade and sat under the rose trellis, where it was cool. Yoyo watched from her perch in the big tree.

"Momma, I love painting."

"That's good."

"Maybe when I grow up I can work for Uncle Pearlie."

"Nah—when you grow up you'll own your own company if that's what you want to do."

"Aunt Wheezie says girls don't do stuff like that."

"Aunt Wheezie's tried to make a lady out of me since I was little. Didn't work. Now she's trying to make one out of you. Don't listen to anybody. Do what you want. Doesn't mean it'll be easy, but go out there and scratch."

"Like a chicken?"

"Yeah. Sooner or later a bug turns up." Juts reached into the deep pocket of her housedress and pulled out a pack of cigarettes. She was glad she smoked, because her other choice would have been to drink too much. That was expensive and it often led to more trouble.

"Nickel, do you know what 'adopted' means?"

"Like from the SPCA?"

"Uh—yes."

"I know we've got Yoyo and Buster but Momma, think of those puppies and kitties. I bet we've got room for one more."

Juts smiled. "Two's enough. You're old enough to know things and you've got some sense in your head. Daddy and I couldn't have children. We wanted a baby something fierce. That's how I got you. Another lady bore you and then Daddy and I adopted you. You're special."

Nickel drank her lemonade, thought a long time, then said, "Does that mean I won't get Christmas presents?"

This puzzled Juts, who had expected a grilling on adoption, mothers, fathers, the whole nine yards. "Now why wouldn't you get Christmas presents?"

"What if Santa Claus is looking for me somewhere else?"

Juts laughed, more from relief than humor. "Santa knows you're here. He knows you belong to me."

"Oh."

"Honey, is there anything else you want to know?"

Nickel shook her head no, finished her lemonade, and walked back to the garage. Once she started a job she liked to finish it.

75

Chessy, left out of the adoption discussion, grumbled, but Juts filled him in on Louise's attacks. She said the time had felt right so she had pressed on with it and Nicky didn't seem to care one way or the other.

He wanted to say something to Nicky. He wanted to tell her he loved her with all his heart and soul, that she was his daughter. But watching her play with the animals, he figured his need to tell her was larger than her need to hear it. Anyway, actions spoke louder than words. He scooped her up, kissed her on the cheek, and played catch with her.

Louise, contrite after her outburst, trudged around town telling everyone she hadn't meant what she'd said. Juts's gags irritated her and pulling one in church just made her see red. Runnymede folks found the spectacle of Louise eating crow as noteworthy as the plastic-vomit episode.

There were those who felt Louise had backtracked, that she had been right in the first place. Others felt she had learned two wrongs don't make a right. Still others wondered if she had grown up a bit, although they agreed time would tell. Newcomers like Pierre and Bob at the Curl 'n' Twirl couldn't understand how the two sisters could be so childish with each other yet seemingly mature with everyone else. People who had grown up with the Hunsenmeir girls shrugged: That's the way they were.

No one expected them to change, and while some would have welcomed it, most people found their antics an antidote to small-town boredom.

The brouhaha died down just as those children born in 1944 entered first grade. Nickel, eager to go, skipped the whole way to school. She wore a neatly pressed plaid dress with dark green smocking on the bodice top. She carried a small bookbag and a lunch pail. She had two new yellow pencils with No. 2 lead, a wooden ruler, a big pink eraser, and a small metal stencil template, containing both numbers and letters.

Juts dragged her feet the whole way. Nickel didn't want to hold hands; she was too busy rushing up to every child on the way to Violet Hill Elementary School. Not even the big kids daunted her. Those children carrying books really impressed her. She couldn't wait to carry books home from school.

At the red-painted doorway to the old brick building, Juts, along with other mothers of first graders, paused and waved good-bye and good luck. As soon as Nicky bopped through the door the tears gushed over Juts's cheeks. She wiped her eyes, then noticed that other mothers were in the same fix.

Charlene Nordness stood next to Juts. "I'm a big bawl-baby."

Lillian Yost sniffed. "They aren't ours anymore. It's their first step into the world."

"Can't they stay little just a bit longer?" Julia wistfully added.

"I'd like to turn back the clock for myself but not for Kirk. I can never wait to get him out of the house," Peepbean's mother replied. He'd been held back a grade and she wondered if this was going to be a pattern. Her recurring nightmare was Peepbean, aged twenty-one, just graduating from sixth grade.

"Girls, let's go to Cadwalder's. An ice-cream float is the best thing after a cry."

They trooped over and who should be sitting at the counter but Maizie Trumbull.

"Maizie, what are you doing here?"

"Aunt Juts, I couldn't stand another day of it. I had to come home from Baltimore. Mom was so proud when I kept working there but I don't like big cities. I can't do it, Aunt Juts. I'm afraid to go home and tell Momma."

"Don't. Let's find your dad first, but the girls and I are going to have ice-cream floats. Want one?"

Vaughn rolled his wheelchair out from the back and was surprised to see Maizie. "Hey, this place is dull without you."

Maizie noticed how green his eyes were. "Can you fit back there to make me my ice-cream float? You do it better than anybody."

"Sure I can. Dad and I rigged up bars so I can do anything I want behind the counter." He guided his wheelchair to the end, grabbed a bar and pulled himself out, then along the bars, his arms huge and muscular now, to reach the ice-cream section. He wore wooden legs but the doctors were still working on getting the fit right and he'd lost muscle tone in his thighs. He could stand well enough though, just swaying a little. He made Maizie her favorite, a chocolate ice-cream soda, and pushed it across the dark marble counter to her.

"The best." She sighed. "You're the best."

Juts, joking with the girls, noticed that Maizie, far from being morose as Juts would have expected, was perky this morning. She was especially perky when talking with Vaughn.

For the first time it occurred to Juts that the Lord moves in mysterious ways.

76

The light in December had an ethereal radiance that compensated for the fact that there was so little of it. Juts hated the short days and the long nights but she appreciated the quality of the light.

She had agreed to go caroling this Saturday, nine days before Christmas. She loved to sing and she'd promised Louise that she'd take Celeste Chalfonte's old sleigh out so that they could sing to people farther from town. Along the way they would give out turkeys to needy people designated by St. Rose of Lima's.

Ever since Juts had egged Nickel into the plastic-vomit caper she'd tried to make it up to St. Rose's. Even Pastor Neely encouraged her to do penance. She countered that having Louise for a sister was penance enough. Still, she performed good deeds. Unfortunately, she couldn't help but call attention to them, which only meant she had to perform more. It wasn't right to put a shine on yourself when serving the Lord.

Juts, upstairs, pulled out warm clothes, a blanket, gloves, and scarves for her and for Nickel. Chester and Pearlie wouldn't accompany them because they were at the firehouse, getting it ready for the Christmas open house after the caroling the following night.

Nickel, downstairs, sat on the floor with a brand-new box of crayons Wheezie had given her. Julia's checkbook proved a unique coloring book.

"Nickel, are you ready?"

Nickel hastily put the checkbook back in Juts's purse.

"Yes."

Juts tromped downstairs, arms full of coats and clothes. She dumped them on the sofa. "Damn, I forgot a hot-water bottle." She ran back upstairs and Nickel put on a sweater, a coat, and her gloves. The inside of her jeans had flannel lining. She pulled on her paddock boots.

Juts returned, the red-hot water bottle filled. "This will keep our feet warm." She studied the paddock boots. "Nicky, how many pairs of socks do you have on?"

"One."

"Your feet will get cold. Here, put this thin pair on, then your heavier pair over them. It will work for a while."

They drove out to Celeste's stables. O.B. had hitched Minnie and Monza to the beautiful sleigh, deep blue with gold pinstriping. He had also tacked up a Percheron named Lillian Russell since both Rambunctious and General Pershing were too much horse for a little girl on a long ride. Of course, Nicky didn't know that. She thought she could ride anything. Huge though Lillian was, she was kind.

Juts and Nicky had decorated the stable the day before with boughs, ribbons, and sheaves of barley, which the horses especially enjoyed. Ramelle, bundled in her sable coat, had watched them prepare.

"Isn't this great?" Julia beamed.

"It's too cold," Louise griped.

"You should be grateful. They say cold tightens the pores and when you age your pores get bigger."

"Shut up. Do you know what Pearlie's getting me for Christmas?"

"If I did, I wouldn't tell you."

"I'd tell you if I knew what Chester bought you."

"Not until you extracted a bribe out of me, like hanging wallpaper in the upstairs bathroom."

"Juts, I did that years ago. You wouldn't let me off the roof unless I gave you my Easter hat—so there."

"Well, he's not getting you any more slips. You have enough to start a lingerie store." She checked her watch. "Twenty-three skiddoo. Ramelle, there's room in this sleigh for one more."

"No. I wanted to see you all off. I love to hear the jingle bells."

"Me, too." Juts hopped up and took the reins.

"Who said you could drive?"

"Louise, you don't even like horses."

"That's not true." Wheezie watched as O.B. lifted Nicky up on Lillian's broad back. "Nicky, you look like the dogs got at you under the porch. Don't you have something better to wear—like a skirt?"

"I hate skirts. Milk of magnesia." Nothing could be worse than milk of magnesia.

"Men like to look at pretty legs," said Juts, who had a knock-out pair.

"Don't care."

"Someday you will," Louise chided her.

"She's warmer this way, Wheezie, and I don't have snow pants and a snow top to match for her. Anyway, no one will care."

"I care."

Juts put her hand to her head as though she were going to swoon. Louise elbowed her hard in the ribs.

"Ouch!"

Minnie and Monza, named for Minnie Maddern Fiske and Monza Alverta Algood, two famous actresses at the turn of the century, turned their beautiful bay heads just enough to see the passengers in the sleigh.

"They're ready." O.B. smiled at Nickel.

"Me, too," she happily said.

O.B. pushed back the big double stable doors, Juts clicked to the girls, and with a scrape or two they slid out onto the snow.

Louise wore a tight-fitting powder-blue coat with frogging and an astrakhan collar, an astrakhan muff, and high boots with soft black gloves to match.

"You told me you didn't have a thing to wear."

"Oh, this?" Louise's voice rose.

"Yeah, that. If I'd have known you were going to dress like a movie star I'd have fussed up more."

"You look fine." Louise inhaled the crisp air. "It's Nicky who looks ratty."

Juts wore a red sweater, red skirt, black pearls, and a soft pair of boots with the tops rolled over like a cavalier's boots. She threw a deep green coat over this with a Christmas-tree pin on the lapel. It was a pretty outfit.

"You girls watch out for the black ice," O.B. warned as he lit the lanterns on each side of the sleigh.

"We will." Juts clucked again and off they went, sleigh bells jingling.

Lillian Russell walked along, puffs of air condensing in clouds from her big nostrils.

People waved as they headed out of town on Baltimore Street. Their first audience was Mrs. Abel, called Hardly Abel by Juts. Her son, a single, unsavory specimen, was called Un. They stopped at the slovenly frame house, sang "The First Noël," and gave Mrs. Abel a turkey. She thanked them and shut the door promptly, for the temperature was plunging.

Juts opened a small flask, enjoying a sip. She offered a swig to Louise.

"No, and you shouldn't, either."

"Just a nip. Wards off the cold."

Five turkey drops later a light snow kicked up. Juts had turned down a side lane to pick up a road west to the Mundis house.

They circled around Runnymede, the ground getting higher as they moved west.

Finally they came to Mrs. Mundis's driveway; her new house sat on a ridge. Gorgeous hickory trees stood like silent sentinels against the sky. Harry had had the presence of mind to build on an old house site so the trees and shrubs were mature. Big elms dotted the pastures, and massive oaks and walnuts shone like tarnished silver against the snow.

Every window of the house flickered with golden light. Mary Miles Mundis didn't need a turkey, but she was giving her traditional Christmas party and the Hunsenmeirs agreed to make this their last stop. They were glad to reach the house if for no other reason than that Juts could warm up the hot-water bottle.

"Julia, don't sing with such tremolo—and don't drink any more."

The huge polished door with brass handles flew open. Mrs. Mundis appeared in the doorway. "Merry Christmas."

Timmy Kleindienst led Minnie and Monza to the stable. He and a groom threw blankets over them after unhitching them. Timmy and O.B. were the best stablemen around.

Once inside Mary Miles's house, Juts, Wheezie, and Nicky admired the fragrant garlands entwined with oranges, apples, grapes, pinecones, holly sprigs, and sprayed-silver oak leaves. Twists of gold ribbon were placed here and there and a big plaid ribbon snaked through the garlands from end to end.

The towering tree, pure white, sported only shiny red balls. Green velvet ribbons tied on the edges of the branches, gold garlands circling the tree, and a star of Bethlehem topped off the decorating.

Louise, after stuffing herself and moaning about every calorie, sat down at the Steinway. She played "God Rest Ye Merry, Gentlemen," "Adeste Fideles," "We Three Kings," and "It Came upon a Midnight Clear."

Juts liberally sampled the eggnog, declaring it the most

delicious she had ever drunk in her entire life. Age jokes followed that, then the talk turned to the lawsuit an insurance company was bringing against the Rife family for setting fire to the meatpacking plant to collect insurance. The investigation by the insurance company was snail slow, but they'd gathered enough evidence to strike.

The snow thickened outside. Juts peered out the window. Louise joined her. "I'm having such a good time, I hate to go."

"We'd better leave." Juts didn't want to either.

Harry called down to the stable. Tim Kleindienst said he'd have the horses ready in fifteen minutes and he'd bring them straight up to the house.

This gave Juts time for another eggnog.

Once in the sleigh, Juts realized more snow had fallen than she'd thought. Nickel, riding on top of Lillian Russell rather than in the sleigh, thought everything was beautiful. Her eyelashes blinked off snow and it tickled.

"Juts, how many eggnogs did you have?"

"Not enough."

"Perhaps I should drive."

"I'm fine." Juts liked having the reins in her hands.

"I had an eggnog," Nickel called out.

"Oh?" Louise's eyebrows arched in disbelief.

"Momma gave me one."

"Julia, how could you?"

"Half an eggnog is not going to turn my child into a raving dipsomaniac. Keep your shirt on, Louise. You're always jumping to conclusions."

"Forcing alcohol down a child's throat is no laughing matter."

"I didn't laugh," Nickel forthrightly said.

"You have a tendency toward these things," Louise warned. "You drank punch at my birthday party." She turned to Juts. "You'd better watch that kid."

"She'll never leave my sight." The sleigh swayed a bit.

"Don't mock me. It only takes a drop if one is so inclined. Yes, it does. Remember when old Uncle Franz, after years of not drinking, sipped a glass of champagne at your wedding? Went on a bender for a week." Wheezie's voice carried that important tone.

Juts hummed.

"Nicky, you promise your aunt Louise you won't drink."

"Yes, Aunt Louise."

"And don't start smoking, either. If God had wanted us to smoke he'd have put a chimney in our heads."

"Yes, Aunt Louise," lied Nickel, who couldn't wait to be old enough to smoke. She thought it was glamorous.

"Where's Maizie tonight?" Juts couldn't bear a harangue on clean living, not when that eggnog tasted so good.

"Out with Vaughn. They went out with their gang. Vaughn keeps close with his Army buddies."

"Maybe she'll marry Vaughn."

"Maybe she won't."

"They'd be happy."

"You think any two people mooning over each other will share a life of bliss."

"You should have had some eggnog. Improve your mood."

"My mood is fine except it's colder than a witch's bosom."

"Tit."

"Bosom."

Nicky giggled.

"Tit, Louise, tit. 'Bosom' takes the laugh out of it."

"I won't talk that way."

"Old age is making you lose your sense of humor, you know that, Wheezie? You're becoming an old fart."

"You're older than I am."

"What?"

Louise jammed her hands in her muff. "Thirty-nine."

"Fine." Juts lifted the reins and gently slapped them against the horses' backs. They picked up a trot.

"Don't go so fast."

"I'm not, but it's getting colder, it's snowing harder, and I want to get home."

"Slow down."

"Louise, close your eyes if you're scared."

"If there's one thing I can't stand, it's a drunk driver." Louise whacked her with her astrakhan muff.

To spite her, Juts asked for more trot and got it.

Lillian, broad-backed, trotted, too. Nicky's short legs barely reached the gray mare's sides. Nicky bounced like a jack-in-the-box.

Juts sang her own words to the tune of "Winter Wonderland." "Fifty years, are you listening? Fifty years, and she's listing. To port I can vow, she looks like a cow, wrinkles—"

"Shut up."

The bays swept their ears back and forward, reaching out with those magnificent forelegs, two trotters in unison. A nasty curve loomed ahead and from there it was a straight shot into Runnymede.

"Momma, I'm gonna fall off."

"You're not a rider until you fall off seven times."

"I did that already. Slow down, Momma." Nicky couldn't get a grip anyway with those flannel-lined jeans.

"Don't take her side, Nicky. I can't stand it when you and Louise are in cahoots."

By now, Nickel lay facedown, holding on to Lillian's mane. Her canter was ponderous but it was a canter nonetheless.

"Grab mane," Juts ordered.

"I am!"

"You'll get us killed," Louise screamed. "We'll be a holiday statistic. We'll be the last people in the state of Maryland killed driving a sleigh."

"Chicken." Juts swung around the curve too fast, hitting the black ice underneath. The sleigh bells jingled wildly.

"I'm gonna die!" Louise bellowed.

"Only the good die young." Juts laughed as the sleigh tipped over to one side and Louise flew into a snowdrift by the roadbank. Juts righted the sleigh by shifting her weight to the other side.

Excited, Lillian decided to take the shortcut home through the Barnharts' field. A strong creek bordered the property. It glittered like a dark mirror. Lillian launched herself over the creek but Nickel dropped like a dead moth from a porch light. She crashed through the ice.

Juts's shoulders ached as she brought Minnie and Monza to a halt about a hundred yards from where Louise had fallen out. The horses' heads bobbed up and down, flecks of foam mingling with snowflakes around their mouths.

The chilling water stopped at Nickel's waist, but she smashed through the ice with such force that the water splashed all over her. Her boots weighed her down as she tried to crawl out. Lillian's hoofbeats faded away as she galloped across the frozen ground.

Nickel wiggled out of her sodden coat and grabbed a gnarled tree root, pulling herself out.

"You all right, Nick?"

"Momma, I'll never catch Lillian. O.B. will kill me."

"Come on." Juts urged her to hurry up as Minnie and Monza were prancing around. She had her hands full.

"Isn't anyone going to ask about me? What if my hip's broken? What if I'm suffering a concussion?"

"You're complaining, Louise, that means you're fine."

"You know, Juts, even black magic can't change a chicken!" Louise sputtered in pure-D rage, leaving her sister and niece to ponder the deep meaning of this statement. She dusted herself off from the snowbank and then, perceiving that Juts might not wait since the horses were restive, sprinted to the sleigh.

Nickel, sodden, hoisted herself up as Juts allowed the horses to walk out.

"Honey, take off your clothes. Wheezie, help her."

"I've twisted my ankle."

"Will you help Nicky?"

Louise removed her expensive gloves and peeled the already-freezing layers off the child's body. Nicky shivered and her skin was cherry red.

"Here." Louise wrapped her in a blanket and put the hot-water bottle on her chest.

The child's teeth chattered.

They rode in silence for half a mile, then Louise giggled. Juts followed. Finally Nickel, shivering uncontrollably, giggled too, but it sounded like a gurgle.

" 'Sleigh bells ring, are you listening—' " Juts started.

" 'In the lane, snow is glistening—' "

The three of them sang at the top of their lungs.

O.B. heard them and pushed open the big doors. Lillian pounding up the lane had alerted him to trouble ahead. Peepbean had joined him.

"Did you girls get in some trouble?"

"Just a tad." Louise waved her muff as he took Monza's bridle.

Peepbean watched as Louise lifted down Nicky to O.B. He put her on the ground.

"Fell off. Fell off," Peepbean chanted.

"Shut up, Kirk, let her warm herself in front of the stove," O.B. instructed his son.

"Go on, honey, I'll be there in a minute. I've got to get your wet clothes out of the sleigh. Louise, don't forget your purse." Juts handed Louise her bag, then plucked out her own. She wanted to give O.B. a Christmas tip, realized she had no cash, reached in and pulled out her checkbook.

Peepbean placed Nickel by the stove. He pulled back the edges of the blanket, which she grabbed and wrapped around herself tightly.

"I won't tell."

"Peepbean, leave me alone."

"I know you've got no clothes on. Come on, let me look."

"No."

He yanked at the blanket and she stood up. "If you don't leave me alone, I'll tell."

He glowered. "I got something to tell you, snot. Your real momma is Rillma Ryan. Little bastard."

"I don't care." Nickel absorbed the news but wasn't about to react in front of him. She remembered Rillma Ryan. She was that nice lady who had come by to see them one day. "Doesn't matter who my momma is—I'm still a better rider than you."

"Fell off."

"Yeah, but I'm not afraid to get back on. Chicken! Chicken! Chicken!"

He grabbed the blanket and fought with her. Louise walked in.

"That's enough!"

Peepbean looked at her like a puppy caught stealing food off the table.

"We were just playing."

"I've got no clothes on. He wants to see me." Nickel told the plain, unvarnished truth.

"She's crazy," Peepbean lied.

"It's Christmas. Do you want me to tell your father so he can give you a licking?"

"No." Fear flickered on his face.

"Then my Christmas present to you is silence." Louise pointed her finger at him. "But if you torment Nickel one more time you won't sit down for a week because not only will your father hide you, I will, too!"

"Nickel!" Juts hollered.

"Yes, Momma."

"Get out here this minute."

Nickel shrugged and waddled out where her mother held open her crayon-enhanced checkbook.

"Did you do this?"

"I'm gonna be rich," Nickel declared.

"You're going to be something, anyway. Did you write in my checkbook?"

"Yes."

Louise peeked at the checkbook and burst out laughing.

"Don't encourage her." But Juts laughed, too.

Nickel grinned sheepishly but she was wondering about Rillma. If Rillma was really her mother, what was so bad about her that her mother had left her?

77

A fearful apprehension seized Nicky. As each day edged her closer to Christmas she worried that Santa would put her presents under Rillma Ryan's tree out in Portland, Oregon—that is, if Rillma Ryan was her mother.

She stared in the gilt-framed mirror in her bedroom. Did she look like Juts? What about Chessy?

Juts didn't notice that Nicky was quieter than usual. Christmas turned Juts into a whirling dervish and besides, Juts wasn't particularly sensitive to other people. Since most of her attention centered on herself she often missed what was going on with others.

Juts's tree, a big Douglas fir, was festooned with huge, shiny balls of solid colors, tinsel, metallic gold garlands, and the occasional hand-carved wooden decoration from the old country.

Since the war was so recent in memory, no one identified which old country.

Spreading out the white sheet around the tree, Juts tugged this way and that but couldn't satisfy her artistic impulses. The "snow" wouldn't lie correctly. Irritated, she crawled under the tree, followed by Yoyo.

"Don't you dare bat a ball off this tree."

Yoyo rested on her haunches, watching Juts grunt and groan. Then Juts backed out. Still not right. She crawled under again. Flat on her belly, she wrinkled the sheet, forming hills and valleys. Then she again backed out and, tired, rested her head on her hands.

Yoyo stayed under the tree. Juts dozed for fifteen minutes, and when she opened her eyes she stared into the fireplace. A small downdraft had created a flutter. She rose, walked over, and leaned into the fireplace to close the flue. She had intended to leave the flue open but she got so busy she forgot to start a fire. When she reached into the fireplace she saw a tiny scrap of paper taped to the interior wall.

She removed it, careful to keep her sooty hand from her clothes.

In a childish scrawl the note read: "Santa I lif here. Nicky." Ignoring the spelling and punctuation errors, she frowned and crumpled the note up, tossing it into the fireplace just as Nickel came down the stairs followed by Buster, who made more noise than she did.

"Momma!" Nickel raced for the fireplace to retrieve her note.

"What if I had started a fire?"

Nickel uncrumpled the paper.

Furious, Juts snatched it from her hand. "You don't need a goddamned note! Santa knows where you live."

"Just in case," Nickel replied in a small voice. "He might get confused."

"He's not confused, you are."

"I really want him to leave me a Roy Rogers holster."

"Stop worrying about your presents. Christmas is more than presents."

But not to a six-year-old. Had Juts been less upset she would have remembered that.

"I've been good and—"

"Oh, Nickel, Santa Claus is a white lie. Don't worry about your presents. You'll get your presents."

Nickel stepped back, ashen-faced. "Mom, you told me Santa would find me."

"There is no Santa Claus, goddammit. It's a story people tell kids to shut them up. I'm Santa Claus, Daddy's Santa Claus. There's no one up there in the sky driving reindeer. Forget it."

Nicky's eyes misted over. "What about the Easter Bunny?"

"Have you ever seen a bunny bigger than a breadbasket? Another whopper. Don't start bawling, Nicky. For God's sake, they're stories. You'll get your presents. That's all you care about."

"That's not all I care about!" Nickel screamed, surprising both Julia Ellen and herself.

Yoyo prudently climbed up the tree. Buster barked.

"I haven't got time for this foolishness." Juts turned and headed for the kitchen.

"You lied to me!" Nickel pointed her finger at Juts like an avenging angel.

Juts spun around. "Don't talk to me like that, you spoiled brat. I'm your mother."

"No, you're not."

That stopped Juts cold in her tracks. Even Buster closed his mouth.

"Rillma Ryan is my mother." Nickel lowered her voice.

Shaking, Juts whispered, "Who told you that?"

"Peepbean Huffstetler."

A long silence followed. Juts put her fingers to her temples. "Rillma Ryan gave you birth. She got in a jam and you were the result. I wanted a baby so I took you. Why I wanted this grief, I don't know. I should have had my head examined." This casual cruelty slid right out of her lipsticked mouth. In fact, she was so mad and upset she didn't even think about the effect on Nickel.

"If you're not my mother you can't tell me what to do." Nickel put her hands on her hips as the tears rolled down her perfectly smooth face.

"Listen, brat. You'd be dead if I hadn't gotten you out of that orphanage." She conveniently neglected to mention Wheezie and Chessy had made the frozen trip to Pittsburgh. "I fed you, clothed you, and saw that you got to church on time. As long as you're under my roof you'll do as I say."

Nickel turned her back on her and walked upstairs.

Juts went into the kitchen and poured a cup of coffee, but her hands were shaking so hard she couldn't get it to her mouth. Furious, she poured the liquid down the sink and then smashed the cup against the wall.

78

A light rap on the front door would have gone unnoticed except that Ramelle happened to be passing through the big hall.

"Nicky." She opened the door to behold the child wearing everything she could think of and carrying her pencil box. "Come in, honey."

"Mrs. Chalfonte, is G-Mom here?"

"Yes. Let's take these clothes off and then we'll find her. This is quite a wardrobe. I know it's bitter out there, but, well—" Ramelle smiled and said no more about it. "There."

She took Nicky by the hand, walking her back to the kitchen.

Cora was cutting out cookies. "Hi. What are you doing here?"

Nicky walked between the two women, her back to her grandmother, and faced Ramelle. "Mrs. Chalfonte, I want to work for you just like G-Mom does. I'm strong. I'm really strong and I'm learning to write. I can sweep and I can—"

Ramelle's laughter rang out like silver bells. "Nickel, you are the most precious thing in the world."

Nickel smiled. "I'll start right now. I brought everything I need."

"Where's your mother?" Cora laughed.

"In Portland, Oregon."

That wiped the smile off both their faces. Cora rubbed her hands on her apron. She picked up some cookies off the platter. "Let's sit over here."

The three sat down in the nook, Ramelle bringing milk.

"First, why don't you tell us why you wore so many clothes?" Ramelle asked in a gentle voice.

"I'm not going back to Momma. I can sleep at G-Mom's and work here all day. I like to work."

"You're a good worker." Ramelle praised her.

"These are good, if I do say so myself." Cora ate a peanut-butter cookie and put her arm around Nickel. "What's this about Portland, Oregon?"

"Peepbean told me my mother is Rillma Ryan and Momma said so, too. I don't like Momma anymore."

"Because she's not your real mother?" Ramelle tried not to make her questions sound as vital as they were. "I mean, your natural mother. A real mother is the one that raises you."

"Momma was ugly to me and I don't like her."

"What did she do?" Cora drummed the tabletop with her fingertips, then stopped. "We won't tell. Cross my heart and hope to die."

Ramelle crossed her heart also.

"She told me there was no Santa Claus, no Easter Bunny, and she said I was a jam."

"A jam?" Cora wondered what this meant.

Nickel nodded her head. "I was a jam and I made her head hurt. I don't have to listen to her."

"Uh—well, let's worry about that later. Right now you eat up G-Mom's cookies. I need to tidy up and I'll be right back." Ramelle left to phone Juts.

"She's what?" came the gasp on the other end of the line. Juts didn't know that Nickel had snuck out the back door. "I'll be right over."

"Julia, that might not be a good idea. Why don't you tell me what happened, especially the jam part? Nickel says you told her she was a jam."

"Oh—" A sharp intake of breath on the other end of the line was audible. "My nerves are raw and—"

Ramelle returned after hearing Juts's version of the story. She sat opposite Cora and Nickel.

"Pretty good cookies, aren't they?"

"Yes, ma'am."

"Nicky, I called your mother and told her you were here. Did you tell her you were leaving?"

"I'm not telling her anything."

"She said you could visit for a while and then she'll come get you."

"I don't want to go home."

Cora shrewdly said, "You can't leave Yoyo and Buster."

"Couldn't they live with me?"

"I don't think so, honey." Cora squeezed her with her arm around Nicky's shoulder.

"And your mother apologizes. She didn't mean that you were a jam, she meant that Rillma got into a jam. It's one of those sayings people use. I think she lost her temper and wishes she hadn't."

"Did you lose yours?" Cora inquired.

"Yes." Nicky cast down her eyes.

"Least you have one. The trick is knowing how to use it."

"I don't want to listen to her."

"She didn't want to listen to me," Cora said. "But that's mothers and daughters. She is your mother. She's not perfect, but she is your mother. Anyway, I'll talk to her and we'll get this sorted out."

"Who's my father?"

A burdensome moment followed that logical and necessary question.

Ramelle, wondering if she was doing the right thing, thought it better to tell the truth than to lie. The child had had enough lying. "Your father was Celeste Chalfonte's nephew, Francis. Rillma told people your father was a man named Bullette, but she did that to protect everyone because Francis was married to someone else."

"Doesn't he like me?"

"He died at the end of the war from overwork and strain. He would love you." Ramelle prayed for guidance since no one, not even Cora, knew the whole story. "He and your mother, your natural mother, worked together during the war and they fell in love. What should have been a wonderful story with a happy ending couldn't be happy because he was married already. The one happy thing to happen was you."

"Oh."

"Only Celeste, God rest her soul, and I knew who your real father was. He gave Rillma the money to move to Portland. It was

Celeste who had gotten Rillma her job with Francis, and she always felt responsible, even though she wasn't. But we are glad you're here. And no one has to know everything."

"Bet Aunt Louise knows. Aunt Louise says she knows all kinds of things."

"Aunt Louise doesn't know."

"Does Momma?"

"No," Ramelle answered.

"Do I have to love Momma?"

"You do—in your heart." Cora sighed, thinking of the conversations she was going to have with Juts and then Louise before Juts got at Louise and another war started.

"How can you love someone when you don't like them?"

"You remember the good times," Cora responded. "And you pray that God will show you the way. You see, people need love when they are most unlovable."

"Like Momma?"

"Well—yes."

"Mrs. Chalfonte, did you ever love someone when you didn't even like them?"

"Many times."

A knock on the door, followed by "It's me," announced Juts.

"Remember—" Ramelle whispered, but before she could finish her sentence Juts was upon them.

She surveyed the scene, then burst into tears. "I'm sorry. Nicky, I'm sorry."

Nickel watched her mother sob. Cora slid out from her seat and hugged her daughter.

"Juts, if only you'd think before you open your mouth."

"I know." Juts sobbed some more.

Ramelle thought of a line written by Paul Valéry: "I loved myself, hated myself, and then we grew old together."

79

Christmas brought Nicky her Roy Rogers gun and holster and Mother Smith an angina attack. She lived. Juts wondered how many more years she'd have to put up with her mother-in-law. She pretended to be happy she'd survived.

Chester wore himself out running between the hospital and home. His brothers, home for the holidays, weren't much help. He came down with a bad cold. Juts put him to bed.

Nicky decided not to go to Jackson Frost's party. Juts dialed the number for her and Nicky got on the phone to tell Jackson that she had to take care of her dad. She did, too. She brought him orange juice, pills, and Vicks VapoRub. She also read to him. He heard " 'Twas the Night Before Christmas" four times in a row and swore each reading was better than the last.

Once when he fell asleep he awakened fitfully to find Nicky sitting on the edge of the bed watching him. She petted his hand as though he were Yoyo.

"Daddy, I'll make you better."

He sneezed. "Yes, you will."

"Daddy, I'd give up my Christmas presents if it would make you feel better."

"You don't have to do that."

"I would, though." She kissed his hand and snuggled up to him. "You won't leave me, will you?"

"Never." He wondered what was cooking inside that curly head.

"You wouldn't give me back to Rillma Ryan, would you?"

"What?" Chester, knowing nothing of the events of the last few days, was jolted wide awake.

"I'm afraid Momma will get mad at me and dump me."

"Don't worry your pretty head, sugar." He couldn't wait to grill Juts. "You belong right here with me, forever and ever."

She nestled her head in the crook of his arm. "I love you."

"I love you, too." He sneezed.

"I'll get you more orange juice. Mom says you have to drink oceans of it."

"Thanks. I've had enough. But you can do me a big favor. Go ask Momma to come in here and keep me company."

"Okay."

By the time Juts's shadow floated across the threshold he had his questions lined up. They sent Nicky down to the kitchen to feed Yoyo and Buster, which meant they had about fifteen minutes.

"Julia, how does Nickel know about Rillma?"

"Peepbean told her."

"Why didn't you tell me?"

"I forgot."

"Shit." He sat upright, his head throbbing. "You tell her she's adopted without me. She finds out about Rillma Ryan. What the hell am I around here, the doorman? You have no right to keep this from me."

"Chester, you're running a fever."

"Don't crawfish!"

"I'm not."

"You should have told me."

"I suppose Nicky did."

"Just now. She wanted to know if you would give her back to Rillma Ryan if you were mad at her. That's a helluva thing for a kid to feel."

Juts waved her hand, dismissing the fear. "She'll forget it. You know how kids are."

"No, I don't. But I know how you are."

"Your mother was put in the hospital and so much happened so fast, I meant to get to it but I didn't. I'm sorry."

"I want the whole story."

"Not now, honey, she'll be back up here in a minute. I promise I'll tell you. Everything."

He flopped back on the pillow. Sweat dribbled down his forehead. Juts dabbed his head.

"I'm going to put ice cubes in a washrag. That ought to help."

He turned his eyes to their wedding picture as she left the room. Did every woman "forget" pertinent facts, or was it Juts alone? He wondered if there was a worldwide female conspiracy to control men, to make them feel stupid.

Juts and Nicky returned.

"I forgot something else," Juts said.

"What?" He half squinted because his head hurt so bad, even his eyes hurt.

"O.B. is putting Peepbean in Catholic school. If he'll be the part-time sexton, St. Rose's will pay for it. Popeye is vacating his sexton duties."

"There's something ignorant about that boy." Chester closed his eyes, the cool washrag on his forehead comforting.

Nicky repeated a phrase she had heard. "He's a new bat in an old belfry."

Chessy and Juts laughed. Somehow it exactly described the situation.

80

A foggy April day in 1952 chased Juts and Louise inside to work. Antsy, Juts pulled out her patterns, the thin paper crinkling.

"I don't like any of these." Louise turned her nose up.

"Me neither."

"I need a new hat. Let's drive over to Hagerstown."

"I can make you a hat."

Nicky, hunched over the porcelain-topped kitchen table doing her sums, watched as Juts left, returning with a falsie.

"And what, may I ask, do you intend to do with that?" Louise asked dryly. "I'm well padded."

"I'll cover it with satin, put a bow here and a little veil. Black or maybe navy blue. Real Tats." Tats was what Juts called the famous milliner, Countess Tatiana.

"Hey—" Louise warmed to the idea. "Black, black with a twist of red in the bow."

"Yeah." Enthusiastically Julia rummaged around in her wicker basket, which held her fabric odds and ends.

"Momma, I want to be in the Soap Box Derby this year so I can win right in front of Aunt Wheezie's house. I'm old enough." At seven she thought she was old enough to do anything.

Through a cloud of cigarette smoke Juts replied, "Girls can't be in the derby."

"Why not?"

"I don't know."

Louise, the voice of authority, boomed, "You'll rattle your ovaries and that will cause problems later."

"Momma, what are ovaries?"

"I haven't the faintest idea." She gave Wheezie the shut-up glare. "Julia, she has to learn about these things sooner or later."

"Later." Juts snipped the black satin with the scissors.

"I want to know now. If they're keeping me from the Soap Box Derby I'll get rid of them."

"Ha!" Louise exploded.

"Will you shut up," Juts warned.

"I don't want them if I can't be in the Soap Box Derby."

Juts slammed the scissors on the table, little bits of satin threads lifting into the air. "Thank you so much, Dr. Trumbull. Now she'll rag me about ovaries the rest of the day."

"What are ovaries?"

Louise cleared her throat. "They are little parts inside you so you can have children. Ovaries are God's gift."

"God can give them to someone else. I don't want children."

Louise's lip twitched. "Someday you'll be glad to have them."

"I'll give my ovaries to someone who wants children. Honest. I don't need ovaries." Nicky pushed her papers aside.

"That does it." Juts opened and closed the scissors, like a potential weapon.

"She can't go about saying she doesn't want her ovaries or to bear children."

"Will you shut up."

A world-weary expression, followed by a slight exhale, informed Louise's every word. "Then again, how would you know."

Juts pushed the patterns, fabric, and falsie on the floor. "Shut up, I said!"

Louise scooped up her "hat" and shouted, "You aren't properly emphasizing the natural part of being a woman. But why should I be surprised?"

Juts lunged for her but Louise jumped behind Nicky. "You've got a mean streak."

"Mean streak! I ought to wring your neck. You have to be the smart one, you know more than I do—" Juts, seething, couldn't even speak.

"I think I'll be going." Louise walked quickly to the mudroom to let herself out.

"Other people are born with wealth, with beauty, with brains. I was born with a sister," Juts complained through gritted teeth.

Seeing that Julia had put the scissors down on the kitchen tabletop, Louise peeked back in from the mudroom. "A sister who has gone through thick and thin with you."

"I did the same for you."

"You can't give this child ideas above her station."

Sarcastically Juts replied, "I'm not trying to be a Chalfonte."

Nicky put her head down on her crossed arms. She *was* a Chalfonte, at least her father was. At that instant she realized she had power over Juts, since Juts didn't know about Francis. She decided that since adults kept things from her, she would keep things from them. Two could play that game.

"She can't race in the Soap Box Derby. It will upset the applecart."

"It's a stupid rule."

"Stupid or not, it's for boys only."

"How come everything fun is for boys?" Nicky smacked her hand on the table. "I can do anything the boys do, and better."

"For now you can," Louise said. "The boys will grow bigger and stronger."

"Aunt Wheezie, I'll wail 'em no matter how big they get."

"There's more than one way to skin a cat," Wheezie said. "Why fight when you can win by just smiling?"

"Your aunt Wheezie is trying to tell you that men are easy to wrap around your finger."

"Is that like being two bricks shy of a load?"

"No, it's different, although many times you will think they're two bricks shy of a load." Louise, thrilled to be the expert, went on. "I'll give you your first lesson in how to control men." She tilted her head upward, hand under her chin, and as she spoke she used that hand to touch her earring. "You are so clever, Paul. I would have never thought of that." Her voice lilted, her every movement suggested delight and deference.

"Here's another one." Juts laughed. "You are so strong. I couldn't even pick that up."

Both sisters laughed.

Nicky didn't. "I'm not doing that."

"Well, honey, let me be the first to tell you, you'll flop with men."

Louise eagerly added, "Once you learn the tricks, they are easy as pie—even the sister boys."

"What's a sister boy?"

"A sissy," Louise answered.

"Like Peepbean Huffstetler?"

"Kinda," Juts filled in. "What Wheezie means is that all men like attention from women, even if they don't want to marry one. You lean into them a little, act as though every word out of their mouth is so-o-o interesting, and that does it." She snapped her fingers.

"They'll know you're faking." Nicky couldn't believe these silly tricks would work.

"Nope," Juts said.

"You're too little right now," Louise added. "The little boys don't care, but once they get, oh, maybe sixteen—"

Julia interrupted her. "Once their voices change, that's the signal. Then let them have it."

Nicky solemnly considered her momma and her aunt. "Can't I be me?"

Louise laughed spontaneously, something she rarely did, a deep belly laugh. "Nicky, having a man love you isn't the same as having a man know you. They don't need to know you at all. In fact, they don't know how."

Nicky couldn't believe that people could live together for years and not know each other. She thought Wheezie was pulling her leg. "Momma, Daddy doesn't know you?"

Juts folded her arms across her chest. "Actually, I think he does, but then Louise and I disagree on the particulars of the subject of men. He might not know why I do something, but he can pretty well tell you what I will do in any given situation."

"Julia"—Louise's voice dropped—"*you* don't even know why you do some of the things you do."

"To get back at you."

"Now, that's the God's honest truth and I have a witness." Louise pointed at Nicky.

"Hey, how about we teach you how to flirt?" Juts was enjoying herself.

"Momma, I don't care about that stuff. I want to be in the Soap Box Derby." Nicky pushed her pencils back, hopped out of the chair. "I'm going upstairs. May I be excused?"

"Sure, Mike." Juts used the old family expression.

As she left, Juts turned to Louise. "I can't figure her out."

A helpless look crossed Juts's face, still youthful at forty-seven. "She doesn't like clothes. I can't get her interested in sewing or cooking. I have to drag her by her heels to get her to attend her friends' parties. Did you ever see a kid that didn't like parties?"

"Not that I recall, but they aren't just like us. Mary taught me that lesson fast enough and then Maizie really drove it home. I'm nervous about this Vaughn thing. He's courting her hot and heavy."

"You should be happy, Louise, what do you want? She's not setting the world on fire as a piano player—and she doesn't have her teacher's license—what's she going to do?"

Louise twisted her wedding ring around her finger. "I don't know. She'll have to take care of him all his life."

"He gets around good." Juts punched her sister on the shoulder. "You're always worried about money. He'll take over the drugstore someday. She'll be set for life."

"I don't know."

"You live to worry, you know that?"

"You'll worry plenty someday when Nicky gets serious about somebody. All it takes is one bad fella, just one."

"Maybe it only takes one for them, too, you know." Juts turned on the faucet and stuck her cigarette under it to put it out. "Who knows what Nicky will do? She marches to her own tune. When I think that blood is thicker than water I remember Rillma as a kid. She wasn't like Nickel at all."

"She sounds like you. She organizes like you," Louise said in a mollifying tone.

"Yeah?"

"I think they're like sponges. They absorb."

"Sometimes I feel like a cook, a maid, a washerwoman, a chauffeur—a nurse, even—but I don't know if I feel like a mother."

"That's what mothers feel like—and don't expect any thanks for it, either."

81

Despite her sister's warning about knowing your place, Juts conspired with Nicky to build a soap-box car. Chessy listened to their arguments and thought, What the hell?

They closed the garage doors and spent the next two and a half months building the car. Chester worked on the aerodynamics of it, creating a low, pointed nose and smooth, sleek sides. Nicky pulled the task of sanding, resanding, and sanding yet again until the surface of the wood shone like glass.

Both Juts and Chessy worried about the steering system. A derby car, going fast, can be hard to hold. Juts had genuine mechanical ability. She crawled under the car, examined the tie-rods and how the wheels sat under the carriage. She drew up designs. Chester pored over them with her, as did Nicky.

The three Smiths drew close together building the derby car. Nicky's favorite time was when they were all in the garage, Buster and Yoyo there, too, and Juts was singing harmony, Chester bass, and Nicky the melody. She didn't worry about Rillma Ryan when they worked together and Juts had been too busy to lose her temper at her.

Nicky was figuring out that if she played with Juts, for she thought of it as play, Juts was happy. They had their riding lesson once a week and afterward Nicky began to accompany Juts on her window-shopping sprees. Bored though she was, she pretended to be interested in the clothes that Juts would bring to her attention.

Now that she was a little older she spent Saturdays with Chessy at the store. Like her dad, she loved building things, but she was careful not to show too much enthusiasm around Juts, for Juts was jealous even of Chessy.

At seven she'd learned caution in expressing her emotions. Possessed of boundless energy and physical courage, she played outside most of the time, did as she was told most of the time, and watched people much more than she listened to them. She'd learned one great and painful lesson about life already, which was that people might like her fine but she had to look out for herself; she couldn't expect other people to do it. Chessy was the only exception to this rule.

Juts didn't care about what was going on inside Nicky. She cared only for the external result. Since she was that way about everybody and everything, there was comfort in her consistency.

Chessy drew the outline of the number 22 on both sides of

the car, now painted gleaming royal blue. Together they painted the 22 gold.

Harry Mundis, head of Derby Day, ran his big empire himself, so slipping one by him wasn't that hard. Nicky entered under Jackson Frost's name, knowing that Jackson would be at the beach on July 4.

The weather, cloudless and with blessedly low humidity, unusual for the season, promised a memorable Fourth.

The square was set up for fireworks, both fire departments participating. Bunting draped the whole town and everybody placed a flag on their front porch or on the lawn.

Quite a few people flew their Maryland or Pennsylvania flags, too, which added to the color.

Men searched for their boaters and Panamas while the ladies fretted over whether they had to wear nylons in the heat. The braver and prettier ones opted for shorts and canvas sandals. Ever since Louise had accused Juts of having varicose veins, Juts refused to wear shorts.

The houses lining the derby route filled with people. Tubs of ice held beer, sodas, lemonade, and for the lucky ones, limeade. Coolers packed with dry ice contained strawberry, chocolate, and vanilla ice cream.

Louise, the lady of the manor, had a crowd at her house. Right across the street, the Wests hosted a huge crowd also. Louise and Pearlie would cross the street and chat, but because Senior Epstein and Trudy partied with the Wests, Juts wouldn't go as long as they were there. If she could avoid socializing with the Epsteins, she would.

The older ladies—Cora, Ramelle, and Fannie Jump, who was going deaf—sat on rockers on the porch. Extra Billy, Doak, and other young men horsed around on the front lawn, playing baseball with a Ping-Pong ball after they'd marched in the parade. Their girlfriends and wives pitched horseshoes. Vaughn was great at pitching horseshoes, beating them all from his wheelchair. The kids mostly screamed and chased one another with the invariable accusations of one pushing the other, one getting more ice cream than the other. The mothers ignored it.

Pearlie stoked up the big brick barbecue he and Chessy had built years earlier. Everyone in Runnymede agreed he sizzled the best steaks in town. Juts and Louise worked together, bringing plates of food to Cora, Ramelle, and Fannie Jump as well as refreshing drinks all around.

The shock wave around town was the insurance company's fingering O.B. Huffstetler as the arsonist hired by the Rifes. Ramelle refused to fire him until proof was positive. She wasn't sure what to do if it turned out he was indeed the perpetrator.

The bands, that morning, marched under cloudless skies. The veterans marched according to what war they'd fought in. Every politician from both counties was there in a convertible, and the county beauty queens waved to everyone. Local businesses provided floats to advertise their products, the plumber's being a giant toilet, which excited comment.

A long banner stretched taut and high over the Soap Box Derby finish line.

Juts checked her watch and sneaked away, easy to do amid the commotion. Nickel, goggles in place, hair slicked back under a York White Roses baseball cap, hurried off with her. Since she was in the peewee races she'd roll down early.

Juts left her at her car and whispered, "Head low."

"Okay."

"And don't talk to anyone. Your voice will give you away. Good luck."

"Thanks." Nicky had a stomach full of butterflies.

Once back at the finish line, Juts whispered to Chessy, who left the barbecue for a minute. Louise shepherded everyone to the curb or the porch, whatever was their preference.

"Where's Nicky?"

"She's around."

Louise fretted. "She never misses a race. Where is she?"

"Probably on the other side of the street. Popeye's over there. See him? Ugh." She pointed out the reporter.

Louise swept her eyes over the crowd across the street, then gave Juts her death-ray stare. "You didn't."

"You're nuts."

"I know you. I know you like a book!" Louise hopped up and down, she was so exercised.

"Pipe down, Wheezie, it's only a Soap Box Derby, for Chrissake. She's not running for president."

The announcer called out, "And in Heat Three, Jackson Frost, Number Twenty-two, and Roger Davis, Number Sixty-one—and they're off!"

As Nicky thundered down the hill after a wonderful running start, Louise knew exactly who was in Car Twenty-two.

"This is a disgrace," Louise bellowed. "You stop her."

"I'm not stopping anything."

"It's not fair to Roger Davis. It won't be a legitimate heat."

"Goddammit, not letting Nicky compete isn't fair to Nicky."

"That's another bag of beans."

"The hell it is." Juts craned to get a view of the cars, Nicky in the lead. "Come on, Twenty-two!"

People were screaming all around them.

"This is not right." Louise bolted out onto the finish line. She held her arms up.

Juts sprinted after her and pushed her out of the way. Chessy tore across the finish line to hold Louise. Of course, they were on the Wests' side of the street, which meant Trudy cast Chester a deep look. Just to be on the safe side, Juts shoved her.

Senior Epstein, horrified, said, "Juts, let bygones be bygones."

"Slut!"

"Old bag." Trudy hauled off and smacked her one.

Juts doubled up her fist, slammed it into Trudy's jaw to send her reeling.

Nicky, in the vibrating car, used every muscle to hold it straight. She'd never gone this fast in her life. She peered up and saw her mother and father, Louise, Trudy, and Senior in a donnybrook that involved more people with every minute. She crossed the finish line ahead of Roger but veered to the right, since the fight was spilling into the street. The rumbling car leapt over the curb, rolling on two wheels, sending Extra Billy and others jumping out of the way. Thank God, Maizie had the presence of mind to roll Vaughn out of danger. People scattered like marbles from a shooter. The Smiths had built a damned good derby car. That sucker was still rolling and finally crashed into Louise's wooden flagpole. Ripped up a good piece of land, too.

While Chester and Senior pulled apart their wives, Louise wiggled free. She ran across the street, her sandals flapping with each step. She pushed through the crowd to yank a dizzy Nicky out of her winning car.

"If your mother won't teach you how to be a lady, I will!" She swatted her hand on Nicky's bottom.

"Mom!" Maizie grabbed her hand.

"It's Nicky. I'm telling you this isn't Jackson Frost, it's Nicky."

Louise grabbed Nicky's goggles. The child jerked her head away, and the goggles snapped back on her face.

"It *is* Nicky." Maizie's jaw dropped.

Nicky removed her goggles. "I won!"

Billy, Vaughn, Doak, and their friends laughed, and Billy put Nicky up on his shoulders.

The announcer, apprised of the mess, droned, "We have a disqualification in the third heat. That winner is Roger Davis."

"I won!" Nicky screamed, now standing on Billy's shoulders. "I won!"

Juts, dragged across the road by Chester and Pearlie, was cussing a blue streak. At the sight of Nicky she clapped her hands. "I knew you could do it."

"They've taken the race from her." Louise spat out the words.

"I don't care. She won and everyone saw her win. That's what matters."

"You're going to spoil that child. She can't go about thinking she can do whatever she wants."

"Ah, Mrs. Trumbull." Extra Billy always called his mother-in-law Mrs. Trumbull. "Give the kid credit for guts."

"And breaking the rules!" Louise's face was mottled.

"Who cares?" Juts, really happy that Nicky had won and satisfied that she had finally laid into that goddamned Trudy Epstein, felt expansive.

"She's made a fool of herself," Louise said.

"Better she do it than someone does it for her," Juts replied.

"This child has enough to contend with in life without you egging her on. You don't have any more sense than God gave a goose."

A little wire snapped in Juts's mind on that one. "As I recall, Louise, you are the last person who should be talking about geese."

Fear washed over Louise, who shouted, "Loose lips!" but Juts rolled on. "Hey, everyone, hey, remember the air raid? It was Canadian geese. Louise blew the siren on Canadian geese and swore me to secrecy. So how about that, Sister, for breaking the rules? You do it, too!"

Louise's goose was cooked.

The riot after that disclosure exceeded the fracas at the finish line. Not only did the story make the *Clarion,* but so did a photo of the battling Hunsenmeirs. Popeye struck again!

82

Ever the drama queen, Louise wore a black veil for two weeks following the Fourth of July revelation. Everyone knew who she was.

Caesura Frothingham, ancient now, declared the veil was a big improvement. Noe Mojo suggested Louise was in mourning.

Juts, thinking at first that blame would bypass her, discovered it was so delicious a taste in the mouth that people were thrilled to give her some, too.

Orrie Tadia Mojo shook her finger in Juts's face and said she had betrayed her sister. Juts snapped right back at her that since Orrie was Louise's best friend, she didn't expect Orrie to give her a fair shake.

Ev Most, back from yet another of her trips, stuck up for Juts although she told her husband that being Julia's friend could be exhausting.

Mother Smith wrote a letter to the editor of the *Trumpet* criticizing public officials who cry wolf. She cited the county commissioner for York County, on the Pennsylvania side, but all of Runnymede knew she meant Louise and Juts.

This stung Cora, who dictated a letter written by Juts to the editor of the *Clarion*. She said, "Josephine Smith is full of shit."

Walter Falkenroth called Cora and suggested she reword her

letter. Ramelle, with a cooler head, helped her so that the letter appeared the day following Josephine's attack.

It read, "Louise Trumbull and Julia Ellen Smith made a mistake. We're glad those weren't German planes."

The next day a letter appeared from Juts in which she said, "Louise screwed up. I covered up. At least we had some excitement."

Louise then pitched a major hissy in print. The Maryland residents sent their responses to the Maryland paper, which bumped up circulation. Louise's detailed reply had to be cut to two paragraphs. The last line read, "I would die for my country."

Wags at the barbershop commented she might have to.

The Curl 'n' Twirl nearly combusted from the gossip concerning the sisters plus the latest on the arson: O.B. had denied setting fire to the warehouse and had hired expensive Edgar Frost to defend him. People figured the money came from old Julius Rife.

Vaughn asked Maizie to marry him, but in the volcanic atmosphere they decided to wait before announcing it publicly. Even Louise didn't know.

Cora quietly told her children that if they didn't hang together they would hang separately. So both sisters, tied at the ankles by Cora, sat down at her kitchen table and wrote yet another letter to the *Clarion*. This time they apologized for any inconvenience they might have caused the citizens of Runnymede.

After they signed the document, Cora released them.

Sullenly they sat at the table.

"Girls, you try the patience of all the living saints."

"I would have gone to my grave with our secret." Louise touched the small gold cross hanging around her neck.

"By the time you get ready to die, Wheezie, you'll be so old you'll have forgotten everything. Only the good die young."

Louise entreated her mother, standing over both of them. "See, she's so smart. Always a comeback. I hate her."

"You started it."

"I did not."

"Louise, you are fifty-one years old—"

"Mother!" Louise wailed.

"Julia, you're forty-seven yourself now. This is no way to behave."

"I told her not to put Nicky in the Soap Box Derby. You try and talk to her. She won't listen," Louise wailed.

"It's not fair. If Nicky wants to race she can race. We didn't commit a crime, Louise."

"Well, you shoved Trudy Epstein. As if letting that child pretend to be a boy wasn't bad enough, you had to publicly attack that woman."

"She said he only stayed with me out of duty. That he really loved her. Dumb bitch."

"Did she really say that?" Louise leaned forward.

"If you hadn't been Our Lady of the Veils I would have told you everything, but you haven't talked to me since the Fourth of July. There's a lot you don't know," Julia said cryptically, knowing that was the way to ignite Louise's curiosity.

"But why would she say that in front of everyone? She takes such pains to be good, poor thing." Louise was no fan of Trudy's.

"How the hell should I know? Probably thought she could get away with it. No one would hear her but me."

"Did anyone hear her?"

"Well, not the first part, but after I clocked her, sure, everyone heard, because she was shouting right along with you, Wheezie."

"I was merely trying to head off an embarrassing situation."

"That's why you ran into the middle of the road? To head off an embarrassing situation? Subtle," Juts dryly replied.

"You weren't going to do anything about Nickel."

"No, because I didn't think we were wrong."

"Boys do what boys do and girls do what girls do."

"Bullshit."

"Next she'll want to play for the Orioles. Actually, she might as well. Why you bother with that bottom-of-the-barrel minor-league team I will never know."

"You just wait, Louise, someday the majors will come back to Baltimore. Just like before World War One. We'll have a real team and then we can beat the Yankees."

"Dream on, sister mine."

"Are you two going to make a united stand? I don't care about who wins what in Baltimore. I want this settled now. No getting off the track." Cora brought them back.

"What's to settle? We wrote the letter." Juts sat sideways in her chair.

"You blew the whistle. That's what's to settle. We wouldn't be in this mess. Julia, it's in other papers, too. People are laughing at us!"

"Let them laugh. At least they're laughing—not crying. I'm performing a public service."

"At my expense." Louise pouted.

"I didn't say geese were German airplanes."

Louise's eyes bulged; the cords on her neck stood out. "You went along with it! That's as bad as making the wrong call."

"Shut up, both of you. Two wrongs don't make a right."

"Yeah, but why should I pay because she was stupid?"

"Julia Ellen, that's not the way to bind this wound."

Louise smacked the table with her open palm. "Wound? Wound? I'll tell you what it is, it's a stab in the back from my own sister in front of the world! Where's your Christian charity? Oh, I don't expect you to be a loving sister. No, I know better than that. You first, everyone else last, but for the sake of sheer Christian charity, you might have spared me this humiliation."

"The last Christian died on the cross." Juts quoted Nietzsche, although she didn't realize it. She just liked the line.

"Julia—" Cora's tone was stern.

"She accused me of being a bad mother!" Juts stood up from her seat. "On her front lawn with eleventy million people around.

I'm not putting up with that shit another minute. She's lucky I didn't kill her."

"I didn't say you were a bad mother."

"The hell you didn't."

"I said you encouraged Nicky to break the rules. And"—she held up her hand for silence—"that she was enough to juggle without adding that."

"Well, aren't you Sissy Tolerance? That's the same as saying I'm a bad mother, which you do behind my back anyway. It all comes back to me, you know. Everything you say comes back to me. This is Runnymede, after all. The last thing to die on people around here is their mouths. For all I know, the stiffs at the undertaker's are still talking."

"I have never said you were a bad mother."

"Excuse me? I guess I've got a hearing problem."

"I have not said that! I have said"—and her voice sounded like a lawyer's in the courtroom—"that you have extra burdens because Nicky isn't yours."

"You told me to have a baby. I did."

"But she's not yours."

"I am still a mother!"

"Kind of."

"Louise, that's just foolishness," Cora interjected.

"Yeah, especially since she was the one who kept telling me I'd never know what happiness was until I had a child. Well, I've got one. Now what do I do with it?"

"See"—Louise pointed at her sister while looking to her mother—"a real mother doesn't talk like that."

"Plenty's the time you came crying to me about your girls. You are getting forgetful." Cora's feet hurt. She sat down. This wasn't going to be over soon.

"I'm a mother. I don't see what's so damned great about it. It's a lot of work. And you conned me into it."

"I did no such thing. You carried on about having a baby

since the day you married. And didn't I tell you not to marry him? He'll never set the world on fire."

"He set me on fire."

"Oh, that." Louise pursed her lips.

"He's a good man. He's made his mistake, but he's a good man." Cora loved Chester.

"You married him to spite his mother," Louise retorted.

"I did not. I don't care one bit about that douche bag."

"I'm going home," Louise announced.

"Not until you two make up."

"How can I make up with her? She's impossible. She wrote in the paper that it was my fault. Bad enough she blew off her big mouth when she did, she didn't have to put it in writing."

"That's not what I said. I said you screwed up and I covered up. One's as bad as the other."

"Oh, sure." Louise crossed her arms over her chest.

"Well—it is. And I wouldn't have done any of it if you hadn't made an ass of yourself over Nicky."

"I'm right about that. Tell her, Momma, tell her that you can't let children do what they want. The derby is for boys."

"I thought it was funny."

"Momma!"

"Oh, Louise, what girls and boys do is like fashions. They change. In my day no woman would show her ankles, much less her calf. People are running around half-naked today. Women go out without hats." Cora shrugged.

Louise interrupted. "Some things never change."

"Name one," Juts challenged.

"Death."

"Okay, name another."

"Women bear children and men don't."

"That's two."

"Taxes."

"They change. When I was young there were no taxes. And it

ought to be that way again." Cora thought of the government as a sanctimonious thief.

"Any more things that never change?" Julia prodded with her finger.

"Don't touch me. The sun rises in the east."

"That doesn't count. People things."

Louise thought, then threw up her hands. "I can't think of anything else. But I still think you were wrong."

"I don't."

"It's not such a big thing. Shake hands and stick together."

"I'm not shaking her hand until she lays off telling me how to raise my kid."

"You ask for advice and then you criticize me for giving it to you."

"Come on, Louise—"

"You weren't cut out to be a mother."

"Well, too damned late to do anything about it now!"

"She's right, Louise. The child is here."

"And the damage is done."

"Oh, great, now Nicky is damaged."

"I didn't mean Nicky. I meant blowing your guts about the warplanes."

"As I see it, we're even."

"Me, too. Now shake and make up and for the love of God, shut up!"

Grudgingly the two sisters shook hands.

That night as Cora drifted off to sleep she wondered if she'd been a good mother. She never could get her two daughters to realize they were both sipping through the same straw.

83

H ere." Nicky handed Juts a yellow-covered manual.

"She'll just lo-o-ove that." Juts laughed, tucking *The Complete Guide to Guitar Prayer* under her arm. "Aunt Wheezie can play anything."

"Mouth organ, too?" Nicky plucked out a harmonica book.

"She's too grand for that. Now come on, we've got to find you a bookbag."

"But I want to get a book for Daddy."

"Daddy's not much of a reader, honey."

"He reads to me."

"That's different. You have to learn that the things you like aren't necessarily what other people like. Daddy would really like a new bow tie. We'll go by the Bon-Ton."

"Okay."

They walked down the aisle, hand in hand, to the back-to-school section. Red bookbags, blue, tan, even bright green ones, filled a row on the shelf. Juts picked one up and replaced it. It was much too big.

"I like this one, Momma."

Juts took the true-red canvas bag and flipped it open. A place for pencils and a ruler was inside the flap. The big interior pocket was divided in half. The strap, sturdy webbing, ought to last one school year. She checked the price: $6.95. That was a little more than she wanted to pay.

"Hold this."

"I like this one," Nicky repeated herself.

"I do, too, but let me just check out these other ones. That one is a little pricey."

She rooted around but couldn't find anything she liked better. The cheaper ones were too flimsy, the more expensive ones out of the question.

Nicky held her tongue. She had learned that pressuring her mother didn't work.

"Well, if I buy this we're going to have to give up something else."

"I don't need a new dress," said the child who hated them.

"Big sacrifice." Juts laughed, then caught sight of Louise pushing open the door to the Five and Dime. "Here, I don't want Louise to see this." She handed Nicky back *The Complete Guide to Guitar Prayer*. "What are you doing here?" She waved to Louise.

"Hi, Nicky."

"Hi, Aunt Wheeze."

"Finished up early at St. Rose of Lima's. That's the first time since the cornerstone was laid that a Ladies' Improvement Society in Jesus' Name meeting ended early."

"You've improved all that you can stand." Juts winked at Nicky, then slipped her arm through Louise's. "I want to show you something." She pointed behind her back that Nicky should take the bookbag and the book to the counter. By the time Juts and Louise joined her there, Verna BonBon, yet another of that numerous clan, had the items in a brown paper bag. Louise bought a pair of hot-coral square earrings with a preserved seahorse in the middle.

They walked outside into the hot hand of late August.

"Where does the summer go?" Louise sighed. "It's almost Labor Day."

"I don't know, but it sure goes faster than the winter." Juts pointed toward a park bench. "Let's sit down. Nicky wants to give you a present."

Nicky eagerly slid out *The Complete Guide to Guitar Prayer*.

"Well, isn't this nice?" Louise kissed her on the cheek, then flipped the book open to "Holy, Holy, Holy." "That's easy. Why, Maizie and I can have duets. I'll play the piano. She gets too carried away on the piano."

"Momma says you and Maizie look exactly alike." Nickel's feet stuck straight out off the park bench. "But I don't look like my momma."

"I guess Maizie and I do look alike. Well, Juts and I strongly resemble each other. Her smile is prettier."

"Your hair is prettier." Juts complimented her back.

"I think you're both pretty. I want to grow up and look like you."

"You'll grow up and look like yourself. Anyway, by the time you grow up, the way we look now will be so old-fashioned you'll laugh."

"You think?"

"I think," Juts answered her.

"Remember those awful high-button shoes we used to wear? We thought they were the cat's meow." Louise laughed.

"Yeah." Juts smiled. "Know what I remember? When we were little, no lady would go out in the summer without her parasol. Actually, it was pretty, remember, walking through the square with Momma and all the ladies had parasols of different colors—some had lace, some had ruffles. People knew how to dress then. The way we're heading, by the time Nicky's grown they won't wear clothes at all."

"The human body was meant to be covered. In the Garden of Eden—"

Juts interrupted. "The Garden of Eden has nothing to do with it. Can you imagine Josephine Smith nude?"

"I'd rather not."

"How about Walter Falkenroth, skinny as a rail."

Louise shook her head in distaste.

"And then there's Caesura Frothingham, that would be like seeing an elephant, with all those wrinkles. She's got to be ninety-five if she's a day."

"What about Harmon Nordness?"

That sent them into guffaws, for the sheriff's gut expanded every year. Soon he'd have to walk and let his stomach ride.

Nicky stared at her legs, the tiny golden hairs catching the sunlight. "What about me?"

"That's different. Children are beautiful," Louise answered.

"Not Peepbean."

"Well, he wouldn't be so bad if his teeth were fixed."

"Beauty's only skin deep, ugly's to the bone." Juts repeated the old phrase.

"Pretty is as pretty does."

Both sisters snapped their fingers and said, "You can't judge a book by its cover." Then they laughed.

"G-Mom says that all the time." Nickel laughed with them.

"We ought to write down her sayings. She was always quoting rules to us. Every now and then she'll fire off another one just like we were still children." Julia kicked off her espadrilles; her feet were burning up.

"Guess we are children, we'll always be children to her, just like Mary and Maizie will always be children to me."

"So, Momma, what are the rules?" Nickel hopped off the bench. The hard slats hurt her rear end. There wasn't much padding there.

"Rules. Okay, here are some rules of the road: Never break your word. Never be disloyal to a friend. Never whine when you lose. I can't think of anything else."

"Pick your friends with care. You can't be everybody's friend. It doesn't work," Louise added.

"What's the Golden Rule?" Juts asked Nickel.

"Do unto others as you would have them do unto you."

"If you forget the others, that one will do. Not that it's easy. Boy, I need something to drink. I usually don't mind the heat but today it's creeping up on me." Juts stood up.

They walked toward Cadwalder's, Nickel charging on ahead out of earshot.

"Nicky thought you'd like the guitar book. She can be very sweet. I didn't have the heart to tell her you might want something different, because she picked it out herself."

"She's bright as a cigar band."

"I wanted to buy her Cootie. All the kids are crazy about that game, but her bookbag cost six ninety-five, so she'll have to wait awhile for Cootie. She calls Peepbean a cootie, which is an improvement on 'asshole.' "

"If you'd stop swearing she wouldn't pick up these words."

"Everybody swears in Runnymede. It saves having to take the time to find the right word."

"I don't swear."

"I forgot about that."

"I don't."

Juts ignored her, her eyes on Nickel skipping now through the square, which must have seemed huge to her. "She's a pistol, isn't she? I love her."

"That's what they need. If more children had love, we'd have a whole lot less trouble in this world."

"I'm trying to be a good mother."

"I know. You are, Juts. I pick at you over little things but the big things, well, you're a good mother. Kids can run you crazy. I'm beginning to think any mother that doesn't strangle her brats is a good one." She waved to Lillian Yost, passing at the edge of the park.

"Chester's so good with her. It's funny, but watching him play with Nicky makes me love him more. I'm starting to trust him again."

"Men play with children because they're children themselves."

"You're too hard on men sometimes."

"Ha!" She snorted. "You show me the woman who invented the income tax. Huh?"

"You got me there."

"Watch!" Nicky called, then spun a cartwheel.

"That's good," Juts called. "That Co-Cola preys on my mind. Come on, Nicky." They stopped at the corner, looked both ways, then sprinted over to Cadwalder's.

After passing and repassing with Flavius Cadwalder and Vaughn, who, unknown to all, including his father, was calling on Paul that evening to state his intentions, the three left, refreshed.

"He's going to ask for her hand." Louise, her intuition on target, was nervous.

"Better than her foot," Juts joked, making Nicky giggle. "Don't fret so much, Wheezie. It's right. You feel it when it's right." They walked to Lee Street, where Juts would turn toward home.

"I guess."

"Here's our corner." She stated the obvious.

Louise stood for a second, then blurted out, "If you have a better answer, tell me."

"About what?" Julia was confused.

"I don't know." Louise clasped her hands. "Sometimes it's like a wave's crashed over me and I worry myself sick. I worry about Vaughn's health and—"

"Louise, two years with the right man is better than twenty with the wrong one. Now, don't fuss up yourself. Really. Look how good Mary and Extra Billy turned out."

"They can fight like cats and dogs."

"Who can't?"

"Paul and I didn't fight like that."

"Oh, yes you did. I recall once he took the car, got drunk, stayed out late, and Chessy had to go looking for him."

"Celeste brought him home on her horse." Louise laughed, remembering.

"If you've got feelings for someone they can heat up. Better than staying cold, you know?"

"I know." Tears glistened in Louise's eyes. "Juts, are we getting old?"

Juts shrugged. "I don't feel old." She put her arm around her older sister's waist, still girlishly small. "Do you feel old?"

"Some days I feel one hundred years old and I don't even know why. And the strangest things float into my mind, like little boats. I remember Aimes and how much Momma loved him." Cora's boyfriend had died in 1917. "I remember Celeste and how she'd lift up her chin, never say a word, just lift up that chin and you knew you'd better toe the line. I remember the straw hats we wore one Easter. You pulled the streamers off mine and I cried. I remember holding Mary in my arms for the first time and I thought that wrinkled red face was the most beautiful thing I'd ever seen. Oh, and I remember the headlines on the *Clarion* and the *Trumpet* when the *Titanic* sank and remember, the list of the missing would be posted outside the newspaper offices every day—" Her voice trailed off, and she made a small gesture with her hand, as if trying to scare off the flood tide of emotion.

"I remember the first time I smelled lilacs." Juts smiled, then hugged Louise. "We're walking encyclopedias."

"But it's all a jumble."

"Everybody's mind is like that. If you asked someone what they ate for breakfast or lunch even two days ago, they couldn't tell you."

"Harmon Nordness could. Two weeks ago, Idabelle McGrail could, while she was alive." Louise laughed.

"You know what I mean."

"I know, but Juts, what happens when I go?" An edge of anguish cut through the air.

"What do you mean?"

"What happens to the memories, to everything I've seen and heard and done and learned? Poof." Tears rolled down Louise's

cheeks. Nicky reached up to hold her hand. She hated to see anyone cry. Louise squeezed her hand but couldn't say anything.

"I have this theory"—Juts smiled to cheer Louise—"that
there's this humongous bank in the sky, the memory bank.
Everything is sorted there, and if some new person like Nicky
wants to learn what you learned, she asks the memory bank."

"Juts, you're silly."

"Well, a library is a memory bank." Juts breathed in the scent
of newly cut grass. "A song is a memory bank. What about 'The
Man Who Broke the Bank at Monte Carlo'? That's full of memories for someone who lived at the turn of the century, like
Momma. All Nicky has to do is hear it. I believe everything re-
mains here in one form or another."

"Except for us."

"Yeah, except for us. I guess we've got to make way for the
spring shoots. Hansford made way for us, even Idabelle McGrail,
the silly ass. They stepped out so we could step in."

"Oh, Juts," Louise was pleading, "I don't want to step out. I
don't want to miss anything—ever."

"Only the good die young, Louise. Have no fear."

Louise stopped a minute, caught a ragged breath, then smiled
through her tears. "We'll live forever."

"Yep."

The sisters kissed each other and separated. Nicky reached for
Juts's hand. Mouse quiet, she finally spoke as they pushed open
the gate into the backyard, seeing Buster stiffly ambling forward
and Yoyo lounging under the big blue hydrangea bush.

"Momma, you won't die."

"Not anytime soon, I hope."

"And Aunt Wheezie won't die."

"Nah." Juts bent over to love on Buster.

"You all won't die because I'll remember you."

Juts laughed. "Sure, kid."

ABOUT THE AUTHOR

RITA MAE BROWN is the bestselling author of several books. An Emmy-nominated screenwriter and a poet, she lives in Afton, Virginia. Her website is www.ritamaebrown.com.